HIDDEN RICHES

Also by Felicia Mason

Enchanted Heart

Testimony

Published by Kensington Publishing Corp.

HIDDEN RICHES

FELICIA MASON

Kensington Publishing Corp.
http://www.kensingtonbooks.com

DAFINA BOOKS are published by

Kensington Publishing Corp.
119 West 40th Street
New York, NY 10018

All Kensington Titles, Imprints, and Distributed Lines are available at special quantity discounts for bulk purchases for sales promotion, premiums, fund-raising, and educational or institutional use.

Special book excerpts or customized printings can also be created to fit specific needs. For details, write or phone the office of the Kensington Special Sales Manager: Kensington Publishing Corp., 119 West 40th Street, New York, NY 10018, attn: Special Sales Department. Phone: 1-800-221-2647.

Dafina and the Dafina logo Reg. U.S. Pat. & TM Off.

ISBN-13: 978-0-7582-0574-2
ISBN-10: 0-7582-0574-0
First Kensington Trade Edition: February 2014
First Kensington Mass Market Edition: June 2015

eISBN-13: 978-1-4967-0150-3
eISBN-10: 1-4967-0150-X
Kensington Electronic Edition: June 2015

10 9 8 7 6 5 4 3 2 1

Printed in the United States of America

For Tom Coe and Steve Kelner, who opened the windows so the light would shine on the artist

and

For Don Maass, who left the door unlocked and the phone line open.

Forget what you've heard about the dead coming back to life.
The dead are just gone. For good. All they leave behind is the mess that somebody else has to clean up. That's when the dead get their due.

Acknowledgments

I have frequently noted in acknowledgments that no book is written in a vacuum. This one is no exception.

First and foremost, to Karen Thomas, Selena James, Steve Zacharius, and the late Walter Zacharius, all of or formerly of Kensington Publishing Company/Dafina Books, thank you for your forbearance.

From the long-time-coming department, the people who heard about Ana Mae before a word was put on a page, I'd like to thank Paula Barnes, Day Smith, and Carolyn Green. For quilting friendships, thanks to Debbie Moore, a die-hard reader, quilter, and all-around great lady with a welcoming smile and a comforting word, and in memory of Eva Washington, quilt teacher, mentor, and friend.

Sylvester "Sly" Washington Jr. years ago uttered a line at a wedding that has always stayed with me; I gave it to Reverend Toussaint, Puddin'. Thank you to David Nicholson, who did a beta read and kept me honest with Clayton and Archer; and to Barista Steffan at Starbucks, who starts reaching for the Tazo Awake tea as soon as I hit the door.

The Pagan River Writers group, Hugh Lessig, Diana McFarland, Sabine Hirschauer, and Tamara Dietrich: Thanks for our monthly Friday night pizza and page discussions near the Pagan, and a fun and productive weekend at The Porches. Of course, the cheering squad of writing pals gets a shout-out: Michelle Fronheiser, Denise Jeffries, Andrea Jackson, and Cheryl Wilson-Bonner; and to Lisa "Merlainne" Barman, it *will* happen for you.

The staff and management at Chanco on the James (www.chanco.org) in Surry County, Virginia, provide a wonderful retreat and respite, the perfect setting in the woods to get a manuscript done. Chef Joe Mack fed me well, and the river was a comfort. And to Trudy Hale, proprietor of The Porches (www.porcheswriting retreat.com), the quiet of your central Virginia retreat center is just what I needed to get the final draft in shape.

Thank you all.

Mortui vivos docent.
Let the dead teach the living.

Ana Mae Futrell   Ahoskie, N.C.

Ana Mae Futrell died Thursday, August 7, in Drapersville, outside Ahoskie.

Ana Mae, a daughter of the late Russell and Georgette Futrell, attended Gibbs High School and worked as a domestic. She was known throughout the county for her quilting and for her prize-winning fried chicken. Ana Mae never had an evil word to say about anyone and always gave strangers a kind word and the benefit of her smile.

She is survived by a son, Howard Futrell, address unknown. She is also survived by three siblings: Mary Josephine Coston and her husband, Lester, of Las Vegas, Nevada; Marguerite Delcine Foster and her husband, Winslow III, of Prince George's County, Maryland; and Dr. Clayton Futrell and his life partner, Archer Futrell-Dahlgren Esq., of San Francisco, California; two nieces and a nephew; a good friend, Rosalee Jenkins, who was like a blood sister to her; and her cats, Diamond Jim and Baby Sue.

The wake for Ana Mae will be Tuesday, August 12 from 6 PM to 8 PM at Rollings Funeral Home and Mortuary. The funeral will be held at the funeral home on Wednesday, August 13, with the Reverend Toussaint le Baptiste, associate minister of the Holy Ghost Church of the Good Redeemer, Drapersville, officiating, and Evangelist Buford Charles reading the Scripture.

The family will be at 2725 Clairmont Road, Drapersville.

1

The Wake

The thing that vexed people the most about the death of Ana Mae Futrell wasn't the secrets she took to the grave with her, but the ones that would come to light after she died.

And the thing that stunned people the most about Ana Mae's passing on to glory wasn't the fact that she'd dropped dead of a burst aneurysm while cleaning Doc Hardison's toilet. What everybody wanted to know was, who the hell was Howard?

Ana Mae's obituary in the Ahoskie Times & Union Report said she had a son. But nobody had ever heard of him. And even fewer people than that believed that Ana Mae had ever lifted the hem of her holiness dress long enough to get knocked up.

Then there was the business about the "life partner." None of Ana Mae's kin still lived in town. They'd all high-tailed it out of Hertford County as soon as they could legally get away—and at least one of them before even that. The baby in the family, Ana Mae's brother, Clayton, was a homosexual. Of course, some folks, the ones who remembered when all the Futrells lived in the little house over on Clairmont where they grew up and that Ana Mae still called home, already knew that. That Clayton was kind of sissy-acting as a boy. But lots of people also carried a quite a bit of latent curiosity about him. Nobody had ever listed a "life partner" as a survivor in the local newspaper. To be honest, most folks were surprised they even let that sort of thing in a family publication.

Needless to say, Ana Mae's wake and funeral promised to be a spectacle—if for no other reason than plain curiosity.

So for the better part of two hours, people from all over the county had been trudging into the Rollings Funeral Home on Maple Avenue in Ahoskie, the "big" town next to Drapersville, to pay their respects to the late Ana Mae Futrell. The family would arrive any minute now.

Ana Mae's kin offered some much-needed entertainment in the town. While many who showed up at the wake wondered about Ana Mae's brother, the homosexual who lived in San Francisco and had the nerve to put it in the newspaper so everybody would know, just as many others wanted to know whatever happened to the two sisters. Nobody had seen skin or teeth of either of them for nigh on about twenty years, though Ana Mae always talked about them like they just ran out to get a pack of cigarettes or some milk from the Day-Ree Mart.

And as at wakes all over the place, some people just wanted to see who all else was there.

Ana Mae was so good at keeping secrets, not even her best friend knew about that Howard thing.

Though she was one of the biggest gossips in town, Rosalee Jenkins prided herself on being able to keep a secret when it mattered. It hurt her that Ana Mae hadn't confided in her about this son of hers. So at Ana Mae's wake, Rosalee stood near the casket and fussed at her friend.

"I'm mad at you for dying, Ana Mae. And I'm mad at you for not telling me about that boy."

"She can't hear you, you know, Sister Rosalee."

The gentle words came from the Reverend Toussaint le Baptiste. He stood tall, slim, and as good-looking as he had been back when they were young and before he'd found the Lord. Many a time, Reverend Toussaint, as most people called him these days, had been asked if he was related to the singers El DeBarge or Christopher Williams. He had the lighter than café au lait skin, the wavy "good" hair, and a slim moustache that added a dashing Errol Flynn touch to features that women gravitated to like honey.

"I know, Too Sweet. I just miss her so much."

"Ana Mae is wearing a crown and walking the streets of gold right now."

Rosalee sniffed.

The minister pulled a tissue from a box discreetly tucked at the side of the coffin. Pressing it into her hand, he said, "I miss her too, Sister Rosalee. I miss her too."

༄

Across the room, a small group huddled, surveying the survivors. "Ana Mae never had no kids," someone whispered loudly.

"Shoot, far as I know she was so holy she never spread her legs for anybody."

The person who said that blanched when the comment earned her an evil-eyed look from Zenobia Bryant. "Y'all ought to respect the dead," Zenobia hissed. She glanced around trying to make sure none of Ana Mae's immediate family had heard the nasty remark.

Truth was, though, townsfolk in Drapersville and Ahoskie, North Carolina, weren't the only ones asking who the hell Howard was. Ana Mae's family wanted to know too.

JoJo, a former showgirl in Las Vegas, stood near the door waiting for a cue from the funeral parlor staff. Her husband, Lester, glanced over his shoulder at his brothers-in-law getting out of the car.

"I was expecting your brother's, uh, er, well, his boyfriend . . ."

"His life partner," JoJo said, as if explaining—again—to a none-too-bright child.

Lester snorted. "Yeah, his partner. I expected him to be more faggy. But he's like a regular guy. Even played some football in college."

JoJo narrowed her eyes at her husband. "You can be so vile."

He raised an eyebrow. "What?" he asked, as she stomped away. "What'd I say? I was giving the man a compliment. For a homo he's not all that bad."

"Don't know what she's all in a huff about," Lester

muttered as he patted his breast pocket for his smokes. He might have time for one before they had to go inside. "She told me to be nice to her relatives."

Twenty minutes later, the Reverend Toussaint le Baptiste cleared his throat at the lectern—for the third time. No one in the funeral chapel paid him any mind.

"Our Father, who art in heaven," he yelled above the din of the mourners come to pay respects to the Futrell family.

By the time he got to "Thy kingdom come . . . ," the place had quieted down, and others intoned the old and sacred prayer with him. After the Amen, the minister clasped his hands around his Bible.

"On behalf of the Futrell family, I want to thank you all for coming out tonight. Sister Ana Mae was a faithful member of the church, and she truly loved her some God."

Heads bobbed in agreement. In the back, near a display of mums and gardenias nearly as tall as he was, Lester muttered to JoJo.

"That's the preacher? What they got in the water down here? Would you look at that? Wrist just as limp as your brother's."

JoJo poked him in the ribs with her elbow.

"Hey!"

"Shh," several people said, turning to glare in his direction.

"Can't you just hush up for half an hour?"

Blood rushed to Lester's neck. "I don't see why we have to do this. Why we even had to come out here. You didn't even like Annie Mae."

"Her name is Ana Mae. And just because we weren't close didn't mean I didn't love my sister. And, Mr. High Roller, I didn't ask you to come here with me."

With a scowl toward the back of the room, an indication that JoJo and Lester's hushed conversation wasn't so shushed, Reverend Toussaint extended his hand toward Delcine.

"Sister Marguerite Futrell—some of you all might remember her as Delcine—is going to say a few words."

Lester rolled his eyes. "Ah, now, here we go. Queen Delcine."

JoJo, with her big teased hair, long false eyelashes, and too-tight, sequined red dress, cussed under her breath, then inched away from her husband.

"Excuse me," she said to a man wearing a camouflage green hunter's jacket. She needed to put some distance between her and Lester before they got into a fight right here in the funeral home.

She paused next to her brother-in-law, Delcine's husband, who silently switched places with her. Clayton took her hand in his and squeezed it.

JoJo offered her brother a thankful smile, then turned her attention to their sister.

Dressed in a royal blue fitted suit that looked like it was tailored just for her and that probably cost more than the trailer that JoJo and Lester lived in, Delcine went to the center of the room, where she could address the crowd of about eighty or so mourners who had ventured out to come to the wake.

"My sister, brother, and I thank you for coming tonight. We know you loved Ana Mae very much. Her passing will leave a void in many hearts."

"Spoken like a true diplomat," JoJo said out of the side of her mouth.

Clayton Futrell smirked. "At least we all showed up. I doubt Ana Mae even expected that."

Delcine cut a glance at her siblings, her eyes narrowed and her lips curved up in her familiar smile-snarl.

Both JoJo and Clayton recognized it as a clear sign that their murmuring was reaching her ears. Flushing, they both looked down at the floor. While JoJo was genuinely contrite, she doubted if Clayton was. He'd never minced words on his feelings about either their hometown or the sister he didn't really know. There were a lot of years separating them. Clayton had always had a closer relationship with JoJo, who was just eighteen months older.

Clayton was gorgeous. He'd gotten the best of the family's genes, and JoJo was proud of all he'd accomplished. From the subtle whiff of an expensive aftershave to the custom suit, he exuded the wealth and the privilege that came of being a successful doctor out in California.

Delcine lived with her family in upper-middle-class suburban luxury outside Washington, D.C. She and her husband both had important and high-ranking government jobs that afforded them a lifestyle JoJo envied only when she was feeling sorry for herself. And that was even though it was never quite made clear just what it was that Winslow—or Delcine, for that matter—did for a living. As far as JoJo was able to determine, Winslow had something to do with government contracts, and Delcine worked as the director or assistant director in some kind of government office.

JoJo was a Futrell who, like Ana Mae, hadn't made much of her life. Yeah, she lived in Las Vegas and used to be a sought-after dancer in the top shows on the

Strip, but that was fifty or sixty pounds ago and before she'd hooked up with Lester. He'd promised her the world, and he'd given her a trailer park and a pack-a-day cigarette habit. She'd kicked the cigarettes to the curb. Now if she could just do the same to Lester.

Too many times now she'd heard tourists exclaim that she looked like a black Peggy Bundy. She couldn't help thinking that that had once seemed like a compliment, but that now, compared to her living-high-on-the-hog and well-put-together siblings, she looked like what she was: trailer trash.

Years as both a bureaucrat and a Beltway wife had taught Marguerite Delcine Futrell Foster how to sound sincere without meaning a word of what she said.

In a way, she was sorry that Ana Mae had died. But part of her was glad. Her last tie to this dismal little town was finally severed and she was freed from the past. Of course, her present didn't rank as anything to be proud of—or to write home about, even if she'd wanted to.

Ana Mae had always been mean to her, as far as Marguerite was concerned. She steadfastly ignored the fact that had it not been for her older sister's little white envelopes arriving a few times every semester, she'd have never made it through college.

But that was neither here nor there now. Water under the bridge. Ancient history. Buried, just like Ana Mae would be before long.

"The services will be here," Marguerite said. "To-morrow, at eleven."

The preacher cleared his throat.

"Uh, pardon me, Sister Futrell."

"Foster," Marguerite corrected.

He bobbed his head, pulled out a handkerchief, and dabbed his forehead. "Sister Foster. The funeral tomorrow will be at the church. Sister Ana Mae wanted a church funeral."

Marguerite bit back rising panic. She glanced at her brother and sister. Clayton was eyeing a young man across the room. JoJo gave her a "don't even think about it" look.

Marguerite gestured for the undertaker. Mr. Rollings glided toward the front of the parlor and sidled next to Marguerite.

She gestured for him to lean down so she could consult with him privately.

"We will not pay for limousine and hearse services to cart that casket all over town."

Rollings opened his mouth, apparently thought better of whatever he was about to say, then bowed his head ever so slightly.

"Transportation is included in the cost of our services, Mrs. Foster."

Marguerite brightened. "Oh, well, in that case." She looked back out at the crowd and a little too cheerfully announced, "Tomorrow morning at eleven at . . . ," she looked at Reverend Toussaint le Baptiste.

"At the Holy Ghost Church of the Good Redeemer," he said. "I think everybody knows where it is."

As restrained and respectful chatter again filled the viewing parlor, Rollings put a hand on Marguerite's elbow, guiding her away from the casket.

"I need to speak with the members of the family," he said. "We can meet in my office. It's about some of Miss Futrell's final wishes."

Delcine's gaze darted to her husband's. She jerked her head for him to join her.

Rollings held out a hand toward JoJo and Clayton, indicating he'd like them to join him as well.

"I'll just wait for you here," said a man standing just behind Clayton.

Like Clayton, he looked ready to be photographed for the cover of a magazine. The dark-blue striped suit, crisp white shirt, wing tips, and cuff links pegged him as a man who paid attention to detail. The clothes, the ice-blue eyes, and his blond hair, slicked back and effortless in its salon perfection, gave him the look of one of those rich white men in Ralph Lauren ads.

"No," Clayton said, reaching for the man's hand. Then, as if remembering where he was, he instead tucked his hand in the pocket of his trousers. "You're my family. I want you to hear whatever it is he has to say."

Marguerite's husband, Winslow Foster, the man of few words, fell into step behind her.

Lester and JoJo Coston followed him.

"This better not be about paying some more money to bury that broad," Lester grumbled.

"You have that right, Lester," Winslow muttered.

Almost simultaneously, JoJo hissed "shut up" to Lester, and on a long-suffering sigh, Marguerite, said, "Winslow, please."

As the family made its way to the undertaker's office, a man in paint-spattered brown pants and a plaid shirt buttoned the wrong way accidentally bumped against Winslow going the other way.

"Sorry 'bout that, bro," the man mumbled, tipping the brim of his rumpled brown hat. "Just coming to pay my respects. Ana Mae helped me find a place to stay."

Winslow didn't say anything, but he brushed at the sleeve of his Brooks Brothers suit jacket.

"Ain't you Mr. Dandy," Lester muttered. "Dude said he was sorry."

If Winslow heard the comment, he gave no indication of it.

Delcine—she'd given up on being called Marguerite while in North Carolina—looked around in distaste as they followed the undertaker.

"What doesn't at all seem likely is that Ana Mae would leave a will or have any final wishes. What in the world could she possibly have?"

"That anyone else would want," her husband Winslow added.

Once the Futrell siblings and their significant others were gathered in the spacious, panel-lined office, JoJo spoke first.

"Mr. Rollings, we had the understanding that all of Ana Mae's funeral and burial expenses were prepaid, you know, in advance."

The undertaker nodded as he indicated for them all to sit.

The office was appointed in rich, coffee-colored leathers, and curiously, Marguerite noted, it smelled of cinnamon. Like somebody was baking something good. But in a funeral home?

She looked around for a source and saw an original oil by a noted African-American artist. The piece she and Winslow commissioned four years ago by the same artist, a 36x24 painting of a black Madonna, had been one of the first things to go.

When she noticed Winslow also studying the painting, she closed her eyes for a moment.

"We'd prefer to stand," she said, responding to

Rollings's invitation. "Why did you need to see us? Is it about some additional . . ."

"And probably jacked up . . . ," Lester chimed in.

". . . expense for your services?" Marguerite finished with a sharp glance in her brother-in-law's direction.

When none of the Futrells opted to sit, Everett Rollings went behind his desk and picked up a piece of paper.

"No, rest assured," he said. "There are no additional expenses for Miss Futrell. Everything has been provided for."

"Well, thank God for that," Lester said.

Winslow, as well, looked relieved.

Marguerite wanted to say "Ditto that," the way her son did when he agreed with a point in a family debate. Instead, she folded her arms. "Lester, please. I'm sure Mr. Rollings is going to get to his point."

Archer smiled. He leaned over toward Clayton and whispered, "You didn't tell me your sister had silk claws."

The edges of Clayton's mouth quirked up, but he didn't say anything.

"Well," JoJo prompted, waving her hand in a forward motion.

"It's the matter of the will," the undertaker said.

Clayton glanced at Archer, then said, "Is that it? Just one sheet of paper?"

Everett Rollings looked down at the paper. "This, no. This is just a reminder about the reading of the will. It will be held at least two days after Ana Mae's funeral. She requested that all of you"—he paused and glanced at the spouses, first Archer, then Winslow, then Lester—"and that includes you," he told the three men, "remain in the Ahoskie/Drapersville area. The reading will take place here, in my office."

JoJo shuddered. "In a funeral home? That's kind of creepy. Isn't there supposed to be a lawyer or something?"

All of the siblings and spouses turned toward the lawyer they knew, Clayton's partner, Archer. In addition to looking good, he was also a partner in a large and prestigious firm in San Francisco.

Archer stepped forward and toward a display along one of the walls. "According to this, Mr. Rollings is quite an accomplished man. He's not only a licensed mortician, but also a man of the law."

"What law?" Lester asked.

"According to what?" Marguerite said at the same time.

Archer pointed to framed degrees on one of the walls in the paneled office. "J.D. from Wake Forest University's School of Law. Good school," he said.

Everett Rollings chuckled. "That's quite observant of you, Mr. Futrell, and yes, Wake Forest is one of the leading law schools in the country."

"Futrell-Dahlgren," Archer corrected.

Rollings nodded, acknowledging the corrected last name.

Lester snorted. Winslow rolled his eyes.

"I beg your pardon," JoJo said.

"Can this procedure not take place directly following the burial?" Marguerite said. "We didn't plan to remain here that long. I'm sure Ana Mae's assets, whatever they are, can be dealt with right after the burial."

"Yeah, it'll just take a strong wind to knock down that shack of a house," Lester said. "We'll be done with everything after that."

Several people chuckled at that.

The undertaker-cum-lawyer picked up a pair of wire-rimmed glasses and settled them on his nose. "Actually, your sister left a considerable estate."

That got their attention.

"Considerable in what way?" Marguerite carefully asked.

Rollings smiled the way lawyers do. "I am not at liberty to say at this time. Two o'clock Tuesday, all of the heirs will hear the reading at the same time."

"Tuesday!" that outburst came from several quarters.

"You said two days." If Clayton sounded like a seven-year-old whining, his tone spoke for all of them.

"I'm not hanging around in this hick town for a week," Lester muttered.

Without blinking, Everett Rollings said, "You will, all of you will, if you want to be a part of your sister or sister-in-law's estate. And it's Tuesday because that's the earliest day that could be arranged with my office. Ana Mae specified at least two days after."

Marguerite narrowed her eyes. "You've said all of you, all the heirs, several times now."

"I noticed that too," JoJo said. "Is this Howard that no one seems to know anything about going to be here too?"

"Two o'clock on Tuesday," the lawyer-cum-funeral director said. "My law office is on Clifton Street, the next one over. Same block. You can't miss it, Rollings and Associates." Then, with a nod to them all that was somewhat reminiscent of one given by a butler or valet, he took his leave without another word.

Grumbling, muttering, and a cuss word or two trailed his path as he departed the office, leaving the

Futrells to return to the viewing parlor where Ana Mae was laid out and awaiting the final words to be spoken over her.

But not a single one of them, the Futrells or their significant others, gave any thought to the woman in the casket. They were all too preoccupied contemplating the contents of her will.

2

The Discovery

"**W**hat the hell is there to give anybody?"

The sisters were back at Ana Mae's house on Clairmont Road, boxing up and clearing out Ana Mae's belongings.

Despite the fact that its guests had belittled it, the house wasn't really ramshackle, just small and cluttered, having lasted through more than six decades of the wear and tear of family living. The property was Ana Mae's now, but their parents had lived in the home for several years before Ana Mae, their oldest, had come along.

Even though there were three bedrooms, the rooms were tiny, two of them just barely big enough to hold a twin-size bed, a nightstand, and a dresser. One was Ana Mae's sewing and ironing room. The other room, while utilized as a sort of catch-all space, still had the bunk beds that JoJo and Delcine had slept in as teenagers.

Faded stickers of flowers, peace signs, and teen-idol pop stars were a lasting testament that the furniture remained the same as it had been all those years ago when they'd first done the "decorating" of their new beds. The change to bunk beds, which their father had worked double shifts for the better part of two months to afford, gave each of the girls their own space. They'd been sleeping together in a twin bed until then, scrunched together, constantly fighting, and generally getting on their own and everybody else's nerves. Delcine, being older, got the pick of upper or lower bunk, and chose the bottom one, which suited JoJo just fine.

Ana Mae had knickknacks and doodads all over the place now. A collection of elephants marched along a shelf on one wall in the front room.

"Do you want the elephants?" JoJo asked. "Isn't that your sorority's mascot or something?"

Delcine paused her sorting of the mail. She had three piles going. The first included magazines, church bulletins, newspapers, and whatnot that she tossed into a box marked "trash." Personal mail went in another box, and bills and notices that looked official went into a third box they'd go through later. Ana Mae had a lot of mail and manila envelopes from the Zorin Corporation. It looked important, so it got dumped in the bills box that they would get back to. The trash box was the fullest by far, partly because it needed to be, given the sheer amount of stuff they had to go through, and partly because Delcine was ruthless when it came to clutter.

She looked at the ceramic elephants. "Leave them for now," she said. "I was thinking about it. But I really don't have a place to put them."

"With six thousand square feet of house, you don't have any place to put them? God, Delcine, just say you don't want them." JoJo said, grabbing a piece of newspaper as wrapping and reaching for one of the figurines.

"It's not that," Delcine snapped. "I just . . . just leave them for now, will you?"

Their tempers when dealing with each other, frayed under the best of normal circumstances, and stretched even further given the nature of their forced visit home to North Carolina, weren't getting any better.

JoJo sighed. She put both the elephant and the newspaper on the sofa.

Patchwork quilts that had seen better days were thrown over the chairs and the sofa in the living room. She looked at a pile of paperback mystery novels and a Thompson Chain Reference Bible resting on a pie-crust-edged table along with a pair of reading glasses.

They'd found four or five pairs of reading glasses scattered around the house. Ana Mae clearly bought them cheap so she could have ready access whenever she needed them.

"How about we take a break?" JoJo said.

This time Delcine sighed. "I think that's a good idea."

Lester and JoJo were staying in the house. Lester wanted to sleep in Ana Mae's room, which had a comfortable-looking double bed, but JoJo refused, saying it disrespected the dead.

Out of habit forged long ago, she'd hoisted herself into the top bunk the first night they'd arrived. But she'd found it a lot harder to climb into it when closing in on forty years old and packing about one hundred eighty pounds. So when Lester fell asleep in front of the TV, she'd claimed the bottom bunk and had seen, for the first time in her life, the night view of the world from Delcine's perspective.

Frankly, JoJo thought it was kind of claustrophobic.

The sisters had spent most of the previous afternoon clearing out the debris that had been Ana Mae's worldly goods, with most of the stuff destined for a nearby landfill via the trash haulers.

The first couple of loads went out the door. Another large pile of giveaway stuff, things Marguerite characterized as junk but JoJo convinced her someone less fortunate might want—"Less fortunate than what?" Delcine had snapped. "Ana Mae was a maid, she *was* the less fortunate"—had been boxed up and was on the back porch. According to some of the neighbors who stopped by with a sweet potato pie or cake, a junk man Ana Mae apparently knew would be around to pick up that stuff in the morning—mostly clothes, books, more knickknacks, household linens, and a couple of quilts neither of them wanted and couldn't imagine Clayton and Archer using in their chic California homes, which were straight out of Architectural Digest.

The sisters went to the tiny kitchen. The refrigerator, in avocado green, looked like the same one that had been there decades ago. At least the gas stove had been updated since they'd lived in the house. They sat at the table in their dead sibling's house. JoJo took a napkin from the plastic holder—it featured a beach scene with MIAMI, FLORIDA scrawled in faded pink stenciling at the bottom.

"Wonder where she got this," JoJo said. "Ana Mae wouldn't get on a plane if you paid her."

"Probably from a junk shop," Delcine said. "Or a so-called gift from one of the families she cleaned for."

The table, like much of the counter, overflowed with Tupperware containers and casserole dishes, all brought to the house by Ana Mae's neighbors, friends, and fellow church members. They'd run out of room in the fridge. JoJo pinched a piece of ham from under a platter. After sampling it, she cut a bigger slice and put it on a napkin plucked from the plastic holder.

"You want some?" she offered.

Delcine shook her head no.

"I remember the last time I talked to her," JoJo said. "We had a fight."

"About what?"

JoJo opened her mouth, closed it and looked away. "It . . . it doesn't matter now. It's not important."

Marguerite studied her younger sister for a moment. For all her boldness, JoJo kept some things pretty close to the vest.

Sort of the way Win and I are doing?

Marguerite ignored the question that was bothering her. She and Winslow literally couldn't afford to stay in North Carolina for any extra days—not, of course, that they would ever admit that to anyone in the family. Pressing matters called for them at home. Now was not a good time for Ana Mae to up and die.

She smiled.

"What?" JoJo asked.

Marguerite shook her head. "I was just thinking how Ana Mae never did anything the way the rest of us did."

"She was happy here," JoJo said. "God knows why. This place was a dump, and from what I've seen so far, it's not that much better now than it was then."

"It's not so bad," Marguerite said.

"Since when did you start loving on Ahoskie and

Drapersville, North Carolina? As I recall, you were the first one up and out of here."

"That's because I was the oldest. Well, the oldest after Ana Mae."

"You got out by going to college," JoJo said.

Marguerite heard the defensive edge in JoJo's voice—even after all this time.

"You could have gone to college if you'd wanted to."

JoJo shook her head. "Mama didn't have the money for that, not after Clay cut out the way he did."

"Well, can you blame him? He was like a leper here."

As the two sisters chewed on that for a moment, JoJo started shredding one of the blue paper napkins.

"I'm glad he made it to San Francisco and that he and Archer found each other," JoJo said. "Archer is good for him."

When Marguerite appeared not to have anything to add to that observation, JoJo continued.

"You know, back home in Vegas there's this street-corner preacher guy off the Strip. He's out there trying to get people to stop gambling and drinking. Nobody pays him much mind. But one day, he was out there screaming about how Las Vegas was the new Sodom and Gomorrah and God was gonna smite down the gays because they chose a lifestyle of abomination."

"Hmmph," Marguerite said. "What did you do?"

"I got right up in that so-called preacher's face and told him my brother was gay and that he wasn't an abomination. That he didn't choose to be gay, he was born that way, and God didn't make any mistakes."

"Good for you," Marguerite said. "What did the street-corner preacher say to that?"

"He told me I was going to hell too."

Marguerite frowned. "Well, that's not very Christian, or charitable." Still frowning, she said, "Maybe I'll ask Clay to talk to him."

"Talk to who?"

"Cedric. He hasn't said anything . . ."

JoJo knew that if her sister was thinking of asking their brother to talk to her son, it could be about only one of two things. Since Ced was still in high school, she doubted it was about a career in medicine.

"You think Cedric is gay?"

Marguerite nodded. "But with everything else going on . . . ," she drifted off for a moment. "How are you supposed to ask your kid if he's gay?"

JoJo shrugged. "I don't know. You just ask, I guess. No one ever asked Clay if he was gay. We all just knew, even when he was a little kid. Hmm, I see what you mean," she said. "You're right. Clay can give you some pointers or talk to him, tell him that it gets better. He sure went through hell here before finding his way. What about Winslow? Are he and Cedric close? Maybe his dad could have a talk with him."

Delcine frowned.

The mention of her husband's name shut down any warm and fuzzies that may have been developing between the sisters. Marguerite gave JoJo one of her icy stares, then looked around the kitchen as if JoJo had not even asked a question.

JoJo took the hint. She'd asked one too many questions of her characteristically aloof and private sister.

Winslow either did not want to acknowledge that his only son might be gay or there was something else going on with them. Winslow Foster never had anything much to say. As a matter of fact, he'd spoken more today at the wake and in the lawyer's office than JoJo ever recalled, not that there had been that many meetings between them all.

"Look at this place," Marguerite muttered.

"It's not like she had anything to leave to anybody," JoJo said after a while.

"Hmm," Marguerite said.

"And it just doesn't seem likely that Ana Mae could have had a kid," JoJo added. "Wouldn't we have known? Wouldn't she have said something at some point over the years?"

"How often did you talk to her?" Delcine asked. Before JoJo could answer she continued. "If it was anything at all the way Ana Mae and I stayed in touch, she could have lived on Pluto and I wouldn't have known. I actually can't remember the last time we talked. But she did keep in touch with the kids. Speaking of kids, how is Crystal?"

"I was in touch with Ana Mae more than I ever was with my daughter," JoJo said despondently. "As a matter of fact, I don't even know where she is these days. Sort of like Clay, she turned eighteen, hit the door, and never looked back."

Delcine winced. "I'm sorry to hear that."

JoJo shrugged. "It's like that sometimes with kids, I guess. She was nine when Lester and I got married. And they never really got along, all they did was fight. Sort of like what Lester and I do."

"Another missing child, like this Howard of Ana Mae's," Delcine said.

"I've been giving that quite a bit of thought," JoJo said. "If she had a son none of us knew about, maybe she also left something of value that we didn't know about either."

As one, the two sisters turned in their chairs, looking over the kitchen, with its avocado refrigerator and stained Formica countertops, as if the said something of value might be in plain sight. The tile on the floor had come up in several places and then been painted over, probably in the hopes no one might notice.

"Yeah, right," Delcine scoffed. "And I'm the Easter bunny."

She got up and cut a piece of one of the pound cakes that had been delivered to the house by one of Ana Mae's fellow church members.

"Would you like some?"

"Why not?" JoJo said. "It's not like another piece of cake won't show."

Marguerite held her tongue on that one. Though she hadn't seen her sister in more than six years, JoJo had definitely collected about fifty additional pounds on her five-foot, six-inch frame. And she'd always tended to be what their mama described as "big-boned."

Thick mascara and eyeliner and overly done lips, cheeks, and eyebrows were the only visible clues to her former profession. If Marguerite hadn't seen her on a trip to Las Vegas a few years back, she wouldn't have been able to guess now about JoJo's talent, nor would anyone else. She could dance, really dance, and with the best of them. She could have made something of herself instead of becoming, well, whatever it was she had become.

JoJo got up and started a pot of coffee. As it was brewing, a knock sounded on the back screen door. Before either of them could answer or even move toward the door, Rosalee Jenkins burst in.

"Delcie? M.J.?" she called. "Y'all home?"

JoJo looked at her sister. "No one's called us by those names in years."

Also lost in the past for a moment, Marguerite only nodded, whether in answer to Rosalee or to JoJo's comment didn't really matter. Delcine had been dead and buried for almost twenty years. There was no need to resurrect her or her spirit right now.

"It's Marguerite," she said as Rosalee bustled into the kitchen. She'd kicked off her shoes in the mudroom off the side porch, slipping into a pair of ratty slippers on the way in.

"And JoJo," JoJo said.

"Uh huh. Okay," Rosalee said, looking at the sisters as if both had lost their minds. "I came over to help y'all with the stuff. I know Ana Mae had a lot of it. And I know you two will probably be throwing a lot away. I can help you figure out what should go out and what can be given away. Ana Mae liked to help people, and if something she had could be put to some good use, I'm sure she'd like that. Like all of her fabric and whatnot."

Marguerite managed to refrain from rolling her eyes. The only decent thing they'd found so far was the blend of dark Arabian coffee in Ana Mae's kitchen. A quick look around when they'd first arrived confirmed that all they really needed to clean out the house were a supply of trash bags and a couple of Dumpsters.

"We were just taking a break from sorting some things," JoJo said. "Would you like some coffee? There's a lot of cake and pie."

Rosalee headed to the counter. "Don't mind if I do," she said, opening a cupboard and pulling down a mug. "Ana Mae always kept a pot going even though she preferred her fancy tea."

After Rosalee settled at the table with a sliver of sweet potato pie and spooned what had to be a quarter of a cup of sugar into her coffee, the three women ate or drank in silence for a few moments. Then, dabbing her mouth with one of the paper napkins, Rosalee glanced between the sisters.

"I'm still trying to get over the fact that she's gone. I just can't believe it or get my head around it," Rosalee said.

She pointed to one of the cakes on the counter. "Did Minnie Evers make that cake? That looks like the Tupperware cake set she uses for the bereaved. Minnie can put her foot in some pound cake. I think I'll get me a slice of that too."

After cutting a generous slice of the rich pound cake, with its lemon drizzle topping, Rosalee came back to the table, pushed the sweet potato pie plate to the side and started working on the second dessert.

Delcine and JoJo shared a glance while Ana Mae's best friend wolfed down the cake. To keep from laughing, JoJo put her face in her own plate.

"So," Rosalee said around bites, "what do y'all all think Ana Mae did with all that money?"

Delcine's head snapped up. JoJo's fork clattered to the table.

"What money?" they asked at the same time.

Using her fork, Rosalee leisurely cut herself another bite and looked from one woman to the other. "You know, the money. The lottery money."

The sisters stared at each other.

Though one was fashionably thin and the other

plump and pouty, with eyes wide, the familial resemblance between them was now unmistakable.

JoJo practically jumped in her seat. Delcine laid a hand over her sister's in a calming gesture.

"Rosalee, let me cut you another nice big piece of cake and you can tell us all about this lottery money of Ana Mae's."

3

The Speculation

That night, in the hotel room in Ahoskie that they couldn't afford but required to keep up the appearances of affluence, Marguerite and Winslow Foster had a fight. It started when Marguerite got back from Ana Mae's to discover her husband propped up in bed with a room service tray at his side.

"Have you lost your mind? There's a ton of food over at the house. I could have brought you a plate."

Winslow grunted. "Could have," he said. "But I see you didn't. So what's the difference?"

"You are working my last nerve, Win."

"So? What else is new?"

"You don't even care, do you? We, your children and I, are about to be thrown out into the streets and you couldn't give a flying rat's ass."

"Now there's an image," Win said from the bed.

The look she gave him would have emasculated another man. Winslow, as usual, just ignored her.

She stripped off her blouse and skirt, carefully hanging the pieces in the closet. After swapping a pair of slippers for the black sling-backs she'd been wearing all day, she headed to the bathroom.

"Latrice called looking for you," Winslow told Marguerite.

"What'd she want?" Marguerite said, her voice carrying.

"What do you think she wanted?"

Marguerite came out of the bathroom, a pink moisturizing cream slathered across her face and neck.

Winslow was propped up on the bed, his hands down his shorts and a pay-per-view porno film on the television.

"That is really disgusting," she said.

He grunted.

"Turn it off," she told him. "There's something you need to know about Ana Mae's will."

Clayton and Archer had a suite in a lovely and four-star-rated bed-and-breakfast inn that Archer had located via the Internet from San Francisco following Clayton's declaration that he would not spend a single millisecond in the Dew Drop Inn of Drapersville.

Archer lounged on a chaise in the sitting room, his leather attaché case and laptop with the law firm work he claimed he needed to do abandoned on the desk. He turned the pages of a hardback book fairly rapidly as he read.

When Clayton got off the phone with JoJo, he went in search of Archer.

"You are not going to believe this."

Archer glanced up from the legal thriller he was reading. "What?"

"Ana Mae had money."

Turning a page, Archer put his attention back on the book. "Everybody leaves a little something."

Irritated at being shut out—again—Clayton went to the sofa and snatched the book from Archer's hand. He flung it across the room.

To his credit, Archer didn't snap, but he did sigh. He looked up at Clayton.

"So, it's going to be one of those nights."

"Why don't you respect me?"

Giving Clayton wide berth, Archer got up and retrieved his book, smoothing the pages that had been bent.

"I'm sorry," Clayton said.

"Yeah, whatever. I'm going to bed."

"In the bedroom?" Clayton asked, his voice low, uncertain of what the answer might be, particularly given his recent display of temper.

"You can have it if you want it," Archer said. "I'll sleep out here."

Clayton closed his eyes. "Since this is our last . . . I mean, why don't you take the bed? I'll stay on the sofa."

Archer met his gaze. "Is that what you really want?"

Shaking his head, Clayton sighed. "Is it really over between us?"

"Only if you want it to be."

It took a few moments for Archer's words to sink

in. When they did, a glimmer of hope unfurled some-where deep inside Clayton. It had been like this be-tween them for months—everything fragile, tentative. As if any abrupt moment or movement on either of their parts would shatter their relationship, more than a decade long, into a million pieces.

Clayton held out his hand. He hesitated for a beat, then Archer took it in his—the apology given and ac-cepted.

"What were you saying about Ana Mae?"

"She left money. A lot of it, according to JoJo."

"Where'd it come from?"

"The lottery."

Archer's brow crinkled at that. "The lottery? The gambling lottery? Holy woman Ana Mae won money from playing the numbers? That doesn't sound right."

"I was thinking along pretty much the same line. Maybe JoJo's had a few drinks or took a pill to calm her nerves."

"Are they here at the inn?"

Clayton shook his head. "Lester and JoJo are stay-ing at the house."

Archer made a face.

"My thoughts exactly," Clayton said. "I don't know why, though. If memory serves correctly, JoJo is aller-gic to cats. I wonder where she put them."

"She must be doped up on Benadryl or something to be able to stay there," Archer observed as they set-tled together on the sofa.

"Probably. None of us were particularly close, but if I had to guess, I'd say JoJo kept in touch with Ana Mae more than either Delcine or I did." Then Clayton said, "Hmm, though now that I think about it, it may have been Delcine who was allergic. We didn't have pets growing up, but Ana Mae was always feeding some stray."

"Is that right?"

Clay nodded and told Archer about one of the strays Ana Mae had been hiding in the house until Delcine or JoJo spent twenty-four hours sneezing and their mother found the kitten.

Archer waved away as inconsequential the topic of the cats and allergies. They weren't staying at the house on Clairmont Road, and that was all that really mattered.

For the next few minutes, the two men chatted companionably. Like surface friends, not at all like the confidants they used to be.

Talking about cats and Ana Mae back in the day meant they did not have to talk about the rift in their relationship, a divide that sprang up from nowhere a few months ago. Clayton, while a prominent, successful, and sought-after physician in his professional life, remained insecure in his personal life. Deep down, he was still the picked-on gay kid from small-town North Carolina, and all this trip did was reinforce that thinking—a character flaw he thought he had shed years ago.

As a matter of fact, if Ana Mae hadn't died, necessitating this trip across country, Clayton couldn't at all be sure that Archer wouldn't have moved out of their Pacific Heights home.

But gathering his courage, Clayton broached the topic that had been on his mind since he'd gotten the call that Ana Mae was gone.

"Thank you for coming out here with me."

Archer took his hand. "I know how much you

hated this place. I didn't want you to be alone. Not at a time like this."

A tremulous smile curved Clayton's mouth. Maybe things between them weren't as bad as he'd imagined. Maybe they would sleep together tonight after all.

But before Clayton could nestle into the comfy crook of his lover's broad shoulder, Archer moved away. Clayton bit back a sigh.

"Do you think Ana Mae knew that her preacher is queer?"

That brought Clayton up short. He almost choked. "What?"

"That reverend. Le Baptiste. He's as queer as you and I."

Clayton shook his head. Getting up, he went to the bar and poured himself a glass of chilled Riesling, then mixed a martini for Archer. "Don't be ridiculous. If there's one thing I know about this town, they do not tolerate homosexuals very well. And definitely not homosexual ministers."

Archer accepted the drink, sipped from it, then muttered, "Well, if he ain't now, he used to be."

❧

In her bedroom, in her house around the corner and down the street from Ana Mae's, Rosalee stared at the ceiling, trying to somehow come to grips with the fact that Ana Mae was gone. Really, truly gone. Tomorrow they would put Ana Mae in a grave.

"They may as well do the same thing with me," she thought.

Ana Mae Futrell was her best friend in all the world. Rosalee didn't know how she was supposed to go on without the routine they'd established. Without coffee over cinnamon rolls. Or dissecting the preacher's sermon while flouring up chicken for frying.

Rosalee closed her eyes. Rocked back and forth in her bed. Trying to hold back the tears. Trying, and failing, to dam all the emotions.

"Think about after," she said. "Just think about after."

She'd been stunned, then flattered when Everett Rollings told her she needed to be at the reading of Ana Mae's will. Rosalee couldn't imagine what her friend had left for her. Even though Ana Mae had hit the lottery, there wasn't never no evidence of it in her house or in the way she lived. She still cleaned houses and ironed clothes for her regulars. Just like her mama did.

Thoughts of Sister Georgette, long gone on to glory, made Rosalee smile. Now there was a true Southern lady. Despite Delcine's airs—imagine wanting people to call her by that fancy name Marguerite? Who ever heard of such—and despite JoJo's over-the-top clothes and makeup, the fact was neither of them could hold a candle to their mama.

Georgette Howard Futrell—Sister Georgette to everyone who knew her—raised 'em all. But only Ana Mae got any common sense and decency. Maybe that was because she always remembered where she came from and gave people the love they needed.

Ana Mae was a friend's friend, and Rosalee's grief, which she kept bottled inside during the daylight hours, came pouring out at night when she realized that Ana Mae was well and truly gone.

"Lordy, Lord," she whispered as the tears started up again. "I'm sure gonna miss you, Ana Mae."

"Trust me," Clayton said. "No preacher of Ana Mae's is gay."

"If you say so."

"What do you think will happen tomorrow?"

"We'll bury your sister," Archer said.

"I mean with the undertaker, or rather the lawyer," he said, sampling his wine. "And that's a perfect example of why I escaped this place. Only in small-town North Carolina would you have an undertaker who is also the lawyer."

Archer smiled, amused. "Actually . . ."

"Don't tell me. You know someone at home who is a mortician-attorney."

"No. What I was going to say is I think the town is kind of charming. Nostalgic even."

The curl of Clayton's lip and the jut of his chin spoke volumes. Clayton despised his hometown. Archer had heard plenty of the horror stories. Returning for the funeral had apparently opened wounds that had yet to heal, even after all these years and miles away.

"Nostalgic," Clayton practically spit. "Let me tell you about nostalgia around here."

He yanked up the sleeve on his shirt. "You see that!" He jabbed his finger at a zigzag scar on his arm. "That's what's it's like to be a fag in a small town. I got sliced there. And there," he said, yanking his undershirt up to reveal the six-inch scar along his side.

"I know, Clay." Archer's words were low, soothing. "It was a long time ago. Things change. People change."

"Maybe in San Francisco, where we aren't an abused minority. Here, it's just like Hell."

"No one is attacking you. No one has even said anything."

Clayton shook his head. "You don't get it, Archer. They don't have to say anything. It's just ingrained deep. Like bone marrow."

Before the argument could blossom into a full-out battle, a telephone call interrupted Marguerite and Winslow in their hotel room. Winslow was now having a heated conversation on the telephone with a creditor while Marguerite listened in on the other line in the room, although she was trying to keep her presence masked from their caller.

"I most certainly am not ducking my financial responsibility," he said. "Remember, it was I who called you today. I could have easily ignored your message."

The way we do all your telephone calls, Marguerite added silently.

"My wife has had a death in her family," Winslow said. "We are about to come into some money."

She glanced at her husband.

We?

In the twenty-odd years they'd been married, he'd set eyes on Ana Mae all of twice—the first time when they'd married, and the second time earlier today as she lay stretched out in a top-of-the-line casket at the Rollings Funeral Home. Now all of a sudden, he was the bereaved brother-in-law.

"I don't know how much the inheritance is," Winslow said. "We have to wait until the reading of the will."

Margaret winced at what the collection agent said.

She saw Winslow's mouth tighten.

"Yes," he said, "I understand."

He replaced the receiver, and then she did the same on the telephone by the bed.

A second later, a crash and a thump made her yelp in alarm. She hit the floor, taking cover.

Her heart pounding, she crawled to the edge of the bed and peeked around it.

"Winslow?"

Her husband was on his knees in the middle of the hotel room floor. The telephone, yanked from one wall and thrown at another, lay on the floor amid pieces of what used to be a lamp.

We're going to have to pay for that, was her first thought after she realized they weren't under attack.

It took a moment for the sound in the room—like an injured animal keening—to register. When it did, her eyes widened.

Winslow was crying. Actually crying.

Marguerite tried to feel his pain, to empathize with him. She too was on this fast-sinking ship, stuck without a lifesaver. But she couldn't cry. She was too angry. Angry that she'd married someone like him. Angry that the life she'd worked her entire life to build was tumbling down upon her, brick by brick, lie by lie.

A cell phone trilled.

Pulling herself up on the bed, Marguerite went to the phone that was charging on the bureau.

"Hello?"

A moment later, she held the phone out to Winslow. "It's Abrams."

She didn't need to hear his side of this conversation. She knew exactly what was being said.

For the second time in her life, Marguerite wished she owned a handgun. It would be so much simpler to just end it all now.

As Winslow talked to his attorney, she bent to pick up the big pieces of the shattered lamp.

The conversation with Abrams lasted longer than she'd anticipated. On Winslow's end, all she'd heard was a curt, "Yes," "No," or "I won't agree to that."

It was over. All over.

Marguerite did the calculations in her head. She had, by necessity, gotten very good at that lately.

If Ana Mae had won one hundred twenty-five thousand dollars, as Rosalee said, she'd probably tithed ten percent off the top to that weirdly named church of hers. Then she'd probably paid some bills. So at most, they were talking about maybe eighty grand left of the lottery money. Even if she'd earned a little interest on it, when the money was split three or more ways, the most they were looking at was thirty grand each. Close, but not nearly enough.

A moment later, Winslow fell onto the camelback sofa. Marguerite sat at the desk in the room, her hands folded together. She didn't look at her husband.

"What did he say?" she asked. "Is it looking any better about the indictment?"

4

The Funeral

The day of Ana Mae's funeral dawned. By nine o'clock the air outside was sticky warm, throwing off the kind of heat that made you want to be not close to anybody—the kind of heat that smelled like tired.

Since Ana Mae had left instructions with Everett Rollings about how she wanted things done, Rosalee and the Futrell sisters didn't have to do much by way of planning a service.

The change in venue from the funeral home to the Holy Ghost Church of the Good Redeemer meant the flowers that had been delivered to the Rollings Funeral Home needed to be taken to the church for the service. There were a lot of them, and Rosalee was the coordinator for the flower girls, the women who carried the flowers from the funeral to the gravesite. On short notice, she'd dragooned Zenobia Bryant into helping her.

The two women were putting several arrangements

in the trunk of Rosalee's car when a big black limousine pulled up. It didn't belong to the Rollings Funeral Home.

"That look like the car the president be riding in," Zenobia said.

"It ain't the president," Rosalee said with some assurance.

"How you know?"

"No po-lice," she answered. "If the president of the United States was coming to Ahoskie, North Carolina, we'd a knowed about it long for now, and there'd be plenty of them Secret Service agents all over town."

"So who you reckon that is?" Zenobia asked.

"Probably somebody done got lost on the way to Charlotte or Raleigh," Rosalee said.

A moment later a car door opened and a tall thin white man strode around the car, opened a back door, and moved to the side.

A portly older white man in a dark suit stepped out of the limo, said something Zenobia and Rosalee couldn't make out, then leaned back into the open door, presumably talking to someone still in the shadows of the car.

"Can we help you?" Zenobia called out.

The short older man stood straight. He plastered a smile on his face and came forward, his hand outstretched.

"He need to get out in the sun a little more often," Rosalee muttered under her breath.

"Good day, ladies. I'm looking for Rollings Funeral Home and Mortuary."

Rosalee pointed toward the sign, big as day on the side of the building. "You found it."

"Splendid," the man said.

The two women exchanged a glance.

"The services for Miss Futrell are here?"

"Not anymore," Rosalee said. "It's over at the church."

"The church? Which church?"

Rosalee and Zenobia exchanged a glance, and then decided if somebody in a limousine was asking after Ana Mae's funeral, it couldn't come to any harm.

They gave him the name, the address, and the directions.

"Funeral start at eleven," Rosalee told him. "Preacher likes to start on time. If you want a good seat, you better get there early."

"Very good, madam. Thank you." The man touched his forehead.

"You got a fever or something?" Zenobia asked.

"I beg your pardon?"

The two women exchanged another glance.

"You know Ana Mae?"

"Thank you for your assistance," the man said. Without another word of explanation, he strode back to the waiting car. He slid into the back. The chauffeur shut the door and walked to the driver's side, and a moment later, the car sped away.

Zenobia put a hand on her hip. "Who the hell was that?"

"Look like Tony Soprano to me," Rosalee said.

"Nah, Tony Soprano had that beefy-looking face."

Rosalee waved a hand. "Whatever," she said. "Let's get the rest of the flowers and condolences and get them over to the church."

The Holy Ghost Church of the Good Redeemer was at standing-room-only capacity. Capacity for the congregation of the small church with the big heart was about three hundred people, plus the amen corner up front, three short pews off to the side for the deacons. Folding chairs lined the back wall and the side aisles, and people were standing in the spaces that were left over and just barely big enough to squeeze into.

The flowers—dozens and dozens of memorial arrangements, from carnations tied with raffia from the children at the Sunday school to bouquets and pots and sprays—just about rivaled the size of Ana Mae's pink casket.

Three church nurses in crisp white uniforms, white shoes, white hose, and jaunty white caps stood at each aisle with tissue boxes at the ready. Plenty of weeping and carrying on from the gathered mourners greeted the small family when they filed in and came down the center aisle for one last glimpse of the not so dearly departed.

Delcine and Winslow Foster followed one of Mr. Rollings's aides; behind them came Clayton and Archer Futrell, then JoJo and Lester Coston. As Ana Mae's closest friends, Rosalee Jenkins and Zenobia Bryant also came in with the family processional.

The siblings, stunned at the public outpouring of grief, wondered if they'd walked into the right service.

They were in the right place, though. Ana Mae, laid out at the front of the church in her pink coffin and wearing what Rosalee declared to the sisters was her favorite blue suit, would herself have been embarrassed and amazed at both the turnout and the genuine grief expressed by the mourners.

Archer leaned into Clayton. "Your sister was awfully special to these people."

"So I'm gathering," Clayton said.

They all sat in the first pew on the right side of the church. Delcine was on the center aisle, with Winslow sitting next to her. Clayton was to Winslow's right, and Archer next to him, followed by JoJo and then Lester. On the second pew behind the Futrells sat Rosalee Jenkins and Zenobia Bryant.

One of the nurses positioned herself in the aisle near Lester as if one of the family members might need medical assistance during the funeral. Not likely. All they wanted to do was get it over with and return to their regular lives, far from rural North Carolina.

After Evangelist Buford Charles read the Scripture, an Old Testament text out of Isaiah and then one from the book of Romans in the New Testament, a stout woman got up. Wearing a black dress and a hat as big as a manhole cover, and carrying a white-lace-edged handkerchief almost as big as her hat, she made her way to the front of the church. She touched Ana Mae's coffin, shook her head sadly, and then faced the congregation.

"Giving honor to God, to all of the ministers and pulpit associates, and to the Futrell family, I want you all to pray for me while I attempt to sing this song for Sister Ana Mae."

She bowed her head, closed her eyes for a moment, and then lifted the microphone from the stand and to her mouth.

Thirty minutes later, when she finished an a cappella rendition of "Amazing Grace," Ana Mae's favorite hymn, there wasn't a dry eye in the sanctuary, and people were hollering out "Thank you, Jesus" and "Hallelujah!"

Delcine and Winslow's hands were clasped and their heads bowed. JoJo was on her feet waving her hands and crying "Glory!" Even Lester was choked up.

The ushers handed out fans, and the church nurses tended to two people who'd fallen out in the spirit in the center aisle.

Archer, while not the only white person in the church, was clearly the only one with his mouth agape. He turned to make a comment to Clayton and was astonished to see his longtime partner swaying in his seat, his eyes closed and his face contorted.

Over the next hour, there was more singing, a lot of praying, a reading of the obituary—though anybody who could read had already done so since it was printed in the funeral program—and condolence messages from seemingly every church official, elected official, and civic group in all of North Carolina.

"We've been here two hours, and they still haven't gotten to the eulogy," Archer whispered.

"Shh," Clayton said. "Welcome to a black funeral in the South."

"Oh, my God," Archer moaned, as he rubbed his temples.

Finally, the Reverend Toussaint le Baptiste rose and came forward in the pulpit.

"Brothers and sisters, we are gathered here this afternoon to say our final earthly farewell to our beloved sister in Christ, Sister Ana Mae Futrell. I'm not going to be before you long . . ."

"Thank God for that," Archer muttered.

The comment earned him a jab in the arm from JoJo and a pinch from Clayton.

". . . but before I begin, I think it's only fitting that

anyone who wants to say a word about Sister Ana Mae have the opportunity to do so."

"Oh. My. God."

"Shh!"

"Now I know this isn't on the program, but I don't think Sister Futrell or the family will mind." He looked at Delcine, who shook her head. A rousing round of "Amens" rolled through the deacons' area, and the organist played softly as people rose across the sanctuary and lined up for a turn to sing Ana Mae's praises.

A bald-headed deacon with pop-bottle glasses passed a handheld microphone over, and the first of about twenty people in line testified about the sweetness of Ana Mae's spirit, the time she cooked dinner for my family when I was laid up by sickness, the quilt she made me, the Sunday school lesson she taught us.

Bringing up the rear was a pudgy white man in his late fifties or early sixties. He resembled the actor Tom Bosley and cleared his throat twice when he took the microphone.

"Good afternoon. My name is David Bell, and I wasn't going to come forward," he began, his voice starting to quiver.

A gasp from the second pew had a few heads turning.

"But when I heard that Ana Mae was gone, I just . . . ," He started crying.

"Take your time, brother. Take your time."

David Bell pulled a monogrammed handkerchief from his pocket and wiped his eyes, then his brow.

"I'm sorry about the display of emotion," he said, "but Ana Mae, she just meant the world to me. I've listened to everyone else say what a good woman she was, and I, I have to agree. We, we've known each other a long time and whenever she came to visit . . ." He sniffed again, and again he got encouragement from the mostly black congregation to take his time.

"Whenever she came to visit, we'd talk for hours, just hours. She loved this town and all of you," he said. "And I, well, I loved her."

He broke down crying again as the congregants applauded his testimonial.

Delcine leaned forward and across her husband to tap Clayton's knee. "Howard's father?" she mouthed.

Clayton shrugged and looked down at JoJo, who was also intensely studying David Bell.

So was Rosalee in the pew behind them, and Reverend Toussaint in the pulpit, and all of the folks who'd spent the last few days wondering about Ana Mae's mystery son.

David Bell was clearly torn up, and he'd intimated that he and Ana Mae spent a lot of time together. Could that have been time between the sheets?

Bell handed the microphone to a deacon and made his way around the flowers and over to the front pew where the family sat. He reached in his suit jacket pocket and pulled out something.

"If there is ever anything I can do for your family, please don't hesitate to contact me," he said, handing a small, cream-colored card to Delcine, one to Clayton, and another to JoJo. "You have my deepest condolences."

One of the nurses, anticipating that he might fall out from grief, stood nearby and walked at his side as David Bell made his way up the center aisle and back to his seat in the rear of the church. Dozens of pairs of eyes followed his path.

Then, as yet another preacher launched into yet another long-winded prayer, the three Futrell siblings and their spouses studied the business cards they'd been given.

David Z. Bell
Chairman And CEO
The Zorin Corporation

The company's Columbus, Ohio, address and telephone numbers were embossed in the same rich coffee-colored ink as his name.

As the man of the Futrell house, Clayton had been designated as the family spokesman today, a job Delcine thought was rightfully hers as the oldest. So when his name was finally called to give reflections on the life of his older sister, Clayton rose.

The pulpit overflowed with preachers and holy women, so many that folding metal chairs from the funeral parlor had been brought in to accommodate all of them. More flowers in sprays and bouquets and memorial tributes filled every other spot.

The flowers alone astonished every single one of the Futrells. Who knew people cared that much about Ana Mae? Since Delcine spoke at the wake and Clayton would now speak at the funeral, JoJo had been the designated family member who would collect the cards. They'd go through them later. Not that any of them actually knew the people who had sent them.

Forcing his mind back to what he was supposed to be thinking about, Clayton unconsciously straightened his tie, then put the first foot on the three steps leading to the pulpit and microphone.

Reverend le Baptiste cleared his throat. Loudly.

Clayton put his right foot on the next step.

Coughing broke out on the dais.

He glanced up. The pastor of Ana Mae's church and about a dozen other clergy members were giving him what could best be described as the evil eye. Definitely a *thou shalt not* look.

Unsure, Clayton paused on the step.

"Brother Futrell," someone said behind him. "There's a microphone for you right here."

Suddenly furious and feeling tenfold the slights he'd endured his entire life in Drapersville and Ahoskie, Clayton refused to let them intimidate him.

"It's all right," he said, stepping up to the pulpit. "I'll just stand here."

Gasps erupted from both the mourners and the preachers, mostly Baptists, with a few Pentecostals and Evangelicals also in the mix.

Three on the dais rose, as if to block the sacrilegious from their holy ground.

"It's all right," Reverend Toussaint le Baptiste said. "Let the boy go on."

Clayton, not knowing that he'd broken a cardinal rule of the black church—thou shalt not step into the pulpit unless ordained—nodded his thanks to the minister and patiently waited for the sputtering from the three and the murmuring from the assembly to quiet down. He glanced at Archer, who smiled at him.

Clayton's mouth dropped open.

It was the first true smile he'd seen from his partner in a long time. A long, long time.

They'd been going through a rough patch lately.

Well, he conceded, it was more than a patch. They were just about splitsville. This trip to the East Coast, to bury the sister Clayton never took time to get to know, was probably their last as a couple. So to see Archer smile, to get that silent encouragement from him meant more than words could ever say.

Tears welled in his eyes. He tried to blink them back, but to no avail.

"That's all right, brother. We understand," someone called from the audience.

Clayton wiped his eyes, wondering for a moment what the person was talking about and when in the history of the church it became acceptable for people to holler at the person standing at the lectern.

Then he remembered.

Ana Mae.

They thought he was crying about the death of Ana Mae.

He took a deep breath, sent a tremulous smile toward Archer, and pulled out the note cards he'd tucked in his pocket.

"First, my sisters and I would like to thank all of you for your prayers and expressions of sympathy. As some of you know, all three of us left Drapersville many years ago. We didn't stay in touch with each other or with Ana Mae as often as we should have."

He paused for a moment and the amen corner encouraged him to "Take your time, son."

Clayton glanced in that direction, saw someone he remembered from a long time ago, and lost his train of thought for a moment. Reginald Crispin, an old lover, apparently remained so deep in the closet that he felt safe masquerading as a deacon in the church.

The hypocrisy galled Clayton. Then the anger started bubbling up again.

In truth, he didn't have that much to say about Ana Mae, but he could and would give these people a piece of his mind for his own peace of mind. He opened his mouth to lambaste the hypocrites.

A throat cleared in the congregation.

Clayton recognized that particular sound. Archer.

He met his partner's gaze for barely a second, and in it he saw what mattered most to him. Clayton smiled, took another moment to compose himself. And with a roll of his shoulders, he let the injustices go. This was about Ana Mae, not about the painful prejudices of his past.

"Yes," he then said, "Ana Mae was the only one of us who stayed. As the presence of each and every one of you here today indicates, that choice she made to stay made this church and this community richer."

Clayton talked for five more minutes about Ana Mae, relating a story about the four of them one summer.

From the pulpit, he glanced down at JoJo and Delcine, then smiled. "I hope my sisters don't mind me telling you all this," he said, "but it really illustrates the type of big sister Ana Mae was to us. There used to be a fair that came through town every year. They'd set up in that field on the other side of the old mill."

"Still do," someone in the congregation yelled out.

JoJo and Delcine, both remembering, sat there smiling and shaking their heads at Clayton.

"One summer, Mama was working and said she would take us over there on Saturday right after she got paid. Well, JoJo and I wanted to go that first night, Wednesday."

"When they give away the free ice cream," another mourner hollered up.

Clayton laughed. "Exactly. Since the ice cream was free, we figured all we needed was bus fare or jitney fare to get over there, since it was too far for us to walk."

"Oh, Lord," Delcine said, to the amusement of the people across the aisle from her.

"Ana Mae was where she usually was on Wednesday nights," Clayton said.

"At church," half the congregation said.

Nodding, Clayton, a natural storyteller, continued. "JoJo and I enlisted Delcine in the plan."

"You mean you co-opted me," she said.

That earned a laugh from the congregation.

"She was supposed to be babysitting until Ana Mae got home from prayer meeting. We, er, well, to put it delicately, we liberated some change from a jar Mama kept on the kitchen counter."

"Oh, Lord have mercy," one of the amen corner residents intoned.

"You've got that right, deacon," Clayton said.

"We took what we thought we would need and headed out and over to the Day-Ree Mart to catch a jitney to the fair. Somebody—and to this day I don't know who—but somebody must have seen us and hightailed it over to the church to report that them three little Futrell kids were running away from home," he said, his voice taking on the Southern drawl of a town tattletale.

"Well, it took Ana Mae maybe all of three seconds to figure out where we were headed.

"No sooner had we paid the jitney and got in the line than we heard a horn blowing and some yelling behind us. It was Ana Mae. With a switch. Waving it out the car window and hollering."

The mourners gathered for Ana Mae's homegoing roared with laughter. They knew what was coming next.

"We were this close," Clayton said, holding his hands about a foot apart, "to claiming that free ice cream when a car screeched to a halt, tires kicking up dust and gravel, and Ana Mae jumped out."

Behind Clayton, Reverend Toussaint was wiping tears of laughter from his eyes. "That was me," he said between guffaws. "Lord, I haven't thought about that in years."

Clayton turned and grinned. "That was you?"

Reverend Toussaint nodded and got a few jabs from the ministers sitting next to him.

"All we knew," Clayton told the congregation, "was that Ana Mae had commandeered somebody's car. She came out of that front seat yelling, 'No ice cream for those three!' and waving that switch like she was gonna give a whupping to every kid standing in that line. The poor carnival man probably thought she was our mother, the way she was carrying on. But we were wrong and all three of us knew it. I was crying by then and JoJo over there," he said, with a nod toward her, "she was whining about the ice cream. And Delcine was saying, 'They made me do it. They made me do it.'"

The sisters were falling over their husbands and Archer, laughing in the pews.

"We piled into the backseat of that car and got a sermon and a half about lying, stealing, leaving the house, and disobeying Mama, who'd said no carnival until Saturday. Frankly, we knew we were dead. But you know what," Clayton said, his voice lowering as he leaned into the microphone.

Folks sat forward in their seats to hear what happened.

Clayton closed his eyes for a moment even as the laughter died down. "Ana Mae never told on us. Not a peep.

"Of course, we didn't know that," he said, standing straight again and chuckling to himself. "We were scared . . ."

"Terrified," Delcine called out to renewed laughter.

". . . about what Mama was gonna do to us. Delcine told us Mama was just biding her time, waiting to punish us. It never came, though, and we learned a valuable lesson that day and week about the love of an older sister."

As he left the pulpit to thunderous applause, the congregants were still chuckling. When he took his seat, Archer beamed at him.

More than an hour and a half later, after the mourners listened to and hollered back at Reverend Toussaint's sermon about the virtuous woman, an altar call—"That we would be dishonoring God and Sister Ana Mae if we didn't have"—and another protracted song about flying away to glory, Ana Mae Futrell's funeral finally came to a close.

Afterward, no one would recall just how the receiving line came to be, but the Futrell family stood in a line in the vestibule getting condolences and healthy doses of "I'm gonna keep y'all all in my prayers."

A brief lull in the line, which had to be at least four miles long, had Archer leaning over. "Does that mean because we're sinners?"

Clayton tried not to crack a smile. He failed.

"That's all right, Brother Futrell. Let it out. Sister Ana Mae enjoyed a good laugh too."

Clayton looked up to see the Reverend le Baptiste. But the reverend's eyes were on Archer. Really on Archer.

Remembering what Archer had said about the preacher, Clayton studied the older man. Well, he guessed he was older. The Reverend Toussaint le Baptiste could have been anywhere from forty to sixty years old. His slicked-back hair—today either straightened with a hot comb or relaxed—was long enough to be in a ponytail. But the look suited him. He was tall, at least a head taller than both Clayton and Archer.

If he ain't now, he used to be.

Clayton couldn't see it. But Archer's gaydar was usually pretty accurate. This time, though, he was wrong. Drapersville didn't suffer homosexuals lightly, and there was no way a gay preacher, no matter how deep on the down-low, could survive if the culture in the black community was the same as it had been when Clayton was coming along . . . and coming out.

His suit, the blue so dark it was almost black, was a throwback to an earlier age. Clayton pegged it as '60s vintage and liked it a lot. What he didn't like was the way the man's gaze seemed to gobble up Archer. Almost as if Clayton wasn't standing right there.

"Reverend!" Rosalee bustled over, breaking both the growing green settling somewhere in Clayton's midsection and the minister's intense perusal.

Clayton looked at Archer, who winked at him.

The playful gesture confused Clayton.

"Be right with you, Sister Jenkins," Reverend Toussaint called. "I am truly sorry for your loss," he said, directing his comment toward Clayton. "Ana Mae was a special woman. We're all going to miss her dearly."

"Would you just look at that?"

"What?"

Bertie and Eula Lee, two of Drapersville's busiest busybodies, had a view of all the goings-on. Their attention at the moment zeroed in on the area where the Futrells greeted the mourners a few feet away. Their lasers trained on the three couples.

Eula Lee looked at Bertie. "You sure he's a little . . ." She waggled her wrist to make her point.

"Oh, yeah. Everybody knew when he was growing up."

"Not him," Eula Lee said. "The other one, the good-looking white boy with him."

"He's the one who was named in the paper. The partner," Bertie said, with emphasis on the word as if it didn't quite sit well with her. "I thought all those sissy boys were, well, you know, sissy-like. But he's looks regular. Real easy on the eyes too."

"Where do you think she got that dress?"

"Who, Delcine? I don't know, but did you notice how fragile she looks? She needs some of them pounds Josephine done picked up."

"Bertie, the woman's sister just died. Don't you reckon she ought to be looking at least a little bit fragile?"

Bertie snorted. "Nary a one of them Futrells ever gave a rat's ass about Ana Mae. Now they're all here, pretending like they cared. If they cared, they would've kept track of their sister."

"How do you know they didn't?"

"Ana Mae told me," Bertie said, her puffed-out chest and chin indicating she had some status with the recently deceased. "Said she hadn't seen that Las Vegas one since their mama died. The fancy one from up north would send a hoity-toity Christmas card every year, sometimes from places like England and Zimbabwe."

"Zem Bob who?"

"Zimbabwe. It's a country over in Russia or something," Bertie added, clarifying for her less-informed friend.

"Actually," Archer said, sidling up and interrupting the ladies. "Zimbabwe is in Africa. The country borders South Africa and Mozambique. It used to be called Rhodesia. Its people are the Shona. And if you don't mind my saying so, I believe the two of you would be treated as queens there."

Eula Lee pursed her lips, distaste marring her red-rimmed mouth. "You're the partner."

Archer nodded. "That's correct. I'm a partner in the law firm of Matthews, Dodson, and Dahlgren. I'm Dahlgren."

Bertie chuckled and nudged Eula Lee. "I like him."

That made Archer smile. He winked at her. "I like you too."

Eula Lee wasn't so convinced, but Bertie had a question that couldn't wait.

"Would you tell me something? I've always wanted to know, you know, if it hurts. Back there. When you . . ." Her words trailed off, but she continued to look him in the eye.

Eula Lee gasped, jabbed Bertie hard with her

elbow. But then looked at Archer expectantly. She too wanted to know the answer.

Archer remained nonplussed. His gaze shifted from one woman to the other, then a slow smile started at his mouth. He waggled a finger toward Bertie, indicating for her to come closer.

She leaned forward. Archer cupped a hand over her ear and whispered something.

Bertie guffawed. Loud. So loud, heads turned toward them.

"What?" Eula Mae demanded. "What'd he say?"

"I'm gonna have to try that," Bertie said.

Archer winked at her and walked away.

Eula Lee grabbed her friend's arm. "What'd he say? What are you gonna try?"

But Bertie's only answer was a lingering chuckle and a self-satisfied smile.

Hours later, long after the funeral and the meeting with Everett Rollings, instead of anticipating their imminent departures from Drapersville, the Futrells and their spouses sat around Ana Mae's house, looking glum.

From among Ana Mae's five hundred plus TV channels Lester found an ESPN network he didn't know existed. Archer and Winslow—two men with less than zero in common professionally, culturally, or socially beyond their relationships with a Futrell sibling—tried to find something to talk about.

Archer eventually gave up.

"I'm going to go make some tea. Would you like some?"

"Tea?" Winslow asked, as if Archer had offered him crack cocaine. "No, thank you. But I'll bet there's some coffee going."

He, clearly, also wanted to escape Lester's play-by-play and dismal company.

"Hey, Archie, will ya grab me a beer while you're up?" Lester called.

Archer didn't deign to reply but made his way to the kitchen where JoJo, Delcine, and Clayton sat at the table, grumbling.

"We're stuck for days in this backwater swamp. Kill me now," Delcine said.

"I thought I'd be halfway back home by then," JoJo said.

"Hey, guys," Archer said in greeting to all of them. "Lester wants a beer," he told JoJo.

"He can get it himself," she said.

"My sentiments exactly," Archer said, heading to the kitchen counter to survey the cakes and rolls and casserole dishes in an array of plastic containers and Pyrex bowls.

Not seeing what he was looking for, he started opening cabinets. A few moments later, "Ah, here we go."

After filling a kettle from the tap and turning on a burner, he leaned against the counter.

"So, what's the plan?" he asked.

Winslow, who had apparently grown weary of Lester's running commentary on NFL game highlights, appeared at the kitchen doorway. "I was wondering the same thing," he said, then to Marguerite, "We're on a timetable."

"I know that," she snapped.

"We have open tickets," Archer said.

"But I hadn't planned to be here for more than three days," Clayton said.

They all grumbled for a few minutes, speculating on how much lottery money might be left for them to split.

When the kettle whistled, Archer made tea. "Anyone want a cup?"

"I'll take one," JoJo said.

"Honey or sugar for sweetener?"

"Whatever you're having," she said.

"Well, the service was nice," Winslow said. "You did a nice job, Clayton."

JoJo playfully hit Clayton in the arm. "I cannot believe you told them about that carnival day."

Clayton got more compliments about his storytelling, and in the way of families across the world, they spent the better part of the next hour or so reminiscing and laughing together, enjoying each other's company while under the surface remained the reason they'd all been brought together: the death of a loved one.

"Hey, Archie," Lester said, appearing in the kitchen doorway. "I thought you were bringing me a beer. What's everybody laughing about?"

The life went out of the party.

Delcine stood up. "Let's head back to the hotel, Win."

"It is late," her husband said.

To Lester, Archer said, "My name is Archer, not Archie. And you can find your beer in the refrigerator."

Muttering under his breath, Lester stomped to the fridge for his long-awaited brew. "If we have to be in this hellhole of a town for two more days, I'm gonna need to find a liquor store."

Later that night, Archer told Clayton about the incident after the funeral with Bertie and Eula Lee.

As Archer expected, the eruption immediately followed.

"That is exactly why I detest this place!"

"She didn't mean any harm," Archer said. "And you won everyone over with your tribute to Ana Mae. Actually, I thought it was quite brave of her to voice her question."

"Brave? Brave? Try bold. Or maybe just damn ignorant."

Archer stripped off his tie, then undid the buttons on his shirt. "Don't be such a bitch. I liked her. She wanted to know something and asked someone who might have the answer."

Clayton harrumphed, but he got distracted when Archer shrugged off his shirt. His gaze met his partner's.

"It's been a long time," he said.

"Yes," Archer replied. "It has. Why don't we take the advice I gave Bertie?"

Making love was the furthest thing from Delcine and Winslow Foster's minds. Intimacy had not been a part of their relationship since Winslow finally confessed to her just how much trouble he (and by extension, they) were in. Worried about her future, Delcine paced the space between the bed and the television.

"You're blocking my view," Winslow said, trying to see the pay-per-view boxing match he'd ordered.

She stopped, standing directly in front of the television.

"We are not down here on vacation, Winslow. We need to figure out what we're going to tell the children."

"The children already know."

Delcine looked stricken. "You told them?"

He scooted over on the bed to get a view unobstructed by his wife. "No. But they're teenagers. It's hard to keep secrets from them."

Putting her hands on her hips, Delcine moved and blocked his access to the television screen again, then turned around and manually hit the power button.

"You mean like the way you kept secrets from me?"

"Oh, here we go again," Winslow said on a sigh.

"That's right, 'here we go again.' Do you even have a plan, or am I supposed to be the one, as usual, to figure out how to keep this family afloat?"

Launched now, their well-worn argument would rage into the night.

5

The Reading of the Will

It was two days later, and one by one the disgruntled heirs trooped into the law offices of Everett Rollings, located on the back side of the funeral parlor—or if you were driving down Clifton Street, the law office was on the front and the funeral home in the back. With one piece of real estate and one office, Rollings had two street addresses and two distinct and prosperous business enterprises.

Rollings and Associates specialized in wills, divorces, and custody cases. The words conflict of interest didn't seem to occur to either the state bar or anybody in town. No hearses were anywhere to be found on the legal side of the property.

The front office, tastefully decorated in pale blues and creams, offered clients a respite from the harried world beyond its doors. Muted music, not quite jazz but not quite classical, soothed the senses.

An assistant, dressed in blue slacks, blue pumps, and a pale blue twinset, matched the décor in a way that had several of the heirs glancing at her twice.

"Welcome to Stepford," Lester stage-whispered.

Clayton glanced at him, surprised that Lester even knew enough to make the reference.

"This way, please," the mannequin said.

A few minutes later, the heirs found themselves in a well-appointed office. Eight leather chairs had been brought in and placed in a semicircle around the room's centerpiece, an oak and teak desk. Already seated in two of the chairs were the Reverend Toussaint le Baptiste, who they hadn't seen since the day of Ana Mae's funeral, and Rosalee, who had come by the house just about every day.

"Well, this should prove interesting," Archer said.

Delcine gave a huff as she stepped around to take a seat as far away from Rosalee and the preacher as possible.

After welcoming them and expressing her condolences, the receptionist stepped out and Rollings strode in.

"Thank you all for coming this afternoon," Rollings began. "I hope not to keep you very long. What we have to do is, however, a bit complicated."

"How complicated could it be?" Lester said. "It's evident from her house Annie Mae didn't have much."

"Ana Mae," JoJo said. "And would you please let the man talk."

Lester stalked over to take a look at a column near the back of the room. "Hey, there're fish in there!"

"It's called an aquarium, Lester," Delcine intoned.

Lester scowled at her, then took a seat in one of the leather chairs next to JoJo.

"In accordance with Ana Mae's wishes, you are all

gathered here to hear the details of her last will and testament."

"You mean the reading of her will."

Rollings lifted his hands and shoulders in a partial shrug. "Well, technically, yes. It is a reading. But Miss Futrell left for her heirs a multimedia presentation."

The assembled Futrells couldn't manage to stifle their groans. The only person who looked intrigued was Archer, the lawyer.

JoJo raised her hand.

"Yes?" Rollings said.

"You said just the heirs are supposed to be here, right?"

"That's correct."

JoJo cast a glance at Reverend Toussaint sitting in the last chair of the semicircle. "Then why is he here? And her?" she added, with a nod toward Ana Mae's best friend.

Before Rollings could answer, Delcine piped up. "Frankly, my thoughts ran along a similar line. Rosalee's presence also made me curious."

Rosalee jumped up. "I got a letter," she said, "from Mr. Rollings. Telling me to be here. Today at one o'clock. Just like you."

Rollings stepped between the two women. "Ladies. And gentlemen. Everyone that Miss Futrell requested be here is present and accounted for. That includes Reverend le Baptiste and Mrs. Jenkins."

With a "hmph!" JoJo settled back into her chair, looking none too pleased. Whatever money Ana Mae had left, it sure shouldn't have to be split five ways instead of just three.

She wasn't the only one in the room thinking that thought.

By Marguerite's calculations, she and Winslow might be able to pull off a miracle—if the leeches didn't claim too much of the cash.

Clayton and his husband were doing all right for themselves—a doctor and a lawyer living high in the tony Pacific Heights area of San Francisco. They didn't need any money. JoJo and Lester were another story. Marguerite hadn't liked Lester when her sister had hooked up with him, and nothing in the intervening years had changed her opinion of him. Rude, crude, and crooked summed him up.

Marguerite's gaze slid to the next chair. Rosalee Jenkins sat there, twisting a white cotton handkerchief in her hands. Had the hankie been paper, it would have been in shreds. Every now and then, Rosalee sniffled and swallowed. She was truly grieving for Ana Mae.

If the truth were known, Rosalee had probably been more of a sister to Ana Mae than either herself or JoJo. So she wouldn't begrudge Rosalee anything that she might get.

But that so-called preacher was another story.

Anxious to get on with the proceedings, Marguerite posed the question on everyone's mind. "What exactly did Ana Mae leave behind?"

Rollings waited for the undivided attention of the heirs. He opened a leather portfolio, took out a sheaf of papers, and made a production of straightening them. He took a sip of water, and then when all of the attention was on him, he began to read from the last will and testament of Ana Mae Berdette Futrell.

"Berdette?" Lester exclaimed. "That's even more country than Ana Mae."

"Hush!" came from several corners.

After getting through the sound mind and body

part and all of the heretofores and other legal mumbo jumbo, he got to the part they were all waiting for.

"To my nieces and my nephew identified as Cedric Foster and Latrice Foster of Prince George's County, Maryland, and Crystal Coston of Laughlin, Nevada, I leave for each the sum of one thousand dollars in cash and some savings bonds purchased for each of them."

Marguerite and Winslow exchanged a glance, smiling. "That's nice. The children will be pleased."

He nodded. "Particularly since they didn't even know Ana Mae."

On the other side of the room, things weren't so rosy. "Crystal?" Lester asked. "Why does she get anything? And since when does she live in Laughlin?"

"Who is Crystal?" Rosalee asked, leaning over toward JoJo.

"My daughter. She left home when she was eighteen. I had no idea she was living in Laughlin. I wonder how Ana Mae knew that?"

Archer, who knew exactly how Ana Mae knew, just smiled to himself.

JoJo was still pondering her daughter's whereabouts and Lester still muttering in general when the attorney got to the second bequest of Ana Mae's will.

"To my friend Zenobia Bryant, I leave the white lace shawl and Japanese fan she always admired. Since she took the fan and never returned the shawl after borrowing it for the missionary tea, she already has both of these items in her possession."

"Oh, that's cold," Lester said on a chuckle.

Rosalee chortled. "Zenobia is gonna be pissed that she messed with Ana Mae's stuff."

"To my dear friend Rosalee Jenkins," Rollings continued reading, "an account has been set up in your name at First Trust and Union Bank. Go have a little fun, Rosalee."

From the portfolio, Rollings retrieved and then handed to Rosalee a slim manila envelope. "The account number, balance statement, and other bank information you will need is all in there," he said.

Accepting it, Rosalee blinked back tears and started to rock in her chair. She didn't open the envelope to check the balance, though; she simply held it close to her chest.

"How much did you get?" Lester asked.

The answer, clearly something that everyone in the office except Rollings wanted to know, did not come from Rosalee.

Her head bowed as she rocked; she was openly crying now, still clutching the unopened envelope containing the bank documents.

"That information is for Mrs. Jenkins to share if she sees fit," Rollings said. "And she is under no obligation to do so now or at any time in the future."

Lester snorted. "That must mean it's a lot."

Archer handed Rosalee a monogrammed handkerchief. Accepting it, even though she had the other hankie balled up in her hand, she wiped her eyes and blew her nose.

"I'm sorry, y'all," she said. "I just . . . I just can't believe she's really gone."

When no one commented on her grief, Rollings cleared his throat, then continued on with the reading of Ana Mae's will.

"I bequest to the Drapersville Piece By Piece Quilting Club the fabrics, sewing supplies, and equipment that is not wanted by my heirs. Rosalee Jenkins should oversee the distribution of these items.

"I bequest all of my household goods, vehicles, and my house and land jointly to Mary Josephine Futrell Coston, Marguerite Futrell Foster, and Clayton Futrell."

"That's like a booby prize," Lester said on a guffaw.

"Shh," JoJo hissed at him.

"To my church, the Holy Ghost Church of the Good Redeemer, a fixed annuity has been established that will provide the church with income to be used at the discretion of the pastor, associate pastor, board, and membership."

"Thank you, Sister Ana Mae," the Reverend Toussaint le Baptiste intoned.

Rollings continued to read, listing Ana Mae's other financial bequests, usually in the one thousand to five thousand dollar range, to various local charities.

Delcine, doing the math, just shook her head.

"And finally," Rollings said, "to my family members . . ."

"All right now, here we go," said Lester rubbing his hands together and sitting on the edge of his chair.

"Lester, please," JoJo said.

Rollings gave him a pointed look, and Lester sat back.

"To my family members," Rollings read, "I leave to Clayton Futrell, Marguerite Delcine Futrell Foster, and Mary Josephine Futrell Coston the sum of ten thousand dollars each."

"Hot damn!" Lester declared.

JoJo shushed him again, but he sat there beaming.

Clayton, looking bored, glanced at his watch.

Delcine sighed.

"When do we get the money?" Lester wanted to know.

"Mr. Coston, please. Let me finish," Rollings said.

Grinning, Lester rolled his hand forward in a "do go forth" motion.

"There is a stipulation," Rollings said.

Lester groaned.

"How much longer are we going to be, Mr. Rollings?" Clayton asked. "I'd like to get back to our bed-and-breakfast so we can pack and catch an earlier flight home."

"Please," Mr. Rollings said. "If I can have your undivided attention for a few more moments."

Clayton sighed and examined his nails.

Mr. Rollings placed the will on his desk blotter and clasped his hands together. "The final part of Miss Futrell's last will and testament is rather complex. She has stipulated for each of you ten thousand dollars, and I have that money here for each of you in the form of a check," he said, tapping the leather portfolio. "However, there is a codicil."

"What's a codicil?" JoJo asked.

"A sort of amendment," he said, surveying the eight people in his office, before focusing on the three Futrell siblings. "Mrs. Coston, Mrs. Foster, and Dr. Futrell, you have five minutes, just five, to decide as individuals if you would like to accept the ten thousand dollars from Miss Futrell or waive it, forfeit it," he added with a nod toward JoJo, "in order to be considered for the rest of Miss Futrell's estate."

"What rest?" Delcine asked.

"I am not at liberty to say at the moment," Rollings said.

"Well, what the hell else can it be?" Lester said. "The thirty grand is about all that's left of that lottery money. She's already given you guys that raggedy house and old car. I think ten grand is a nice little farewell gift."

"I don't know, Lester," JoJo said, getting up to pace the office. "Let me think."

"What's there to think about?" he said. "We can sure as hell use ten thousand dollars about now."

As the three couples began to review their options, Rollings retrieved a few items from a desk drawer and placed them on the desk top.

Delcine leaned forward to consult with Winslow. She kept her voice low so their conversation was private.

"I hoped there would be more," she said.

"Yes, so did I."

"Like Lester over there, I was doing a tally as he named beneficiaries. It looks like her church and probably Rosalee got a big chunk of whatever was left of the lottery money."

"Ten thousand isn't going to help us," Winslow said. "It's not even enough to hold them off for a month or two."

Delcine sighed again. Then, "What do you think this remainder of the estate is?"

Winslow shrugged. "I don't know. It could be anything. Maybe it's some land that's worth something. Or maybe she made some wise investments. She was your sister, what do you think?"

Delcine rolled her eyes. "Ana Mae and investments? Those words don't belong together. She died cleaning somebody's toilet, Win."

Conceding the point, he nodded. Then added, "But you never know."

"We've got nothing to lose," Delcine added. "I'll waive the money on the hope that there's something of value that can be sold for the amount of money we need."

Winslow nodded in agreement.

While his sisters discussed or argued with their spouses, Clayton got up to look at one of the paintings on Rollings's wall. Muddied browns and greens depicted three hounds at the hooves of a big bay horse carrying a rider with a rifle. Looking at Archer, he muttered, "I've never understood the appeal of these country hunt scenes."

"It takes all kinds," Archer said.

"Hmm. Well, what do you think?"

"What do you think is the question?"

"We don't need the money," Clayton said.

"No."

"But ten thousand dollars is ten thousand dollars. That was nice of Ana Mae."

Archer remained silent.

"You really have no opinion?" Clayton asked.

Archer grinned. "I have lots of opinions. You know that. But on this, it's a decision solely for you to make."

Clayton shrugged. "I really don't care. I just want to get out of here. But I am curious about the rest of her so-called estate. What kind of estate does a domestic worker leave behind?"

"I'm sorry," Rollings said. "But your time is up. I will need your decisions now."

The heirs all returned to their seats—except Lester, who stood sentinel behind JoJo's chair.

Rollings opened the portfolio and picked up three manila envelopes identical to the one he'd given Rosalee.

"Mrs. Foster?"

"We'll . . . I'll waive," Delcine said.

"As you wish," Rollings replied, placing one of the envelopes back on the desk.

"Do we still need to be here, Mr. Rollings?" Rosalee asked, leaning forward. Her manila envelope fell to the floor. "It looks like you're done with me and Reverend Toussaint."

"Please remain until we have concluded the proceedings," Rollings said.

Rosalee sighed and sat back.

The minister picked up the envelope and handed it to her. Rosalee looked at it a moment as if she'd forgotten all about it. Then she opened it and pulled out the papers.

Rosalee gasped.

Eyes wide, she glanced at Rollings as if for confirmation and then shoved the bank statement back into the envelope.

"How much did you get?" Lester asked.

Rosalee opened her mouth, but no words came out. She just clutched the envelope to her chest.

The edges of Rollings's mouth curved up for the briefest of moments, then he asked, "Mrs. Coston, what is your decision in the matter?"

Before JoJo could answer, Lester placed a hand on her shoulder.

"All right, Lester," she said, shrugging off his hand. "God, you can be a pain in the ass."

"The decision is yours, Mrs. Coston," Rollings reminded her.

"I'll take the money."

"That's my girl!"

Lester bent over and kissed the top of her head like a good luck charm. "You're gonna be sorry, Margie . . ."

"It's Marguerite," she said, ice dripping from each syllable.

". . . you should have taken the cash," he said. "I bet this is gonna be just like 'Let's Make a Deal.' You've traded ten grand for a chicken coop."

His chortles filled the office.

"Ana Mae did like her game shows," Rosalee said. "She got that fancy satellite TV just so she could get the Game Show Network."

"Oh, God," Delcine said.

Winslow too practically moaned his disappointment.

Clayton and Archer looked at each other, and Archer raised a brow in question. Clayton shrugged. "That doesn't change anything," he said.

"I sure hope not," Delcine muttered.

Rollings handed JoJo one of the two remaining manila envelopes.

"Suckers," Lester taunted.

"Mr. Coston, please have a seat," Rollings said.

"And shut up," Rosalee added.

Even Reverend Toussaint cracked a smile at that.

Lester sat, and JoJo, looking glum, handed over to him the envelope with the check.

Grinning, Lester settled down.

Rollings turned toward Clayton. "Dr. Futrell, that leaves your decision."

Clayton glanced at Archer who simply said, "It's up to you."

"All right," Clayton said. "I'll play. I'll waive the money and see what the big mystery is."

"Another sucker," Lester said not quite under his breath.

"Mr. Coston."

The warning from Rollings came in the tone of a principal giving a recalcitrant pupil one final warning before consequences were meted.

"All right. All right." Lester pinched his thumb and forefinger together and ran them across his mouth to indicate it was zipped.

Rollings picked up the envelope Delcine rejected and, in a deliberate motion, placed it with the one Clayton turned down and tore them both in half.

Delcine sighed, as if resigned to the fact she'd made a bad decision.

The lawyer then aimed a remote control at a paneled wall, and it opened to reveal a large flat-screen television.

"Miss Futrell left final messages to you via a video recording," he said. "She did this on my advice and recommendation so there would be no misunderstandings given her, well, as you'll see, her rather unusual wishes. These statements were filmed at her home with myself and another attorney from the firm present as witnesses."

Rollings glanced around at the heirs. Seeing or hearing no objection so far, he gave a nod, then said, "Here now, in her own words, she will explain about the rest of her estate."

A moment later, Ana Mae Futrell popped onto the fifty-two-inch plasma screen.

"Hey, everybody!" she hollered, waving energetically.

Rosalee and JoJo gasped.

"Oh, for God's sake," Delcine muttered.

The men—Reverend Toussaint, Clayton, Archer, and Lester—just stared. Rollings watched all of them.

Ana Mae, wearing a floral print dress, spoke to them from her front porch. At her side a round pie-crust-edged table held a pitcher of lemonade and a glass. It looked like a sunny day in the spring.

"If y'all all are watching this," she said, "it means I'm gone on to glory. Don't shed any tears, though . . ."

Delcine harrumphed. "As if."

". . . 'cause I'm walking with Jesus now," Ana Mae said.

"Hallelujah," Reverend Toussaint responded with a holy wave of his hand.

"Everett shoulda done read all that legal stuff to you. Now we get to the good part." She grinned as a cat jumped into her lap.

"That's Baby Sue," Rosalee said. "Diamond Jim is probably on the railing. He likes sunning himself up there."

"Shh."

"This here is one of my cats," Ana Mae said. "This is Baby Sue. Diamond Jim is around here someplace," she added, looking around for the animal. "Anyway, back to this will and estate stuff.

"But first, I wanna tell y'all all how much I love each and every one of you, Delcine, JoJo, and my Clayton. You all made me so proud to be your big sister."

Here, Ana Mae got choked up. She put the cat down and reached for a napkin on the round table beside her. She dabbed at her eyes. In Rollings's law office, JoJo swiped a finger at her own eyes, and Rosalee put Archer's handkerchief to use again.

"I wish I could have seen each of you one more time, just to give you a big hug."

Reverend Toussaint cleared his throat and pulled a

handkerchief from his suit coat pocket. Even Delcine looked choked up and damp-eyed.

"As Mr. Rollings should have told you by now, I had a little money and wanted to make sure everybody got equal. So that's what the ten thousand was for. Everybody equal. No matter what, I want everybody to be happy with the decision you made."

On the screen, Ana Mae chuckled to herself. "The good Lord knows I wish I could see y'all all right now 'cause here's my news: There's a little bit more than that thirty thousand."

"Huh?" Lester said. "What was that?"

Ana Mae poured herself some lemonade from the pitcher that had lemon slices floating on the top and then took a sip from the glass. After drinking, she let out an "ahhhh" and put the glass back down.

"I hope all three of you turned down the ten thousand because only Too Sweet and the ones of you who did can go on for the rest. In all," Ana Mae said, "I got about three point eight million dollars in cash."

6

Regrets and Recriminations

"**S**on of a bitch!" Lester hollered, jumping up as if his behind was on fire.

"Oh, my God," Delcine whispered. She clutched Winslow's arm so hard he winced.

"Did I hear that right?" Clayton asked, looking dazed.

"Y'all all heard me right," Ana Mae said from the TV. "I have almost four million dollars, but there's . . ."

"Son of a goddamned bitch," Lester said, running his hands through his hair and pacing the office in frantic steps.

"Mr. Coston, please," Reverend Toussaint said. "I have tried to be patient and understanding given the circumstances, but the profanity here is an abomination to my ears. And taking the Lord's name in vain is a blasphemy I will not be privy to."

"I agree," Rollings said. "Mr. Coston, please be seated."

"Shh," Rosalee said. "We can't hear what she's saying."

With a look thrown in Lester's direction, Mr. Rollings rewound the video a bit.

"Y'all all heard me right," Ana Mae said again. "I have almost four million dollars, but there's a catch."

She leaned forward and pulled what looked like a blanket from the porch railing.

"Only the ones who figure out the clues in this here quilt I made can get all or a share of the money. That's the big money, I mean. And if nobody figures it out," she said, "the money goes equally to Diamond Jim, Baby Sue, and Too Sweet."

The preacher jumped up and hollered "Glory! Glory!"

Rosalee's mouth dropped open. "What?"

Clayton looked at Archer. "Is that another cat?"

On the flat screen, Ana Mae stood and shook out the quilt so they all could see it. "Good luck, y'all. Somebody's gonna be rich."

The television screen went dark.

"Oh, my God," JoJo said. "What have I done? What have I done?"

Lester, back on his feet despite the warnings, was pacing and looking for all the world like he wanted to punch something or someone, specifically Ana Mae. His glares in Rollings's direction gave testament to the living target he had in mind.

"We were tricked," he said.

"No, you were greedy," Rosalee said. She settled back in her chair, looking satisfied.

"Says she who's probably over there sitting on a cool million."

Rosalee sniffed.

"One more outburst from you, Mr. Coston, and you will be physically removed from this office."

As if to enforce the threat, the office door opened and a giant stepped in. He stood close to seven feet tall and looked like an NFL linebacker.

"You need me, Mr. Rollings?"

Rollings let his associate's presence cover the room for a moment. "Not just yet, Clyde. But do stand by."

"Yes, sir," he said with a nod.

When the door closed behind Clyde, Rollings looked at Lester, who'd suddenly turned a bit pale.

"Did Ana Mae really have three point eight million dollars?" Clayton asked.

"Yes," Rolling said.

"And what's Too Sweet? Is that another one of her cats?"

"No," Reverend Toussaint said, grinning. "That would be me."

Despite his warning, Lester fell back in his chair with a moan.

"Honey, are you okay?"

The question came from Winslow and was directed not toward his brother-in-law, but at his wife. Delcine was almost doubled over, hyperventilating.

Clayton jumped up and was at his sister's side almost immediately.

"Get her some water," he told Winslow. "Hey, Del. Take it easy. Deep breaths," he said, taking her pulse. "That's it. Take deep breaths and relax. Relax."

Rollings poured a glass from a sideboard and handed

it to Winslow. Water sloshed from the sides as Winslow hurried back to his wife.

A moment later, Delcine sat up and started fanning her face with her hands. Winslow pressed the glass of water into her hands.

"Thanks," she said. "I'm fine. Really."

"She's just a little overwhelmed by the news," Winslow added helpfully.

"That's one way to put it," Delcine said, taking a sip of water.

Clayton checked her pulse again. "If you feel light-headed, put your head between your knees again."

"I'm fine," she assured her brother. "Thank you."

"Mrs. Foster? Are you sure you're all right? I can call the paramedics."

"No," she said, nodding. "I mean, yes, I'm fine. Really. Paramedics aren't necessary. Go ahead with"— she waved an uncertain hand—"with whatever."

"What have I done? What have I done?" JoJo was still muttering. She was up and at the door. With a hand at her mouth, she appeared to be biting her finger— maybe to keep from screaming.

With a flick of the remote control, Rollings closed the panel housing the television screen and faced the heirs of Ana Mae Futrell.

"I'm sure you have questions."

That was an understatement. Everyone started talking at the same time.

"We were cheated."

"How soon can we get the money?"

"Where did Ana Mae get four million dollars?"

"One at a time, please," Rollings said, holding out his hands to halt the verbal assault. "First, Mr. Coston, you were not cheated out of anything. As the heir of

Miss Futrell, your wife, Miss Futrell's sister, was the person who ultimately made the decision to accept the guaranteed cash offer from Ana Mae."

JoJo leaned against the door as if it were the only thing supporting her. Tears were in her eyes.

"To answer your question, Mrs. Foster, the money, which as of August the seventh, the day Miss Futrell passed," Rollings said, returning to his desk and the file with the last will and testament, lifting a piece of paper, and reading from it, "came to exactly three million, eight hundred fifty thousand seven hundred twenty-six dollars and thirty-four cents. It will be available immediately to the heir or heirs who solve the quilt clues. It can be a cashier's check, although a wire transfer is recommended."

JoJo pressed a long-nailed hand to the door and whimpered.

Lester pounded the arm of his chair in mute frustration.

"Thank you, Jesus. Thank you, Jesus. Thank you, Jesus."

Everyone in the office heard Delcine's thankful and whispered prayer.

"And," Mr. Rollings said, turning to Clayton. "In answer to your question about the source of Miss Futrell's wealth, that, Dr. Futrell, is something you will have to determine."

"I don't understand."

"It's very simple," Rollings said. "The quilt Ana Mae created contained information she wanted you to know. All you have to do, individually or collectively, is decipher the clues she left behind. When someone believes he or she has interpreted the clues, we shall reconvene here for an analysis."

Rollings took his seat behind the desk and clasped his hands together. "I tried to get Miss Futrell to leave the quilt here since it is a part of her will, but she said she liked looking at it at the house. I'll ask you to retrieve it from her home and deliver it here for safe-keeping," he said. "The person or persons who claim the inheritance will receive it."

"And what if no one does?" Archer asked.

"Then the quilt and the money go to Reverend Toussaint . . . and the cats."

The minister, now over his initial glee, sat looking dazed.

"I saw Ana Mae making that quilt," Rosalee said. "She never said it was anything special. But she did call it her legacy project."

From the door, JoJo took a tentative step forward and then paused. "Uh, Mr. Rollings, can I have a word with you?"

The question from JoJo brought all eyes to her. She stood, shifting her weight from one foot to the other and looking pitiful. It was pretty clear to everyone what she wanted to talk to the lawyer about.

"I'm sorry, Mrs. Coston," Rollings said. "You made your choice. Ten thousand dollars is, in my opinion, a very generous personal bequest."

JoJo shook her head. Then she hazarded a glance at Lester who, dejected, simply bowed his head.

"I'm sorry, Jo," he said. "I didn't know. I just didn't know."

"No one knew," Rosalee snapped at him.

But Reverend Toussaint reached out and patted Rosalee's hand in a calming and comforting gesture. There was already enough tension in the room.

"Mr. Rollings, I really need to speak to you. In private," JoJo added.

Rollings rounded his desk. "All right, Mrs. Coston." To the others, he said, "If you'll excuse us for a moment."

He ushered JoJo out of the office.

The room erupted behind him.

"I still don't get where Ana Mae got that much money," Clayton said.

"Maybe she hit the Powerball or something," Rosalee offered.

Reverend Toussaint shook his head. "Sister Futrell told me she never played the lottery before or after she won that scratching ticket. And I believed her."

"It's called a scratcher, Reverend," Rosalee said.

Reverend Toussaint shrugged.

Delcine and Winslow were again huddled together, whispering.

"This is the answer to a prayer," Delcine said. "If we get this clue business out of the way today, we'll be able to get that wire transfer on Monday."

She smiled, the sight rare and radiant.

"I wonder what she's out there talking to him about?" Reverend Toussaint said.

"Getting us part of that money. That's what," Lester mumbled. Then he quickly turned around as if expecting the bouncer Clyde to bust through the door and take him down.

But when the door did open, JoJo came through followed by Mr. Rollings. He looked ashen, and JoJo was wringing her hands.

"What's wrong?" Archer and Lester asked at the same time.

Mr. Rollings guided JoJo to her chair and then, after again taking a seat behind his desk, clasped his hands together in what the siblings now recognized as his "serious" pose.

He cleared his throat, then took a deep breath.

"What happened?" Delcine asked, her joy of just a moment ago dissipated.

"Mrs. Coston has informed me that the quilt has been disposed of."

"Disposed of?" Rosalee echoed.

"Oh, God," Delcine moaned.

"This just keeps getting better and better," Archer said, shaking his head in wonder.

"The quilt," JoJo said. "I threw it away. I thought it was junk. There are so many throws and quilts and blankets and whatnot in that house. How was I supposed to know that that one was special?"

For a moment, no one said a word as the reality sank in.

They were on a treasure hunt and no longer had a map or a compass or any clue to what they were actually looking for.

Then, almost simultaneously, the outbursts:

"How could you be so stupid?"

"What are we going to do now?"

"I'm sorry. I'm sorry," JoJo said, practically wailing herself.

Clayton got up and came over to his sister. He knelt at her chair and took her hand in his. "Hey, Jo. It's okay, sis. Really. Don't worry about it."

"Don't worry about it," Delcine screeched. "That's almost four million dollars she threw away."

"Hey, stop yelling at her," Lester said, coming to his wife's defense—even though he'd done his own share of yelling and berating. "That house is full of junk. It was an easy enough mistake to make."

"That's easy for you to say," Rosalee said. "You have ten grand."

Lester whipped around for a comeback, but caught Rollings's eye. Without a word, he sat down and ran the zipper across his mouth again. But a moment later, he raised his hand, asking for permission to speak.

Rollings sighed. "Yes, Mr. Coston?"

"What if she found it?"

"I beg your pardon?"

"What if she's able to find the quilt?" Lester clarified.

Delcine, on her feet and now standing behind Clayton, glared down at her sister. "Do you think you know where it is?"

The question, which could have come across as a gentle query from Clayton, barreled out of Delcine like the demand it was.

Lester, still focused on Rollings, made an appeal. "If she finds it, let us back in the game for the big money."

"Mr. Coston . . ."

"It's only fair," Lester said. "She finds it and we give back the envelope." He was already reaching for the manila envelope. Not finding it in his chair, he leaned over and grabbed it from the edge of JoJo's chair cushion.

Lester thrust the envelope at the lawyer.

"There was no contingency. . . ," Rollings started saying.

But Clayton piped up. "That's fine with me," he said giving JoJo's hand a gentle squeeze. "If she, if we, find the quilt, JoJo is allowed back in the clue hunt."

He turned around to glance up at their remaining sibling. "Delcine?"

Holding her head as if she had a migraine and looking generally disgusted, Delcine scowled and then just said, "Whatever."

Clayton took that as acquiescence and rose, turning to Archer. "That's legal, right?"

Archer looked at Rollings. "As long as all of the invested parties agree, I don't see a problem. Do you?"

"Well, there was no contingency for this scenario," Rollings said. He mulled it over for a moment, then, apparently, like Archer, coming up with no legal objection, nodded.

"Reverend le Baptiste, do you agree?"

"Absolutely," the preacher said.

"Mrs. Foster?"

Delcine sent daggers in the direction of JoJo and Clayton, then gave Lester a lethal dose of her glare. "Yes, that's fine," she finally said. "If we find it."

"Then it's settled," Lester said rubbing his hands together and grabbing his wife's hand. "Come on."

"I'm really, really sorry, everybody," JoJo said.

Rollings stood. "I suggest that you all go back to the house and reconstruct the events that led to the, uh, disposal of the quilt. If it's found . . ."

"When it's found," Lester interjected.

"When it's found," Rollings conceded, "please immediately bring it here. That is not negotiable. Does everyone understand? The quilt is to be retrieved and returned to this office immediately."

He got everyone to verbally agree. For a moment he turned toward his desk, looking as if he might draw up a contract to that effect for each of them to sign. But in the mere seconds it took him to think the thought, the heirs were dashing for the door.

For the first time since arriving in North Carolina, Marguerite felt that her world might not be imploding around her. While the others went outside, she'd hung back for a moment in order to ask Rollings a question.

His assurance—that the money would immediately be available to the winning heir or heirs—eased her trepidations. While little could be done about the indictment Winslow faced, with the promise of three point eight million dollars, she could stave off the creditors and the foreclosure.

With shrewd eyes she assessed her brother and sister. JoJo was trying to hide it, but she and Lester probably needed money as well, judging by the way Lester pounced on the offer of ten thousand. Then there were the other signs. The too-done makeup could be attributed to JoJo's former profession. But cheap clothes couldn't be masked with costume jewelry and Payless shoes.

Her glance then slid to her brother Clayton, the only Futrell who'd actually made it.

The irony didn't escape Marguerite. Neither did the resentment that their mother, and even Ana Mae, always seemed to favor the boy in the family. It was something of sweet justice that he didn't turn out to be the man their mama thought he'd be. Marguerite couldn't begrudge him his success, though. A doctor "married" to a lawyer. Wasn't that every girl's dream, to marry well?

She thought she'd chosen wisely with Winslow. But time proved just how wrong she'd been. And how stuck she was now.

It was pretty likely he'd go to prison. Where would that leave her? The scandal ruined friendships that had been built on professional achievement rather than true caring or sentiment. And it was highly possible that the lies on which she'd built her own history and reputation would come to light when reporters started digging around into Win's crimes.

There was but one way to put a positive spin on her current situation, just one way to resolve all of her problems: She had to be the one to get all of Ana Mae's money.

In a stall in the ladies restroom, JoJo was thinking similar thoughts, a fact that would have set Marguerite's teeth on edge had she known.

She'd had to hock her wedding rings to get the fare to North Carolina. Unfortunately, it hadn't been the first time she'd made her way to Vegas Thrifty Pawn. The owner there, who'd been sweet on her way back when, always gave her a good rate and didn't mind if she was a bit late getting her stuff back.

This time, though, JoJo probably wouldn't claim her jewelry. What was the point? Her marriage was all but over. The only reason Lester even showed up in Drapersville at all was because he had a sixth sense for sniffing out money. And, boy, had his nose been working overtime this go-round—almost enough to make JoJo wonder, if just fleetingly, if he actually could claim some level of psychic talent or ability.

She quickly dismissed that, though. Lester's primary skill was conning people out of their hard-earned money, whether by sleight of hand or one of his "psychic" readings.

There was a lot JoJo could do with the kind of money Ana Mae left them, even if it had to be split up three ways.

Clayton didn't need it. He was a doctor with a successful practice back in San Francisco. And his sexy sweetie, Archer, made a ton of money suing people or doing whatever it was he did.

No, the only Futrell who hadn't lived up to her—or anybody's —potential was Mary Josephine. It was time her luck changed, though.

Time indeed.

Out on the sidewalk on Clifton Street, the heirs sort of stood around looking stunned.

"Three point eight million dollars," Lester muttered. "That's like four million bucks. And it's all cash?"

Marguerite narrowed her eyes at her brother-in-law. "For some of us. Her direct heirs."

Lester slipped his arm around his wife's shoulders. "And my baby here is gonna get her cut."

"Girl, what possessed you to throw out that quilt?" Rosalee asked.

JoJo shrugged out of her husband's embrace. "It was ugly. The squares made no sense. It looked like something from the country."

"The last time I checked, this was the country," Winslow said on a dry note, uttering the most words he'd spoken around any of them since arriving in North Carolina. "There's not a decent coffeehouse within thirty miles."

Marguerite rolled her eyes. "Winslow, please."

"We need to find that quilt," Rosalee said.

"We?" Marguerite inquired.

Rosalee nodded, smug. "That's right. I'm reckoning if JoJo tossed it out as a rag, none of you will be able to figure out any clues. That leaves me."

"Over my dead . . ."

"Excuse me," Archer interjected before either Rosalee or Marguerite landed the first slap, push, or pull of hair. "We, as the people who were witness to the reading, need to stop arguing and set about finding this quilt."

Clayton leaned over, whispered something in Archer's ear.

Seeing the two, JoJo's husband smirked. A pack of cigarettes materialized in his hands. He tamped down the Newports, then slipped one from the package. Before Lester could reach for a book of matches, JoJo plucked the cigarette from his lips and snapped it in two.

"Hey!"

"You're supposed to be quitting."

"You're the one who quit. Don't take your cravings out on me."

Clayton nodded to Archer and then announced, "We're leaving. I guess this is something like a treasure or scavenger hunt."

"Yes, rather so," Winslow added with one of his sage nods.

"And may the best team win," Lester said.

Even though Clayton had put the suggestion in everyone's head that they were on a scavenger hunt, it took the Futrells about a minute for them all to realize they had to find the quilt before they could divide and conquer anything.

Eventually realizing that Ana Mae's house was the best place to begin, they headed there.

Marguerite put on a pot of coffee as the heirs, Rosalee, and Reverend Toussaint crowded into the kitchen.

"Would she really leave all that money to a couple of cats?" JoJo asked.

Rosalee nodded. "Ana Mae loved all animals and spent a lot of time over at The Haven, the no-kill animal shelter. But she loved Diamond Jim and Baby Sue the best. She loved 'em like they was her own kids."

JoJo shuddered. "I don't see why. Cats are scary creatures."

"That's just 'cause they make you sneeze," Lester said.

"I've been doped up on Benadryl from the first day I walked into this house," JoJo added.

Archer gave Clayton a told-you-so glance.

"You should have stayed at a hotel," Clayton offered.

JoJo flushed, then glanced guiltily at her husband. "Well, yes, but, uh, someone needed to be here."

As if picking up steam for her explanation, JoJo pointed to the countertops still overflowing with food from neighbors and friends. "Somebody needed to be here for when people dropped by."

She smiled broadly, as if suddenly satisfied with that explanation.

"JoJo, start from the beginning," Marguerite said. "Tell us what you did with the items to be donated or destroyed."

The field marshal's command put them all back on track.

JoJo bit her lip and looked around as if just seeing the kitchen for the first time. "Well, first I gathered up all the stuff that was over there." She pointed toward a corner where an ironing board was set up in a little alcove.

"That's where Ana Mae did her work," Rosalee pointed out.

"Work?" Marguerite said, trying—and failing—to keep the sneer or the haughtiness from her tone.

Rosalee sucked in her breath and stood straight and tall. All five foot two inches of her challenging the taller, sophisticated woman. "Ana Mae and me did honest work. Every single day. Ain't nothing wrong with washing and ironing clothes and cleaning houses."

Marguerite closed her eyes for a moment, trying to gather her composure.

"Unless you punch out in a toilet," Lester said with a nudge at Archer.

"Out!"

"I was just funning," Lester said.

"Actually," Clayton said, sending a brief glance in Archer's direction, "would you all give us a moment, please? Just the siblings. JoJo. Marguerite."

The sisters exchanged a look, wondering at the authoritarian tone in their otherwise docile brother's voice. After a moment, Marguerite nodded.

"I think that's a good idea," she said. "We, the three of us, need some time alone."

Muttering under his breath and pulling out his cigarettes, Lester stomped off.

With a long and lingering look at Clayton, Archer took his leave, giving Clayton plenty to wonder about the message his partner was trying to send telepathically.

Pulling out a pipe, Winslow excused himself and headed out the back door.

When just four of them remained, as one the Fu-trells turned toward Rosalee.

"I got to leave too?"

"Please," Marguerite said.

"You don't have to be snappish about it," Rosalee said. "I know where I'm not wanted. I just wonder if any of you all know that. You're acting all brotherly and sisterly now that Ana Mae is in the ground. But not a one of you cared a whit about her while she was alive."

"Be that as it may," Marguerite began.

Clayton's hand on her arm stayed the rest of her comments. Marguerite cleared her throat.

JoJo just watched the byplay, feeling, as usual, much like a third wheel with a broken spoke.

When Rosalee left, slamming the side screen door on her way out, the three looked at each other.

"Three point eight mil," JoJo said. "That's a lot of money."

"It's not ours yet," Clayton reminded them. "First we have to find that quilt you tossed out."

Even under the heavy makeup, JoJo's face turned red. "I'm sorry, all right. How many times do I have to say that?"

"Well, just be glad we cut you back in," Marguerite reminded her.

JoJo bit back a comment. Marguerite had always been the uppity one, the one they all figured would make it out of Drapersville and on to something grand. She'd even married well. To that fancy Winslow with the big government job. For a while, it seemed like every time JoJo went to her mailbox there was a post-card with Marguerite's schoolteacher-perfect hand-writing coming from some exotic locale or a country that only people on the TV news seemed to know how to find or pronounce.

If JoJo hadn't gotten knocked up, and later been stupid enough to marry Lester, maybe she would be the one with the fancy house, the fancy car, and the fancy, but kind of dull, clothes.

She should have been the one to marry a good man who provided well for his family. Instead she'd picked Lester.

But not for long.

Lester didn't know how much she wanted to leave Las Vegas and move somewhere . . . maybe even back home. And if there was nothing else, she knew how much Lester thrived in a place like Vegas and would wither in a small place like Ahoskie or Drapersville, which was all the more reason to move to North Carolina. On a whine, he'd already asked, "What do people do here?"

A broad smile transformed JoJo's face. The image of Lester black and withered up like a dead vine on an otherwise thriving houseplant filled her with . . . joy.

"What are you over there grinning about?" Clayton asked.

"Just imagining a different life."

The three fell silent. And just for a moment, it was like it was when they were kids—young at heart, but old of spirit, and all dreaming about the day when they could escape the confines of small-town life, small-time attitudes, and small-minded thinking.

Life had a funny way of turning itself around and biting you on the ass, though, JoJo thought, because all three of the Futrells, though they had successfully escaped once, now found themselves right back where they'd started from—in Drapersville, North Carolina, with the future looking dismally like last call would be hollered in this place, and when the lights came up, they'd find themselves alone in a dingy bar wondering what had happened to the evening's luster.

"Let me think a minute," JoJo said, as if she hadn't been wracking her brain from the moment they left Rollings's office. "There were four boxes of giveaway stuff. Some clothes, shoes, household goods."

"And?" Delcine prompted.

Nervous and getting even more anxious about her transgression, JoJo bit her lower lip and closed her eyes, concentrating hard.

Then, suddenly, she smiled.

"What?"

"I remember what box it was in," she said.

Seeing the Futrell sibling's men outside, a neighbor strolled over to get a better look at them all. She couldn't get off work and had missed Ana Mae's funeral, but she'd heard plenty about it. It was time to get a good look-see at the folks who were the topic of such juicy speculations over at Junior Cantrell's place. Junior's side-by-side businesses specialized not just in haircuts and the best barbecue in town, but in the latest gossip; served hot and juicy, like his ribs.

"Afternoon everybody," she said, with a wave toward the three men. "Thought I'd come over and give my respects."

"Good afternoon," Winslow said.

She lifted a brow, wondering if this one was supposed to be the homosexual. He sure was proper. "I'm Thelma Whitherspoon. I live right over there across the street. Saw y'all out here and thought I'd come on over.

Couldn't make Ana Mae's funeral, and I hadn't stopped over yet. I sent a card, though," she added, defending her negligent neighborliness.

Archer offered a hand to the woman. "It's a pleasure to meet you, Miss Whitherspoon. Thank you for your regards."

She smiled up at this one. With those luscious blue eyes and that I want to lick-you-all-over stare, he was one fine man.

"Marguerite, JoJo, and Clayton are inside."

Lost in Archer's gaze, it took Thelma a moment to register what he'd said. "Marguerite? Who is Marguerite?"

"That'd be the one you people call Delcine," Lester added.

At the "you people," Thelma's gaze left the sexy one and slid over to the big man with the cigarette. This had to be JoJo's husband, Lester. The talk about him wasn't all that good. Now she saw why.

He was one of them light-skinned Negroes who thought they could pass for white but wasn't fooling anybody, not even white folks, who sometimes couldn't tell. She sniffed, dismissing him, as she turned her back to him.

"I've been keeping an eye out on the house while y'all was away," she said. "Some folks just leave stuff on the porch if nobody's home. But only the junk man went around back like he always do."

As one, Archer and Winslow said, "The junk man?"

Lester tossed his cigarette into the grass and watched it burn, then, frowning, went to stub it out.

"Yeah," Thelma said. "He always stops over here the day before trash day. Ana Mae would leave him stuff he could take to sell. You know, stuff she'd been given from some of her people but couldn't find a use for or somebody to give it to."

"And he took things from the back porch?"

Thelma looked Winslow up and down. "That's what I just said."

Sensing her dislike of his brother-in-law, Archer smiled at Thelma, pulling her attention away from the man who was supposed to have had some sort of experience in the diplomacy field before taking his current and vaguely unspecified position in the Federal Department of Housing and Urban Development. So far he had proved to be anything but diplomatic in his dealings with the people of this small town.

"Miss Witherspoon . . ."

Coyly she tapped his arm. "Shoot, honey. You just call me Thelma."

"Thank you, Thelma. Do you know where we might be able to locate this junk man's store or yard?"

"Shoot, yeah. Everybody knows where Eddie Spencer's place is."

The three men leaned forward. Winslow pulled a slim leather notebook and fountain pen from his inside suit jacket and asked, "Would you mind giving us directions to his place of business?"

It didn't take long to track down the box. Long being relative, of course.

And it didn't take long for word to get out about what Ana Mae left behind.

Next door to the barbershop at Junior's Bar and Grille—where the "E" on "grille" fancied up the place, at least in Junior's mind—the talk swirled in so many different directions that it was hard to keep up with all the tracks.

Junior was doing his best, though, based on what his honey pot told him. Seeing Rosalee on the side benefited Junior in more ways than one. If Rosalee got some of that money, she'd share some with him. Junior's broad smile widened even more, making him appear more than a little slow. Despite his looks, Junior Cantrell was a sharp tack. He could do numbers faster than a calculator and didn't ever need to write down an order, even if there were several going at once. Since his back room hosted a small-time numbers operation, the skill came in handy.

"I'm putting my money on JoJo," somebody said. "She always knew how to smell out a buck."

"Yeah," Luther, another regular, agreed. "Too bad she hooked up with that beer-belly good ole boy."

"He ain't white."

"Damn sure look like it."

"So does your mama. And she ain't white."

That shut him up for a moment 'cause it was true. "He the palest brother I ever seen then."

"You just mad cause JoJo Futrell wouldn't go to the senior dance with you."

Luther snorted. "Shoot, ain't thinking about that. That was nigh on twenty-some years ago."

"And you still ain't got over it."

Though ostensibly watching the baseball game on the TV above the bar, Junior had taken note of the conversation. The business opportunity mentioned therein didn't slip his notice.

Leaning toward the two patrons, he refilled their

drinks, adding, "On the house. If you want a little action on that."

Two brows furrowed. Then Luther grinned, getting it.

He reached in his back pocket for his wallet. "Junior, I think I'd like to order a full rack to go." He slipped a bill onto the bar top and nudged his friend. "You in?"

The man nodded. He eyed Junior for a bit, trying to guess how he might handicap the outcome of the race for Ana Mae's millions. "I'll take a full too," he eventually said. "But I want mine for here."

Junior pocketed the money, smiled at the men. "I'll have your orders delivered when they're done. One to go, one for here."

He knew word would get around to the right folks. Those who wanted to bet on the relatives would place their money on the house—for "here"—getting the cash. Those who thought the relatives would lose, would place their orders "to go."

Whether Rosalee came out ahead or not, Junior Cantrell knew he would. He took a thirty percent commission on any and all action at his place. In return, his payoffs and his percentages were the highest among those who dealt in The Business.

At the Holy Ghost Church of the Good Redeemer, the Reverend Toussaint le Baptiste stood at the altar in the sanctuary. He'd been trying to pray, but his mind kept wandering back to the lawyer's office. Seeing Ana Mae on that video had been hard. Harder than he'd expected. Their relationship went back a ways, a long ways. She had been there for him when no one else believed in him. She'd had enough faith for the two of them and then some.

It was because of Ana Mae Futrell that the man formerly known as Too Sweet—and not because he liked the ladies back then—today was a devout man of God.

And it was because of Ana Mae that this church, this house of God, would continue to rise up as a beacon in the community.

If he closed his eyes, Toussaint could imagine the new sanctuary, with plush and cushioned pews for several hundred more parishioners. The choir loft would be to the right, instead of behind the pulpit, with a brand-new Hammond and a top-of-the-line drum set.

And his robe. A grin split his face when he envisioned the robe he'd always wanted. He'd described it to Ana Mae once, and she'd called it Toussaint's Robe of Many Colors. She'd offered to make it for him, but Toussaint had demurred, saying that was something he wanted to get for himself.

He nodded as he closed his eyes and lifted his hands toward heaven. In her will Sister Futrell left the Holy Ghost Church of the Good Redeemer a goodly amount. So even if he didn't claim a portion of the rest, there was a lot to thank God about.

The only thing that ate at Toussaint had been first the news of Sister Futrell having a son, and then the boy not having the decency to show up at his own mama's funeral.

Toussaint le Baptiste prided himself on knowing all about the members of the church, even if he wasn't the senior pastor. As director of outreach ministries, he came in contact with most of the everyday members or

their families more often than Reverend Leonard did. It
enabled Toussaint to better serve their ministerial needs.
That Ana Mae had kept a detail as important as a son secret even from her associate pastor was a blow he took
personally.

"But praise God anyhow," Reverend Toussaint said,
his voice echoing in the empty sanctuary. "Through
Sister Futrell, the Lord has provided for his own."

After considerable squabbling, the heirs decided to
go en masse to Eddie Spencer's place. The spouses
stayed behind, though. They didn't want to tip off
Spencer that he had something very valuable to them.
But the three not-exactly-mourning siblings would be a
different story.

Seeing the car drive by her house, Rosalee followed. She didn't plan to let them get away with anything.

7

Let the Games Begin

Eddie Spencer looked up when the bell over the door to his place jangled. With a sigh, he put down the hot roast beef and cheese sandwich he was just about to sink his teeth into. He had a side of mashed potatoes and brown gravy steaming on the plate. Customers, rare as they sometimes were around here, weren't to be ignored—even for roast beef and potatoes hot from Junior's kitchen over at the grill.

"Well, I'll be damned," he muttered when he saw who it was.

All three of the Futrells—looking like they'd just stepped off a spaceship and onto a foreign planet. Tall, snooty Delcine was still tall and snooty. She'd barely walked in the door and her nose was already turned up as if she smelled something bad.

Josephine Futrell was another story. He felt some

rumblings down there just looking at her. She'd put on a lot of weight since he'd seen her last, but Eddie liked a woman with some meat on her bones. Doing Delcine would be like having sex with a brittle scarecrow. But JoJo. Now that was a lot of good woman.

He hoped she hadn't turned snooty like her sister. Since they'd been back in town, Eddie had heard some things about Ana Mae's relatives. None of it was good.

"Howdy. What can I do for you folks?"

"Good afternoon," Marguerite said, designating herself as the official spokeswoman. "My name is . . ."

"I know who you are, Delcine. And your brother, Clayton, and this must be little Josephine." He grinned at her, giving her another thorough once over from the big hair to the big tits and on down to the big hips. "You sure done growed up since I last saw you."

JoJo peered at him, as if trying to place him. "Have we met?" she asked.

Eddie chortled.

"Now I ain't changed that much, have I, Josephine? Remember that time at Doc Henry's office?"

JoJo's eyes widened. Then on a squeal like a high school girl being asked out by the winning quarterback, she flung herself into his arms.

"Eddie Spencer! Oh, my, God. I didn't make the connection. Spence, just look at you."

"Look at you, darling. You're a sight for these sore eyes. How've you been doing?" Before she could answer, he remembered the reason the Futrells were all back in town. "Oh, I'm sorry," he said bowing his head for a moment. "I was real, real sorry to hear about Ana Mae. She was good people. Y'all all from some good blood."

Clayton raised an eyebrow. As JoJo and Eddie Spencer reminisced, Clayton eased around to get a better look at the man.

Spence. That name he too remembered. And also in connection with Doc Henry's place.

Dr. Henry Miles was one of two black doctors back in the day. He made house calls and carried a black bag, just like Marcus Welby on television. He put quarantine signs on the doors when anybody came down with the measles or the mumps, and he carried peppermint sticks in that medical bag. If you didn't make a fuss during the examination, he'd give you one.

His office was an addition built onto his house. And next to it was a little shed that had been converted into a hangout for his son.

It was in that shed behind Doc Henry's place that Clayton first discovered he liked boys much better than he liked girls. But it was with an older man named Daniel. Was this Daniel Spencer's younger brother . . . or his son?

JoJo preened under Spence's gaze. Marguerite cleared her throat.

"Oh!" JoJo said, as if her sister had pinched her. "Eddie, we've come by looking for some things that we need . . ."

Marguerite interrupted. "They were mistakenly left in the place where apparently Ana Mae always put things out for you."

JoJo nodded. "Spence, I didn't know that you and Ana Mae had a system. I was just trying to clear some things out of the house until we could sort them better."

Spencer rubbed his chin. "Yeah, I picked up some stuff from the house. It's over there."

As one, the Futrell trio turned, following the direction of his finger. Trying not to appear nervous or anxious—and failing miserably—they dashed toward the corner.

Eddie chuckled. His sandwich forgotten, he sat back and watched them. He knew what they were looking for. Rosalee had called on her cell phone and said they'd all been running around like chickens with their heads cut off after throwing out that quilt. That's what they get for thinking ill of Ana Mae, God rest her soul.

The first shriek came from the snooty one who now called herself Marguerite and put on even more airs than she did back in the day.

"This is outrageous!"

"What?" Clayton said.

"Look at the price!" Marguerite shoved the tag on a patchwork quilt into her brother's face. "Five hundred dollars. For this!"

Clayton took the quilt and shook it out. It had nine blocks with pictures on it. "Are we sure this is the right one?"

"It's the right one," Delcine said.

Eddie Spencer didn't blink an eye. "You're in the antiques section of the place. That quilt is an antique. Hand-stitched. Fine workmanship, too."

Clayton lifted a brow, then peered at the stitching.

Marguerite narrowed her eyes and stalked back toward the counter where Eddie stood. "I happen to know antiques, Mr. Spencer."

"Do tell." He grinned at her. "Then I'm sure you know the value of that particular item. I'm giving you a bargain . . . considering the circumstances."

Sure that they were being played but unable to prove it, Delcine gave him the evil eye.

After a few more empty threats and posturing to no

avail, JoJo and Delcine looked at Clayton, who sighed and paid the man—in cash. Eddie wrote up a receipt and beckoned JoJo closer for a private word.

"You need anything, Josephine, anything at all while you here," he said, his eyes dipping to her bosom, "you just give ole Spence a call, you hear."

He slipped her a piece of paper ripped from the edge of a lined notebook. "Anything," he repeated. "You know, for old times."

JoJo glanced at the paper, saw a phone number, and gave him a smile like they were the only two people in the place.

"I'm married now, Spence."

He grinned. "Shoot, honey. So am I."

After the Futrells had been gone about five minutes, Eddie Spencer was still grinning when the bell on the front door of his shop jingled again, and Rosalee bustled in.

"Did they get it?" she called out.

Spencer waited until she got to the counter. Then he held out and ticked off the crisp one-hundred-dollar bills. "One. Two. Three. Four. Five."

"Get out of here!"

He handed her two of the Benjamins. "You were right. They came in here like hell on fire."

Rosalee held up the bills. "You sure?"

"If you hadn't of called me letting me know what was up, they'd have gotten it for nothing," Eddie Spencer said. "I didn't mean to pick up something that weren't meant for me."

"Ana Mae sure would get a chuckle out of one of her quilts selling for five hundred dollars—and to her own kin, to boot. She always gave them away." After another look at the two hundred-dollar bills, Rosalee tucked the money into her bra. "Who paid?"

"He did. You know, Rosalee, he looks more like a tennis player or one of them dudes who rides around on a horse saying 'tallyho.' "

Rosalee shrugged. "You should see his . . ." She wrinkled her brow, uncertain. "I wonder what they call themselves." Shrugging again, she added, "You'd never guess by looking at him that his boyfriend is like that. Ana Mae always said Archer just hadn't met the right woman before Clayton found him."

"Well, I ain't got nothing against them dudes," Eddie said. "You know my brother was like that. Couple of years before he died I went to one of them marches with him. I got a button that said 'My bro's gay, and that's OK.' I wore that button to his funeral."

Rosalee patted his hand, and they both gave a little moment of silence to Danny Spencer's memory.

"I don't think Clayton is the type who'd go to them marches with the men dressed up like women," he said.

"You're probably right." Then, perking up, Eddie grinned. "I thought Delcine was gonna have a stroke right here on the floor when she saw that five-hundred-dollar tag."

"You know, she's all fancy now," Rosalee said. "Goes by Marguerite." She held up her pinkie and adopted what she supposed was a French accent to pronounce the name.

Eddie Spencer rolled his eyes at that. "Yeah, and my name is Eduardo. I wish she hadda been the one to pay. I'll gladly lighten her stuck-up load."

"So, how'd it go down?"

"I'd just gotten over there and changed the tag

from five bucks to five hundred. I was trying to change the five to a dollar sign and ended up adding a couple of zeroes. I just barely got back to the counter before they came in. Clayton didn't look too happy about it. But I knew he was gonna be the one to pony up the cash."

"How'd you know?"

"Delcine and JoJo both looked at him with this . . ." He put his hands on his hips and cocked his neck imitating a pissed-off woman. " 'And you don't expect me to pay for that, do you?' "

Rosalee chortled. "Good for you."

She finally took note of the congealed gravy on the mashed potatoes on his plate and wrinkled her nose. "Eddie, I think I'm gonna treat you to a fine meal over at Junior's tonight." She whipped the money from its hiding spot. "I can afford it."

"It's a date," he said. Then, apparently remembering who she saw from time to time, "Well, you know what I mean. I ain't stepping on Junior's toes."

Rosalee grinned and waved a hand, letting him know no harm had been done. "I better get back on over to Ana Mae's and see what they're up to now."

Rosalee left Eddie Spencer's place. Outside, she squinted as she looked up the street, trying to figure out which way to go. Since the Futrells had the quilt in hand and all of them were together, she figured they wouldn't go to the lawyer's first. That would be after they'd had a good look at Ana Mae's treasure map.

Rosalee chuckled at that thought, then looked up toward the heavens. "A treasure map. Girl, you sure are keeping things lively down here."

Gripping the steering wheel on her Cavalier, she fussed at her friend. "Ana Mae, you let me see all your quilts. How come I didn't know nothing was special about this one? The most important one. This don't make any sense, girl." She let out a loud hoot. "But you sure 'nough made a profit on that quilt."

She fell silent at a stoplight, then nodded.

"I know, I know," she said, as if Ana Mae were sitting right beside her, riding shotgun. "Ten percent belongs to the Lord. And if it'll make you happy, I'll drop fifty in the offering plate on Sunday."

A bark of laughter followed that. She glanced around, looking to see if anybody had been looking at her talking to herself. Tears welled in Rosalee's eyes, and she shook her head.

"Ana Mae, girl, I sure do miss you."

8

The Legacy of Ana Mae Futrell

"**I** wouldn't pay five hundred dollars for that pile of raggedy scraps," Delcine said, as the trio piled into the Lincoln Town Car that Clayton and Archer had rented at the airport in Norfolk.

The seventy-mile drive from Norfolk International Airport in Virginia and across the border into Clayton's North Carolina hometown had been made in stony silence since he and Archer had little to say to each other these days. Now, however, with his bickering sisters going at it, Clayton longed for the solitude of a peaceful drive.

"First of all," JoJo said from the backseat, "you didn't pay for it. Clayton did."

JoJo, relegated to the back seat because Delcine claimed she got carsick if she didn't ride up front, was already pissed about being in the back, so her attitude should have been expected. There was no point in saying that riding in the back seat was like being chauffeured. JoJo wouldn't see it that way, not with Delcine riding shotgun.

Clayton bit back a small smile. It was like the years had fallen away and they were all kids again. Then he remembered, although vaguely, somebody throwing up all over the floor of a car, maybe a taxi, and getting cussed out by somebody. The memory, hazy around the edges, could have come from thirty years ago—or last month when he was in L.A. at a medical conference.

He couldn't recall and, on a sigh, decided it wasn't worth the effort expending any more mental energy to figure it out.

Squabbling sisters, gotta love 'em.

"And secondly," JoJo said, "whether you'd pay five dollars or not is irrelevant. Ana Mae thought it was important enough to leave us this quilt."

"Which," Delcine added, "Clayton wouldn't have had to pay five hundred dollars for if you hadn't thrown it away in the first place."

"Hey, guys," Clayton said, "can we not fight? The important thing is we have it, and now we can figure out what it means. Let's just get it over to the lawyer's office."

The mention of the lawyer shifted the conversation and elicited twin harrumphs from the sisters.

"What kind of name is Too Sweet for a preacher?" JoJo asked.

"I think his initials are T.S.," Delcine said. "Toussaint something or other."

"I'll bet he was named for Toussaint Louverture," Clayton said.

"Toussaint who?"

"God, JoJo," Delcine scolded, as she turned around

long enough to roll her eyes at her sister. "Were you paying any attention at all in high school? He was that guy down in Jamaica . . ."

"Haiti," Clayton corrected.

"Whatever. He was in the Caribbean and led a slave revolt."

"Well, I'm gonna lead a revolt right here in Drapersville and Ahoskie if that preacher walks off with all of Ana Mae's money," JoJo said. "And I still don't know why somebody who calls himself a man of God would let people run around calling him Too Sweet."

Delcine twisted to the left so she could see JoJo in the backseat.

"It's a nickname, JoJo. Like 'JoJo.' You know how folks are around here. Forty years ago, he probably gave some girl a dandelion weed in the schoolyard and she said, 'Oh, Toussaint, you're just too sweet.' "

The falsetto of Delcine's voice and the baby-doll singsong had both Clayton and JoJo smiling.

"And from that moment on and until the undertakers close his casket and put him six feet under, a grown man can walk the streets of North Carolina, be a pastor at a church, and still be known to one and all as Too Sweet."

Laughter filled the vehicle as the siblings nodded, knowing that Delcine's summation had more than a ring of truth to it.

Delcine always could mimic people, and her take on the origin of the nickname was probably as spot-on as her imitation of a smitten little girl all those years ago.

Facing front again, Delcine looked out the window. They rolled past cotton fields on one side of the road and a large, dilapidated trailer park on the other.

The landscape was as depressing as ever, and she said so.

"What did you think was going to change?" Clayton said. "Think about it. We've been gone from this hellhole for a long time. And we all live in large, vibrant cities. North Carolina is just as backwoods country as it's always been."

"Not all of North Carolina," JoJo said from the back seat. "I hear Charlotte and Raleigh are pretty nice."

"What's the address for the lawyer's office?" Clayton asked.

"It's right behind the funeral home on Clifton Street," said JoJo, the family's internal GPS system. "That's weird too. The undertaker is a lawyer."

Clayton chuckled. "I thought the same thing. But Archer says it's not that odd. Think about it. Undertakers deal with a lot of legal issues. And it's a really small town. You've been in Vegas and out of Carolina too long, sis."

JoJo grunted.

"You have that right," Delcine said. "I'm getting twitchy just being back here."

Clayton glanced over at her. "I thought it was just me."

Ten minutes later, the three of them were standing in front of Ana Mae's quilt in the lawyer's office. Rollings and his secretary used fat binder clips to secure it along the back of two flip-chart easels.

The Futrell siblings wanted to immediately begin dissecting the quilt blocks, but Everett Rollings put them in a small waiting room while the other heirs and the spouses were summoned to his office.

"We should have just gone straight to Ana Mae's house from that junk store," Delcine fumed.

"It's too late now," JoJo said.

Clayton was near the window, tapping furiously on his phone.

"What's he doing?" JoJo asked.

"Probably having a fight with his boyfriend."

"I can hear you, Delcine," Clayton said.

"We know," JoJo answered back and winked at her sister.

Clayton went back to his texting, and they all cooled their heels for almost thirty more minutes before Everett Rollings's secretary, Maria, summoned them into the conference room at the law office.

Delcine and JoJo nodded at but didn't say anything to Rosalee.

Toussaint le Baptiste was standing in front of the colorful quilt, gazing at the images as if transfixed by the colors.

At the bottom was a large tree. Its leaves carried through the entire quilt, almost as if there were two images in one: a traditional quilt with nine picture squares, and then the flowering tree encompassing it all.

"It's pretty, isn't it?" Maria said.

Reverend Toussaint nodded. "Ana Mae always did like a lot of color. Look at the flowers," he said, pointing toward the base of the tree, where flowers in vibrant reds, golds, and oranges bloomed in profusion. "There's a lot going on in this quilt."

Everett Rollings approached. "And there's a lot at stake," he said. Then, "Reverend le Baptiste, if you'll take a seat. Everyone, please."

When all of the heirs were seated at the table, the lawyer/undertaker picked up a long, thin pointer and walked to the quilt. From where he stood, all of Ana Mae's heirs had unobstructed views of the piece.

"As you can see, Ana Mae's quilt was made up of nine blocks, each approximately twelve inches long and wide. The quilt will remain here . . ."

"But . . . ," three people began in protest.

Everett held up a hand to stop the assorted and varied objections. "But," he said, "my assistant has taken digital photos of the front, the back, the label, and detail images of each block. You each will receive a copy of all of the photos. That way, you can review them at your leisure. The original quilt will remain here, secure, until your quest is completed. Are there any questions?"

There being none, he nodded. "All right, now to review."

Several groans, the most audible from Lester, echoed around the room.

"You're free to go at any time, Lester," Clayton said. "You're only here because you think you can claim some of Ana Mae's money."

Lester pointed a stubby finger at his brother-in-law. "That's right, and I predict you don't get a dime. We're gonna win this game," he said with a gesture toward JoJo.

"Lester, please," JoJo said.

But Delcine jumped into the defense of her sister. "The only reason you are even here, Lester, is because . . ."

"People," Everett Rollings interjected, "there is no need for this division. Ana Mae's will is very specific about who will inherit and why. Let us take a moment to review."

When everyone had settled back into their seats— Lester quiet but with his arms folded and a scowl directed toward Delcine and Clayton, who sat next to each other—the lawyer started again.

"The stipulations of the last will and testament of Miss Ana Mae Futrell are clear. The person or people who individually or collectively solve the mystery of the quilt will equally divide and inherit the full estate, less the personal bequests noted the other day. In addition, the person who solves the mystery of the quilt will receive the quilt as well."

"What if we solve it together?" JoJo asked.

"That's what collectively means, Jo," Archer said, his voice gentle and not mocking, as Delcine's would have been.

JoJo nodded. "Oh. Okay. Go on, Mr. Rollings."

The lawyer splayed his left hand toward JoJo. "Just as you cut a side deal with your siblings to be allowed back in the quest, I am sure you all will overcome your differences. If you would like to establish a contractual agreement, someone here in the office can do that, or we can refer you to another firm in the area for independent representation."

Clayton looked at each of his sisters, who shook their heads, and then at the lawyer. "That won't be necessary."

"Hmmph," Lester muttered. "Maybe it will be. You got your own personal lawyer sitting right there next to you."

Archer didn't take the bait, and under the table he placed a restraining hand on Clayton's thigh to still his likely reply to Lester.

"Do you need time to discuss the matter?" Rollings asked them all.

"We need to get on with what we're supposed to do with that quilt," Reverend le Baptiste said.

Delcine glared at him, but JoJo tapped her sister's arm. "He's right," she said. "Let's just get on with it."

Rosalee cleared her throat—loudly, but she could have been biting back laughter.

Rollings looked at each of the heirs, holding the individual gazes for more than a moment. He had a few ideas about what Ana Mae was after here, but it was not his place to say. He had been keeping Ana Mae Futrell's secrets all these years. As far as Everett was concerned, he would keep on keeping them—just as she had kept his about his own sons.

He doubted that any of the people in the room had a clue. Maybe Rosalee Jenkins, Ana Mae's dearest friend. But, Everett Rollings knew, even Rosalee did not know Ana Mae's biggest secret.

His secretary, Maria, came into the room, her arms full with spiral-bound booklets. Everett had paid extra for a rush on the job to get the photographs for the heirs.

"Here are your photocopies," he said, as Maria began passing them out, one each to Clayton Futrell, Marguerite Delcine Futrell Winslow, Josephine Futrell Coston, Rosalee Jenkins, and the Reverend Toussaint le Baptiste.

Rosalee raised her hand.

"Mrs. Jenkins, you have a question?"

Rosalee looked at the siblings, then at Toussaint le Baptiste, and finally back at Everett Rollings. "I just want you to explain one more time what my stake in this is. Ana Mae left me that bank account. Am I supposed to be going after the quilt clues too?"

The solicitor consulted a sheaf of papers on the table, then met her gaze. "I'm sorry, Mrs. Jenkins. I encouraged Ana Mae to be more specific, but she only said what she did. You are to oversee the distribution of her sewing supplies and equipment and be present at the reading of the will. Since this meeting is a part of that process, I made sure you were also invited."

"But Too Sweet, I mean, Reverend le Baptiste does have a stake?"

"Yes," Rollings said, "he does."

Rosalee nodded, as if the answer confirmed some unspoken assessment. She reached for her pocketbook and rose. "Well, there's no need for me to be here as far as I can see."

Toussaint reached out. "Stay, Sister Rosalee. Please. You can be my guest."

She looked at him. "But . . ."

"Moral support," he said, flicking his eyes toward the siblings.

For a moment, Rosalee hesitated. And then she smiled. "Okay, Too . . . I mean Reverend Toussaint. For moral support and in memory of Ana Mae."

Clayton narrowed his eyes, considering the preacher and Rosalee Jenkins. Maybe le Baptiste was one of those pimp in the pulpit types. Rosalee was over there batting her eyelashes like a woman flirting with an available man.

For his part, Toussaint le Baptiste didn't look like a typical black Baptist preacher. He was tall, a few inches taller than Clayton's own six-foot frame, and more wiry than thin. He sported a thin moustache and wore his still-thick hair combed straight back, a slight wave evident and a curl at the ends as if he were overdue for a visit to the barbershop. Toussaint put Clayton in mind of a much older El DeBarge.

If Clayton were to guess, and he did, there was some biracial or tri-racial ancestry in the preacher's blood, his

French-Creole name further advancing the theory of a mixed lineage.

Maybe it was just one of those things where women were attracted to their ministers. Clayton didn't get it.

Toussaint settled Rosalee back in her chair, then folded his large hands on the tabletop.

"So I'm in the hunt," Rosalee said, looking at the quilt.

"Yes, helping me."

"Well, that appears to be settled," Rollings said as a way to draw them all back together. "Let us begin with the overall quilt," the lawyer said, again using his pointer to indicate the areas of note on the piece hanging between the easels. "Some time ago, Ana Mae let me borrow the quilt for a few days so I could photograph it and gather additional information in the event it was needed. Since I knew little about quilts or quilting, I took the liberty of consulting the owner of an area quilt shop to be able to give you a more accurate description. The dimensions are seventy-six inches by seventy-six inches. This quilt was hand-pieced and machine-quilted by Ana Mae."

He reached down and lifted the bottom-right edge so they could all see the back of the quilt. "As you can see here, and in your booklets on page four, there is an elaborate label stating just that. The motif of a full-leafed flowering tree seen on the front of the quilt is continued here. In addition, the label provides the name of the quilt, which is The Legacy of Ana Mae Futrell, the date and place where and when it was made here in North Carolina, and the following quote: "Love must be sincere. Hate what is evil. Cling to what is good. Be devoted to one another in brotherly love."

"Amen," said the preacher.

"All of the words on the quilt label are embroidered rather than using a fusible printing method or a fabric pen. Mrs. Elnora Rogers, the quilt shop owner I consulted, said Ana Mae put as much work into this label of the quilt as she did into each of the blocks."

"What's a block?"

"Why is the label on the back so important? It's the front with the clues that matters, right?" Clayton asked.

Several heads bobbed, echoing the question.

Everett consulted a legal pad on the table. "The second question first," he said. "Mrs. Rogers said the label of a quilt is, in many cases, more important than the actual quilt. The label provides authenticity by citing, at a minimum, the name of the quilter and the date the quilt was made. In this case, as you can see, Ana Mae took special care to include additional information about the piece. She wanted you to know this information. And the label on the back side of the quilt is the same size and dimension, that being twelve inches by twelve inches, as the quilt blocks on the front."

"We have a group of quilting ladies over at the church who use the fellowship hall for meetings every month," Reverend Toussaint said, his voice a little wistful. "I remember one of them saying how Ana Mae always liked to make the back of her quilts as special as the front."

No one said anything for a moment, then the lawyer cleared his throat.

"As for what's a block," he said. "Each square you see here," using the pointer to outline one of the nine focal points on the front of the quilt, "is a block. Sometimes, I am told, quilters cut up large pieces of fabric into small pieces of fabric and then sew them back to-

gether in designs to create a block. That's calling piec-
ing."

Rollings consulted his notes again, then pointed to
another of the nine main blocks. "But Ana Mae used a
technique called appliqué, which, in a nutshell, is sewing
fabric pictures onto other fabric. The material between
the blocks is called sashing."

Lester sighed.

"Is any of this really important to finding the
cash?"

Before anyone could scowl at him, Delcine said,
"Frankly, I was wondering the same thing."

"It is my fiduciary duty to ensure that all of you be
equipped with any information that will aid you in
your endeavor."

"Well, if that's the case," Clayton said, "Just tell us
the magic words now so we can be done with this and
get home."

Several "yeahs" sounded in response.

Rollings bit back a sigh. "It will not be that easy, I
am afraid. Are there any questions thus far before we
review the blocks?"

Once again thwarted in the effort to bypass Ana
Mae's last wishes and claim her hidden riches, the anxious heirs huffed and sat back in their seats around the
conference table.

"As I was saying," Rollings continued, indicating a
strip between the blocks, "this fabric is called sashing.
And this is a border," he said, pointing to a large strip
of fabric that went around the entire edge of the quilt
blocks, "and this is the binding." He indicated the outer
edge of the quilt. "One other thing that the quilt shop
owner thought it would be important for you to know is
that a quilt is essentially a sandwich."

"That don't look like anything to eat," Lester said.

"Shush," JoJo hissed at him.

"A quilt sandwich is a front layer, a back layer, and something in the middle, usually batting. Mrs. Rogers said Ana Mae always used a high-quality cotton batting for her work."

The lawyer turned a few pages in the booklet. "If you will all go to page five, we shall begin with the block in the upper left of row one, then we will review the blocks in the second row and finish with the third.

"The first block and clue is a plate of fried chicken."

"Maybe she decided to have that rather than a sandwich," Lester said.

Several mouths quirked up, but no one said anything.

"The second block and clue is a North Carolina Lottery scratch-off lottery ticket."

Rosalee leaned over to Toussaint and whispered, "That's the game Ana Mae won all that money on."

"What was that?" Delcine asked from across the table.

"Nothing," Rosalee said.

To the lawyer, Delcine asked, "And why is she here again?"

Rosalee leaned forward and pointed at Delcine. "If it hadn't been for me," Rosalee declared, "y'all wouldna even known Ana Mae had any money, Miss High and Mighty."

Toussaint patted Rosalee's hand in a calming gesture. "Mrs. Jenkins is with me," he said in answer to Delcine's question.

Delcine pursed her lips but didn't say anything.

"The third block," Rollings said, moving on as if

the skirmish hadn't even happened, "features images of Diamond Jim and Baby Sue, Ana Mae's beloved cats."

"More like bedeviled," JoJo said to no one in particular. "Even with the Benadryl, I'm still sneezing."

"Look at that detail," Reverend Toussaint murmured.

"Indeed, Reverend," Rollings said. "Mrs. Rogers, the quilt shop owner, told me the workmanship is impeccable."

"See, it was worth the five hundred dollars," Delcine said.

"That blanket is worth a helluva lot more than five hundred," Lester said.

Rollings jumped in. "The fourth block is a teapot and a teacup."

Clayton leaned over to whisper something in his partner's ear. Archer smiled in return.

"Why don't you share the joke, Clay?" JoJo asked.

"Let's not hold up Mr. Rollings," Clayton said.

"Thank you," the lawyer intoned. "The fifth block and clue is the center of the quilt and features an opened Bible with the words Matthew 25:14–18 embroidered across the bottom. The embroidery is like that found on the label on the backside."

"What is that Bible verse?" Archer asked.

"That's where the man was burying his talent," JoJo said.

Lester looked at her, his mouth open. "Since when did you start reading the Bible?"

"Probably the day she married you," Delcine said on a dry and flat note.

"Very good," Rollings said in acknowledgment of

either JoJo's assessment of the Scripture reference or Delcine's wry analysis, and again interjecting to keep the bloodshed among the heirs to a minimum.

From a shelf, he plucked a burgundy-colored leather Bible. "This is the King James Version, but we can supply a New International Version if anyone prefers that interpretation."

Again hearing no objection, he opened the holy book and began reading the Scripture text referenced on Ana Mae's quilt.

"For the kingdom of heaven is as a man travelling into a far country, who called his own servants, and delivered unto them his goods. And unto one he gave five talents, to another two, and to another one; to every man according to his several ability; and straightaway took his journey. Then he that had received the five talents went and traded with the same, and made them other five talents. And likewise he that had received two, he also gained other two. But he that had received one went and digged in the earth, and hid his lord's money."

Rollings closed the Bible and placed it on the table.

"Amen," JoJo said. "And may the Lord bless those who hear his word."

All eyes shifted to her, but JoJo merely clasped her hands together on the tabletop.

"What's that supposed to mean?" Delcine asked. "Is Ana Mae saying she buried a talent she had or that one of us did that?"

"Mrs. Foster, it is your task to interpret the quilt. As I said, the passage I read is from the King James Version. We can supply a copy of the Scripture to anyone who needs it." Using the long pointer, he indicated the block again. "The block on Ana Mae's quilt simply says Matthew 25:14–18, which may or may not mean that that is what she wanted you to look up or refer to. I just wanted to supply you with the information."

"Yeah, your fiduciary duty," Lester muttered.

"Precisely," Rollings said with a broad smile. "The sixth block on the quilt is of a sewing machine and a basket of fabric. And the seventh block is an illustration of a man, presumably Jesus, with little children around him.

"Now, based on what Mrs. Rogers noted, I'll point out the ninth block before returning to the eighth one," the lawyer said.

The ninth one had a mop and a bucket appliquéd on it.

"This one," he said, going back to the one he'd skipped, "the eighth block by position, has, as you see, a gravestone. Etched on the stone is R.I.P–A.M.F. with a large flowering tree in the background."

"Rest in peace, Ana Mae Futrell," Toussaint said softly.

"Possibly, Reverend. I am not at liberty to offer any explanations for any of the quilt blocks."

"Well, any idiot can see that's what that one means," Lester said.

Toussaint's gaze left the quilt and focused on Lester.

"Oh, sorry. Not you, Rev. No offense. I just meant that . . ."

"We know what you meant, Lester," his wife said. "Now please, let Mr. Rollings finish his presentation."

"But because of the tree, this block is something of an anchor, according to Mrs. Rogers. Note how the tree's branches, leaves, and flowers spread out and touch just about every other block."

"She put a lot of work into this quilt," Archer said.

Clayton glanced at his partner.

Rollings nodded. "Yes, she did. I must say, before consulting with Mrs. Rogers I had little knowledge of quilts other than their usefulness on a bed for warmth. There are many types of quilts, from art pieces to functional ones and whimsical ones and those that mark occasions, such as a wedding. But I digress," Rollings said, again consulting his legal pad. "And please note that carved in the trunk of the tree is a heart with the word *HOWARD* printed inside, in embroidery, of course," the lawyer said.

"That's our family name," Delcine said. "Howard was our mother's maiden name."

"Yes, I know. My father served the Howard family for many years."

"Served them what?" Lester asked.

"As family solicitor."

"Well, la de dah," Lester muttered under his breath. "For a bunch of dirt-poor folks, you all sure have a lot of lawyers running around."

Everyone ignored him.

"Mr. Rollings," Clayton said, "is there anything else that we should know about the quilt or about what we're supposed to be doing?"

"I fear not."

The muted refrains of a Puccini opera suddenly filled the room. Everyone looked around for the offending mobile telephone. Delcine took her time reaching for the handbag housing the cell. She glanced at the display, winced, then punched a button and tucked the phone back into her bag.

She made eye contact with her husband for the barest of moments.

"Mr. Rollings," Delcine began, as if there had been no interruption, "do you have any idea why Ana Mae decided to take this insane treasure hunt approach to fulfilling her last will and testament?"

"Yeah," JoJo piped up, "why is she making us do this?"

"First," Rollings said, "this is not a treasure hunt, and second, it is well within the rights of any person to stipulate how or even if his or her assets are to be distributed upon death. As for why Miss Futrell chose this particular method, I am sure your sister's motivations will become apparent as you work through the process of deciphering the quilt squares."

When no one said anything, Rollings consulted his notes again, then referred the group to a page in the back of the booklet.

"We have taken the liberty of creating copies of this page," he said, as his assistant handed out a sheet of paper to each official heir. "It is a quick reference for you in the event you don't want to take the full booklet around with you."

The single sheet had a color photocopy of the quilt on one side, and the back listed the subject of each block under a heading labeled "Appliquéd blocks of the quilt *The Legacy of Ana Mae Futrell*."

Block 1: A plate of fried chicken
Block 2: A replica of the winning scratch-off lottery ticket
Block 3: Ana Mae's cats, Diamond Jim and Baby Sue
Block 4: A teapot and teacup
Block 5: (center square) An open Bible with the Scripture reference Matthew 25:14–18

Block 6: A sewing machine and basket of fabric

Block 7: Jesus with little children

Block 8: A tombstone inscribed R.I.P–A.M.F at the foot of a large flowering tree. In the center of the tree trunk is a carved heart with the word *HOWARD*.

Block 9: A mop and bucket

"I have a question," Rosalee said, raising her hand like a schoolgirl.

"I need another copy," Reverend Toussaint said at the same time.

"For what?" Delcine snapped.

Rollings held up a hand to stave off any other outbursts. He nodded to his assistant, who without question gave the minister a second copy.

Delcine's glower made her impression perfectly clear.

"Yes, Mrs. Jenkins?"

"How long is this supposed to take?"

"Until someone calls me saying he or she has completed the task. At that point, I will convene a meeting of all the heirs."

"Are there any other instructions before we begin, Mr. Rollings?"

The question to get them back on track came from Clayton.

They had all been obsessing about the why of Ana Mae's actions. All Clayton wanted to do was get the ordeal over with as quickly as possible so he could get the hell out of North Carolina and back to civilization. For half of his life, he'd dreamed of one day escaping and never, ever coming back. Now he was stuck here in

Drapersville and Ahoskie, fooling around with Ana Mae's torture from the grave.

What should have been a two-day—three-day at the absolute maximum—trip to North Carolina was now turning into what quickly and clearly was stretching into a prison sentence. A sentence with no parole.

He should have opted out, taken the ten grand, and walked away. That would have been the smart move.

"As a matter of fact, yes," Rollings said, answering Clayton's question.

Resigned to purgatory, Clayton released a heavy sigh and sat back in his chair.

Archer placed a hand along the back of the chair. Their gazes met for a moment, and Clayton's heart kicked over. He relished the small intimacy and dared not move even an inch.

"Everyone has a booklet with the images of the quilt," Rollings said. "I estimate that it may take you approximately a week to . . ."

"A week!"

Clayton and Delcine shrieked simultaneously.

". . . do what you need to do. Please leave with Maria telephone numbers where you can be reached. And Dr. Futrell and Mrs. Foster, a week is just an estimate. If you would like to take longer, that would be fine."

"Longer? Here in Drapersville and Ahoskie?" Clayton looked horrified. "I don't think so."

"And as I told Mrs. Jenkins, you may find that you do not need more than an afternoon."

"That's more like it," Clayton said, jumping up. "Let's get this farce over with."

He didn't want to spend a moment longer than he

had to in this hick town. He'd sworn off North Carolina and all of its tiny hamlets a long time ago. And he had absolutely no intention of getting stuck or sucked back into one at this point in his life.

He couldn't stand it, and his relationship with Archer wouldn't survive it.

"What's wrong, Clay?" Archer asked.

He was having a hard time, that's what was wrong. "I didn't anticipate that we'd have to be here that long."

Toussaint studied the younger man, then looked at the quilt, his brow furrowed.

Noticing the minister's focus on Clayton, Archer asked him. "Something wrong, Reverend?"

"No, son, nothing's wrong. I was just admiring Ana Mae's quilt."

In truth, Toussaint was wondering why Ana Mae had him involved in this treasure hunt. That's all that it really could be called, despite what Everett Rollings said. Sister Futrell had already made a generous contribution to the church—several, in fact—which were far and above a ten percent tithe. Did she mean for him to win and keep the money personally?

Lord, just the thought boggled his mind.

But knowing Ana Mae, and they went way back, maybe the millions were for the building fund. The Good Lord knew that without a serious infusion of cash, it would take another ten or so years for the congregation to raise the money that would let them build without debt. There were so many souls out there who needed saving. Ana Mae knew that.

The additional money from her estate could carry on the kingdom business of bringing souls to Christ . . . or giving them a step up in the world. Everybody needed a little help now and then. Ana Mae Futrell knew that and spent much of her life doing something about it in her own way. The Holy Ghost Church of the Good Redeemer focused on providing that help and uplifting the community through its various outreach ministries.

Ana Mae also knew what it meant to sacrifice. That concept was one most people either glossed over or didn't even believe in these days. Going without so someone else could benefit was anathema to most folks. Ana Mae, however, was different. She'd always been different, and that was one of the things he'd always liked about her, even when they were kids, growing up poor and black in a poor and mostly black town.

"Does anyone have any additional questions?"

Rollings's query drew Toussaint le Baptiste out of his reverie and back on the challenge before him. Right then and there he committed himself to the challenge from Sister Futrell.

With Rosalee's help, he knew he would win.

9

Secrets to Keep

Trey Rollings's main problem working at his father's funeral home was that no one believed that he had actually followed his father into the family business. While Everett Rollings tended to look the part—a mix of somber empathy and concern—Trey seemed to always come across like a frat boy doing community service before heading out for his next wild weekend of debauchery. He was the exact opposite of his homebody brother, who had to be coaxed to leave Drapersville long enough to go away to college.

Not for the first time since starting his mortuary apprenticeship, a potential client eyed him with distrust. For today's client meeting he wore a gray suit instead of the blue blazer, gray slacks, and shirt of a mortuary intern. Dressing the part helped his image as a competent professional.

"I thought Mr. Rollings was going to be handling

the arrangements for my brother," the octogenarian said. "Are you sure you have enough experience? Everything has to be just perfect for Waldo."

"Mrs. Weatherby," Trey said deliberately, slowing his un-Southern tendency to talk fast, a trait directly attributed to his Yankee mother. "I assure you that the full service and attention to detail that has always been a hallmark of Rollings Funeral Home will be focused on you and your family's needs."

He wanted to call her on the fact that he too was a Mr. Rollings, but he knew better than that, so he did the next best thing. Trey pulled a business card from a small case in his suit coat pocket and handed it to her.

Taking the card, Annie Weatherby eyed him, her brow furrowed in concentration. "You don't look much like your daddy. As a matter of fact, you tend to favor somebody else. I just cannot put my finger on who, though."

He bit back a sigh. He'd heard that before from people of a certain age who believed in blurting out whatever rude thought crossed their small minds at any given moment. Unlike his father, who steadfastly refused to believe anyone knew their little secret, Trey was sure that plenty of people around town knew but were too polite to say anything.

Mrs. Weatherby pulled up her glasses from the beaded chain on her neck and peered at the business card.

"Everett H. Rollings the third," she read aloud.

"Yes, ma'am. But people just call me Trey for short."

"Hmmph," Mrs. Weatherby said, clearly not approving of nicknames, or at least his nickname. "Is Mr. Rollings a junior? I didn't know that."

Trey pulled on the reserve of patience his mortuary mentor tried to instill in him. "Yes, ma'am, he is. But since his own father passed away many years ago, he doesn't use the 'Junior.' "

For what it was worth, not that Trey would tell the clearly grieving in her own busybody way Mrs. Weatherby, his father didn't use the "Junior" moniker even before that. Everett Rollings was no one's junior. On official documents, he was listed simply as Everett H. Rollings II.

"I find it peculiar that you refer to the elder Mr. Rollings as your father's father rather than as your grandfather."

Trey knew where this was going and had no intention of playing her game. He simply smiled at her.

When her comment didn't elicit the favored response, Mrs. Weatherby looked at the engraved business card again. "And what does the H in your name stand for?" she wanted to know.

Trey was saved from having to answer or engage her any further when the door was pushed open.

"We're all ready for you, Mrs. Weatherby," said Christopher Coles, the senior family counselor who was training Trey.

"Mrs. Weatherby, I was glad to be of assistance to you. And again, I am very sorry for your loss," Trey said graciously.

"Hmmph," the old woman said, as Trey assisted her from her chair and handed her off to Christopher. "Mr. Rollings sure has a lot of help around here. Does he do any work anymore? I'm not paying good money to have a passel of trainees and amateurs . . ."

The rest of her complaint mercifully faded away as Christopher led her into the adjoining showroom—not that Everett Rollings allowed any of his employees to call it such. The only reason Trey had been stuck with the old biddy in the first place was to allow another grieving family time to complete making their casket choices and be ushered into one of the client lounges.

It was the end of his workday at the funeral home, and Trey couldn't wait to get out of the suit. He had a date in Virginia Beach that night and had no plans to keep the lovely lady, a woman he'd met while doing his other job, waiting a moment longer than necessary.

In his room at the bed-and-breakfast, Archer Futrell-Dahlgren considered his options. As a lawyer, he knew how to obstruct and/or obviate the truth without breaking either the law or client confidentiality. And for the last eight months, he'd been doing just that. Clayton would be furious. But, Archer wondered, would his longtime partner consider the sin of omission enough to convict him?

Yes.

Did Archer care?

Hmm. Therein lay his moral dilemma.

Clayton was a wonderful man, and Archer did indeed love him. Was it, however, enough?

For the last dozen years he and Clayton had been devoted to each other, for ten years as domestic partners. They owned a spectacular home together as well as a weekend pied-à-terre in Monterey. Of all their friends and acquaintances, gay and straight, their relationship was viewed as the most solid. But it had all changed eight months ago when his sister-in-law Ana Mae Futrell contacted him.

She wanted him to do some legal work for her.

At first, he'd been flattered that she'd sought him out. Although they had not been successful in getting her to come to California to visit, she kept in regular touch via the occasional telephone call, and she always remembered their birthdays and their anniversary.

When she'd explained to him what she wanted him to do, Archer had had his doubts. Taking Ana Mae on as a client meant one hell of a conflict of interest.

"Why are you telling me this?" he'd asked her.

Ana Mae's answer had been as simple as it was profound. "Because you love him as much as I do," she'd said.

Recalling the conversation now, Archer sighed.

She had not expected any of this to matter for a long, long time. How could she have known that an aneurysm would take her at such a relatively young age?

Archer sighed again. What he knew could change everything.

Everything.

The question eating at him was a simple one: Was he willing to trade all they had now for a chance to get more?

He zipped open the hidden compartment on his carry-on bag, extracted the damning evidence, and carried it to the bathroom of their suite at the bed-and-breakfast.

Before ethics kicked in, before he changed his mind, and before he could conjure the hurt sure to be in Clayton's eyes, he lit a match to destroy the evidence.

But it was already too late. He couldn't do it. Not even for a client. The match burned down and licked at his finger. Archer dropped it in the toilet and shook his hand, rubbing the area that had been singed by the small flame.

The document, embossed with the seal of the Commonwealth of Virginia, was still in his other hand. It should have been incinerated, with the other charred bits of paper now floating on the surface of the water. But he couldn't do it. Not this.

He expected guilt to assail him.

It was the first time in his career that he'd ever betrayed a client. He thought he might feel a stab or at least a twinge of guilt.

None ever came.

For the first time in her life, Rosalee Jenkins was alone. Really and truly alone. Ana Mae had always been like a sister to her; the two were closer than if they'd been birthed by the same mother, closer than Ana Mae was with either Delcine or JoJo.

Now, with Ana Mae gone, Rosalee didn't know how she would survive. At least five times a day, she'd reach for her phone to tell Ana Mae something funny she'd seen on TV or overheard at the post office.

There had been no secrets between them—at least that's what Rosalee always believed. Until the obituary appeared in the *Times & Review.*

Ana Mae had a son.

Who the hell was Howard?

In all the years the two had been road dogs, Ana Mae had never, ever, not even once, so much as hinted that she'd had a child.

"Why'd you leave that part out, sister?"

Rosalee stared up at the ceiling as if expecting Ana Mae's voice or visage to come from above.

She sighed, knowing better, but still missing her friend.

Then there was the business of that quilt. It was all pretty ordinary, a simple telling of Ana Mae's life in stitches and fabric. Ana Mae had made far prettier ones, and instead of selling them, she'd simply given them away as gifts.

Rosalee smiled. Except for the one the Futrells paid five hundred dollars to get back.

It was wrong what she'd done. Purely out of spite toward that hateful Delcine. Rosalee had hoped that Miss High and Mighty would have to pay for the quilt over at Eddie Spencer's place, but Clayton had ended up doing it. She wasn't too happy about that, especially since she'd always liked Clay.

There sure wasn't anything special about that quilt, except for all the appliqué. And if anyone would know, it was Rosalee, since she'd seen Ana Mae working on the thing and had given it no more thought than any of the other projects in Ana Mae's sewing baskets. It had taken a long time for her to make that quilt. It was Ana Mae's never-ending project.

"Just a little something for me," she would tell Rosalee.

Ana Mae called it a legacy.

Little did Rosalee know or realize just how much of a legacy that quilt would be.

"Are you playing some kind of game with your kin, Ana Mae?"

The question, like all her queries to her dead friend, was directed heavenward.

That seemed the only logical explanation Rosalee had come up with since the day Everett Rollings dropped that bomb of a will.

She couldn't fault Ana Mae for leaving her money to her family. She'd gifted Rosalee with a more than generous amount that was now sitting in the First Trust and Union Bank. What hurt, what Rosalee took as a personal insult, was the secret of Ana Mae's son, Howard.

Heaving a sigh, she pushed herself up out of the chair in her living room. "Come on, Rosalee. You can sit here feeling sorry for yourself, or you can go find some answers."

The self-directed pep talk spurred her into action.

Clayton, Delcine, and JoJo could run around town figuring out quilt clues and stuff that made no natural sense at all, since it was clear as day what the quilt meant. Rosalee would solve the real mystery. And she knew just where to start.

10

Sweet Memories

Rosalee wasn't the only one thinking about what Ana Mae left behind. It didn't take Ana Mae's neighbors, friends, and fellow church members long to figure out that something pretty extraordinary was going on with the Futrells. And the next thing everyone knew, a story in the Drapersville Times & Review told about the big-city visitors who'd returned to their hometown and had to stick around for a while because of something Ana Mae did from the grave. Then an "anonymous source"—which everyone who was anyone knew was Rosalee Jenkins—was quoted in the paper saying Ana Mae had left a significant monetary inheritance to the heir who deciphered the clues left in a quilt.

Odds at Junior Cantrell's and the barbershop ran three to one that the snooty Marguerite would get the money. "She's the one don't need none," one sage said.

"But that boy got a good head on his shoulders, even if he is that way. I think he's gonna get it," another handicapper declared, laying down twenty bucks on the ten-to-one odds of Clayton claiming the money.

Thanks to Eddie Spencer's explanation of how she'd tossed out the valuable quilt as trash, JoJo, the Vegas show girl, was universally viewed as a flake and about as likely to figure out how to win the cash as she was to fit into her old high school majorette uniform.

Debate raged about just what the Reverend Toussaint le Baptiste had to do with it all. Since Ana Mae was known to be a devout churchgoer, half the folks making wagers decided his presence was about Ana Mae giving the church even more money than she already had. The other half was split down the middle, some saying Ana Mae and the preacher had a side thing going on and the others just as vehemently strident that it wasn't nice to say such bad things about the dead, especially seeing as how holy Ana Mae was.

Then someone would say: "Well, what about that Howard son of hers? Apparently, she wasn't always holy. Didn't she used to talk to one of them Jenkins boys before they moved over to Greensboro?"

And the debate would relaunch all over again while more money exchanged hands and the odds shifted.

"For such a small house, Ana Mae sure had a lot of stuff. What is all this crap?"

Delcine and JoJo were at Ana Mae's house, still going through her belongings. More careful now that millions of dollars were on the line, they maintained a diligence that would have been unwarranted a few days ago when they unceremoniously tossed out papers, knickknacks, and other seemingly worthless trash.

Now they meticulously reviewed every piece of stray paper, opened envelopes, and shook out magazines lest a critical clue be overlooked or thrown out the way the treasure quilt had been.

They'd decided to work in their older sister's bedroom today, JoJo handling the closet and Delcine focusing on the dresser drawers and the overflowing bureau top. The gilded frame of the mirror on the bureau dresser was barely visible under snapshots and ticket stubs from movies and sporting events.

"The good thing is at least it's halfway organized," Delcine said. "Just think if she'd been one of those hoarders like on television."

"What's a hoarder?"

Delcine paused in sorting scarves and gloves from one of the drawers. "You mean you haven't seen any of those hoarder shows? People have so much stuff that only a path is clear in their house and junk is piled up to the ceilings. Frankly it's pretty sickening. And sad."

"We don't watch a lot of TV," JoJo said.

Delcine rolled her eyes. "Oh, yeah. That's right. Lester's too busy working the Strip with his fake psychic bit while you're putting in eighty-hour weeks at the casino to keep a roof over your heads."

"My work weeks aren't that long," JoJo said, a note of defensiveness in her voice. "I do get some overtime every month, though, and that helps a lot."

The last thing she wanted to have with her wealthy and successful sister was a conversation about money. JoJo paused and looked at her hands. They were no longer the soft and pampered hands of a woman who regularly indulged in manicures and spa treatments, and her nails, kept short by necessity, were those of a woman who labored. In addition, her hands were bare. No rings adorned them. And she'd be buried in Antioch Cemetery right next to Ana Mae before she ever let Delcine know that she'd had to hock her wedding rings just to afford a one-way ticket to North Carolina for the funeral. She planned to discreetly ask Clayton to pay her fare to get back home.

So when Everett Rollings said Ana Mae had left her ten grand, JoJo thought for sure that she had won the lottery. She knew Lester was already calculating how much he'd "invest" in his latest get-rich-quick scheme. But when they'd found out there was so much more than ten thousand up for grabs, Lester had been furious, claiming they'd been tricked out of their portion. He didn't see the irony in what he did to tourists in Las Vegas every day. That was trickery at its finest. But she knew he wouldn't see it that way.

"You okay in there?" Delcine asked.

JoJo wiped at a stray tear that somehow had sprung to her eyes.

"I'm fine," she lied.

She had no idea if the sudden tears were for Ana Mae, for her own lost hopes and dreams, or because Delcine was being such a bitch.

JoJo pulled out a large wooden box from one of the two shelves in the closet. Carved on the top was a scene of a hunter in a duck blind; pussy willows and lily pads surrounded the banks of a knoll overlooking a pond. "Ana Mae didn't hunt. I wonder where she got this."

"What is it?" Delcine said from the doorway.

"Some kind of hunting box."

JoJo put the box on Ana Mae's bed, the double

mattress covered with a lightweight but colorful, scrappy quilt, likely made by Ana Mae herself, although there was no label on it.

The sisters looked at the eight-by-twelve-inch box, then at each other.

"Diamonds?" Delcine guessed.

"A week ago I'd have laughed at that," JoJo said. "Now, who knows?" She lifted the lid to reveal a layer of white tissue paper protecting the contents.

"What is it?"

Peeling back the tissue, JoJo uncovered a bundle of letters tied with a pink satin ribbon, a small Bible, a couple of dried flowers, and other mementos, including a handful of photographs.

She placed each item on the bed, pausing a moment to glance at the old snapshots, including one with a couple of smiling teenagers waving a flag. She smiled at one from an Easter Sunday years ago. Clayton was a little kid, maybe four. Delcine was pouting and JoJo grinning, and Ana Mae looked like the boss of them all.

"Remember this?" JoJo said, handing the photo to her sister.

Delcine looked at it and nodded. "I was mad because you got to wear the bonnet I wanted."

"It was too small for your head!"

"Hmph," Delcine grunted, before displaying a pout much like the one in the long-ago captured moment.

Delcine reached for the ribbon-bundled packet. "Love letters? To Ana Mae?"

"I don't know," JoJo said. The photographs put aside, her attention was back on the remaining items in the wooden box. Her own handwriting was on one of them. "Well, I'll be."

"What is it?"

"She kept them," JoJo said, wonder in her voice.

"Kept what, Jo? Is it something to do with the money?"

JoJo bit her lip in a vain attempt to staunch the tears that again sprang to her eyes. "No," she said. "They're Christmas cards."

"Christmas cards?"

"Uh huh," JoJo said sniffling.

She flipped through and pulled out three envelopes, two with the postmarks identifying when they were sent and the third made of a rough paper that JoJo now remembered.

A brown paper bag.

She couldn't find envelopes anywhere in the house, so she'd made them for her Christmas cards that year from a Piggly Wiggly grocery bag she'd claimed before Mama folded it up to use for trash later on. She needed envelopes to go with the cards she'd crafted for her mother and her sister.

That's the envelope JoJo opened now, by far the oldest one in the box. As she lifted the flap and pulled out the card, the years fell away, and she found herself remembering the moments she'd enjoyed the most as a kid. On the floor, with her back against the twin bed and her feet almost touching the yellow wall of the bedroom she shared with Delcine. Her craft supplies she kept in an old cigar box that Mama gave her for her treasures. In the box, kept under her bed until she needed it, were her crayons, glue, the sparkly glitter, a pair of childproof scissors with rounded ends, and a couple of markers, the tools required to create master-pieces from scrap pieces of paper.

Tears welled in JoJo's eyes at the sight of that first

handmade card. She'd painstakingly made it from construction paper and cutouts from Christmas dream catalogs.

I LOVE YOU ANA MAE FROM YOUR LITTLE SISTER JOSEPINE

JoJo smiled at the misspelling of her name. She always used to forget the H, one of the reasons she quickly adopted the much easier to spell nickname of JoJo. But the message, scrawled in the big block letters of her five- or six-year-old self, brought back the memory of the moment when Ana Mae opened and read the card.

"Do you really love me, Jo?"

She'd nodded, sure of the unfailing devotion and love that only a much older sister could engender.

"How much?" Ana Mae had asked.

"This much," the young JoJo said, spreading her arms wide.

"And I love you, this much," Ana Mae said repeating the gesture with her longer arms and then wrapping them around her baby sister in a big hug.

Ana Mae must have been about nineteen or twenty then, but she always had time for JoJo.

"What's that junk?" Delcine asked.

"It's not junk," JoJo said, clutching the card to her breast. "I made it and gave it to Ana Mae. I've made a Christmas card for her every year since I was little. This is one of the early ones. She saved them all, every single one."

"You make cards? How . . . crafty of you."

JoJo was sure Delcine was going to say something else, but quickly substituted crafty for whatever derogatory thing had initially crossed her mind. As it was, she made the word crafty sound provincial and lowbrow.

Delcine didn't know that JoJo's greeting cards now supplemented her income. She'd picked up rubber-stamping as a hobby, and her talent had quickly turned it into a part-time job. She made her own cards and took orders from other people, but the holiday greeting sent to Delcine, Winslow, and their kids each year was always carefully selected from the Hallmark store, the sort of thing that Delcine would consider tasteful and proper. JoJo knew not to waste any of her original Christmas cards and designs on snooty Delcine. All she would do was what she'd just done—make a not-so-subtle dig designed to belittle and degrade.

JoJo considered her sister, wondering if Delcine's attitude came as an unintentional or a deliberate part of her personality. How Winslow stood it, JoJo couldn't figure out. He was a nice enough guy.

I guess it takes all kinds, JoJo thought.

While Delcine went back to the drawers, JoJo sat on the bed and walked through the years of Christmases she'd been apart from Ana Mae. Las Vegas was a long way from Drapersville, North Carolina. And like her other siblings, once she got out of Carolina, there was little to compel her to come back. Except Ana Mae.

She studied the cards she'd made for her sister. There was the year she'd experimented with non-traditional Christmas colors, making cards that were neon orange and honeydew yellow, and the year she was obsessed with the iris folding technique of manipulating paper. Ana Mae had kept them all.

Now that it was too late, she wished she'd spent more time with or just talking to her older sister. Two cards a year, at Christmas and for her birthday—if JoJo even remembered that one—and a brief call every now and then was no way to treat family. Her chance to do right by Ana Mae was gone, just like her chance for her own hopes and dreams.

But her older sister loved her, and that was a gift she could always treasure.

11

Sibling Rivalry

The offices of the *Drapersville Times & Review* were on the second floor of a bank building downtown. The Greek Revival architecture of the First National Bank of Drapersville stood out like the proverbial sore thumb it was. Milton Draper's visions of grandeur for the town he'd founded couldn't be contained in just the six-bedroom mansion he'd built for his bride. With money some said he'd stolen from a gold coach out west, Milton settled in North Carolina, opened a mill, a bank, and a mercantile. In other words, he owned the town.

By the 1940s, hard times had come, and his grandchildren had little of their former wealth. Between the Great Depression and the war, the Drapers hadn't fared very well. Milton would have been enraged over the way they'd squandered his legacy. But his bank building remained, and the grandchildren let out the two unused floors to maintain a steady income. That plan, like most hatched in the town, didn't last. And it took until 1958, when a Draper great-grandson returned home from up North, that things began to look up for both the family and the town.

He kick-started life into the newspaper and converted the third floor of the bank building into offices and two apartments. He kept one for himself rather than move into the mansion on the bluff with his bigoted and bitter cousins. He leased the other to what the townspeople called a never-ending stream of liberal hippies, artists, and musicians.

By the Summer of Love in 1967, Drapersville, North Carolina, was the hidden gem and getaway of the Beat Generation. But by the late 1970s, all the hippies were gone, and the town once again settled into sleepy oblivion reminiscent of its undistinguished existence in the 1950s, and it remained that way through the turn of the new century.

When Rosalee Jenkins got off the elevator on the second floor, the glory days of the *Drapersville Times & Review* greeted her.

Yellowed and faded front pages of the newspaper hung in frames along the wall along with clippings from more recent editions of the now weekly publication that was "Your source for Hertford County News." It didn't seem to matter that its sister paper, the *Ahoskie Times & Union Report,* claimed the same thing.

Rosalee made her way to the front counter, where Matilde Adams had manned the receptionist's desk since Jimmy Carter was president. The blue and pink polyester pants suit she sported came from the same era and had probably been purchased on sale at Zayre's back when that was the place to shop.

Matilde's pop-bottle lenses of her eyeglasses made

her look blind, but she had a razor-sharp memory and knew more about the village of Drapersville and the city of Ahoskie than most people.

"Rosalee Jenkins, I declare. I haven't seen you since you and Ana Mae Futrell took out that ad looking for . . ." She abruptly stopped mid-sentence and reached out a hand to Rosalee. "Oh, Rosalee, I'm so sorry about Ana Mae. I know the two of you were close."

"Thank you, Matilde," Rosalee said, placing her pocketbook on the counter. "But that's actually why I'm here."

Matilde pushed her glasses up as she rose and straightened, a professional ready to provide the best customer service to a longtime subscriber. "What can I do to help?"

Rosalee explained what she had in mind, and Matilde Adams led her back to the newspaper's morgue, where all of the back issues of the paper were stored.

Toussaint le Baptiste didn't quite know what to make of everything that had transpired over the last couple of days. Ana Mae Futrell's death and funeral had knocked him for something of a loop. And the meetings with Attorney Rollings and the family sent him down for the count.

He and Ana Mae had a history, a very personal one. But it reminded him of the poem by Robert Frost that he'd learned in school. He and Ana Mae had traveled different roads. Looking back now, he wondered what might have become of them had they walked the same path. He'd chosen college and seminary and the single life of an ascetic devoted to ministry and service. Ana Mae Futrell had her pick of boys back in the day. But after she found the Lord, she sent them all packing. She eventually followed in her mother's footsteps. She worked hard and lived a Christian life.

He knew Ana Mae won some money playing the lottery. She'd come to him to confess the sin.

"Reverend, I swear, on my Mama's grave and in Jesus' name, that I've never gambled before. I never even went to the bingo games at the Catholic church even though I cleaned up after them. I just saw all the people in the Day-Ree Mart talking about a new scratch ticket, and I figured it wouldn't hurt to spend a dollar on one."

Toussaint smiled at the memory. Her one-dollar ticket ended up being a big winner. Embarrassed, she gave the church her tithe and more just as soon as she cashed the check from the lottery office.

Had she gotten hooked on playing the lottery and won another big payday?

Where else would she have gotten close to four million dollars to give away?

He closed the Bible on his desk and flipped forward a couple of pages on the yellow legal pad. Reverend Leonard yielded the pulpit to the associate pastor one Sunday a month, and it was Toussaint's Sunday to preach. So he was supposed to be writing his Sunday sermon, but his mind kept straying to Ana Mae and the Futrells. Instead of jotting notes on the Scripture text he planned to preach from, Toussaint did some ciphering.

If memory served correctly, Ana Mae won a hundred twenty five thousand in the lottery. She paid her tithe, handed out a couple of scholarships to church kids headed to the local community college, and bought some books for the library and the recreation center.

Even if she'd invested wisely, he still couldn't figure out how she had so much.

Every year she took a little trip, but nowhere exotic. He knew that because she took the bus and was always back in time for the next Sunday service.

"You were a mystery to me in life, Ana Mae, and you're keeping it up in death. God rest your soul, sister. God rest your sweet, sweet soul."

Lester sluiced water over his head, then shook himself like a dog.

"Hey," JoJo squealed. "Watch it."

They were both squeezed into Ana Mae's small bathroom trying to get dressed for the day. The space, though tight, was actually a little bigger than the bathroom in their trailer back in Las Vegas.

JoJo looked at her husband, who finger-combed his hair in the mirror. "What are you supposed to be today, a Mafia boss?"

Lester snorted as he smoothed an errant tuft behind his ear.

JoJo grinned in the mirror.

"What?" he asked.

She paused in the process of putting on her fake eyelashes. "You're trying to copy Archer's hairstyle."

"I am not," Lester declared, indignant.

But the red crawling up his neck called him a liar.

Lester, who was actually biracial, looked more like his Irish father than his Jamaican mother.

"He did look good at the funeral," JoJo said, again picking up her eyelash implements.

"Hmph."

Lester wiped his hands on one of Ana Mae's pale blue bath towels, then patted his wife's plump butt.

"Stop," she said. But she was smiling when she said it.

"Is there a Walmart around here?"

"What do you need a Walmart for?"

He shrugged. "I just need to pick up some things. Maybe they'll help with the search."

Suspicious now, JoJo turned to look him in the eye. "Things like what?"

"A map, to start with," he said. "I've never been here, and it's been what, more than ten years, almost twenty or so, since you were here. If we have to stay around, I wanna know how to get around."

"Lester, we don't have to stay. I do. You can head home anytime. Don't you have a couple of shows booked?"

He grinned, then leaned in to kiss her on the cheek. "I don't want to leave you in your time of need. I'm gonna take Ana Mae's car. I'll be back in a flash. Since you all decided to start the hunt together—something I disagree with, by the way—I wanna make sure we have everything we need."

"Everything like what?"

"Just stuff," he said evasively.

JoJo didn't like the idea that he was already claiming Ana Mae's belongings as "theirs." And she sure as hell knew he was up to something besides picking up a map at Walmart. Lester's steady gig doing a psychic show at an off-Strip local casino brought in a little cash. It was his Vegas street work that brought in the most money. He and a partner, a sleight-of-hand magician, scammed tourists on a regular basis. She had no doubt that he was up to something. Drapersville and Ahoskie were too small for him to pull a big con, and without Mickey Davenport, his partner in crime, or as he put it, his business partner, Lester was limited and at a disadvantage. Which, as far as JoJo was concerned, was itself a blessing.

She did, however, know that the lure of Ana Mae's millions would keep him on the straight and narrow for a while at least.

What JoJo had not yet figured out was how to claim all the money before Delcine, Clayton, or that preacher did—and permanently get rid of her husband. Back home she knew how to find people who, for the right price, incentive, or chip to cash in later, could make problems disappear. Here in North Carolina, though, she had to play a different set of cards.

She heard the screen door slam as Lester left the house. A moment later she heard Ana Mae's old Bonneville reluctantly kick over. And then she remembered the offer from Eddie Spencer.

Imagining Eddie in the role of an old-time Vegas gangster, she grinned. The offer he'd made to her for "anything you need" was just the sort of thing one of those guys from Las Vegas's organized crime days would say. Back when she looked like she did in her dancing days, it was easy to picture the way it would all go down. She'd put on something clingy, making sure to show off the girls to their best advantage. Then, knowing full well she'd have to pay up one day, she'd ask one of the boys for a favor—to arrange an accident for her husband.

Once Lester's car blew up or he was escorted out to the desert for a one-way trip, she'd be free to live her life the way she wanted to.

A Lester-free life. The very notion lifted her spirits.

But reality set in a moment later as she stared in the mirror. She could no more kill Lester than she could fly. A girl could dream, though.

At one point in her life, JoJo thought she needed a man, someone to take care of her, to make her complete. Time, marriage to Lester, and being here in North Carolina had changed her perspective.

She would give Eddie Spencer a call, though. Maybe he could give her some suggestions on the job outlook in the county.

Once it arrived in JoJo's head, the notion of staying here appealed to her . . . a lot.

"You clearly don't give a damn about any of this or any of us," Delcine told her husband.

Winslow didn't bother with a reply. Instead, he reached for the remote control for the television.

Delcine snatched it from his hand and hurled it across the room. It hit the wall and the batteries popped out. A dent in the wall and tear in the wallpaper testified to the force she'd used.

The argument between them had been raging for the better part of an hour. The hotel's front desk had already phoned once asking them to keep it down because complaints were coming in.

In response, Delcine cranked the volume on the perky morning TV host, and when the commercials came on it was a battle to determine which was louder. Winslow, fed up with the argument and the TV noise, just looked at her, then manually turned down the volume.

"What do you want me to do, Marguerite? What do you want me to say? We're screwed. Okay. Does that make you happy that I said it?"

She put her hand on her forehead, clearly trying to gather her patience with her husband. Taking a deep breath—and then another one—she went to the area near the room's full-length mirror and bent to pick up the batteries and the back cover of the remote.

"Dammit," she said seeing the crack in the cover.

Then, standing, she brandished the broken piece of plastic. "See this? Do you see this?"

"Yes," Winslow said. "It's something else we'll have to pay for."

That did it.

"We?" she said advancing on him. "Don't you even go there, you trifling excuse for a man. This is what our lives have become, a cracked and broken mess, and all because of your greed and stupidity."

"That's enough, Marguerite."

She stopped and stood ramrod straight, cocking her head just a bit. "Or what? What are you going to do? Hit me?"

Winslow looked at her in disgust, then stomped around her and to the closet. A moment later, he was back with his garment bag and two suits in hand.

"Where are you going?"

"Home. The funeral is over. There's really no need for me to stay down here."

"Oh, no, you don't," she said, reaching for the hanger. "You're not running out on me now."

Winslow actually laughed at that.

"Run out on you? Hardly, Marguerite. I'm not stupid, despite what you may think. You're about to inherit

three point eight million dollars. I'm not going anywhere."

"Your ass is going to jail. For a long time."

"There's been no indictment," Winslow said.

"Yet," she taunted right back. "And when it comes,
you are going down. At least you'll have a bed in prison
to sleep on. The kids and I won't even have that, thanks
to you."

"I'm not going to prison."

As if he hadn't uttered a word, Delcine kept talking. "And don't go claiming Ana Mae's money. We
haven't even started figuring out what that heap of rags
is supposed to mean. That preacher and those damn
cats are likely to get all of the money."

Winslow moved around her again, this time to get
his underwear and socks from the drawer he'd placed
them in. A moment later he went into the bathroom and
came out with his shaving and toiletries kit.

Hands on hips, Delcine watched him. "This is how
you handle every problem that comes your way in life,
isn't it? You just walk away."

"Yes," he said, calm as a poker player bluffing a
low pair.

Fully packed, he picked up his Ray-Bans from the
dresser top, slung his garment bag over a shoulder, and
headed toward the door. "Later."

Delcine threw the batteries at him as he walked
through their hotel room door.

Archer and Clayton finished off the last of the eggs
Benedict in the dining room of the bed-and-breakfast.
The booklet of quilt photos from Everett Rollings was
open on the table.

"Where should we start?" Clayton asked.

"Are you sure you mean that *we?*"

Clayton's gaze met his partner's. "After last night you have to ask me that?"

"Just checking," Archer said. He turned to the beginning of the booklet to find the image of the overall quilt. "My guess is that your sisters will start with the first block and work from there. We can begin with a different one, maybe one of the ones on the bottom row."

But Clayton wasn't really paying attention. His thoughts were on Ana Mae. "She was almost like a mother to me, you know."

"Who?"

"Ana Mae." Clayton dabbed his napkin at his mouth and placed it on the left side of his plate. "Mama was always working, and Daddy was gone by then. I remember when I was about nine or ten, I'd gotten into a fight with a couple of boys at school."

"A faggot fight?" Archer said, a knowing sympathy in his voice.

Clayton nodded. "I was constantly beat up. But that one was especially brutal. Mama was cleaning somebody's house, but Ana Mae was home, doing some of the extra ironing that Mama took in."

Archer reached for and took Clayton's hand in his. "What did she do?"

Closing his eyes, Clayton gave a little half-laugh. "She sat at that same rickety kitchen table that's there now and cried with me. Then she got a rag and cleaned my face, made me a cup of tea with honey and a little bit of something else that she knew Mama wouldn't like . . ."

"A touch of medicinal hooch?"

He smiled. "Something like that. And then she said the most remarkable thing."

Archer squeezed his hand, and Clayton reveled in the support and the love from his partner. "She told me that God made me just the way he wanted me. That I was special and perfect just the way I was. Ana Mae taught me how to be gay and proud in a time and place when being either was virtually impossible."

"She was a special lady," Archer said.

Swallowing, Clayton nodded. "It's funny how I've tended to forget that. Being here has brought it back."

Archer reached for the napkin and pressed it into Clayton's hand. Dabbing his eyes, Clayton said, "I took her for granted and then ignored her because she was poor and uneducated and represented everything that I wanted no part of."

"Shh," Archer said. "She loved you and knew you loved her."

"But I never told her," Clayton said, the tears now openly falling.

"Yes, you did."

Clayton shook his head, denying the words.

Archer took Clayton's chin in his hand to make him look into his eyes. "Yes, you did, Clay. You became a success. You're a doctor. Do you know how proud she was that her baby brother was such a big shot? And he married a lawyer."

That got a chuckle out of Clayton.

"Hey, no more shoulda, coulda, woulda. Not only isn't it productive, it's pointless. If she didn't love all three of you, she wouldn't have left you all anything in her will."

"The cats will probably end up claiming all the money," Clayton said.

Archer's mouth quirked up at that. "You're probably right."

"We don't need the money," Clayton said. "Not the way I think JoJo does."

"Her husband is a revolting man."

"Has been from day one," Clayton said. "I don't know what she sees in him."

"And I'll bet there are a lot of folks in this town saying the same thing about us."

Both men laughed out loud at that. Then, since no one was around to see, they shared a tender kiss.

From around the silk screen that separated the dining room from a small prep area at the bed-and-breakfast, Nan March peeked out when the talking stopped. A fresh pot of coffee in her hand, she stifled a gasp when she saw the two men kissing. Never having witnessed anything like that before, she was caught between fascination and revulsion. Because of what was in Ana Mae Futrell's obituary, she'd known they were that way. But knowing something and seeing it with your own two eyes was altogether different.

But the kiss wasn't what shocked Nan the most.

There had been a lot of speculation around town about what was going on with the Futrells. Now she knew for certain.

As she'd refilled their breakfast plates, she'd gotten several glimpses of the booklet they referred to throughout the meal.

Eddie Spencer had been right. One of Ana Mae's quilts had something to do with a whole lot of money she'd left for her family. But apparently there was a catch, and each of the Futrells was trying to beat the others to claim it.

Nan slipped back into the kitchen. She put the coffee carafe on the counter and picked up her cell phone, hoping it wasn't too late to place a bet at the barbershop.

12

That Fisher Boy

The siblings agreed to work through the puzzle as a team—the rationale being they could get it done faster that way. The plan was to meet up at Ana Mae's after breakfast and then start a diligent search. They worked at a disadvantage, having been away from Drapersville for so long. And the Lord only knew what Rosalee and Reverend Toussaint were up to. So a united front seemed the best bet.

But Archer and Clayton, figuring that the girls would want to start with the first quilt block, opted to do their own analysis from the opposite end. So far neither of them had been able to decipher Ana Mae's message on the block featuring a mop and a bucket.

"I wish Rollings had given us some more guidance on how we're supposed to figure out all of this," Clayton said.

The booklet with the images from the quilt was propped open on the car's dashboard in front of him.

Behind the wheel, Archer stopped for a light. "Ana Mae worked as a domestic. So that's a start."

Clayton frowned. "That seems too easy."

"In the legal profession, sometimes we find that the easiest explanation to a problem usually works," Archer said. "Go to the front with the picture of the whole quilt."

As Archer made the left turn onto the street to Ana Mae's house, Clayton flipped back to the beginning of the book.

"The quilt really is pretty," he said. "I remember Ana Mae always liked color and lots of it." Clayton smiled as he traced the images on the paper with a finger.

"Fried chicken," he said looking at one of the blocks. "Ana Mae made the best you've ever eaten."

"Maybe you can look for her recipes when you get to the house."

Clayton caught the singular in Archer's voice. "Where are you going to be?"

"I'm going to drive around a bit. Explore the area. Then hopefully get some work done back at the B and B." He glanced over at Clayton, "This is a journey for you and your sisters, Clay. Something that the three of you need to do together."

"But . . ."

Archer stilled the objection with a hand on Clayton's thigh. "I'm still going to be here with you and for you," he said. "But this is a time for you, Marguerite, and Josephine to reestablish your connections. You're scattered all over the country, and none of you likes North Carolina, so in addition to saying good-bye to

Ana Mae, this might be the last time you see your remaining sisters, too."

Clayton stared straight ahead and then closed his
eyes for a moment.

"I never really thought about it that way," he said.
"But you're right. The only one of us who loved this
place was Ana Mae."

Archer weighed his next words carefully. Then, nodding toward the quilt booklet on the dash of the rental,
he said, "And maybe Ana Mae wanted you to know
that."

ᏑᎱ

When Delcine finally arrived at Ana Mae's house,
JoJo was sitting at the kitchen table flipping through a
small yellow box. The coffeemaker burped and drib-
bled its last drops of java as a kettle on the stove began
its windup to a full whistle of boiling water.

"Where's Lester? I see the car is gone."

JoJo looked up. "Hey. He went to Walmart. What
took you so long?"

"Winslow and I got into it," she said. "He's headed
back to D.C. . . . to, uh, check on the kids."

JoJo's eyebrows rose, but she didn't say anything.

Delcine had never even so much as hinted that she
and Winslow had anything but the picture-perfect marriage, coordinated by Martha Stewart and as solid as a
Norman Rockwell painting. They were living and
breathing the American dream in a huge house in one
of Maryland's wealthiest counties. Their neighborhood
was so exclusive and expensive it was called an *enclave* on the site JoJo googled for information.

JoJo and Lester lived in an enclave too: the Brighton
Beach Mobile Home Community. That was a laugh. The

whole dump was in the middle of the desert and far from bright.

"Clay will be here in a bit. He called when they left the bed-and-breakfast."

Delcine rolled her eyes at that. "As if this backwoods metropolis would know what a suitable B and B was."

JoJo shrugged. "I drove by. It looks real nice."

They were spared what JoJo knew would be Delcine's caustic comment on their differing definitions of the word nice by Clayton's knock on the screen before he came in.

"Good morning," he said, and headed straight to the counter. "Thanks for putting the water on," he said over his shoulder to JoJo.

"I pulled some tea down."

He looked at a box of Lipton tea bags on the counter, near the chipped mug she'd set out for him.

"Archer found and used some tea leaves the other day. I'm going to brew a cup of that."

"Tea leaves?" Delcine said. "Is that what that stuff is? I thought Ana Mae had a stash of marijuana. I almost threw it out, but the container was pretty."

She pointed to where Clay would find the tea tin amid the clutter of the kitchen counter.

"Sister Ana Mae Futrell of the Holy Ghost Church of the Good Redeemer would not be having any of that mari-jay-whanna in her house," Clay said, hands on hips mimicking an indignant church lady.

He measured out tea leaves, added them to an infuser, and then found a proper teacup and saucer in the cupboard.

JoJo laughed at his antics.

"Well, that is true," Delcine conceded. However,

unwilling to lose ground, she added, "but we didn't think she played the lottery either."

Chuckling, Clayton went about preparing his tea. "You have a point there."

He added a touch of honey and then sat at the table. "So, what's the plan?"

By mutual agreement, the Futrell siblings decided to start their search together, and they would begin at the place where it all started—with the lottery ticket.

Since Lester had Ana Mae's car, Delcine drove. Clayton claimed the backseat before JoJo could start whining. It didn't take long for them to get to the Day-Ree Mart, where Ana Mae bought her winning ticket. It had been in the same place for the last four decades and hadn't changed much in the intervening time.

"I always wondered if it was spelled like that because they didn't know how to spell dairy or if they were being cute," Clayton said from the backseat.

"I'd go with the former," Delcine said dryly.

"You're both wrong," JoJo said. "It's named after the first owner's parents."

Delcine glanced over to look at her but quickly got her eyes back on the road.

"And you know this because . . . ?"

" 'Cause I used to, um, see Billy Ray Jarrett."

"Billy Ray Jarrett? Who was that?" Delcine asked.

"R.J.," Clayton said from the back. "He had the most gorgeous eyes."

"That wasn't all that was gorgeous about that man," JoJo said on a knowing purr.

"Well, who was the Day and who was the Ree?"

"His daddy was Dayton and his mama was Maureen, but apparently everybody called her Ree."

"Does anybody in this godforsaken place just have a normal name?" Delcine said.

"Welcome home to Carolina, sis," Clayton said.

The Day-Ree Mart had actually been updated over the years. These days, the North Carolina lottery was a big part of its business. Much like Junior Cantrell's place and the barbershop, the Day-Ree Mart served as convenience store, gas station, meeting place, and all-around spot for anyone who wanted to know what was going on.

The lottery ticket Ana Mae purchased had come from here.

Inside, they passed a crammed display of Doritos, Cheese Doodles, fried onions, bags of pork skins, and potato chips in no less than six different flavors. And right next to the salty items were all of the sweet ones: boxes of Little Debbie snacks and a lot of oatmeal cream pies and the southern favorite Moon Pies. Not a piece of fruit could be spied in the place.

Hot dogs, sausages, and other high-fat processed meat items rolled on a grill that was constantly kept supplied. The Day-Ree Mart still made the best hot dogs in all of Drapersville.

"Umm," JoJo said, inhaling the scent of hot dogs. "Remind me to get one of those before we leave. I love me some Day-Ree Dogs. And Lester likes oatmeal cream pies."

Delcine did her eye roll as Clayton approached the clerk behind the counter. His name badge read "Roscoe."

With a single question, the convenience store clerk pegged them as outsiders. "Y'all all need to get the way up to Virginia Beach?"

He reached under the counter and came up with a piece of paper about the size of an index card. "Here you go," Roscoe said, handing it to Clayton. "Just make a right up at the light and follow them there directions till you get there. We get a lot of folks like y'all all who take a wrong turn and wind up here. We got a special going if you wanna get some snacks for the road. Buy two Day-Ree Dogs, get a snack cake free. Any one of them over there," he said, pointing to yet another overflowing display of high-calorie items.

"No, thank you," Delcine said.

At the same moment, JoJo said, "I'll take one of the specials, and I need a couple of boxes of those oatmeal cream pies to take home."

"God, JoJo," Delcine mumbled.

Several customers came in then, half of them making a beeline to the expansive lottery ticket display and the others queuing up at the hot dog grill.

Roscoe greeted them all by name before turning back to the out-of-towners.

"We're not here for directions," Clayton said. "My name is Clayton Futrell, and we'd like to speak with the store manager."

"Futrell? Y'all all related to Ana Mae?"

"Yes, she is, was, our sister," Clayton said.

Roscoe put his hand across his heart. "My sympathies to all y'all. Ana Mae was some good people. God took an angel on home when he tapped on Ana Mae's shoulder."

Clayton and Delcine shared a glance.

JoJo busied herself inspecting the rest of the junk-food items in the mini market.

"That's what we're here about," Clayton said. "We wanted to talk with someone who knows about the lottery ticket Ana Mae purchased here."

"Shoot, man, everybody knows about that." Roscoe's

grin said he ranked among the everybody. "Ana Mae sure was generous when she hit big too. 'Course it was a scratcher and not the regular numbers, you know. But ain't nobody I ever heard of won even that much on the regular numbers—a hunnerd and twenty five Gs. That's a lot of money."

Delcine pushed forward, bracing her hands on the front counter. "What do you mean she was generous?"

"Well," Roscoe said, scratching his chest for a moment, "Loretta sold her the ticket, and Ana Mae give her five hunnerd just as soon as she got the check from the lottery people. Me and Butter was working that shift too. I was stocking and Butter was out . . ."

Distracted, Delcine asked, "Butter?"

Roscoe's grin grew wider. "That's just what we calls him around here. His name is Robert. But like I was saying, Butter was out fixing the propane for a customer. But since we was all working that shift, Ana Mae gave us a reward too," he said pulling a long vowel on the word so it sounded like reee-ward.

"She gave each of you five hundred dollars?"

"Shoot no," Roscoe said. "That was just for Loretta, who sold her the ticket. Ana Mae gave me and Butter a hunnerd bucks a piece. I thought that was real nice since she didn't have to give any of us nothing at all."

The Futrell siblings looked at each other. There was clearly a disconnect somewhere. Delcine expressed it.

"Are you sure Ana Mae won just one hundred twenty-five thousand?"

Roscoe narrowed his eyes at the thin woman. "Just? I don't know where y'all all from, but a hunnerd and twenty five thousand dollars is a lotta money round these here parts."

Seeing that Delcine neglected—yet again—to don kid gloves when dealing with people, Clayton asserted himself as the man of the family.

"That's not what she meant," he explained. "What my sister was trying to ask," Clayton said, giving Delcine a sidelong look that said please, shut up, "was do you know if Ana Mae shared any of her winnings with other people?"

Roscoe shifted his bulk a bit so his attention focused solely on Clayton, giving a none-too-subtle cold shoulder to Delcine.

"Sure," he said.

JoJo stacked three boxes of oatmeal cream pies on the counter and flashed Roscoe a broad smile. In an instant, his grin was back, and he zeroed in on first her ample chest and then her face. "You gonna need some help eating those, sugar?"

"I always like to stock up," she said. "You never know when the urge might hit you."

"Oh, for God's sake," Delcine muttered.

A second later, she let out a small yelp and hopped on one foot.

"Clayton!"

Clayton ignored her, hoping he hadn't really done much damage to her foot when he stepped on it to shut her up. His focus was on getting as much information as possible out of Roscoe.

JoJo gave a little shimmy, as if she needed to get a little more comfortable in her tight jeans and the pullover sleeveless shirt that showed off her bosom the same way a tight sweater might.

"And you wanted a Day-Ree Dog special too—right, sugar?"

"Yes, indeed," JoJo said, licking her lips in anticipation.

"Who else did Ana Mae give money to?" Clayton asked.

Roscoe talked as he stepped to the hot dog grill to make JoJo's order. "Her church, the school. You want the works on your dogs—right, sugar?"

"Give me everything you've got," JoJo said.

Delcine rolled her eyes, but stayed quiet.

"And that Fisher boy," Roscoe said. "I heard tell she gave him some of the lottery money. But I don't know how much. He's one of them inventors or something. Always making stuff from things other people throw away. He sure helped Loretta, though. She's the manager here at the Day-Ree Mart now. But she off today. That Fisher boy, he made some kinda contraption for her that made her so happy she told him he could get a Day-Ree Dog for free for life, anytime he come in. He don't eat meat, though, that Fisher boy. He got a good head on him, but he's a little different, if you know what I mean."

"He's gay?" JoJo asked.

Clayton gave her a look.

"Naw," Roscoe said, taking a sidelong glance at Clayton, "leastways not that I know of. He don't eat meat. He be one of them, whatchacallit, vegetablians."

"Vegetarian?" Clayton supplied.

"Yeah, that's it. Don't eat meat or eggs or anything normal like. He just always tinkering and building and, well, he just ain't too sociable. But he and Ana Mae, they got along like cornbread and grits."

"What's his first name?" Clayton asked.

"Gerald or Jeremy or Jerome. Something like that. Maybe George. Most people just call him the Fisher boy."

Roscoe placed JoJo's hot dogs next to her oatmeal cream pies, then turned toward the two conference-size tables set up with lottery slips, pencils, and displays where a couple of people were sitting, filling out their numbers.

"Hey, Paulie. What's that Fisher boy's first name?"

"Jeremy," the answer came back.

"Yeah, that's it," Roscoe said. "Jeremy Fisher."

Clayton was able to get a little more out of Roscoe, including the fact that to the clerk's knowledge, Ana Mae hadn't won any more money from the North Carolina Lottery, nor ever even played again.

Armed with JoJo's purchases and the directions to Jeremy Fisher's house, the three headed across the gravel parking lot to the car.

"You know, Delcine, you don't have to be so condescending to people," Clayton said. "You can catch more flies with honey than with vinegar."

"Look," she said, "I didn't come back to this godforsaken town to win friends and influence people. I want to get the money Ana Mae left for us and then get the hell out of here. I have a life waiting for me."

"I think we were better off working in individual teams," JoJo said.

They pondered that for a bit, each one silently agreeing or disagreeing.

When they got back in the car and Delcine fired up the air conditioning, she let go with something that had been bugging her. "What is with the y'all all around here? Don't these people know that that's a redundant, not to mention incomprehensible, phrase. You all all. God, that's irritating."

JoJo tore open one of the oatmeal cream pies. "You know what he meant, so it's not incomprehensible."

Clayton smiled. "Can I have one of those?"

She passed the box back to him.

"I cannot believe the two of you are going to actually eat those things."

"Do you know the way to the Fisher place?"

"It shouldn't be hard to find with those directions from Roscoe," Delcine said shaking her head in disgust. "Make a left at the combine and a right when you see the house with the double rooster weathervane. Welcome to Hooterville."

"Once again," JoJo said around bites of her treat, "you know exactly what he meant."

"Hey, guys. Let's not fight," Clayton said.

"And what was with you stepping on my foot like that?"

"We needed to keep him talking. We're already at a disadvantage over the reverend, who knows all of these people. And he has Rosalee working with him. We need all the help we can get," Clayton told Delcine. "And you were antagonizing the man."

An unladylike grunt assessed her opinion of his opinion.

JoJo wiped her mouth with a napkin. "I forgot how friendly everybody could be here."

"Friendly?" The echoed question rang through the confined space of the car.

"If you'd stuck out your boobs any farther he'd have been able to breast feed on them," Delcine said.

JoJo laughed and did a quick boost of her breasts, as if positioning them in one of her old showgirl costumes. "Don't hate on me because the good Lord was generous with me and forgot to give you some."

"The good Lord made those silicone implants, did he now?"

"All natural, hater. This is all natural."

From the back seat Clayton laughed out loud.

"This reminds me of growing up," he said. "You two were constantly going at it. And Ana Mae had to break up the fights."

Heading out of the Day-Ree Mart lot, Delcine started following the directions they'd gotten from Roscoe to get to the Fisher place. "Remember the time you took Mama's silk scarf and I grabbed it?"

JoJo turned in her seat, propping one leg up so she could see both Clayton and Delcine while they talked. "Yeah, I had it wrapped around my head and hanging down the back. I think I was being 'I Dream of Jeannie' or something. You went to pulling and tugging on that thing, and before long we were rolling on the floor, scratching like cats and dogs."

"Who won?" Clayton said.

"Neither one of us," Delcine said, chuckling. "Ana Mae came in, saw us. She stomped out of the room and came back with a big pair of pinking shears and the next thing you know that silk scarf was in two pieces not big enough to do anything with."

JoJo picked up the story. "She handed half to me and half to Delcine and said, 'There's some Solomon justice for you. Now both of you hush up.' "

"No, she didn't," Clayton said. By now he too was laughing. "But what about Mama's scarf?"

"When she got home, we ran to tell her what Ana Mae had done. And you know what she did?"

Delcine and JoJo looked at each other, and both fell out laughing.

"What?" Clayton pressed.

"She, she told us, 'Well, Solomon was right.' "

"And JoJo is crying now because she doesn't have the scarf and Ana Mae isn't getting in trouble for cutting it. So she goes to Mama, 'Who's Solomon?' "

"Oh, Lord," JoJo said, wiping her eyes. "What did I ever want to say that for?"

"We both had to go not only to Sunday school and morning service for the next six weeks," Delcine said. "Mama made us go to Wednesday night prayer meeting and Friday night praise and worship with Ana Mae. Said she couldn't believe she was raising such heathen children, and since we didn't know who King Solomon was, we could sit in church until we did."

"You better believe I learned all of those Bible stories," JoJo said, still chuckling.

By the time they got to the house on Evers Street, they'd shared two more stories about their interactions with Ana Mae.

"She sure loved us a lot," JoJo said, as Delcine parked at the curb. "I wish we'd stayed in better touch through the years."

"Me too," Clayton said, subdued and more than a bit contemplative about the sister they'd just buried.

A few moments later, they stood at the curb in front of a white frame house. Freshly painted with green shutters and a well-manicured and lush green lawn, the house looked loved and lived in. The front porch held two white wicker rocking chairs with a small table between them.

A garage, adjacent to the house, had clearly been turned into a workroom. The garage door was up, and the sounds of some kind of saw and hammering came from it, so they gravitated there.

"Maybe we'll get an answer here to how Ana Mae

turned one hundred thousand and some change into almost four million."

"I was wondering the same thing," JoJo said. "It sounds like she gave away a lot of the lottery money."

"I've been keeping a tally," Delcine said. "So far we know she tipped the convenience store people. Knowing Ana Mae, she probably gave her church way more than a tithe."

"How much is a tithe?" Clayton asked.

JoJo let out a hoot. "Now who needs to be going to remedial Bible study? A tithe is ten percent, Clay."

"Ten percent? You mean right off the top she gave ten grand to her church? Man, no wonder those TV evangelists rake in the millions."

"And remember, we're talking about Ana Mae here, so it was probably more," Delcine said. "A lot more."

"Well," Clayton said taking each sister by the hand. "Let's go see if we can find out what this Jeremy Fisher knows."

"Hellllooo!" Clayton called out as they approached.

The man in a pair of jeans, hiking boots, and a plaid shirt clearly didn't hear them. Safety goggles covered his eyes as he worked at a bench.

When he paused to check an angle, Clayton called out again.

The man looked up and smiled. He turned off the saw, pushed the goggles to his forehead, and swung his leg around.

"Hey there, y'all. Just a sec."

He went across the room and turned off a machine from which the hammering noise emanated.

Aerosmith suddenly blared from all directions.

Delcine covered her ears.

Jeremy snatched up a remote and pointed it toward a corner. The garage instantly fell silent. Wiping his hands on his jeans, he came over to greet them. "Sorry about that," he said. "When I have all of the machinery going I forget about the music being up. It's programmed to play louder than whatever I have on."

He reached out a hand to Clayton and shook it. "I was so sorry about Ana Mae. I sure loved that woman," he said.

Whatever the Futrells had been expecting, this wasn't it.

Jeremy Fisher was about twenty-five, twenty-six at the most, had sandy blond hair, and toffee-colored skin that pegged him as either biracial or somebody who spent a whole lot of time in the sun. That he knew who they were without introduction also seemed to throw them for a loop.

"You loved her?" JoJo said, staring at him like he might hold the secret to the Holy Grail.

"I sure did. With all my heart," Fisher said. "She believed in me when no one else did. Nobody else paid me any mind, but Miss Ana Mae, she was different."

He stuck out a hand to both Delcine and JoJo. "I'm Jeremy, by the way. I know we haven't met or anything, but I'd know you all like my own family. Ana Mae talked about you all all the time. You're Clayton," he said, grabbing Clayton's hand again and pumping it. "You're the successful doctor out in California. And you're Josephine from Las Vegas, star of the stage. And you're Marguerite from PG County." He pronounced the nickname of Prince George's County, Maryland, as if it were Buckingham Palace and he was honored to meet the queen.

"Delcine," she corrected, forgetting that she preferred to be called Marguerite.

"Are you Howard?" Clayton said, voicing the question they were all wondering about.

Jeremy Fisher was about the right age to be Ana Mae's son. And since he was biracial, that might explain why no one knew anything about Ana Mae having a child. Maybe she'd been seeing a white man in town. But who? Was that David Bell from the funeral his father and Ana Mae his mother?

"Howard?" Jeremy asked. "No, I'm Jeremy. Jeremy Fisher. I'm an inventor, and Miss Ana Mae invested in my company."

"Your company?"

"Fisher Innovative Solutions. But these days I run FDE, Inc., Fisher Design and Electronics," he said, sweeping a hand to encompass the garage. "It doesn't look like much, but with high-speed Internet and FedEx, it's all I really need. And thanks to Miss Ana Mae, I can devote all of my time and energy to my passion."

"Your passion?" The question came from Delcine.

"Come on in the house. Mama will be pleased to have company, and I can tell you all about it."

"Mama?" Delcine asked.

Jeremy nodded and then turned to secure something on his workbench.

"Is he Howard?" JoJo mouthed to her siblings.

Both Clayton and Delcine shrugged.

"Mama, we've got company," Jeremy called as he escorted the Futrells into the house.

"Back here, honey."

Jeremy led them down a wide foyer and into a spacious great room.

"Holy cow!" JoJo said.

A back wall of windows opened to an unexpected oasis, a large in ground infinity pool surrounded by lush greenery and a waterfall.

"Wow," breathed Delcine, who was not easily impressed. "You can't tell from the front of the house that all of this is here."

Jeremy grinned. "Cool, isn't it? I figured out how to use rainwater for the waterfall. It looks like it's flowing into the pool, but it isn't. The water is actually irrigating the fields."

"The fields?" Delcine asked, walking, uninvited, deeper into the room, which was decorated in an eclectic mix of French country and traditional furnishings.

"Well, not really fields like a farm, but we do grow our own vegetables. Tomatoes, cucumbers, three varieties of lettuce, beans, and corn. Plus sunflowers. Those are just for fun."

"Jeremy, I doubt our guests want to hear about your crop experiments."

The woman who entered the room came in soundlessly, which was surprising since she was in a motorized wheelchair.

Seeing at least JoJo's expression, she laughed.

"No sound, I know. Freaks out some folks. But I love sneaking up on people," she said. "Hi, there, I'm Nell Fisher."

Clayton and JoJo shook her hand. Delcine waved from the window.

The familial resemblance between Jeremy and his mother couldn't be mistaken. While her wispy blond hair and pale blue eyes made her seem fragile at first glance, there was a strength in Nell that Jeremy also exhibited. In her mid-fifties to maybe early sixties, she had a twinkle in her eyes that put them all at ease with her disability.

"Welcome to our home," Nell said. "I'm so sorry for your loss. Ana Mae spent many hours here talking about you all."

She turned the chair to her son. "Jeremy, where are your manners? Invite our guests to sit down."

Nell shook her head. "Kids. It doesn't matter how old they are." She steered toward a seating area with two large sofas, a chaise lounge, and big comfy chairs.

"Thank you, Mrs. Fisher," Clayton said. He waited until she slid into a spot clearly designed to let her engage with guests in the space.

"Oh, it's just Miss. I never married. But call me Nell."

"I like that," JoJo said.

"That my name is Nell?"

Seeing the laughter in her hostess's eyes, JoJo grinned as she settled on a cushion. "That you're an independent woman."

"Mano will be bringing us some tea in a moment."

"He's one of my best creations," Jeremy said.

And sure enough, a few moments later, a robot about the size of a third-grader pushed a cart into the room. A pitcher of iced tea and a plate of cookies were displayed on the cart's tray. Underneath in an open storage area were glasses and napkins.

After Jeremy and Mano served everyone, the humans munched for a few minutes, talking about the weather and other banal pleasantries.

"Well, I know you all probably have some business

to discuss," Nell said, "and I have some tomatoes that need harvesting. It's been lovely meeting all of you. I'm just sorry it took this sad occasion for us to get together."

With Mano the robot following behind her, Nell left her son and the Futrells in the great room.

"That little man is so cool," JoJo said.

"Miss Ana Mae liked it too," Jeremy said. "We've been testing out a new model, one that would help her . . ." His voice trailed off, and he blanched. "I'm sorry. I still can't quite wrap my head around the fact that she's really gone. She was like my big sister and other mother and best friend and confidante all rolled into one."

Jeremy laughed then. "We made quite a pair. The gospel-singing black cleaning lady and the long-haired geeky vegan white boy. 'Here they come,' " he said in a spot-on imitation of Eddie Spencer. " 'Ana Mae and that Fisher boy.' "

Shaking his head, Jeremy added, "You know, I don't think many people in this town except Ana Mae and my mama even know my first name. They all call me That Fisher Boy."

"That's how we found you," JoJo said.

"The Day-Ree Mart?" Jeremy guessed.

"Yep."

"We understand Ana Mae invested in your company," Delcine said in an effort to end the chitchat and get to the point of their visit.

Jeremy grinned. "Absolutely. I have, well, had five investors, including Mama. But Miss Ana Mae was far and away the biggest shareholder in the company. We had quite a run together, the two of us."

"What, exactly, is it that you do?" Delcine asked.

That question apparently was all the encouragement Jeremy Fisher needed. He launched into a detailed description of his company that had them wishing for an executive summary.

"I started tinkering with things when I was a little kid. I was always trying to come up with something that would make Mama's life easier.

"She has MS," he explained. "When I was young, well, younger," he amended, looking at the three of them, "I was always coming up with things that would make it easier for her to get around the house and do things in the kitchen. I just never stopped tinkering," he added with a self-effacing shrug.

"How did you meet Ana Mae?" JoJo asked.

"When I went away to college," Jeremy said. "I did two years here at Roanoke-Chowan Community College so I could stay at home to help Mama. But when I transferred to Chapel Hill to finish up the undergrad degree, Miss Ana Mae came over a couple of days a week to check on Mama and do any heavy cleaning that needed to be done. There usually wasn't any since Mama insisted on being independent. You sure got that right, Miss JoJo," he said, shaking his head in mild disgust.

"One time I came home on break and Miss Ana Mae asked me about some of the things around the house that I'd done for Mama. She asked me if I could come up with a better approach to a mop and bucket. It took me a while, but after graduation from Chapel Hill, I did."

"So you're a preacher too?" JoJo asked.

The question earned her a blank look from Jeremy and an inelegant "Huh?" from Delcine.

"At chapel school. That's where you learned how to be a minister, right?"

"Oh, for God's sake," Delcine muttered.

"I don't understand," Jeremy said at the same time.

Clayton, who did understand, took the diplomatic approach. "He means the University of North Carolina at Chapel Hill," he told JoJo. "Chapel Hill is the name of the town. It's about, what two or three hours from here?"

Jeremy nodded. "Almost three."

"You were telling us about Ana Mae," Delcine prompted.

Jeremy nodded. "She tested it out and loved it. The next thing you know, she's telling her friends and they all want one. I was working on the first generation of Mano then, so the cleaning solutions stuff was a sort of side thing. But before you know it, that was taking all of my time. The mop and buckets were selling well. I needed capital to expand Fisher Innovative Solutions. By that time, Miss Ana Mae had tested out some of my other inventions, and when she won the lottery money, she invested in the company. Well," he added with a shrug, "she really invested in me. She believed in me when everyone else called me that crazy Fisher boy."

For a moment, Jeremy looked as if he might cry. Then, his voice unsteady, he told them, "Even after all this time, it seems a little odd to call it the company, like it was some big thing. There were really just three of us—me, Mama, and Miss Ana Mae."

Delcine's eyes scrunched up as if she were trying to figure out a missing element. "And the assorted projects and products you created? You took them to market?"

Jeremy nodded and gave them a big smile. "Yep.

And the rest, as they say, is history. When the Day-Ree Mart and the hardware store downtown started carrying the cleaning caddy and some of my other stuff, the *Times & Review* did a big story."

Delcine rolled her eyes, a reaction Jeremy missed because he'd hopped up to go to a console behind the large sofa. He returned with a scrapbook and opened it to a page featuring a clipping from the *Drapersville Times & Review:*

Local Man Invents Cleaning Caddy

A photo of Jeremy outside the front of the Day-Ree Mart and another of him in front of a display of his mop and bucket caddy inside the Jefferson Brothers Hardware Store went along with the article.

"I'm sure you were very proud," Delcine said.

If he caught the flat note of sarcasm in her voice, Jeremy didn't let on.

"Yes. Mama and Miss Ana Mae were right there with me. They're both quoted in the story. If it hadn't been for them—especially Miss Ana Mae believing in me and supplying that initial capital—I wouldn't be where I am today."

The Futrells thanked him for his time, and they all got up to head for the door.

"Jeremy!" Nell called. "Wait. I have something."

A moment later, she appeared with a basket on her lap. It brimmed with tomatoes, peppers, and corn. "Fresh grown," she said. "Please, enjoy the harvest. Ana Mae always did. And she made the most wonderful sauces with vegetables grown right out back."

Accepting the gift, Clayton thanked them for it, their time, and their friendship with Ana Mae.

Back in the car, Clayton hefted one of the tomatoes. "This will be great in a salad," he said.

"Hmmph," Delcine grunted. "That was more than an hour of wasted time."

"No, it wasn't," JoJo said. "We have another quilt clue solved, and we met some nice people who knew Ana Mae. It's kind of fun to find out about this Ana Mae we didn't know."

Delcine took her gaze off the road long enough to roll her eyes at her sister.

"It was a waste of time if you ask me," Delcine said. "I still don't get where she got almost four million dollars. That Fisher boy didn't sell that many of those bucket things at the Day-Ree Mart."

"Well," Clayton said, taking a bite of the tomato and chewing it, "look at it this way: we have seven more quilt blocks to figure it out."

13

Digging Up The Past

When Clayton, Delcine, and JoJo got back to Ana Mae's house after their quilt-clue hunting, it was to find Ana Mae's car at the curb instead of in the small driveway adjacent to the house. They pulled into the drive only to spy Lester, in jeans, sneakers, and a sweat-stained white T-shirt, digging up the yard.

Mounds of dirt like abandoned molehills clumped and cluttered the side yard. Soil, unceremoniously dumped, strangled the flower beds that Ana Mae had carefully tended. The jonquils and daylilies, the tea rose bushes, and all of the brightly colored annuals she put in every summer—marigolds in a riot of yellows, golds, and oranges—all of them buried or bent under the dirt.

On the bottom step of the side porch, a metal bucket filled with ice and bottles of Budweiser beer sweated about as much as Lester did.

"What the hell are you doing?" Delcine shrieked.

Lester looked up and grinned. With the back of one hand he wiped his brow. The other hand gripped the shovel he'd clearly used to dig a giant hole in the ground. He was working on the second hole when they interrupted his labor.

"Took you all long enough to get back. I started without you. Haven't found anything yet, though. But I know it's here."

"What the hell are you doing?"

This time the demand came from Clayton.

JoJo went to one of the flower beds. She tried to squat in her tight jeans, thought better of that notion, and used her foot to try to knock some of the dirt off the flowers. "Oh, Lord, Lester. Look what you did to Ana Mae's pretty flowers."

"What do you care about a bunch of flowers? He might care," Lester said nodding toward Clayton, "but I'm looking for the money."

"What the hell did you say?" Clayton demanded.

"You have no right to . . ."

Delcine, so indignant she actually sputtered, advanced on her brother-in-law and snatched the shovel from his hands and reared back. "You ignorant son of a bitch."

"Lester," JoJo said, cutting off her sister and grabbing her husband by the arm. She yanked him a few steps away from Delcine and the shovel, and from Clayton, who looked like he was ready to go twelve rounds with Lester.

"Who the hell does he think he is?" Clayton said.

Delcine tossed the shovel to the ground. Then, her hands on her hips, she just looked around in disbelief at the destruction wrought on the pin-neat little yard in just a few short hours.

"I'm calling the police," she said, stomping up the side steps.

The screen door creaked and then slammed behind her.

Her cussing matched Lester's as JoJo lit into him.

"Have you lost your ever-loving mind, Lester? This isn't a treasure hunt where X marks the spot."

"How do you know? That fancy lawyer-undertaker sure wasn't offering much insight into how to go about looking for the money."

"It's not your money to find, Lester," Clayton said.

"Now see here, you little . . ."

JoJo cut him off. "Clay's right, Lester. You are way out of line here."

"Out of line? I don't think so. That Bible verse clearly said the money was buried in the earth. That," he said pointing to the ground, "is the earth. And I'm digging it up to get at that money Annie Mae buried."

"Ana Mae!" JoJo and Clayton practically yelled.

Lester shrugged. "Yeah, whatever."

"What's going on over there?"

The new voice had them all turning toward the driveway entrance. Ana Mae's next-door neighbor was hanging out her back door, but someone they all knew was coming across the lawn.

"Oh, great. It's Reverend Holy Ghost," Lester said.

JoJo hit him in the stomach with the back of her hand. "Hush. You've already caused enough trouble."

"Is everything all right?" Reverend Toussaint asked. "I was passing by and heard some commotion."

"Hi, Reverend," Clayton said.

A moment later, a siren heralding a Hertford County sheriff's vehicle could be heard racing down the street.

JoJo hit Lester again. "Now look what you've done."

"I didn't do it. That sister of yours called the cops."

The deputy pulled partially into the driveway. He turned the siren off but left the lights flashing.

"Lord, have mercy," the next-door neighbor hollered. Her hair was in pink curlers and she had on a housedress, but that didn't stop her from coming closer. "Has something else happened?"

"Howdy, folks," the deputy said. "We got a call about some trespassing and destruction of property."

"I called," Delcine said, coming out the side door. "Arrest that man," she said pointing at Lester.

"Wait just one minute," Lester declared. "I didn't do anything."

"Ana Mae may have been country, Lester, but she sure wasn't crazy," Delcine said. "Even you have to know she wouldn't be fool enough to bury almost four million dollars."

The deputy's eyes bulged. "Did you say four million dollars? In cash?"

"No!"

The emphatic answer came from all of the would-be heirs.

"Ana Mae buried four million dollars?" the neighbor asked.

"No!"

Eyeing each one of the suspects, the law officer reached for his radio. "I think I better call Sheriff Daughtry."

"That won't be necessary, Deputy Howard," said

Everett Rollings, undertaker-cum-lawyer, striding toward them.

Dressed in a black suit, black shirt, black tie, and black shoes, he looked more like a Mafia don than a funeral director or attorney-at-law.

And that's when the Futrells, Reverend Toussaint, and the sheriff's deputy all noticed the crowd of neighbors and onlookers who had gathered in front of Ana Mae's house. Word spread quickly, with the police car at the house and probably aided by the next-door neighbor's speed dial. The profanity, the police, and the prospect of money buried in Ana Mae's yard brought them all to the scene to see what would happen.

At the same time that that fact registered, so did Rollings's greeting. Delcine was the first to make the leap.

"Did you say 'Officer Howard'?"

The young deputy, who couldn't have been more than twenty-five years old, gave her an odd look. "Yes, that's my name, ma'am."

"Howard," Clayton said.

Reverend Toussaint, closest to the deputy, peered into his face. "Howard?"

The deputy, cautious and suspicious, put a hand on his service revolver and took a step back. "Mr. Rollings, what's going on here?"

"Everything is okay, son," Rollings said. "I think I can clear this up quickly enough."

He motioned for everyone to gather around, including all of the curious onlookers. Archer, who'd pulled up behind Delcine's car at the curb, excused himself, and a path opened for him. All the onlookers knew he belonged to Ana Mae's bunch. He made his way to the group of heirs.

"What's going on?" he whispered to JoJo, who just shook her head.

"Let me be perfectly clear," Rollings said. "Ana Mae Futrell did not, I repeat, *did not* bury any money or any other valuables in her yard or anywhere else. All of her financial assets are in secure bank accounts, just as they should be.

"So if anyone has any ideas about coming over here in the middle of the night and digging up the rest of the yard," he said with a pointed look first at Lester and the shovel and then at a few of the folks in the crowd most likely to launch a late-night expedition, "let me spare you both the trouble and the trespassing charges."

"Yeah, that's what you say," Lester muttered.

"It is the truth," Rollings said, lowering his voice so just the heirs and the deputy heard him. "If I had, for even a moment, thought that someone would come to that conclusion, I would have told you during our meeting. This is not a buried treasure."

"Who thought that?" Reverend Toussaint asked.

All eyes turned toward Lester, who maintained a belligerent stance.

As usual, he didn't look at all convinced that the fancy-schmantzy undertaker was being straight up with them.

"I just stopped because I heard a commotion when I passed by Sister Futrell's house," Reverend Toussaint said. "If you'll excuse me, I'm late for an appointment down the street."

He scurried through the gathering of neighbors.

"Go home, people," Rollings told the onlookers. "There is nothing more to see here."

"Get out of my way!" a woman said.

The group of about thirty people crowding the front yard parted like Moses at the Red Sea to make way for Rosalee Jenkins. She took one look at the yard, grabbed her head, and let out a wail.

"Look what you did to Ana Mae's garden!"

"Here we go again," Lester said.

Delcine and JoJo quickly went to Rosalee to comfort the woman, who was actually shedding tears over the destruction of the yard.

Lester pursed his lips and set the shovel up against the side of the house. "For real, Mr. Rollings? There's no money buried?"

"No, Mr. Coston. There is no buried treasure or anything else buried here in this yard. Do I make myself clear?"

"Well, damn," Lester said, pounding a hand on his jeans. "I thought for sure that that was the clue."

He plucked a beer from his makeshift cooler and with a twist screwed off the top to take a long slug.

"Mr. Rollings?" the deputy said.

"Howard!" the Futrell siblings all exclaimed at the same time.

This time the deputy took two steps backward. "Why do they keep saying my name like that?"

"Who's your mother, deputy?" JoJo asked.

"And what year were you born?" Delcine added.

The young lawman's eyes darted from one to the other and then to the one person he actually knew. "Mr. Rollings?"

"Just answer their questions, son."

"My mom is Lucy Howard, and my father is Kenneth. Why?"

Rosalee glanced around and then let out a bark of laughter.

"You all can stop scaring the man," she said. "He's not that Howard. His last name is Howard. And I remember when he was born. I was working at the county hospital then and remember his mama in labor."

"What Howard?" the deputy asked. "And my name is Tyrone. Deputy Tyrone Howard."

"Just a case of mistaken identity," Rollings assured him.

The deputy pulled out a small black notepad and jotted down a few things.

"Do you want to press charges?" the deputy asked Delcine, who appeared to be in charge.

"Yes," Delcine declared.

"No," JoJo and Lester said.

"I believe the differences have been resolved," Archer said. He stood off a bit and to the side, leaving Clayton room to maneuver physically and emotionally.

This was not San Francisco, and there was enough stress and drama already without being overt about their relationship in front of all of the more-than-curious neighbors.

"And who are you?" the deputy asked.

"He's with me," Clayton said.

The two shared a fleeting look, and then, almost blushing, Clayton glanced away, a small smile at his mouth.

"All righty, then," said the deputy. "About the charges?"

"Everything is fine, son," Rollings said.

"This yard isn't fine," Delcine said. "Somebody is

going to put it to rights, and that somebody is the imbecile who tore it up in the first place."

"You tell him!" someone from the yard yelled.

"Yea," another neighbor hollered. "Disrespecting Miss Ana Mae that way ain't right."

"Well, under the circumstances," the deputy began.

"He'll be doing the repairs," JoJo said, nudging her husband. "Right?"

Lester didn't look too happy about it, but he acquiesced. "Yeah, I'll fix it back to the way it was."

"And I have pictures to make sure you do it right," Rosalee said, still visibly upset over the upturned earth and destroyed flower beds.

The young deputy dispersed the reluctant-to-leave crowd while Everett Rollings turned to his client's would-be heirs and ushered them toward the side door of the house. He waited as they all filed inside, Clayton and Archer followed by Rosalee, JoJo, and Lester, with Delcine bringing up the rear.

"Thank you for handling that, Mr. Rollings," she said.

"Anytime, Marguerite," he replied.

"It's Delcine here," she said.

He gave a slight bow in an "as you wish" gesture reminiscent of English butlers. Then, pulling something from the pocket of his trousers, the lawyer-undertaker stepped around Lester's bucket of beer bottles and closed the screen door behind him.

No one but Rosalee had ventured beyond the kitchen, where JoJo was pulling trays and foil pans out of the refrigerator.

"There's still a ton of food from the neighbors and Ana Mae's church folks, so y'all all need to make a plate and eat," she said, placing the ham on the table.

But with one glance at Clayton and Delcine, the three siblings started laughing.

"What's so funny?" Lester groused.

"It's nothing, Lester," Delcine told her brother-in-law. "Just something we were talking about earlier in the car."

"You too, Mr. Rollings," JoJo said. "It's about lunchtime, so you need to get yourself a plate as well."

Rollings was still near the door, though, frowning and looking around at the floor.

"Mr. Rollings?"

"Where are the cats?" he asked. "Where are Diamond Jim and Baby Sue?"

He held up a couple of fish-shaped cookie-looking things. "I always bring a treat for them when I stop by. They like the salmon bites."

"You know, I was wondering the same thing," Delcine said. "For two animals who'll inherit millions if we mess this thing up, they've been conspicuously absent since we arrived."

"I forgot about the cats," Clayton said.

Suddenly, everyone was looking around the house. Moving chairs in the living room, looking under the sofa and under the beds and cushions, in a small basket near the window, the corners of the rooms, and on top of the refrigerator and cabinets, all of the places cats were known to frequent.

The search came up empty. And from the living room and kitchen all eyes, including Lester's, turned to JoJo.

"What?" she said, around a bite of ham sandwich.

"You're allergic to them," Clayton said.

"Did you send the cats to the pound?" Delcine demanded.

"I believe it's dogs that go to the pound," Archer said.

"Why would I do that?" JoJo asked. She dropped the sandwich on a paper plate and stared down her accusers.

"Well, Jo," Clayton said in a let's-be-reasonable voice. "You did throw out the quilt. Maybe you sent the cats off too."

"I never did anything of the sort."

"Uh oh," Lester said.

"What now, Lester?" Delcine asked.

"You know, in that Men in Black movie, the cat's collar held the secret to the universe. Maybe Annie Mae . . ."

"Ana Mae!" the siblings said in exasperation.

Undaunted, Lester continued. "Maybe the cats have diamond collars, and now they're at the pound about to be tossed into the incinerator."

"You are so vile," Delcine hissed.

The toilet flushed then, and a moment later Rosalee appeared. "Whew, I needed to go," she said smoothing her slacks. "Turned out I really needed to go."

Delcine frowned.

Lester grinned. "Yeah, I put some of that air freshener in there. I got it over at the Walmart when I picked up the shovel."

"I saw that," Rosalee said.

"Rosalee," Delcine said. "Have you seen Diamond Jim and Baby Sue?"

"Sure," she said, heading toward the cupboard near the refrigerator and oblivious to the parade of Futrells and company following behind her.

"Oh, I see you pulled out the food. Good. There's sure plenty of it." She proceeded to pull down a glass and then help herself to a plate heaped with collard greens, ham, and a double helping of macaroni and cheese. "Sister Ettrick made this mac and cheese. She sure knows how to put her foot in it too."

Everett Rollings stayed her hand. "Mrs. Jenkins, the cats?"

Rosalee gave him an odd look, then noticed the others peering at her. "What's going on with you people?"

"Are the cats alive?"

"Of course the cats are alive. What else would they be?"

"Where are they?" the impatient question came from both Delcine and Lester, for different reasons, though.

"At my house. Where else would they be?"

Rosalee put her plate in the microwave and punched in a few minutes of warm-up.

"How did they get to your place?" Clayton asked.

"I took them there right after Ana Mae died. They were a howling and carrying on like they knew she was gone. So I took 'em home with me to care for 'em. They both doing just fine and having fun with Snookie."

"Snookie?"

"That's my tiger cat. She's a bit older than Diamond Jim and Baby Sue, but they all gets along just fine."

"What kind of collars do they have?" Lester asked.

Rosalee scowled at him. "What kind of fool question is that? Ana Mae's cats don't have no collars."

"Damn," Lester said.

"Mr. Coston, I told you before that Ana Mae did not . . ."

Lester cut him off. "You were talking about buried

money then, not diamonds on cats. Why else would the thing's name be Diamond Jim?"

"Diamonds on cats?" Rosalee asked, her brow crinkled in confusion.

"Because it has a white patch that is sort of in the shape of a diamond," Rollings said.

Lester deflated. "Oh. Well, my bad."

"As usual," Delcine said.

After declining a plate for the third time, Rollings reminded them all that there was nothing buried anywhere, no jewel-encrusted cat collars or anything else untoward about Ana Mae's last will and testament.

"And other than bequests specifically mentioned in the will, the only piece of tangible property Ana Mae left for you is the quilt," he said. "It's all you need."

"And a fat lot of good that's doing so far," Lester mumbled.

Delcine and Clayton shared a glance and then looked at JoJo, who nodded. The unspoken message among them was clear: The day's findings shouldn't be mentioned in front of the enemy—the enemy being Rosalee, who would undoubtedly take any information she gleaned straight to the ears of Reverend Toussaint le Baptiste.

Since neither JoJo nor Lester wanted to see to the welfare of the cats while they were staying at Ana Mae's house, it was mutually agreed that Diamond Jim and Baby Sue would remain in Rosalee's custody.

"Because this has morphed into a meeting of the heirs, I will see to it that Reverend le Baptiste is apprised of all that has transpired since he left," Rollings commented.

"Great," Lester mumbled.

In their rental car, with Archer again behind the wheel, Clayton and Archer talked on the ride home.

Archer waved at the people sitting outside the barbershop. The straight-back chairs couldn't be all that comfortable, but the customers looked as at ease as if they were at home stretched out in their La-Z-Boys and Barcaloungers.

"You know, Lester is definitely a fish out of water here in East of Mayberry, but he sure seems to be making himself comfortable."

Clayton laughed at that, then waved at Eddie Spencer, who was loading a dresser onto his pickup truck.

"There's something else I noticed about that man your sister married. For someone who doesn't really have a stake in this, Lester is awfully vocal about his opinions."

"He has just as much stake as you do," Clayton said.

"Thank you for that. But I'm just here as your other half."

"My better half."

They shared a smile, and Archer reached for Clayton's hand to hold.

As they headed back to their bed-and-breakfast inn, Clayton caught Archer up on what he and his sisters had learned that morning, first from Roscoe at the Day-Ree Mart, and later from Jeremy Fisher, the young inventor and entrepreneur.

"Ana Mae was generous with her time and her money," Archer observed.

Clayton nodded, but his eyes were squinched together as if he were suffering a migraine.

"What's wrong, hon?"

A moment later, Clayton slapped the dashboard. "That's it! I should have known."

"What?"

"Did you hear what Rollings said?"

"When?"

"Back when he first came in back at the house. Telling you about the Fisher boy's garage made me remember it. Rollings said he always brings catnip treats for Ana Mae's cats. If he's at her house so often that the cats know him and he's bringing them cat snacks, maybe there was more to his relationship with Ana Mae than simply attorney-client."

When Archer gave him a blank look, Clayton spelled it out.

"The elusive and mysterious Howard. Rollings has kids. There were at least a couple of young men on the mortuary staff who could belong to him . . . and to Ana Mae. He could be Ana Mae's baby daddy."

Archer didn't look convinced.

"Those words—Ana Mae and baby daddy—don't even belong in the same sentence, Clay."

"Well, somebody is Howard's father. He didn't just hatch."

"Besides," Archer added, "Ana Mae and Everett Rollings? No disrespect to your sister, Clay, but Ana Mae was a domestic. She died cleaning a toilet. I don't think she was the persnickety Mr. Rollings's type."

"You weren't my type," Clayton pointed out. "I was into muscle boys, not brainiacs."

Archer looked at him when they came up on the light. "You do have a point there. Where to now?"

"Let's swing by the funeral home and see who resembles the two of them."

But their hunch couldn't be verified—at least not that afternoon.

When they arrived, the staff was busy getting ready for a viewing, and the only males in sight were either too young or too old to be Ana Mae's Howard.

Clayton took a gamble, though.

"Is Mr. Rollings's son here?" he asked one of the attendants.

"Not at the moment," the young woman said. "Trey should be in this office tomorrow, though."

Thanking her, Clayton and Archer left the Rollings Funeral Home.

They had a name.

※

While the Futrells, Lester, and Rosalee were having it out at Ana Mae's house about dug-up flower beds and missing cats, the Reverend Toussaint le Baptiste finished up a call on a sick and shut-in church member, then headed to a place he hadn't been in a lot of years. If his hunch was right, he knew what he would find there based on the message Ana Mae had left for him in her legacy quilt. Should it turn out he was wrong, he'd pray on the matter some more and go from there.

Reverend Toussaint found himself at something of a loss, not knowing exactly what his role was supposed to be in Sister Ana Mae Futrell's after-death wishes. Among the most perplexing was why she'd included him at all.

As children growing up in Drapersville, they had been close once. Very close. But that had been a long, long time ago. Before either of them found the Lord.

Before he'd gone off to college and she'd moved on to boys who could love her the way she deserved.

At Ana Mae's wake, Rosalee Jenkins slipped up and called him Too Sweet, the nickname he'd carried throughout his high school years. He didn't call her on it. He doubted she even realized she had said it. The moniker, with its double-edged meaning, brought back a lot of memories, most of them of the unpleasant variety.

But Ana Mae calling him Too Sweet was something he cherished. When she'd said it, it was not the derogatory nickname tagged onto a teenager questioning both his sexuality and his place in the world.

While some of the older folks in town might remember him from those days, he had worked long and hard to shed that image, living a life and lifestyle that was above reproach. It was also why he chose to remain a celibate bachelor, devoting his life to God's work. And, rather than pursuing a pastorate of his own, he chose to be an associate minister, not the senior pastor of a flock. The Lord called his children to different purposes and ministries in the kingdom.

Toussaint le Baptiste had found his and took joy in the work his did with the various outreach programs of the Holy Ghost Church of the Good Redeemer. In addition to being the church's Sunday school superintendent, he coordinated the meals and jobs programs, and served as overseer of the Good Redeemer Academy. In short, the work as director of outreach ministries kept him busy and fulfilled.

"Ana Mae. Ana Mae. Ana Mae," he said on a wistful sigh.

He'd loved her like he loved all of the members of the congregation. There had, however, been a time in his life—in their lives—when his feelings for her ran much deeper. But that was ancient history, long ago and done with. They had both moved on, matured in their lives and their walks with God.

While he couldn't get a grasp on her wishes, something about her last will and testament quilt, *The Legacy of Ana Mae Futrell*, called to him . . . and nagged at him. The colors, so bright and cheerful, like the woman herself, and the leaves, they too especially called to him.

He wanted to touch the quilt again. To feel the smooth fabric under his fingers. Somehow, being near it and able to touch the soft material comforted him. He would have been hard pressed to explain to anyone the why of that, especially now. Toussaint was not even sure it was something he could articulate to himself, let alone someone else.

He glanced at the booklet from Everett Rollings on the passenger seat. The extra copy of the quilt image he'd requested of Mr. Rollings was taped to his fridge at home. Something about it nagged at him.

Ana Mae had made plenty of quilts through the years. Every year she donated one to the church's annual bazaar. And she'd made an outstanding one for Pastor and First Lady Leonard's tenth church anniversary, which coincided with their twenty-fifth wedding anniversary. Double wedding ring was the pattern, if he recalled correctly. But Ana Mae had put her own unique spin on it by adding a cross in a center medallion to symbolize their everlasting love of each other and of Christ. That blue, gold, and cream quilt was lovely and hung on their family room wall as art rather than cover a bed.

But something about the quilt Ana Mae made for herself—for her heirs—was truly special.

Toussaint le Baptiste didn't covet anything in this world, but he wanted that quilt. It spoke to him in ways he didn't quite understand. All he knew was he desperately wanted to possess that piece of the late Sister Ana Mae Futrell.

14

Surprises from Ohio

Since Rosalee knew more about sewing than Delcine and JoJo combined, the siblings agreed to let Rosalee go through Ana Mae's sewing room the next day.

"What's to say she didn't already take the good stuff before any of us got into town?" Delcine asked. "It's clear she's used to coming and going in this house as she pleases."

"That's what friends do," Clayton said. "Or so I'm told."

He couldn't imagine any of their San Francisco friends, even the neighbor who had a key in the event of an emergency, just wandering into their home for grins and giggles or because of sheer curiosity. But here in the South, well, things were done a little differently than on the rest of the planet.

"What good stuff?" JoJo demanded. "It's a room full of fabric. Let her take it all."

"What are we going to do about the house?" Clayton asked.

That was a question they'd all been avoiding. Clearing out Ana Mae's stuff had kept JoJo and Delcine busy since they'd arrived in North Carolina, but to what avail?

Delcine looked around. "Even with a couple of coats of paint and some new appliances, it's not going to fetch much on the market."

"And the market is still pretty lackluster, especially around here," Clayton said. "I looked it up before we left California."

JoJo cleared her throat. "Uh, actually, guys, I've kind of been thinking about this."

Her siblings turned to her, eyebrows raised in question.

But a knock at a door and Rosalee's "Hey, y'all, anybody home?" interrupted.

"We're back here," Clayton hollered toward the kitchen since Rosalee usually came in the side door.

A moment later, she bustled into the room, followed by two plumpish women who could have been sisters or twins or mother and daughter.

"I brought a couple of the ladies from the Holy Ghost Bee over to take a look at the fabric."

Clayton stepped out of the room to give the women more room to get inside. JoJo was near the window, Delcine sitting in the chair at the sewing machine. Two of the walls were lined with built-in cubbies containing all types and colors of fabrics. One wall served as a design space, with blocks and fabric pinned to it. There was even space for a couple of shelves of pattern books and binders and a small television. And a camera bag hung from a hook next to a corkboard that held all manner of magazine pages and pieces of paper ripped and pinned up.

"Lord, have mercy," one of the women exclaimed. "It's like Elnora Rogers's store."

"Better than Elnora's," her companion said, squeezing over to fondle the fabric. "Look at these batiks."

Rosalee grinned. "I told you all Ana Mae had a sewing room to die for."

If she realized the irony of what she said, neither Rosalee nor her guests gave any indication.

"It look like a rainbow threw up in here."

Delcine and Clayton scowled at that one.

"Betty and Hetty Johnson, these here are Ana Mae's sisters and brother."

Rosalee made the rest of the introductions. One of the Johnsons embraced Delcine in a hug that clearly wasn't reciprocated. But JoJo hugged her back hard.

"I sure was sorry to hear about Ana Mae," Betty or Hetty said. "But her homegoing was something else. She woulda loved that service. And you," she said, letting JoJo go and heading over to Clayton. "That tribute to her," Hetty or Betty patted her chest. "You done Ana Mae proud, Mr. Clayton. You done her proud."

When tears welled up in the woman's eyes, Clayton glanced at Rosalee. But she was busy pointing out some aspect of Ana Mae's sewing machine to the other Johnson. Clayton murmured a few words that sounded consoling and offered the woman a tissue from the box on a shelf.

A few minutes later, the sewing room was cleared of Futrells. JoJo went off to make coffee for their guests, while Clayton and Delcine went to the living room to talk.

"Have you and Archer made any progress on any of the other clues?"

Clayton moved a box of newspaper-wrapped knick-knacks out of the chair and onto the floor before taking a seat.

"Not really," he said, deciding to keep the Everett Rollings as Howard's father theory private for now. "And despite what that idiot Lester did, I think Rollings was being straight up. I don't think any of these so-called clues are really tangible things."

"What do you mean? The quilt is a tangible item; so was that lottery ticket that launched all of this."

"Speaking of that ticket," Clayton said. He got up to peruse the carefully labeled boxes. He paused at the one marked *IMPORTANT PAPERS*. "We need to figure out what Ana Mae's connection is with David Bell."

"We know already," Delcine said. "He's from that Zorin Corporation in Ohio."

"But how did they meet? What was she visiting him for?"

Delcine snorted out a half-laugh. "Well, seeing as how our big sister apparently led a life that none of us knew anything about, I'd say she was going to get her some."

"Some what?" Clayton said. Then, "Oh." He scowled. "Since when do you talk like that?"

Delcine shrugged. "Apparently, North Carolina is a bad influence on me."

Clayton pulled out one of the envelopes in the important papers box, a large white one. Inside he found an annual report. On the cover and in the middle, almost like a quilt medallion was a big Z. Photographs, presumably of customers or people important to the company formed the inside of the Z. He peered at it more closely.

"It can't be."

"What?"

Distracted, Clayton moved closer to a lamp, leaning down to see better. Sure enough, among the photos was Ana Mae. David Bell had his arm thrown around her shoulder, and the two grinned at the camera from one of the collage of photographs.

"Hey, you all," JoJo called. "Come take a look at what we found!"

Clayton and Delcine glanced at each other, then, almost as one, dashed to the sewing room.

"What is it?" Delcine said, beating Clayton to the doorway.

They both clearly expected to find riches hidden among the bolts and cuts of fabric. But the Johnsons, Rosalee, and JoJo were all focused on a binder.

"It's the quilts," JoJo said, wonder in her voice. "Every single one that Ana Mae ever made."

"Huh?"

"She kept a record," Rosalee explained. "It's a quilt journal. She tells the story of every quilt she ever made and gave away to someone. There are even pictures."

"And this one," JoJo said, holding up an identical large three-ring binder, "has all of the quilts that she ever entered in a contest or fair, and even the prizes she won."

One of the Johnsons, Hetty or Betty, stood over JoJo's chair. The other one stood next to Rosalee as they thumbed through the binder. Each sheet, in a page protector, had a photo of a quilt. On the other side was information on the dimensions of the piece, small cuts of the fabric used to make it, the date it was made, and whom it was made for, as well as the techniques used and whether it was an original design or made from a pattern. Some of the back sides featured pictures of Ana Mae with the quilt recipient, both smiling, with the quilt also prominently displayed.

It was a study in provenance and background.

"There are two more binders just like these," Rosalee said, pointing to the shelf. "I never knew Ana Mae paid so much attention to these details. Shoot, I've made stuff and given it away and couldn't tell you who I made it for or gave it to if you paid me."

"Ooh, look at that one," JoJo exclaimed, pointing to a photo in the binder Rosalee held. "That is gorgeous!"

The blue, gold, and cream king-size quilt had a cross in the middle of it.

Rosalee looked over. "Oh, she made that for Pastor and Sister Leonard's anniversary. They don't use it on their bed, though. They said it was too pretty for that, so they have it hanging up on the wall, like a picture."

"A tapestry," Clayton said.

None of the women paid him any mind.

"Here's my favorite one," Rosalee said. "She made this for my niece when she graduated from the Duke University law school. She's a lawyer up in D.C. now, working for the government in the Justice Department. That's my sister's girl, and we're all really proud of her. Ana Mae put a lot of love into that quilt."

JoJo fingered the image of a quilt made with blues and yellows. The color combination reminded her of a picture she'd seen of a French countryside. She'd decorated her own kitchen in the color palette. It amazed her what Ana Mae could create with just the stuff in this room.

Fabric and thread. A sewing machine. And a lot of love.

"I think she put love into all of her quilts," JoJo said.

❦

It did not take a genius to see that the Futrells were causing a stir in Drapersville. But the spectacle that had been Ana Mae's funeral paled when compared to the law being called out to her house for crowd control the previous day. And unfortunately for Everett Rollings and Sheriff Dan Daughtry, the weekly *Drapersville Times & Review* had gotten wind of the call and made it the lead story on the front page. The story was written by Eric Peters, the owner and editor of the paper.

Reluctantly, Everett Rollings admitted to himself that he would have done the same thing if he'd been the editor of the newspaper and something like that had happened right on deadline for the next edition. Nothing that interesting had happened in Drapersville in quite some time.

That did not, however, mean Rollings had to like it. And now he hoped to get in a bit of damage control, even though the damage had clearly already been carried out in the name of the First Amendment and that most sacred of Southern commandments, interpreted as a constitutional entitlement—the people's right to know their neighbors' business.

"Dammit, Everett. Why didn't you give me a heads-up about this?"

"Because there was nothing to give you a heads-up about."

Rollings tossed the newspaper on Sheriff Daughtry's desk. This was the sort of conversation that needed to take place in person, so he'd driven to the county government building before a consultation with a newly bereaved family.

"That photograph makes it look like two hundred people were gathered there. That is just not true. And despite that headline," he said pointing to *HIDDEN RICHES?* in big, bold type, there is not any money buried in Ana Mae Futrell's yard."

The sheriff eyed the photo. "How do you know for sure? Deputy Howard said it was like a mob over there."

Rollings threw up his hands. "Oh, for God's sake, Danny. You are sounding like that idiot brother-in-law of hers. You knew her, and she was not a foolish woman. All of Ana Mae Futrell's money is right where it should be, in banks and investments earning compound interest for her estate."

"Hmm. She really was rich?"

Rollings nodded. "But the only tangible assets of financial value are the savings bonds she purchased for her two nieces and her nephew. And those are going out to each of them from my office via certified mail first thing in the morning."

That comment drew the sheriff's attention away from the newspaper and to the lawyer and undertaker.

"Certified mail? Why? That's pretty expensive for a couple of savings bonds."

If Rollings's skin wasn't so dark, the man would have blushed. As it was, he cleared his throat a couple of times. "Well, sheriff. To say it is a couple of savings bonds is rather disingenuous."

The sheriff frowned at the complicated word, but refrained from saying anything.

"In truth," the funeral director-cum-lawyer said,

"she had been saving up and buying bonds for the kids for years, ever since they were infants. I told her there were better ways to invest for them, better returns that she could get on her money. But she liked what she called 'good, old-fashioned United States of America brand savings bonds.' She bought them like clock-work—years ago in small denominations, but later in one-hundred- and two-hundred-dollar-face-value cer-tificates. The Treasury Department doesn't even issue paper bond certificates anymore."

Sheriff Daughtry leaned back in his chair but care-fully eyed Everett. "How many years' worth of savings bonds?"

"The oldest niece is twenty-one or twenty-two years old now, and the other two are teenagers, fifteen and seventeen or sixteen and eighteen."

Daughtry whistled. "That's a sweet gift from Aunt Ana Mae."

Rollings leaned forward as if he was about to share a confidence, which was true. "And the best part," he said, his voice a bit lower even though they remained the only two people in the office, "is the parents have no idea. The oldest one is JoJo's, the other two, the teenagers, belong to Marguerite."

"Who is Marguerite?"

Rollings just managed to avoid rolling his eyes. "Delcine Futrell."

"Oh," Daughtry said. "I didn't know her well." He shook his head. "But from what Deputy Howard told me and what was in his report, and in Eric's," he said jerking his head toward the newspaper, "the relatives don't exactly get along."

"No. They don't," Rollings said. "And that just broke Ana Mae's heart."

The two men fell silent for a moment, each lost in his own thoughts about life, death, and family. Then Sheriff Daughtry pushed aside the copy of the *Drapersville Times & Review*.

"Well, no matter what they like or don't like about each other, we have to do something about this," he said.

"We? I came to you for help. You are the law enforcement."

Daughtry frowned as if to say, "Don't remind me." But he instead replied, "And just how did this hairbrained idea get hatched?"

Rollings sighed.

Thanks to the junk man, Eddie Spencer, who was probably aided by Rosalee Jenkins, the details of the legacy quilt were in the newspaper story. He did not think he would break any client confidentiality by telling the sheriff about the quilt blocks.

Daughtry listened to the story and then shook his head. "You're right, that Lester is an idiot, and I don't appreciate you calling me one too, in case you think I was letting that slide."

"Sorry about that," Rollings said. "This has just all been so . . ."

"Idiotic?"

Everett grinned. "Something like that."

"Well, tell you what. I'll get a man to sit there overnight so no treasure hunters—relatives, neighbors, or otherwise—go digging up the yard again."

"With all due respect, I do not believe that one night of increased patrol is going to solve anything."

"Yeah, I know," Daughtry said. "That's why I'll keep a man out there for a bit. Until things die down and the relatives go home. Maybe until I can convince

Eric Peters to write an article that clearly says there is no money to be found buried in Miss Futrell's yard or anybody else's."

"Thank you, Sheriff."

"Don't thank me," Daughtry said, picking up the newspaper, then tossing it into the trash bin next to his desk. "I'm gonna be billing you and Eric Peters for the overtime."

Later that evening at the bed-and-breakfast, Clayton pulled out several of the Zorin Corporation envelopes he'd taken from Ana Mae's house. Particularly interested in the annual report that had his sister's photo on the cover with the CEO, he wanted to know more about the company and Ana Mae's involvement in it.

When Archer came in an hour later, packages in both hands, Clayton looked up. "Hey there."

"Hi, Clay. I found the best gallery ever. Who would have known that your little hamlet could produce this?"

From one of the shopping bags he whipped out a piece of abstract sculpture. "It's by a sculptor named Pablo Diego Muñoz. Wonderful stuff. I got a small piece for the beach house, too," he added, unwrapping a second piece of art.

"I also got the artist's information and Web site. We should commission a piece," Archer said.

He then pulled out a long beige cashmere scarf and draped it around Clayton's neck. "It's a little warm now, but this, my dear, will be perfect for those cool San Francisco nights."

Clayton smiled his thanks and caressed the sumptuous fabric. "It's lovely."

Archer kissed Clayton, then sat cross-legged on the floor in front of him. "What has you so pensive?"

"I've been going through some of this Zorin Corporation stuff from Ana Mae's house."

"So what kind of company is it?"

"Cleaning products," Clayton said. "Apparently they supply a lot of businesses all across North America. And, according to this annual report," he said, picking up the glossy publication that had Ana Mae's picture on the front, "they'll be branching out into the consumer market this year."

Archer studied the cover of the booklet. "Is that Ana Mae and that crying man from her funeral?"

"Yep. And guess what other name I found in there?"

"Who?"

"That Fisher boy. Jeremy, the inventor."

Archer was quiet for a moment. Then, "Are you thinking what I'm thinking?"

"Yep," Clayton said. "I think Jeremy Fisher neglected to tell us something about Ana Mae's investment in his company."

❧

Rather than all of them calling David Bell at different times, Clayton and Archer decided to tell the girls about the discovery. Delcine would join them after checking out of her hotel. But on the drive from the bed-and-breakfast to Ana Mae's house, Archer bowed out of the meeting.

"This, as I said before, is something between you

and your sisters," he said. "I'll drop you off and then head back to the suite to get some work done."

"Work?"

Archer glanced at him. "Yeah, that lawyerly stuff I've been neglecting for shopping, reading . . . and you."

Even though he did not want to voice the suggestion for fear Archer might actually take him up on it, Clayton bit back his reservations and made the offer that he knew needed to be made.

"You can head home if you'd like," he said. "Winslow left to head back to D.C. There's no reason you need to hang around Drapersville."

"Oh, really?"

Clayton didn't know quite what to make of the tone of Archer's question. Was it sardonic? Or was it just a question that Clayton managed to read far more into than actually existed?

"Clay, I'm here in North Carolina because you're here. You just lost your sister. I'm not going anywhere until you do."

The joy that filled Clayton could only be described as rainbows and fairy tales, the stuff of good dreams and happily ever afters with the one you loved.

"Thank you."

The simple expression of gratitude seemed all he could manage at the moment.

Archer took Clayton's left hand in his and pressed a kiss to it. "Besides," he added, "there is no way I would leave you alone and defenseless against that idiot brother-in-law of yours."

Clayton chuckled. "Lester is as much your brother-in-law as mine."

"Don't give him to me. I'd rather adopt dull and dour Winslow."

"You know," Clayton said, as Archer turned onto Ana Mae's street, "there is definitely something going on with them."

"With JoJo and Lester?"

"Well, yeah, them too," Clayton said. "But I was referring to Marguerite and Winslow. I think they're having money trouble. I overheard Winslow on the phone at the funeral home."

"You and her husband are the only two people who call her that, you know?"

Clayton shrugged as he undid his seat belt. "Who am I to deny someone the right to call themselves whatever they want?"

"Touché," Archer said, as Clayton opened his door. "Call me."

"Will do. Love you."

"Love you more."

Archer tooted the horn as he pulled away. Clayton walked up the driveway to the house with a big smile on his face. Whatever had been bothering Archer these last few months seemed to have resolved itself.

North Carolina had been on Clayton's most loathsome list for so long that he found it on this side of surreal that this place where he'd been shunned was the same place that was restoring energy into his relationship.

He glanced to the sky, mostly clear and blue with a few fluffy clouds languidly drifting by.

"Thanks, Ana Mae."

"Hey, guys," Clayton said, greeting his sisters and Lester when he came through the side door and into the kitchen at Ana Mae's house.

"Hi, Clay," JoJo said. "The water is on for tea, and I just made a pot of coffee."

The women sat at the table, Delcine with her hands around a coffee mug and JoJo with coffee and a generous slice of pound cake.

"Thanks," he said. He sent a chin-up nod toward Lester, who stood near the refrigerator. Lester nodded back. There were never many words between the two men.

Clayton wasn't happy to see Lester there with Delcine and JoJo. He thought it would just be the siblings going over things. A glance at Delcine, who was scowling in Lester's direction, confirmed for Clayton that she had been under the same impression.

Lester seemed incapable of detecting nuances, particularly the kind directed toward him. Winslow had left for home. Why couldn't Lester take the next flight back to Vegas?

But Clayton knew the answer to that. It was because millions of dollars were at stake and Lester intended to claim what he considered was "his share." Resigned to the fact that his obnoxious brother-in-law would be with them, Clayton took a seat at the kitchen table after making a cup of tea.

"So, what exactly is this Zorin Corporation?" JoJo asked.

Clayton explained what he'd read in the company's annual reports. He pulled out his mobile phone and typed in a few things. A moment later, the company's Internet site popped up.

"Listen to this," he said. "The Zorin Corporation, based in Columbus, Ohio, in the United States, is the leading manufacturer and distributor of innovative solutions for businesses and industries."

Lester, leaning against the refrigerator, tapped a cigarette from his ever-present pack. "What does all that bullshit mean?"

"Don't smoke in the house, Lester," JoJo said.

"Do not smoke in this house," Delcine said at the exact same time.

Lester scowled at the two women, then tucked the cigarette behind his ear.

Clayton turned and held the phone out so Lester could see the image displayed on the screen in high definition.

"Cleaning supplies," he said. "The company makes and sells cleaning supplies."

"So?"

Clayton was about to answer when JoJo stood up.

"Hon," she said, walking over to her husband. She placed a hand on his paunchy stomach. "I think we're low on beer. Can you make a run over to the Walmart to get some?"

The fate of running out of that essential had Lester erect and looking alarmed. He yanked open the fridge door.

"Shit," he said. "You're right."

Moving as fast as any of them had seen him go since the day Everett Rollings said Ana Mae had left three point eight million dollars, Lester was making tracks to the door.

"Sure thing," he said. "I'll pick up some more smokes, too. I cannot believe how cheap cigarettes are here. Hmm," they heard him say as he pushed out the side door. A few moments later, they heard Ana Mae's car start up.

"Oh, Lord," JoJo said.

"What?"

"Now he's gonna be thinking about how he can make a buck running cigarettes," JoJo said.

"Well, at least he's gone so we can talk," Delcine said. "And that is truly a thriving business up where we live. People run guns and cigarettes from Virginia, where they're both cheap and easily accessed, and haul them straight up Interstate 95 to New York."

"Yeah," JoJo said, "I saw something about that on 60 Minutes or one of those news shows. They were talking about how shootings in New York City were done with guns bought in Virginia. I wondered how that happened."

"Girls," Clayton said in an attempt to rein them in and get them back on track before JoJo could launch into another of her as-seen-on-TV moments.

"Oh, yes," Delcine said. "We were talking about cleaning supplies. And, by the way, smooth move, Jo, getting Lester out of the house."

JoJo beamed at the praise.

"Ana Mae cleaned houses," she said.

"And that Fisher boy . . . ," Delcine added.

"Jeremy," Clayton supplied.

". . . that Fisher boy invented things that made cleaning easier."

"Exactly," Clayton said. "So I'm thinking . . ."

"Oh, my goodness," Delcine exclaimed. "I think you're right."

She'd clearly made the leap, but they'd left their younger sister behind—as usual.

"What?" JoJo asked. "He's right about what?"

Clayton and Delcine exchanged a glance, then Clayton outlined his theory.

"You saw that garage of his. He makes all kinds of things. What if he made something and sold it to this Zorin company, made a lot of money, and split it with Ana Mae?"

Delcine's lip curled. "Why?"

"Huh?"

"Why would he split the money with Ana Mae?"

"I don't know," Clayton said. "It's a theory. Maybe the thing he made was Ana Mae's idea. He said she invested in his company."

Liking the hypothesis, Delcine nodded. "That would explain why Ana Mae had so much money."

JoJo didn't look convinced. "Or maybe she hit the lottery again. That's happened, you know. People winning a big jackpot and then winning another one. I've seen it happen at the casinos too. Somebody hits for a really big jackpot on the slots and then . . ."

"Well," Clayton said contemplating the theory, "we won't have to speculate much longer." He used his mobile phone to place the call. They reached a receptionist, who said Mr. Bell was unavailable.

"May I have your name and number for a message, sir," the polite woman said.

Clayton gave his number and then said, "My name is Clayton Futrell. I'm in North Carolina at the moment."

"Futrell? Futrell! Oh, Dr. Futrell, I am so sorry for your loss," the receptionist said, her voice changing from cool but professional brush-off mode to warmth-infused sympathy.

Clayton frowned.

"What?" JoJo said. "What's he saying?"

Clayton waved her away. He punched a few buttons, putting the phone on speaker and then set it in the middle of the table so JoJo and Delcine could hear the conversation.

"We all just loved Miss Ana Mae. Her death is such a loss," the Zorin Corporation receptionist said.

Identical dumbfounded expressions marred the faces of the three surviving Futrells. It was clearly one thing to have David Bell crying like a baby at a funeral, but even the receptionist was choked up.

"Mr. Bell is in Virginia on business at the moment, but I know he would want to speak with you. I'll get your message to him right away," she promised. "And again, you have my deepest sympathy."

"Thank you," Clayton said, before punching the phone off.

"What the hell?"

Delcine got up. "I'm going to get some more of that Zorin Corporation mail. Ana Mae sure had a ton of it."

Clayton's phone rang a moment later.

"That was fast," JoJo said.

She got up to cut herself another large piece of the remaining pound cake, pour coffee, and start brewing Clayton's tea.

"Hello?" Clayton said, answering the phone.

A second later he was waving for his sisters to join him.

"Yes, Mr. Bell. Thanks for getting back to me so quickly."

Delcine raised a brow. "Wow. That was fast."

He listened for a moment, and then said, "My sisters are right here. Do you mind if I put you on speaker phone?"

"Not at all," David Bell said.

JoJo sat down with her coffee and cake, and Delcine returned with a stack of the large white envelopes from the box of Ana Mae's mail that was in the living room.

"Quarterly reports," she mouthed to Clayton, who nodded.

"Her passing just leaves a huge void in our company and in my heart," Bell was saying, his voice again breaking as it had at the funeral.

"Thank you," Delcine said. "This is Marguerite Futrell Foster, and we were wondering about your relationship with Ana Mae."

JoJo hit Delcine's arm. "Just be blunt," she hissed.

"Shh," Delcine said.

"Being blunt is just fine," Bell said with a chuckle.

JoJo's eyes widened. "I'm sorry. I was talking to my sister," she said. "This is Josephine."

"Yes, JoJo," Bell said. "Ana Mae always spoke so fondly of you. I could never get her to join me in Las Vegas, though. She wouldn't get on a plane, neither my private jet nor a commercial one."

This admission earned him another speculative glance from the three at the table.

"And to answer your question, Delcine," he said, adopting the familiar nickname for Marguerite, "my relationship with Ana Mae was one of the few true joys in my life. I was so hoping to be there for the wake so I could speak with all of you in private. I am so glad you called. I am up in Richmond, Virginia, for a meeting."

"Mr. Bell . . ."

"Please, call me David," he interjected.

". . . This is going to be another blunt question," Delcine said.

JoJo was shaking her head, but Delcine ignored her, and Clayton clasped her hand. JoJo sighed.

"You may have noticed in Ana Mae's obituary that she had a son. His name is Howard. We're looking for him and thought you might know where we could find him."

She gave a "so there" huff in JoJo's direction.

She'd skirted the direct question, apparently deciding it was too blunt for a conference call on a cell phone.

"Well, actually . . ." Bell began.

15

New Interpretation for Old Realities

About ten minutes later, the three Futrells sat in stunned silence at Ana Mae's kitchen table.

Clayton opened his mouth. No words fell out.

JoJo still stared at Clayton's mobile phone in the middle of the table.

Delcine recaptured speech first, but it was unsteady, like all of their heartbeats. "Do, do you know what this means?"

But Clayton had a question now too. "Do you think Rollings knew?"

"He had to have known," Delcine said. "He's like the Wizard of Oz, controlling everything from behind his little curtain."

"I don't understand," JoJo confessed. "Does what David Bell just said mean Ana Mae had even more money than the three point eight million?"

Clayton nodded. "A whole lot more."

"But what are the options he kept talking about?" JoJo wanted to know. "Choices to what?"

For a moment, Clayton just looked at her. Then he shook his head. "Not options like choices," he said. "Bell was referring to stock options."

"I'm glad you figured out what she was talking about," Delcine muttered.

"There's no need to be so damn condescending, Delcine."

JoJo sniffed. "Thank you, Clay."

Delcine folded her arms and sat back in her chair while Clayton explained. "Jeremy Fisher took stock options as well as a cash deal when he sold his company to the Zorin Corporation. Since Ana Mae invested in his company, she profited from that sale. And a stock option means if you get a share of stock for five dollars and the stock price rises to, say, one hundred dollars, you can exercise your options and you've suddenly made ninety-five dollars."

"But we're not talking about a five-dollar stock value, are we?" JoJo asked.

"Far from it."

"And the beneficiary of those options is this damn Howard."

JoJo narrowed her eyes. "Did you all notice how he just tap-danced all around that question about Howard?"

Delcine nodded. "That's because he's Howard's father. And I bet he's figured out not only where this elusive Howard is but a way for their son to transfer the money back to the company."

"Well, at least we found out what the plate of chicken on Ana Mae's quilt means," JoJo said.

Delcine raised an arched eyebrow, but Clayton voiced the question. "What are you talking about?"

The "now" was left unsaid but implicit in his half-irritated tone.

"The fried chicken," JoJo said, as if that explained it all. She pushed her chair back and headed into the living room, talking all the while. "Ana Mae always took David Bell a basket of her fried chicken. He said he was really going to miss it."

JoJo returned with her copy of the quilt booklet. She flipped to the page with the block featuring the plate of fried chicken. "See."

"JoJo, there was no mention of chicken, fried or otherwise, in that conversation with Bell."

"Yes, there was," JoJo insisted. She turned to her brother for support. "Tell her, Clay."

But Clayton's face was scrunched up as if he were trying to draw on a distant memory. "JoJo, I don't know . . ."

"He did," she insisted. "It was right when . . ."

"Dammit," Delcine said.

"What's wrong?"

"Rollings told us this back at the reading of the will."

"About the chicken?" JoJo asked.

That earned her one of Delcine's smile-snarls, this one clearly conveying that JoJo was clearly the "slow" Futrell who needed things spelled out in large block capital letters for her to understand.

"The stock options," Delcine snapped.

"How do you figure?" Clayton asked.

"He kept asking if we wanted an attorney. Someone to set up the agreements. He knew there was going to be this issue. God damn that man."

"Don't use the Lord's name in vain like that," JoJo chastised.

"Who are you, the Sunday school teacher now?"

"Girls," Clayton said, again trying to avert an all-out brawl between the sisters.

JoJo took a deep breath.

"I don't understand why she continued to live like this," Delcine said. "Look at this place. It's practically falling down. And for God's sake, Ana Mae was still cleaning toilets. She was a multimillionaire, and she had her hands stuck down somebody's toilet when she died. She could afford a mansion and an entire staff to wait on her hand and foot."

Clayton finally reached for and pocketed his mobile phone. "She wasn't one to live an ostentatious life."

Delcine cut her eyes at him.

JoJo bit back a smile.

Clayton—apparently not even realizing he had insulted Delcine, or knowing and not caring—missed the byplay between the sisters. His mind was on the implications of all they had discovered thus far.

Ana Mae lived a simple life by choice. Who did that in this day and age? And who helped her navigate the world of high finance?

Even JoJo, as world-weary and wise as she was living and working in Las Vegas, didn't know what a stock option was.

"How did Ana Mae know how to do any of this?" Clayton wondered aloud.

"Rollings."

The word came out as a curse and almost simultaneously from Clayton and from Delcine, who had been doing her own deductive reasoning.

Clayton reached in his pocket for his phone, but

Delcine was already up and reaching for Ana Mae's wall telephone receiver.

Only JoJo sat at the table, wondering how her siblings had completely missed David Bell's reference to the fried chicken.

They demanded a face-to-face meeting with the "funeral director slash charlatan"—Delcine's phrase.

Even so, he kept them waiting in his law office for ten minutes before entering the conference room.

"Good afternoon," Everett Rollings said.

Today's pinstripe suit was a charcoal gray, matched with a gray shirt and a darker gray tie. He looked ready to be laid out in one of his caskets in the funeral parlor. "What can I do for you?"

"Sit down, Mr. Rollings." The order came from Delcine.

He braced his large hands on the back of one of the chairs. "What can I do for you this afternoon, Dr. Futrell and Mrs. Coston?"

"You can ignore me all you want, Rollings," Delcine declared, "but we are on to your little game and the North Carolina State Bar and the funeral directors' association is going to hear about this."

A fleeting smile curved his mouth for a nanosecond. "And what, exactly, is the nature of your complaint, Mrs. Foster?"

"Your dereliction of fiduciary duties."

Rollings made a deliberate gesture of checking his watch. "I have an appointment in a few minutes," he said. "If one of you would kindly be specific, I will attempt to address your concerns."

"You didn't tell us about the stock options in the Zorin Corporation," Clayton said.

Rollings gave a full smile now and took a seat at the table across from them. "Ahh, so you have completed the interpretation of all nine quilt blocks. Excellent. I will have my assistant contact the other . . ."

"We don't have all nine blocks figured out," JoJo supplied.

"Is that so?" Rollings asked, moving to rise again. "Well, there is nothing further to discuss until . . ."

"Mr. Rollings," Delcine said, standing and stalking to his side of the table, "do not trifle with me. We know that Ana Mae had unexercised stock options worth about five times the money in her so-called will. When she died, those options reverted to this phantom Howard. I believe there is no Howard. You just cooked all of this up to make a grab for the money. That's why I'm going to the state bar to report your sorry ass."

JoJo's eyes widened. The North Carolina was coming out of Delcine now.

Rollings rose, gave a tug on the sleeve of his suit jacket as if it were more important than his former client's relatives.

"Mrs. Foster," he began, enunciating each word, and with a glance toward the still seated Clayton and JoJo, "Mrs. Coston, and Dr. Futrell, your sister was explicit in her wishes. My duty as her attorney was to see that those wishes were carried out according to her desires."

He strode around the table and reached for the quilt block booklet in front of JoJo. "May I?"

She nodded.

Rollings picked it up and turned to the page with the photograph of the entire quilt. "This quilt, *The*

Legacy of Ana Mae Futrell, tells a story," he said tapping the full-color image of Ana Mae's stitching. "She wanted you to figure out that story. If you know about the stock options, then you know the story behind *one* of the quilt blocks. You still have eight to go. Call me when you have done all of your sleuthing."

With that, he placed the booklet on the table, bade them "Good day," and walked out of the conference room.

"That son of a bitch," Delcine said.

Clayton held his hand up to halt the tirade. "But he's right, Del."

"What do you mean he's right? Look, I need . . . I mean, we need to get all of this sorted out so we can get the money and get back to our lives."

"I'm not so sure that's what Ana Mae wanted," JoJo said quietly. "We've learned a lot about Ana Mae that we didn't know before. That has to count for something."

Clayton reached for the booklet. "By my estimate," he said, "we have a long way to go."

"Please don't say that, Clay," Delcine said looking weary and pained. "I just don't have the time."

"What's going on with you and Win?" he asked.

But Delcine just shook her head.

Clayton gave her a pointed look, then turned his attention to the images. "We figured out the lottery ticket by talking to those folks at the store. Jeremy Fisher and David Bell represent the mop and the bucket, the cleaning supplies. That still leaves seven blocks."

"Don't forget Lester digging up the yard," JoJo said. "That was an interpretation of the middle block in the quilt."

"An interpretation all right," Delcine intoned, "but clearly an incorrect one."

"Be that as it may," Clayton said. "The faster we get this thing worked out, the faster we can go our separate ways. I suggest we spend the rest of the day chasing down some of these other clues. We didn't get much done yesterday."

"Thanks to Lester," JoJo said glumly.

A world-weary sigh came from Delcine. She opened her Gucci handbag and pulled out her mobile. She sent a text, then placed the phone on the table. In an uncharacteristic move, she placed both of her elbows on the table and dropped her head in her hands.

"What's wrong, sis?" Clayton asked again.

She shook her head and sighed again. "It's too complicated to get into right now."

Her phone pinged. She snatched it up, read the message, and sighed again. She furiously typed out another text and dropped the phone into her purse.

"Let's get out of here," she said.

JoJo remained silent on the ride back to the house. She sat in the backseat with no complaint. She knew Clayton and Delcine figured she was sulking because they—well, Delcine really—had put her down. But JoJo's mind was awhirl on more important matters than Delcine and her attitudes.

The lottery ticket quilt block and the bucket and mop quilt blocks weren't the only clues that had already been solved. JoJo knew for sure the answers to at least two other clues from Ana Mae's legacy quilt, and maybe another—the chicken.

On the phone, David Bell said he loved Ana Mae's

home cooking and that she always brought him a bit of North Carolina when she visited. JoJo interpreted that to mean Ana Mae's chicken and probably some of the other food she specialized in. If there hadn't been so much food in the house from Ana Mae's neighbors, church members, and friends, JoJo would have enjoyed trying out a few of the recipes she'd flipped through in Ana Mae's little yellow recipe box. As it was, she planned to try out Ana Mae's secret ingredient the next time she made fried chicken.

Delcine thought she was trailer trash without a brain. But Mary Josephine knew more than either of them credited her with. Her mama didn't raise no fool.

So while Miss Hoity Toity Delcine was running around like a chicken with her head cut off, trying to figure out seven more of Ana Mae's messages from the grave, JoJo had only four, and maybe just three, to solve before she could claim the three point eight million.

If she got it, she'd gladly share with Clayton and Delcine. But Lester. Well, he posed a problem.

The image of gangland Vegas mobsters came to mind again, which made her think of Eddie Spencer. Maybe it was time to see what Spence could tell her about settling down here.

Lester better be back with Ana Mae's car when they returned to the house.

Delcine dropped off Clayton at the bed-and-breakfast inn. They didn't make plans to meet up for dinner or breakfast. Everyone was in a reflective mood after the phone call with David Bell and the brief meeting with Everett Rollings.

The stakes had gotten higher, much higher.

Their initial curiosity about Ana Mae's alleged son had turned into something else. Each Futrell now had a lot more to lose.

"I'll call you later," JoJo told Clayton, as she reluctantly got in the front seat and powered down the window.

He closed the door. "Okay, sis. I'll see you guys later."

Delcine pulled away before Clayton even cleared the curb.

"Why did you check out of your hotel?" JoJo asked. "I thought you didn't want to stay at the house."

"I changed my mind," was all Delcine would say.

"Where do you want to sleep?"

Delcine glanced at her. "I'll stay in our old room."

"That's where Lester and I have been," JoJo said.

"You two have been sleeping in bunk beds? Why? There's a perfectly good double bed in Ana Mae's room."

JoJo shrugged. "I don't know. It felt weird, you know. It just didn't seem right for anyone to be in her bed. You know, like she was still there."

Delcine snorted. "Ana Mae is six feet under over at Antioch Cemetery. She is not haunting her house."

"I didn't say she was haunting it. It just," JoJo shrugged again, "it just didn't seem right."

"Hmmph," Delcine said. "Ana Mae may not have cared about living in a fancy house, but she sure had top-of-the-line tastes when it came to her bedding. She slept well."

"What do you mean?"

"Didn't you notice her sheets? They are eight-hundred thread count Egyptian cotton. And not just the ones on the bed; all of her linen is top notch. And that bed, oh, my God. It's the same brand Winslow and I have. Believe you me, those do not come cheap in any size. Ours is a king, of course, but it doesn't matter. Best sleep ever. I'll gladly stay in her room."

JoJo didn't know anything about fine linen. The sheets on the bed in their trailer back home had come from Kmart about five years ago. Leave it to Delcine to be noticing sheet thread counts.

That was okay, though. When JoJo collected the millions, she'd get herself a new mattress and some Egyptian sheets too.

✂

What JoJo didn't know and what Delcine had no intention of sharing was that the bedding she bragged about, as well as all of the furniture in their big house in upscale Prince George's County, was days away from being repossessed, right along with the house, which was days away from being foreclosed on.

Winslow hadn't, as she'd told her siblings, high-tailed it back home to check on their children, who were old enough to be home alone for a few days. They were just fine, considering.

While they'd had a big fight, he'd also left to try to get as much stuff as possible out of the house and into a storage unit before the bank padlocked the house or the police came to arrest him. He was also going to tell the kids what was happening. They had managed until now to keep the worst of it from Cedric and Latrice, although as Winslow said, Marguerite suspected the kids already knew more than they let on.

How could they not, with bill collectors calling all hours of the day and night, threatening letters from law firms overflowing the mailbox, and parents arguing behind closed doors?

Plus, all of the stories in the *Washington Post* and other media about corruption in their father's division at the U.S. Department of Housing and Urban Development couldn't have escaped them, especially Latrice, who had already asked "What's going on with Daddy's job?"

Daddy screwed himself and them, Delcine had wanted to tell her daughter. But she'd kept that to herself and spent her own lunch hour that day trying to find someplace for them to live other than a homeless shelter. But she had little cash and their credit cards were at or near the max, and finding a house to rent in the Washington metro area had not proven an easy task.

The news that Ana Mae had left a significant estate buoyed their hope that they could salvage their financial situation. But it was taking far longer than either of them anticipated for Ana Mae's money to get cleared.

Marguerite loathed the idea of staying at Ana Mae's house, but she could not afford another night at a hotel. She and Winslow couldn't afford the four nights they had already put on an American Express Platinum card, a card that would go into default when they failed to pay off their hefty balance at the end of the month.

She glanced at her sister. If Clayton hadn't insisted she be let back in the hunt, Ana Mae's money would have been split only two ways instead of three.

Clayton and Archer didn't need the money. With two hefty professional salaries, two million-dollar homes, and Lord only knew how much stashed away—Clayton had been tight with a dollar even when they were kids—Ana Mae's money would for them be cash for investing in property that would bring in rental income or donating to one of their gay causes. Delcine needed the money to keep a roof over her head and to feed her kids.

And right now, the only way she could see to do that was to beat out her brother and sister in claiming Ana Mae's legacy.

Their mama, God rest her soul, always preached that what one had they all had. But that thinking, Delcine now knew, was nothing less than shortsighted and designed to keep them all in poverty.

She'd escaped from Drapersville, North Carolina, once before and had no intention of ever, ever finding herself trapped in it or any place like it ever again. So she would do exactly what she needed to do to secure her future.

Just as soon as she dropped off JoJo at the house, Delcine planned to head out to see that Fisher boy one more time. She had an offer that would appeal both to his inventor's heart and to her negative-balance bank accounts.

"Are you having a good visit to Drapersville and Ahoskie?"

The deep male voice came from the right. Clayton paused near the reception desk at the bed-and-breakfast.

An elderly man who looked vaguely familiar sat in the Queen Anne wing chair closest to the arched entrance of the parlor. His blue-and-brown-striped sweater vest seemed a bit much for the heat, but the ensemble, which included a cream-colored shirt, brown slacks, and tasseled loafers, suited him. He had the air of a professor at an Ivy League university.

"Not particularly," Clayton said.

"That's unfortunate," the man said. "If I recall correctly, you had a rough time here years ago. I had hoped things would be better for you now."

Clayton cocked his head, considering the man. Then he crossed the lobby area and approached the stranger.

"Have we met?"

The man placed a hardback book on a side table and rose. "It's been many years," he said, extending his hand. "Ambrose Peterson. I was a guidance counselor at . . ."

"The high school," Clayton finished.

He clasped the man's hand and pumped it. "Yes, I do remember you. Hello, Mr. Peterson. Oh, my goodness. It's been years. I thought you looked familiar. I've been away so long I wasn't sure. Are you here at the inn visiting Mrs. March?"

Mr. Peterson shook his head. "No, no. I'm a guest at this lovely establishment. I retired and moved farther south. Join me for coffee?"

Mr. Peterson indicated the coffee and tea service on a mahogany sideboard.

Clayton hesitated, and glanced at his watch. "Well, I . . ."

"Oh, I'm sorry. You probably have plans for the evening."

It took Clayton less than a moment to make up his mind. A cup of coffee with someone from his Drapersville, North Carolina, past who didn't evoke anger or bitterness was a rare treat.

"Mr. Peterson, I'd love to chat with you. How have you been?"

Clayton went to the sideboard and poured two cups of coffee from the carafe. "Cream? Sugar?"

"No, thank you," Mr. Peterson said. "Just black."

Clayton added two teaspoons of sugar and a touch of half-and-half to his own cup, then balanced cups and saucers as he went to the matching chair. He placed both his own and his old guidance counselor's coffee on the side table, then returned to the sideboard for napkins and a few of the homemade cookies baked fresh each morning by Mrs. March.

When the two men were comfortably settled and had sipped on their coffee, Mr. Peterson asked, "So, what brought you home to North Carolina?"

Clayton looked startled for a moment. The town was so small and the newspaper story about Ana Mae's legacy so prominent, he would have thought everyone knew.

"My older sister, Ana Mae, she died August seventh."

Mr. Peterson's cup clattered on its saucer. Clayton reached for it to right it before the hot liquid spilled.

"I'm so sorry for your loss, Clayton," the older man said. "I didn't know."

"It's okay. And thank you, Mr. Peterson. The funeral was last Wednesday. We, my other two sisters and I, we're still here wrapping up some family things."

Mr. Peterson nodded, then he sighed and reached for his coffee cup. "Yes, there is a lot to do following the death of a loved one." He brought the cup to his mouth.

But something in his voice caught Clayton's attention. Maybe it was knowing the sadness of losing someone close. Clayton's loss seemed to be almost personal for him.

That's when the memories came rushing back. The social outcast gay teen he'd been in high school had always found a few moments of refuge and peace in the study room off the guidance counseling center's office. It was Mr. Peterson who always encouraged him to spend as much time as he needed in there. Although officially called a study room, the space was more lounge than study hall. The hard desks and chairs that furnished the high school's other study rooms were absent, replaced by a crate-style sofa, chairs, and a coffee table piled high with college catalogs, military recruitment brochures, and study-abroad pamphlets.

Clayton had spent many an hour in that room crying, hiding, wishing he were dead.

It clicked then.

All of the small kindnesses, the empathy.

"You're gay," he said. It wasn't a question.

Mr. Peterson smiled. "Don't tell me you're just now figuring that out."

Clayton's mouth dropped open, but he quickly recovered. "I . . . you know, I guess part of me always knew, but I didn't know. You were kind to me."

"The world is not always a pleasant place for homosexuals," Mr. Peterson said. "And a small Southern town can be especially brutal for a young person just coming into his or her sexuality, especially if it's outside society's accepted norm."

Something, a forgotten memory, nagged at Clayton.

"You knew? About me?"

Mr. Peterson nodded. "Probably before you did," he said. "I tried, to the best of my ability, to look after my little birds. There were several of you throughout the years. But you, you seemed to struggle the most."

The nagging memory came back to Clayton.

"But I thought you and Miss Hughes, the librarian . . ." Clayton's voice trailed off.

Mr. Peterson and Miss Hughes were known to be the school's longtime sweethearts. They were even seen out and about on dates in Ahoskie.

Clayton closed his eyes, the reality settling in. Miss Hughes, the pretty and soft-spoken librarian was what . . . Mr. Peterson's beard? It didn't seem to fit.

"Did you figure it out yet?" Mr. Peterson asked gently.

Just as when Clayton was a teen, the guidance counselor guided rather than directed. Then he knew. It did fit. The high school's faculty and staff members would have as much, if not more reason to hide behind shields. Their jobs and livelihoods were at stake.

"She was gay too?"

Nodding, Mr. Peterson confirmed. "My best lesbian friend. She still is and will be delighted to know I've run into you."

"Tell her I said hello," Clayton said, then shook his head as if trying to grasp the idea of not one, but two of his high school mentors being homosexual right under everyone's noses. "Why didn't I see this?"

"Don't be too hard on yourself, young man. Most teenagers are so self-absorbed or wrapped up in their own, their families', and their friends' personal dramas that they rarely have time to analyze what's going on in the lives of adults who are not their parents. And that is a fact more true today than it was when you were coming along."

"Thank you."

Mr. Peterson sipped from his coffee cup. "For what?"

"For being a positive influence even though I didn't consciously realize it."

The statement apparently pleased the former guidance counselor, because his smile grew broad.

"So how did things turn out for you?"

It was Clayton's turn to sport a wide grin. "It got better," he said. "Much, much better."

They spent the next twenty minutes chit-chatting about this and that. Clayton bragged on Archer, and Mr. Peterson congratulated him on his longtime partnership.

Mr. Peterson, who had long since retired to Florida, had traveled to Raleigh for a reunion of high school guidance counselors. He was so close to his old school that he'd decided to make a little side trip to Drapersville to see the old neighborhood.

The conversation made Clayton reassess the entirety of his teen years. Were things really as bad as he remembered?

"Hell, yes," he said out loud.

But he had both Ana Mae and Mr. Peterson running a sort of interference for him, roles he hadn't even recognized then.

What else may have been right under his nose all along without him realizing?

That question remained with him as he entered the suite upstairs.

Archer wasn't back yet from his shopping, but he'd clearly been hard at work for a while. His laptop was open, and several files were spread out on the desk.

His mind still on what Mr. Peterson said today—and what he hadn't said but what he had done all those years ago—Clayton pulled out the booklet featuring the quilt blocks from Ana Mae's legacy quilt. The lesson from Mr. Peterson was that everything isn't necessarily as it seems at first glance. Look deeper and you'll find new interpretations to old realities.

You don't have to buy into the interpretations you were taught as a child.

The quote, one that had stayed with him from a long-ago sermon he'd heard at a Metropolitan Community Church, finally made sense. And maybe it applied to Ana Mae's quilt as well. Maybe the interpretation of the quilt was as simple as it seemed. The blocks were about his sister's life. What else was she trying to tell him?

He opened the booklet to look at the individual images. His sister wanted him to know about her life. Clayton decided it was time he got to know more about Ana Mae.

16

Reading the Tea Leaves

It was Archer, not Clayton, who figured out the block on Ana Mae's quilt that featured the teapot and teacup.

Because he didn't trust anyone except the owner of his favorite tea shop in San Francisco to blend tea properly, Archer had packed enough in a tin to last a good week. So far, he had managed to refrain from bringing his own leaves and infuser into the dining room at the bed-and-breakfast.

This morning, they and another couple were enjoying the last moments of a sumptuously prepared breakfast in the inn's dining room.

The tea the innkeeper brewed wasn't bad, but his refined palette knew the subtle differences. As he watched her place a pot on the table before them, the tea cozy made from the same quilted fabric as a table runner along the sideboard, it dawned on him.

"Clay?"

"Hmm."

Clayton, absorbed in the booklet featuring the close-up and detail images from *The Legacy of Ana Mae Futrell*, did not even look up.

"Can I get you anything else, Mr. Archer?"

He found it amusing that the innkeeper Nan March either had apparently given up on trying to pronounce the Dahlgren part of his hyphenated last name or just thought referring to two men as Mr. Futrell more than she could handle.

"As a matter of fact, Mrs. March, there is."

He reached for the teapot, loosened the cozy, and held it up. "Where do you get the tea you brew? I'm something of a connoisseur, and I have especially enjoyed this breakfast blend."

She beamed. "I'm so glad you like it. Most of our guests are coffee people, so it is always a special delight to find someone who appreciates a nice cup of tea made the right way."

Clayton glanced up at all of the sudden chatter. "When he says he's a tea connoisseur, he really means a tea snob. You'd think the man owned stock in the tea shop near our house. He's always there for tastings and parties and is forever bringing home teapots of every shape and size."

"Really?" Mrs. March said. "Then you must stop by the Carolina Tea Company before you leave. It's where I get the tea you like," she said, nodding toward the pot Archer now poured from.

"Where is it?" Archer asked.

"Not terribly far, although some people think I'm crazy to drive way over there just for some tea. Carolina's place is just about thirty minutes from here. She has the most darling little tea parties for girls."

Nan March suddenly blushed, as if she'd inadvertently made a gay slur against her debonair guests.

"I adore tea parties," Archer said, his voice a little higher and lispier than usual.

Looking relieved, Mrs. March beamed again. "I can get the address and number for you and print off some MapQuest directions if you'd like to visit. Carolina loves to meet people who are as passionate about tea as she is."

"Carolina is a person, I take it?"

The innkeeper nodded. "Her parents were apparently infatuated with state names. She's Carolina, she has a sister named Georgia, and I think there's a brother named Arizona or Utah or something strange like that. She told me all about their names when I asked how she'd come up with the name of the tea shop. You know, living in North Carolina, it's just perfect."

"Just perfect, indeed," Clayton muttered.

"I would love the address and directions, Mrs. March. Maybe we'll be able to make a trip over there."

Clayton leaned back in his chair and gave a mock groan. "Now you've done it, Mrs. March. We've just lost a day to his infatuation with tea leaves."

Archer playfully hit Clayton's arm, then gave Nan one of his most charming smiles, the type that made heterosexual women completely forget that he wasn't the least bit interested in them. "Pay him no attention," he said. "I don't."

A schoolgirl giggle escaped her. Then, hailed by one of the other guests in the dining room, she excused herself.

Clayton closed his quilt booklet and lifted a brow. "What was that super-gay act all about? You 'adore' tea parties," he said, using the same patently and clichéd gay tone that Archer had used on the innkeeper.

"The tea," Archer said.

Clayton spread his hands in a "what about it?" gesture.

"It's the tea," Archer said again, reaching across the table for the booklet featuring Ana Mae's quilt and its individual blocks.

He flipped forward until he found the page featuring the teapot and teacup. "The tea," he said again. "Ana Mae's tea. Don't you remember?"

"I have not the first clue as to what you're babbling about," Clayton said. "And," he added with emphasis, "we cannot spend all day at a tea shop. I have clues to . . ."

His words fell off when Archer gave him a pointed look. A moment later, the lightbulb went on for Clayton.

He clasped his hands together on the table, serious now and his voice bearing it out. Clayton said. "Tell me about the tea, Archer."

"Remember the other day at Ana Mae's house? I found tea. Really excellent tea. A box of those vile bags that people call tea was on the counter, but I found Ana Mae's good tea while hunting for a coffee cup. I'd decided to bear coffee rather than submit to a Lipton tea bag."

Nodding now, Clayton clearly remembered. "The tea in the tin that Delcine thought was marijuana."

"Marijuana?"

Clayton waved away the question. "The thing is . . ."

"Where did Ana Mae get tea leaves? Real tea. Really good tea," Archer finished. "Clearly it didn't come from the Piggly Wiggly or the Food Lion."

Clayton grinned. "Quilt block number four is about the Carolina Tea Company."

Archer nodded, grinned, then took a sip from his cup.

ॐ

Slipping away from both her sister and her husband proved easier than JoJo ever would have thought. Delcine slept like the dead, complete with eye mask and earplugs. When JoJo tried to rouse her to tell her she was running out, Delcine muttered something that sounded like a swear word or two and turned over in Ana Mae's bed.

Lester had been even less trouble when she announced that she needed to go get a few feminine things.

Her rude, crude husband would sooner agree to be given a blow job by a midget in a clown suit in the middle of the Las Vegas Strip than walk into a store and buy tampons. That aversion served JoJo nicely as she gave a final touch to her lipstick, then spritzed her neck and between her breasts with an alluring scent. She blew a kiss into the bathroom mirror, then for extra measure cupped her big breasts and thrust them up in her already low-cut, white-lace-edged blouse. Satisfied, she made her way in kitten heels and tight jeans to Ana Mae's car.

Not long afterward, she parked in the side lot adjacent to Eddie Spencer's junk store and sashayed her way inside.

She didn't worry that he might not be open so early. It was barely nine in the morning. He was, however, expecting her.

And it looked like Eddie had also spruced himself up in anticipation of their get-together. His hair, recently barbered and shaped up, had a nice wave pattern in it. He was clean-shaven and had on a pale blue shirt, jeans, and boots.

"Josephine."

"Hey, Eddie," she said.

The hug he gave her included a slight butt grab that made JoJo wince.

Maybe coming here hadn't been such a good idea, after all.

"I was real glad to hear from you, Josephine," he said leading her through the store.

As they passed through, JoJo caught glimpses of furniture that should have been sent to the dump rather than put up for sale, a lot of dishes and bicycles, and even a couple of lawnmowers.

"To tell you the truth," Eddie Spencer said, "I didn't think you'd call since you told me you were married."

He led her into his back office—a space that, unlike the front of the store, was actually decorated with some class. The desk, made of a dark hardwood and truly an antique, as opposed to one of the clapboard pieces for sale out front, gleamed with the care of frequent polishing. A telephone, a tablet and pen, and a laptop computer were the only items on the surface. A nice picture of a flower garden, not a print but made with real paint, hung in a frame that almost matched the wood of the desk. Eddie produced a couple of cups of takeout coffee with the Day-Ree Mart logo and a bag of doughnuts. JoJo sat on the loveseat and angled her body a bit so that she was sitting on the edge while Eddie settled back, getting comfortable. He took a sip from his cup before putting it on the floor and placing a hand on her knee.

"But there are some things I'm still very much interested in," he said. "You being one of them. I never got over you, Josephine."

She patted his hand. "Don't be silly, Eddie. We were always just good friends."

He licked his lips, took her hand in his, and said. "And we still can be. Good friends, that is."

"I didn't mean that kind of get-together when I called you, Eddie."

His face fell, and he let go of her hand and bent to retrieve his coffee.

In that moment, JoJo realized two things.

First, he'd gotten a haircut and shave and probably put on clean underwear in anticipation of a romp with her. And second, maybe someplace deep in her subconscious, she really wanted it to be that kind of reunion.

She'd never cheated on Lester—although she couldn't be entirely sure Lester had been faithful to her—and she didn't plan to start breaking her vows now. That would come via a Nevada state judge's signature on a divorce decree. Until then . . .

"Eddie, it's been a long time. I just thought we could catch up."

So they did, over the next twenty minutes or so, laughing and reminiscing about high school and old friends until JoJo got around to the real reason she wanted to reconnect with Eddie Spencer.

"Since I've been home for the funeral," she said, "I've been doing some thinking and wondering about something."

"What's that, darling?"

JoJo glanced at him, shy and hopeful and wondering why it was easier to talk to an old flame about this rather than to her own flesh and blood.

She took a deep breath and then let the words tumble out before she lost her nerve. "Ana Mae left us the house, and I know neither Delcine or Clay will be interested in it. So I've been, well, I've been thinking about moving back here," she said. "You know, to Drapersville or Ahoskie, or maybe even Murfreesboro or Elizabeth City. I've been in Vegas for a long time. The life there is . . . ," she shrugged, "well, it's fast and it's rugged, and I think I'm ready for a change."

"Well, now, Josephine," he said on a low drawl, "I personally would love to have you back in town."

"Eddie, I told you . . ."

"I know, I know. Just friends, 'cause you're married. But something tells me that husband of yours might not be all that interested in moving to North Carolina. From what I hear tell, he's a big-city kind of fella."

JoJo pursed her lips but did not confirm nor deny the speculation.

Eddie Spencer grinned and patted her jeans-clad knee before getting up to go to his desk. Bending over, he started opening drawers.

Not quite sure what he was doing or looking for, JoJo continued, although a bit wary now. Eddie Spencer used to be kind of wild, the sort of guy who knew people who could make things happen to people.

For a moment, she conjured the image of the old-time Vegas gangster. She could easily see Eddie, though he was black, in that role.

Was he looking for a gun?

"I, I was wondering what it's like here now," she said. "You know, jobs and the economy and whatnot."

"Somewhere in here is a . . . ah, here we go," Eddie said. "I knew I hadn't tossed it out."

He pulled out a pocket-folder envelope with a

white glossy cover and handed it across the desk to JoJo. She glanced at the cover and saw both the North Carolina state flag and a couple of logos she didn't immediately recognize.

"What's this?"

Eddie came around and leaned on the front of his desk.

"The Chamber of Commerce put those things together a while back," he said. "It's like a newcomer's guide to the county, with info about housing and jobs and things to do. They wanted all of us to learn some of the facts and share 'em with customers. As if anybody who comes in here is a tourist."

JoJo opened the folder and found slickly produced color brochures and multiple rainbow-hued pieces of paper. Flipping through, she saw information about living, working, visiting, and vacationing in Hertford County, North Carolina.

"Thank you," she said. "This will be helpful, I'm sure."

Eddie folded his arms. "Waste of a few trees, if you ask me. But I held onto it, and now you need it, so I guess it was a good use of their money. 'Course, the truth is that's just a bunch of propaganda. We're all struggling here, just like everybody else in the country. The whole of Hertford County is about twenty-four thousand people or so. I'll bet one of them big hotels in Vegas has that many people in it on any given night."

JoJo nodded. "You're probably right, counting all of the employees, guests, and people in the casino, restaurants, bars, and shops."

"We don't have a lot of crime, and that's a good thing," Eddie said. "Every now and then somebody will up and go crazy and do something stupid that brings down all the TV reporters from Norfolk. But mostly folks around here still go about their business just like they did back when y'all all lived here. Not much in the way of jobs, either. And if you're looking for a big-city paycheck like you're probably used to out there in Las Vegas, you're gonna have to go to Raleigh or Charlotte, 'cause we ain't got nothing much here."

JoJo almost laughed out loud at that.

People tended to think that everybody who lived and worked in Las Vegas raked in the cash like a slot machine paying off a big jackpot. The reality was that working-class folks were the backbone of the city and worked hard just to keep a roof over their heads and food on the table.

The slower pace and lower cost of living in this part of North Carolina appealed to JoJo on a lot of levels.

Surprising her with his knowledge, Eddie gave her some more statistical information about Drapersville, Ahoskie, and Hertford County. He may not have realized it, but he was actually a good pitchman for the area.

What JoJo didn't realize when she left, about ten minutes later, was that as soon as she drove off in Ana Mae's car, Eddie Spencer pulled out his mobile phone and called over to Junior Cantrell's place.

He had some inside information now. He wanted to make a long-shot bet and to put his money on JoJo.

17

A Theory About Howard

Emily Daniels missed Ana Mae Futrell's funeral, but she wanted to pay her respects to the family. Because Emily took her mission very seriously, she kept meticulous records about all activities at The Haven.

Miss Futrell, one of The Haven's biggest supporters, played a key role in its expansion and was to receive the Volunteer of the Year award. Now that Ana Mae had died, though, Emily wanted to make sure that Miss Futrell's family received the posthumous honor and knew all that she had done for the defenseless residents who found shelter at The Haven.

She put the finishing touches on the package. Then, remembering a photo the family might like, she went to her computer and found the file. A quick glance at the clock told her she'd have enough time to make a nice print and find a frame.

"Melinda, I'm going to run out for a bit. Will you be okay by yourself until Sam gets in?"

The college student who worked at the no-kill animal shelter in the summer and during school breaks planned to be a veterinarian, and Emily knew she was more than capable but wanted to check just in case. Emily tended to worry.

"Oh, sure, Ms. Daniels. I have a few more kittens to see to, but I should be all right."

Max, a long-haired Persian found abandoned after a hurricane and named by shelter volunteers after the storm, brushed against Emily's leg. She knelt and gave the cat a bit of love, then picked up the materials for the Futrell family. "I shouldn't be too long. You have my number if you need anything else."

"We'll be fine, Ms. Daniels."

Emily, already rehearsing what she would say to the bereaved, waved as she left The Haven.

"I don't want to impose," she said a while later.

Emily caught Clayton just as he was leaving Miss Futrell's house. He was about to get into a car in the driveway when she pressed on her horn at the curb and got his attention.

It had taken much longer than she anticipated to select a frame that went with the photograph. And then, it seemed only natural to have the entire presentation gift wrapped. Choosing the right paper and ribbon had taken an inordinate amount of time.

"It is no imposition," he said. "Come on in."

Emily's heart beat a little faster. He was a handsome man. Not quite as handsome as her Howard, but still . . .

He opened the door and held it for her. When she walked by, Emily caught a hint of a manly fragrance that brought back so many memories. It had been a long time since she had known the comfort of a man, felt the yearning stir within her core and lost herself to the magic of unbridled passion.

Her breathing grew deeper.

"Miss Daniels?"

It took Emily a moment to remember where she was, with whom and why. Then, embarrassed, she blinked and cleared her throat.

"You, you remind me of someone I used to know," she told him. "I, I was thinking of him."

"Pleasant thoughts, I hope."

"Oh, yes," Emily said as she entered the small mudroom and then through it to the kitchen. "Very pleasant memories."

∾

"We need to go out to the cemetery."

"The one where Ana Mae is buried?" Archer asked.

"Yes. I think we'll find our mysterious Howard there."

Archer closed his laptop and grabbed the keys. "If you say so."

On the drive to Antioch Cemetery, Clayton shared what he had learned from the odd Emily Daniels. "She is a cat lady in every sense of the word," he said.

"Meaning?"

"Mid-fifties, obviously single, and she was wearing one of those long peasant skirts. Cat hair was all over it."

"I wondered why you peeled out of your clothes the moment you hit the door. I thought maybe you just couldn't resist me."

"There is that," Clayton said with a grin. "But before she left, she grabbed me in this extreme hug. She was cuddling me, Arch."

"You're cute. But remember, dude, you're gay and you're mine."

Clayton thrilled at the declaration, but couldn't resist adding. "She wanted me."

Archer rolled his eyes. "So why are we going to the cemetery?"

"Howard."

"Howard is at the cemetery?"

Clayton nodded. "At least I think so. Emily Daniels came by to tell me all about Ana Mae's work at an animal shelter called The Haven. Apparently, Ana Mae gave them a lot of money and volunteered there. That's where she got Baby Sue."

"Baby Sue?"

"The cat. It and the other one are over at Rosalee's."

Archer nodded. "Ah, yes. The cats. They would be the ones that dear Lester believed had jewel-encrusted collars."

"I do not see what JoJo sees in that horrid man."

"It's probably the sex," Archer said. "Never underestimate the power of what goes on between the sheets."

"Archer."

"What? You know, Clay, this place is turning you into a little Puritan."

Clayton snorted. "Not likely."

"Back to the cemetery," Archer said, prompting Clayton again.

"The cat lady said Howard disappeared. He was apparently her boyfriend. And, according to Miss Daniels, I resemble him . . . a lot."

"I thought you said she was in her mid-fifties. Isn't that a little old for any son of Ana Mae's?" He paused. "Ah, the cat lady is a cougar."

"Bingo," Clayton said.

"So what makes you think her guy is, first, our guy and, second, dead?"

"She said Howard disappeared about six or seven years ago. Left town without a trace."

"She probably wore him out and he needed to escape."

Clayton laughed. "That could be likely. But it was the photograph that made me think of the cemetery."

"What photo?"

"I left it at the house," Clayton said. "She had it in a really nice silver frame. But it's of Ana Mae and a lot of cats and kids, and in the background is Antioch Cemetery."

Archer glanced over at Clayton. "All right, Hercule Poirot. You are going to have to explain it a little better for the unwashed masses here. What does a picture of Ana Mae with some cats have to do with this missing nephew of yours?"

"Well, it might sound a little crazy," Clayton said.

"Humor me."

Clayton knew his theory was kind of out there. But the entire situation was out there. This made more sense than digging up the backyard or cats wearing diamond collars.

"Well," he began tentatively, "you know how in Ana Mae's obituary it says Howard's address is unknown?"

Archer nodded.

"Well, Ana Mae was a serious churchgoer."

"To quote the good Reverend Toussaint le Baptiste—or, as Lester calls him, Reverend Holy Ghost—'Sister Ana Mae loved her some God.' "

The right-on-target impersonation of Toussaint at Ana Mae's wake made Clayton smile. "Yes, she did. And if a son of hers wasn't churched or saved or whatever when he died, Ana Mae wouldn't know if he went to heaven or to hell. Hence, address unknown."

Archer's mouth dropped open. He did not say a single word.

"Well?" Clayton prompted.

"Well, what?"

"What do you think of my theory? It works, doesn't it?"

Archer just shook his head. "I'll tell you this about that theory of yours, if that's how that medical doctor brain of yours thinks and processes information when you're not at the clinic, I think you entered the wrong profession. We could use that kind of nonlinear thinking in our litigation department at the law firm."

Clayton knew a long-winded compliment when he heard one. He leaned back and smiled.

They were both surprised to find another visitor at Ana Mae's gravesite. The headstone that Mr. Rollings's people said had been preordered was not yet installed. However, flowers from the funeral—some in their baskets but now dried in the summer sun—still covered the mound at the grave. But a fresh bouquet of wildflowers in bright pinks, yellows, reds, and purples stood sentinel at the top, where the headstone would eventually be.

"Good afternoon, gentlemen."

Reverend Toussaint le Baptiste extended a hand to greet Clayton and Archer.

After shaking the minister's hand, Archer took a step aside. "I'll start looking over here," he said.

"All right," Clayton said. Then, "What brings you here today, Reverend?"

"Probably the same as you," Reverend Toussaint said. "Paying my respects."

Clayton nodded toward the new bouquet. "Pretty. Are they from you?"

If he heard the question, the minister ignored it. "This is a nice quiet place to think," he said. "I come here often, usually to sit by the creek over there and meditate on the goodness of the Lord."

"I don't know much about that," Clayton said. "I generally leave religion alone."

The two men—both tall, but one slim and in a dark suit and the other athletically lean and in casual clothes, even though they were pressed jeans and a polo shirt— stood at the foot of Ana Mae's final resting place.

"Why is that?" Reverend Toussaint asked.

Clayton thought of all the hypocrisy he'd encountered in the church while growing up. In the pulpit the preacher would condemn homosexuality but didn't seem to care if everybody knew the choir director was a flaming queen on Friday and Saturday nights and holier than thou on Sunday mornings. He thought about Deacon Reginald Crispin, who'd been sitting up all righteous with the deacons at Ana Mae's funeral. That one was still in the closet, living a lie and calling himself a Christian. Clayton and Archer belonged to an open congregation back home, a congregation that didn't put labels on its members. He'd leave that kind of religion to Reverend Toussaint and folks like Ana Mae.

"Religion, organized religion, is a solace for those who need it and a crutch for those who are trying to hide or absolve themselves of their hypocrisy," Clayton said. "People who need to believe that there's a great magician in the sky controlling the universe, making decisions for us, laughing as we fail."

"You think the Lord is like the Wizard of Oz?"

Clayton smiled. "I did not quite mean it that way," he said, "but now that you mention it."

"Faith isn't like that," the preacher said.

"There is no God," Clayton said.

"How do you know?"

Clayton laughed, but little if any humor went with the sound. "If there's a God, he surely has a sick sense of humor. Making me gay. Making me come back here to this godforsaken town."

"For someone who doesn't believe in God, you . . ."

Clayton held up his hand. "Reverend, I don't mean you any harm or disrespect, but this is not a conversation I wish to have at the moment."

Or any other moment, Clayton added to himself.

Reverent Toussaint nodded. Then he bowed his head. "All right."

Before Clayton could say anything else, the minister was praying . . . out loud. Clayton sighed.

"Lord, we come to you today with bowed heads and open hearts. We don't know your ways, but we know and believe that you alone are worthy of all of our praise and honor."

Clayton may not have been religious, but he knew

enough to be respectful. His Mama had taught him that much.

The thought of the late Georgette Futrell made him glance around, even as he kept his head bowed while Reverend Toussaint droned on.

". . . the path may be rocky, but the journey is divine. Order their steps, Lord . . ."

Their parents were buried somewhere out here at Antioch Cemetery. It hadn't crossed his mind to look for their gravesites the day Ana Mae was buried. The only thing on Clayton's mind that afternoon was getting it all over with and returning to California as soon as humanly possible.

The fact that he was still stuck in North Carolina did not sit well with him in the least bit.

". . . and lift him up, Lord. Brother Futrell and his, uh, his friend. Bless the whole family, Lord, and give them the strength they'll need in these coming days. Hallowed be thy name and thy son Jesus' name. Amen, and amen."

"Amen," Clayton said, not meaning it in the least. He glanced around and saw Archer about one hundred feet away, looking at gravestones and not paying any attention at all to Clayton and Reverend Toussaint.

"Thank you for your prayers, Reverend. But I don't need them."

"Everybody needs prayer, son. Even those who don't believe. I'll leave you now."

The minister placed a fedora on his head and turned to leave.

"Reverend le Baptiste?"

Toussaint turned.

"Thank you for everything you did for my sister."

The minister nodded. "She was a good woman. A Godly woman."

Long after the Reverend Toussaint le Baptiste slipped away, Clayton remained staring down at Ana Mae's grave.

While he hadn't been paying much attention to the preacher's prayer, a line of it remained with him. *The path may be rocky, but the journey is divine.* The words, in their simplicity and truth, gave Clayton pause. His entire life, from birth until this very moment, seemed encapsulated in that single sentence.

A shout from Archer pulled him from his musings.

"Clay, I found something!"

18

The Lady Who Loved Little Kids

Feeling vaguely let down by her encounter with Eddie Spencer, JoJo drove around town as aimlessly as her thoughts were wandering. She didn't have a lot of options open to her. Las Vegas had long since lost the appeal and cachet it had had for her in her youth, back when she knew—was certain, without any shred of doubt, misgiving, or lack of conviction—that her star would rise over the Vegas Strip, that she would be the principal of several shows and managing her own stable of young impressionable and talented wannabe stars.

Life had had a few other opinions, though, and before JoJo could claim her piece of the star-studded rainbow, she was knocked up and struggling, not even sure who the father was of the baby she carried.

"Ana Mae."

She said her sister's name as if it were a prayer.

Too terrified to tell her mother that not only had

she run away from home to be a showgirl in a low-budget Las Vegas review but that she was also now pregnant, JoJo called her big sister.

While a sermon on the virtues of chastity and holiness might come from Ana Mae, that punishment, JoJo decided all those years ago, was infinitely better than the bitter disappointment she knew she would find in her mother's eyes.

As far as JoJo knew, Georgette Futrell died without ever knowing that she had a granddaughter. Ana Mae had kept JoJo's secret. And since apparently Ana Mae knew that Crystal lived in Laughlin, less than one hundred miles from Las Vegas, JoJo could only wonder what other secrets Ana Mae took to the grave with her about JoJo's daughter. Crystal was so close geographically and so far away emotionally.

JoJo gave a little snort, a half laugh of self-derision.

"You kept my secrets, Ana Mae. I wonder if you tucked away any secrets for Clay or for Delcine?"

She didn't expect an answer but was half surprised to find herself in the parking lot at the Holy Ghost Church of the Good Redeemer. Several cars and minivans filled the lot, not so many as to indicate a service might be going on inside, but enough to tell her people were there during the day.

A late-model Lexus with the personalized North Carolina license plate REV T made her immediately think of the Reverend Toussaint le Baptiste.

With her mind on the sins of her own past and curious about the place where her sister had spent so much of her time, JoJo parked Ana Mae's car next to the Lexus and made her way to the church.

The front door was locked.

Her own church back home was a little chapel occupying a former storefront that used to house a souvenir shop. The front entrance and a back door were the only two ways to get in, and the fifty or so congregants used the front door. A church like this, a real church even if it had a strange name, would have more than two doors.

JoJo hadn't been paying that much attention at Ana Mae's funeral. Her mind was pretty much on other things than entrances and exits to the church, but she tiptoed on aching feet—her sexy shoes to entice Eddie Spencer were not made for traipsing across parking lots—back to the parking lot, then looked around. The kitten-heeled open-toe mules she'd put on looked great and felt like sheer hell.

But sure enough, just as she was thinking she'd go on home, she saw an entrance a ways down and near where many of the other vehicles were clustered.

An awning the same color as the red brick of the church covered a walkway.

A few minutes later she found herself in a hallway. The sounds of children singing and a phone or two ringing gave her courage.

What exactly it was she feared she would not have been able to name. But a bit of trepidation washed over her.

Guilt. Not fear.

"I'm sorry, Lord," JoJo whispered.

She felt guilty about wishing she could put a hit out on Lester. She felt guilty about not staying in better touch with Ana Mae.

The singing drew her. The melody of the children's song was familiar, but the words escaped her.

"May I help you?"

JoJo started. Then she turned to see a petite woman

in a blue-jean dress with a smock covering part of it coming out of one of the rooms.

"Hi," JoJo said. "I'm, I'm looking for Reverend Toussaint la Baptist."

"Le Baptiste," the woman said, correcting JoJo's pronunciation. "His office is right down here. I'll show you. But he's probably just about ready to go in with the kids right now."

"Thank you," JoJo murmured.

She had not come to see the minister, Ana Mae's and Rosalee's childhood friend. But with no better excuse and the teacher-looking lady staring at her, that's all that came to mind. The way things were in the world right now, the last thing she wanted was the lady thinking she'd come to kidnap a child or something. Crazy people were everywhere, including in small towns in the South.

The woman led her to an office that had the door pulled to, but not completely closed. She knocked. "Reverend T?"

JoJo smiled. So the Lexus out in the parking lot probably belonged to him.

"Yes, Delia?"

The woman pushed the door open. "There's someone here to see you."

She guided JoJo into the small space and departed.

"Sister Josephine," Reverend Toussaint said, standing and coming around his cluttered desk to greet her. "What a surprise and pleasure. Come on in."

Shaking the minister's hand, JoJo smiled.

"I hope I'm not disturbing you," she said.

"Not at all. Have a seat," he said, indicating two cushioned folding chairs in front of his desk.

JoJo settled herself on one and put her big purse on the other.

Reverend Toussaint took his seat again, then clasped his hands together and gave her a smile.

"How are you doing?" he said.

JoJo gave a half shrug. "I guess I'm okay, you know."

"Then tell me, what can I do for you?"

JoJo absently noticed that he was a really nice-looking man with that wavy hair and those smoky eyes. Then, remembering she was in the Lord's house even if it was an office, she opened her mouth to answer him. She closed her mouth. Opened it again and then started crying.

"Oh, dear," Reverend Toussaint said. "Sister Josephine, what's wrong?"

She sniffled. "I'm sorry. I just . . . I've made such a mess of my life. Nothing turned out the way I thought it would."

Sitting right there with this kind man, it all just bubbled up and over in her. Ana Mae was gone. She was broke. She wanted out of her marriage to Lester. Her own daughter hated her.

Her life wasn't just a mess, it was a hot mess. And the tears now came in a steady and heavy flow.

"Sister Josephine, everything will be all right. Our God is a wonder-working God."

He got up and came to sit on the edge of the chair next to her—and accidentally pushed over her handbag. It fell to the floor with a clop, the contents spilling out.

"Oh, dear. I'm so sorry," he apologized, bending over to get her bag.

One of the things that fell out was a small Bible,

one of the little New Testament volumes that also included the Psalms and sometimes the book of Proverbs. She'd gotten it from a street-corner preacher back home. He'd been passing them out one Saturday afternoon, and JoJo liked the idea of having a Bible in her purse. It made her feel a little closer to God.

JoJo leaned over, but Reverend Toussaint had already scooped up the Bible, a lipstick, a pen, and the purse. He handed her the loose items and placed the bag on his desk. With a quiet "Thank you," JoJo put the lipstick and ink pen back inside and rummaged for a tissue.

She dabbed at her eyes for a bit, hoping she hadn't messed up her makeup, then finally sat back with the Bible.

"Sister Josephine?"

She batted her eyelashes, not flirting, but trying to hold fresh tears at bay. She felt one of her false eyelashes slipping. With a sigh and a few more tears, she closed her left eye and pulled it off.

"I need a better-quality glue," she said by way of explanation.

Reverend Toussaint, apparently used to women weeping in his office, gave her a few moments to get herself composed.

After a few more dabs at her eyes and a few sniffles, JoJo sighed.

"I'm a poor excuse for a Christian," she said.

"We are all sinners saved by grace," Reverend Toussaint said.

"If you say so."

He smiled. "I say so. So tell me. What prompts these tears? What is on your mind and heart today, Sister Josephine?"

She sat silent for a while. Then, answering a need

to get it all off her chest, she told him, as if she were in a confessional with a Catholic priest.

"I miss Ana Mae," she said. "I wish I had been a better sister to her. I don't love my husband. I want to stay here in North Carolina and live in Ana Mae's house. It's where I grew up, you know. I just don't know what I'm going to do with my life."

Reverend Toussaint patted her hand. "That's a lot going on," he said.

"Tell me about it," JoJo harrumphed, getting some of her usual aplomb back. "Since I've been here in Drapersville, I've found out more about Ana Mae than I knew in all the time she was alive. What kind of sister loses touch like that? I just wish . . ." A few additional tears sprouted, and she quickly and defiantly swiped them away.

"Josephine," he said, taking her hand, "Ana Mae loved you very much."

"How do you know?"

"Because she was always bragging about you. About all three of you. She was so proud of what you, Clayton, and Delcine accomplished in your lives."

JoJo snorted. "Accomplished? I haven't accomplished anything."

"That's where you are wrong," he said. "And I can prove it. Come with me."

He stood up and beckoned for her to follow him.

JoJo grabbed her bag and tucked the small Bible inside. She slung the heavy tote over her shoulder and followed him down the hall and into an open and colorful multipurpose room filled with about twenty or so kids sitting on blue and yellow mats on the floor.

"Hi, Reverend Toussaint!"

"Good afternoon," he said. "Your practice has been

excellent today. I even kept my office door open so I could hear you," he told the children, using the voice adults sometimes adopt when talking with elementary- and pre-school-age little ones.

"I have a visitor with me, and maybe she would like to hear your song."

The aide in the room lifted her arms, and the children scrambled up and got into a three-line formation.

"Ready," the teacher said. "On three—one, two, three."

The children, who ranged in age from about four to seven or so broke into a rousing rendition of a song in the round.

"Make new friends, but keep the old, one is silver and the other gold."

When they finished, JoJo and Reverend Toussaint both applauded.

"That was wonderful, children," he said.

"I agree," JoJo exclaimed. "I remember that song from Girl Scout camp with my sister Ana Mae."

A hush suddenly fell over the room.

One of the older children, a girl, ran forward. "You knew Miss Ana Mae?"

JoJo glanced at Reverend Toussaint, but answered the girl.

"Yes, she was my older sister. I came home for her . . . ," she paused. Death did not exactly seem like the right topic to address with kids this little. But JoJo's mouth dropped open with a little boy's next words.

"We miss her a lot," he said.

"Miss Ana Mae went to be with Jesus," a girl said.

"Yes, I . . . ," JoJo looked to the preacher and then the teacher for some guidance.

"Why don't you show Miss Ana Mae's sister the book you all wrote with Miss Ana Mae?" the teacher said.

JoJo turned to Reverend Toussaint. "Ana Mae wrote a book?"

He grinned and nodded as a little person grabbed JoJo's hand and tugged on it. JoJo followed to a table in a corner that had bookcases three shelves deep in an L along the walls. The boy pulled out a large volume on the top shelf, and a little girl guided JoJo to an adult-sized rocking chair.

"She always sat here when she read to us," the girl said. "My name is Suzy Swindle and that's my brother Joshua."

"My name is Josephine," JoJo said.

As if on cue, the class yelled, "Good afternoon, Miss Josephine."

"You're Miss Josephine?" Suzy asked eyes wide in wonder.

When JoJo nodded, the girl started jumping up and down, saying "Ooh. Ooh!"

JoJo looked to Reverend Toussaint, but Suzy was suddenly talking a mile a minute. "Ooh. I'm gonna be a dancer like you when I grow up."

The child then did a perfect pirouette for her.

"A dancer? But how did you know?" JoJo's gaze darted between the little girl's and Reverend Toussaint's.

"Granna Mae told us all about you. She said you performed for thousands of people," Suzy said. "And I told her I wanted to be a dancer too."

"I told you," Reverend Toussaint said.

Delighted, JoJo grinned.

The teacher clapped her hands twice. "Get your mats for the story," she said.

All of the children ran and grabbed their mats to settle down in front of JoJo, who was guided into the rocking chair.

Reverend Toussaint stood behind the rocking chair, and young Joshua, who had designated himself the reader, stood to her left.

"The title of this book is *The Lady Who Loved Little Kids*."

He showed the cover to all of the assembled children, and then made sure JoJo got a good look at it.

The cover was clearly drawn by someone young. Its crayon design had stick-like images of children with big smiles and colorful hair. A larger stick figure with an even bigger smile and a pouf of curly, brown-crayon hair stood behind the kids, with enormous arms wrapped around all of them.

JoJo swallowed and blinked back the sudden tears that threatened to fall again. She recognized those big arms, even when drawn in crayon. They were the very ones that so often wrapped her in big-sister love.

"That's us," one of the kids said.

"And Granna Mae is giving all of us a hug," another piped up to clarify, in case their visitor was not sure about the identities of the people.

"Granna Mae?" JoJo said, sending the question to Reverend Toussaint.

He smiled and nodded.

"She said all of the kids here were her honorary grandchildren. Those who did not have biological grandparents close by or just didn't have any at all could claim her. She always said she had plenty of love to go around."

JoJo nodded and pointed toward the book cover. "Love big enough to surround all of them like on the front of the book?"

"Exactly."

JoJo mulled that for a bit. It seemed her big sister lived a full and satisfying life here in Drapersville, a life filled with the things that JoJo had once taken for granted. And now that she didn't have them—a daughter who loved her as much as these kids adored Ana Mae, a husband she loved and who loved her, a life not encumbered by debt and regret and enough what-could-have-beens to fill a book—those were the things she wanted most.

She hoped Crystal had made a good life for herself in Laughlin. And right there, JoJo vowed to herself that she would get her daughter's address from Mr. Rollings. If Ana Mae knew it, he knew it. And nothing was going to stop JoJo from making amends with her only child.

Ana Mae had apparently died not even knowing where her own son, Howard, was. That tragedy would not be JoJo's legacy.

"Sister Josephine?"

"Huh?"

Lost in her thoughts, JoJo glanced at Reverend Toussaint.

"The story."

Her brow wrinkled for a moment, and then she remembered what they had been doing. She gave the little reader a smile, and he turned to the first page of the book.

"Once upon a time there was a lady who loved little kids."

The boy was an excellent reader. He and the others clearly knew and enjoyed this story.

"But the lady was sad," Joshua said.

He then held the picture out so all of the kids on their mats could see the stick-figure image of Ana Mae with the curly hair and a pocketbook the size of a suitcase on her arm. The expression on the face was clearly a cheerless one, and there appeared to be a big tear—or what passed for a tear when drawn by a six-year-old—rolling down her face.

"Why was she sad?" JoJo asked.

"He's coming to that part," one of the children on the floor said.

Joshua patted her hand. "Don't worry, Miss Josephine. The story has a happy ending."

She couldn't help but smile at his youthful optimism.

Maybe the story in the children's picture book had a happy ending, JoJo thought. But Ana Mae's own story didn't. Not when she was in a casket buried six feet underground over at Antioch Cemetery. Not when her only living relatives were running all over town trying to see who could claim her wealth first.

And JoJo had been daydreaming of a life without Lester in it—permanently.

Joshua continued the story.

"The lady was sad because she had no little children to love."

The boy kept reading and showing the book's illustrations. The story was a joyful tale.

"One day, she met a whole room full of children, and before long, the lady smiled all the time."

At the end of the simple tale, illustrated by several young artists, the lady was happy because she had lots of kids to love who also loved her back.

Such an uncomplicated way of looking at life, JoJo thought.

"Out of the mouths of babes," she murmured.

"Thank you, children," Reverend Toussaint said, dismissing them.

"It was nice meeting all of you," JoJo said. "Thank you for being such good friends with my sister."

The children scrambled up and replaced their mats. Several of them gave JoJo a hug and whispered words of encouragement to her.

"Don't be sad, Miss Josephine. Granna Mae is with Jesus."

"I'm glad you came to see us today."

"I miss her so much."

That one brought tears to JoJo's eyes. She hugged the girl closer and whispered back. "I miss her too, sweetie. I miss her too."

And to Suzy after a big hug, "you keep practicing that ballet, okay?"

"I will, Miss Josephine."

JoJo had not pulled into the Holy Ghost Church of the Good Redeemer's parking lot with any sort of mission in mind. But she left feeling richer for the visit.

Reverend Toussaint walked her to her car, parked next to his in the lot.

"The kids really loved Sister Ana Mae," Reverend Toussaint said. "She spent a lot of time with them, reading stories and listening to their concerns and problems. She always used to say that just because a person hasn't lived a long time doesn't mean they don't know trouble." He smiled wryly. "She was the closest thing we had to an in-house therapist. The kids really opened up to her, and I like to think she did the same to them in a way."

"What do you mean?"

He shrugged. "The young people enrolled here at the Good Redeemer Academy were, in a way, her . . . ," he paused, clearly uncomfortable.

"Her what, Reverend Toussaint? I'm trying to understand this part of my sister's life. It's important to me . . . to understand, I mean."

He nodded. "I can comprehend that," he said. "Try to remember, though, that you all—you, Delcine, and Clayton—well, you all just weren't here. Sometimes I, well, I just got the impression that you all had shut her out of your lives even though the one thing she loved more than anything in the world was you all. Whether deliberately or by accident, all of you left her. And all I know is that there was something like a hole in Ana Mae. And these children here, these precious little ones, filled up that hole in her. They were her adopted family. She called them her grandchildren of the heart."

He looked pained to have to say it, but it was something JoJo had already come to realize.

A boy, about eight, ran over to where they were standing. "Excuse me," he said.

"Did you get permission to leave the building, Dwight?" Reverend Toussaint asked sharply.

"Yes, sir. Miss Graham said it was all right just for today to come out. I needed to see you."

"All right then, son. What can we do for you?"

The boy, whose hair was in mini-dreadlocks, thrust a piece of paper at JoJo. "I made this for you, Miss Josephine."

Bewildered, JoJo accepted the proffered item. "What is it?"

"It's a picture," Dwight said. "I just drew it for you. I signed it too, just like Granna Mae told me to do on all my drawings."

JoJo's gaze fell to the lower right corner of the page and saw in neatly printed magic marker or Sharpie, DWIGHT HENDERSON. His signature was followed by the year.

"I don't want you to be sad, Miss Josephine," the boy said. "So I drew you a picture of Granna Mae. See," he said, pointing a small brown finger to a figure high up on the page.

It was then that JoJo grasped the entire image, which included a large building, grass, cars. Dwight was clearly the artist who created the cover of the picture book about Ana Mae. It was of the same stick-figure-ish woman featured prominently, except this time she was flying in the sky above a large church and school, the big purse still hanging on her arm and a grin as wide as the one on the picture book. A flowing white and purple robe replaced the floral dress. But the most important addition in the image was wings.

He'd drawn Ana Mae as an angel looking down on the Good Redeemer Academy.

19

Secrets Revealed

JoJo Futrell's visit to the Good Redeemer Academy sparked a long-forgotten memory for Reverend Toussaint. Not a man who dwelled in the past, he had no reason to believe his life would be better for the road not taken. He had done a lot of things as a younger man that, if he did not quite regret them, he would not do again, not since giving his life over to the Lord Jesus Christ. But JoJo reading that book with the children somehow brought one thing back.

Not sure he even trusted his memory on this, instead of going to his car Reverend Toussaint made his way from his office at the Holy Ghost Church of the Good Redeemer and to the now darkened multipurpose classroom. The children and teachers of the Good Redeemer Academy were gone now, and the large room, without their boisterous energy, seemed curiously barren.

For a moment, he stood in the doorway just staring, but not seeing the colorful mats stacked in a corner, the motivational posters on the wall, the shelves with neatly stored games and athletic equipment.

Instead, Toussaint le Baptiste saw the past . . .

"See, when I put this right here, it'll be a sign for everyone who sees it that my heart is taken."

"For sure?"

"For sure," he told the girl standing right next to him.

Her smooth brown skin beckoned his touch, and it was all he could do to keep his hands off of her—for now. The summer day, hot and humid with the stickiness that accompanied Southern heat, might have been unbearable except for the exquisite company. The girl—his girl—at his side.

Well, he hoped she would be. Maybe after today.

Sheathing the pocketknife he had used to carve their initials in the old oak tree, he slipped it back into the pocket of his blue jeans. The dungarees were new, ordered from the Sears, Roebuck Company catalog. He'd worn them hoping to impress her.

It worked.

She'd said he looked mighty handsome.

But she, she took his breath away, the only girl who knew that what they said about him wasn't really true—mostly.

As they stood before the tree, an ancient live oak just on the outskirts of town, he took her hand in his.

"A kiss to seal it?" he asked.

Her shy smile encouraged and emboldened him.

It also caused the erection in his jeans to swell

even more. He wanted her, but he didn't want to move too fast or do anything that might scare her off. She was special to him in so many ways.

Lifting their clasped hands, he placed them over the heart and the initials he had painstakingly carved into the tree's thick trunk. And then, leaning forward, he pressed his lips to hers.

The rockets going off in his head had nothing at all to do with the Fourth of July fireworks exploding behind and overhead.

When he finally pulled back, she was smiling at him.

They gazed into each other's eyes for what seemed an eternity before turning to the tree. Slowly their hands traced the outline of the heart and the initials within it before pulling away to reveal the tribute carved there.

"What did you find?" Clay said, sprinting to where Archer stood in Antioch Cemetery. "Is it Howard?"

Instead of answering, Archer just waited for Clayton to reach his side.

"Oh," Clayton said when he looked down. Reading the first headstone and then the one next to it in the adjoining plot, his demeanor changed from excited anticipation to somber contemplation. "Oh," he said again.

Archer lifted a hand to Clay's shoulder to offer a measure of comfort. But his hand failed to connect as Clayton squatted low for a level view of the gravestones.

Georgette Howard Futrell   Russell Clayton Futrell
Wife, mother, friend   Husband, father, wanderer
March 18, 1939–June 5, 1999   Dec. 24, 1927–Feb. 29, 1988

For long moments, Clayton didn't speak at all. Archer, silent as well, gave him the room to grieve.

"Mama said Daddy died the way he lived. On his own terms," Clayton finally said. "Only he would pick a leap year day to die."

"What's the reference to being a wanderer?" Archer asked.

Clayton rose off his haunches, smiling a little, but not with mirth.

"Daddy was what we today call a player with a capital P, or what I suppose Rosalee and Ana Mae would call a Mack Daddy. I was sixteen, about to turn seventeen when he died. I was pissed because he lived his life leaving Mama and cheating on her."

Shaking his head in disgust, Clayton said, "They had some kind of understanding. Basically it went like this: Whenever he showed up, she understood he'd be around until he left again. She welcomed him home like he hadn't been gone for six months or a year. He once went three whole years without us seeing hide nor hair of him. No postcards saying, "Hi, thinking of you." No birthday greetings, and forget about Christmas. I never did understand why she allowed him to do that to us, to her."

"Because she loved him," Archer said.

Clayton snorted.

Taking a few steps to his mother's marble head-stone, he ran a hand over the smooth stone, caressing it as if he were drawing comfort from her presence even now.

"I remember this kid, everybody called him BoBo because of the cheap shoes he wore. Anyway, he was picking on me, making fun. He said my father only stayed around long enough to knock up my mom before he disappeared and went back to his real family. I was so pissed. I told him what Mama had always told me. That my Daddy hadn't abandoned us. He was out working in a place far away, like the father on 'Good Times.' And like a fool, I believed her, and I wanted BoBo to know the truth."

"What happened?"

"He laughed in my face. Called me a faggot who believed in fairy tales. Then he beat the hell out of me."

They were quiet for a moment, Clayton reliving the pain and Archer hurting for him.

"I knew Mama would never tell me the truth, so I asked Ana Mae about it," Clayton eventually said.

"What'd she say?"

Clayton smiled and gave a little half laugh. "She told me that Daddy loved us and Mama in his own way and that he provided for us in his own way."

"Pretty cryptic for the straight-shooting Ana Mae. What did she mean?"

"I asked her that," Clayton said. "But she just smiled at me and shook her head.

"When he died, Delcine refused to come home for the funeral. She was either still in college or had just graduated, I can't remember which. JoJo and I said if she didn't have to go, we didn't have to go either. But

Mama was tore up to pieces over his death. Ana Mae sat us both down and told us no matter what we thought about Daddy, we needed to be there for Mama."

"So you went."

Clayton nodded. "And I spent the whole service looking around at the other women crying their eyes out. I wondered which one of them and her kids were my father's other family. How many half brothers and sisters I might be sitting with in that church and not even knowing. I'd never forgotten what BoBo said."

"You shouldn't torture yourself over the lives your parents lived," Archer said. "They made their own choices, ones that might not seem reasonable to us right now, but decisions that made sense to them in their own minds and time. They made their own choices, Clay."

Clayton's gaze met his partner's, and this time his laugh held good humor, even though it may have included a tinge of the self-deprecating variety. "That's the same thing Ana Mae told me."

Clayton and Archer left the cemetery with a bit more information. Three plots away from where Georgette and Russell Futrell lay buried they found the gravesite of the mysterious Howard. The stone had no first name and no last name, just Howard, 1979–2005.

Since Clayton was planning to drop Archer off at the inn and then to go back out to see Jeremy Fisher again, he was behind the wheel of their rental.

"Well, at least we got that Howard thing solved," he said. "He died at twenty-six. Young. And the right age to be Emily Daniels's much younger lover. The nephew I never knew I had."

"Hmm," Archer said.

"What?"

"If that was Ana Mae's son buried there, why was he so far away from the rest of the family? Your parents were right next to each other."

"Oh, he was with family," Clayton said. "That whole area, about ten graves on each side, was family—older cousins, mostly Mama's generation, a couple of aunts, and their husbands and their kids. We didn't really know them. A lot of them had moved away from North Carolina. They went north to New York and Philadelphia for jobs and better lives. But they wanted to come home to be buried."

"When I die," Archer said, "please cremate me and spread my ashes in the sea, preferably off Carmel."

Clayton gave him a look. "Don't even play like that, Archer. We are going to live forever."

⌇

After dropping off Archer, Clayton went out to the Fisher place. He was stunned to see Delcine getting out of her car.

When she saw him, she flushed and then scowled and yanked the strap of her small shoulder bag.

"What are you doing here?" she demanded, as she slammed closed her car door.

"I could ask the same of you," he said, pocketing his keys.

Delcine sighed, her shoulders slumping. "I, well, I had a few more questions for Jeremy."

No way was she going to admit to her wealthy younger brother that she was here to try to play on Jeremy Fisher's memory of Ana Mae in order to get money from him to cover her financial situation. Delcine's pride wouldn't allow her to take that step. She would rather grovel at a stranger's feet than divulge to her baby brother that she—well, her husband—had completely screwed up her life.

"Funny, so did I," Clayton said slapping his thigh with a booklet he was holding. "We must be thinking along the same lines."

I doubt it, Delcine thought.

Indicating the booklet, she asked Clayton, "What's that?"

"The annual report. There's something I want Jeremy to explain," he said, heading toward the garage. "Come on."

No Aerosmith or any other rock music blasted the air, and they quickly realized they needed to try the house.

As they made their way to the front door, Delcine, not at all comfortable with Clayton knowing something she didn't, again asked, "So what is it you want to know from Jeremy?"

"Just some questions that came to mind from the annual report of the Zorin Corporation."

Clayton rang the doorbell as Delcine fanned herself with one hand.

"David Bell's company? The one in Ohio? He already told us about Jeremy."

"Something doesn't add up," Clayton said. "I figured going straight to the source could clear up the confusion."

Other than Ana Mae having so much money, Delcine couldn't think of any confusion.

The door opened, and Nell Fisher beamed up at them. "Clayton, Delcine—I mean Marguerite—how wonderful to see you again. Come in, please. Get out of the heat."

She backed up in the wheelchair, and the Futrells followed her inside the blessedly cool house. Nell led them into the same great room she'd entertained them in during their last visit.

"Call me Delcine."

Nell smiled. "Thank you. I know you prefer the other, but Ana Mae always called you Delcine."

"You just missed Jeremy," she added. "He had to go to Texas to meet with a supplier. Is there something I can do for you?"

Delcine sighed at the news that Jeremy wasn't home. But Clayton stepped up. He held out the Zorin Corporation's annual report to its shareholders.

"I was reading through this and noticed that Jeremy is on the board of directors. Ana Mae was also affiliated with the company," he said. "Her picture is even right here on the cover with David Bell, Zorin's CEO."

Nell beamed. "He's such a nice man. It's a shame about his son, though. But Ana Mae was helping him work through that. They were very close, you know."

"We know," Delcine said.

Mano the robot came in then, again bearing a cart. This time it held a pitcher of lemonade.

After refreshments were served, Clayton tried to get Nell Fisher back on point.

"How did Jeremy end up on the board of Zorin?"

Nell waved a manicured hand. "Oh, that was part of the deal," she said.

"The deal? What deal?" Delcine asked.

For a moment, Nell looked confused. "The deal," she said. "When Zorin bought out Fisher Innovative Solutions, Jeremy secured two six-year terms on the board and, of course, an equity stake in the company.

They offered a one-term board position to me and to Ana Mae as well, but neither one of us wanted that kind of responsibility."

"Oh, my God," Delcine said, the pieces finally coming together. And judging from Clayton's expression when he glanced over at her, he got it too.

"How much did Jeremy's company go for?" he asked.

Nell leaned forward in her wheelchair and grinned at Clayton and Delcine. "Can you believe they paid almost twenty million dollars for a little gadget company that started right outside in what used to be our garage?"

Delcine gasped.

"They initially offered twelve million, but Jeremy held firm. He got an M.B.A. at Chapel Hill, you know. And he knew both the value of Fisher Innovative Solutions and what it was worth. So he held out, and they met his number. He got the bulk of it—in cash," she said. "Since Ana Mae and I were just minority shareholders, we both just got almost five million and some stock options."

Overwhelmed, Delcine sat back in her chair, her mouth agape. Clayton's guess had been right.

Nell giggled like a teenager. "I say 'just' as if either of us expected anything like that much money to come out of that mop-and-bucket caddy or any of Jeremy's other little things he made for me and Ana Mae. Neither of us was complaining, though. Ana Mae and I were too busy laughing and crying together."

It was not until later that night—much later, as she lay in the bunk bed of her youth in the house where Ana Mae had lived her entire life—that it dawned on

JoJo. She got up and padded to the kitchen, where she'd left her booklet from Mr. Rollings with all of the quilt blocks reproduced in it. She looked at the picture of the quilt and then flipped to the page with the seventh block on it.

With just the light from the stove to illuminate the room, she saw it, and she smiled. She knew she now possessed the secret of the seventh block on the quilt. The image Ana Mae created in fabric and thread was of Jesus with little children. By embracing the children, the least of them, Ana Mae followed the example he set.

That was the secret of the quilt block. It may even be the secret of the whole thing, JoJo thought. The treasure she was already getting was that she got to know her big sister better, even though Ana Mae was gone now. And she'd had some time to get to know Clayton and Delcine. The three of them had never been particularly close, but now, as adults, they were discovering plenty of shared memories that made their growing-up years in Drapersville seem not quite as bad as remembered.

There had been good times and good moments.

Lester thought they were looking for a hidden or buried treasure. JoJo now realized that her sister . . . it was Ana Mae who was the treasure.

JoJo smiled.

Closing the booklet, she placed it on the kitchen table and made her way back to bed humming a Sunday school song she recalled from her youth: "Jesus loves the little children, all the children of the world."

And so did Ana Mae.

In Ana Mae's bedroom, Delcine held a heated but whispered mobile phone conversation with Winslow.

"It's not that easy," she hissed. "And since you have failed to in any way come up with a plan to get us out of this mess, staying here to get the money is the only way I see out of the problem."

She listened to her husband for a moment, and then grunted.

"That's easy enough for you to say, Win. What do you think is going to happen to all of those memberships when your face is plastered on the six o'clock news, huh? Did you think of that? I already cannot bear the thought of what's being said behind my back at my women's club. We're probably laughingstocks already."

She was silent for a moment as Winslow countered. Then, "Fine!" she yelled. "Fine. Do whatever the hell you want to do."

She threw the cell phone across the room and heard a clunk as it hit the dresser. A moment later, a soft knock came at the door.

"Great," Delcine muttered. "Just great." Then, louder, "I'm fine, JoJo."

But Delcine was anything but fine, and the tears she had refused to shed all of these months came gushing down like water from a levee breached in a hurricane.

"Delcine?"

JoJo pushed the door open a bit. She saw the state her older sister was in and went into the bathroom. She returned with a length of toilet paper that she handed to Delcine.

Sitting on the edge of the bed, she waited for the tears to subside.

"I'm okay," Delcine sniffled. "You can leave now."

"No, I won't. And no, you're not okay."

Delcine sighed heavily, then wiped at her eyes and blew her nose. "When did you get so bossy?"

"I took lessons from you."

The words could have been harsh, uttered with the disdain and condescension Delcine usually meted out on others. But there was a note of compassion in JoJo's voice, and fresh tears fell from the woman who, as Marguerite, was cultured, wealthy, confident, assured, and more than a bit bitchy. Delcine was a skinny and poor black girl from the country. In less than a week, Marguerite had disappeared, and Delcine had taken over the life she once knew . . . and cherished.

"My life is a lie," Delcine said.

JoJo tucked one leg under the other at the end of the bed.

Without her makeup and the power suits and designer dresses, Delcine looked vulnerable, like the sister JoJo remembered her being before they became virtual strangers.

Sensing that this was a time to listen rather than a time to talk, she, for once, just waited. Whatever Delcine decided to share, she would in her own time and way.

The wait did not take long.

"Winslow and I are broke," Delcine said.

Of all the things she had expected to hear, that was not among them. JoJo anticipated news of an affair—on Win's part, since she didn't think Delcine had any passion in her at all. Broke was something else entirely. Something that JoJo could relate to. But before JoJo could respond, Delcine continued.

"And when I say, broke, I don't mean we just can't

afford to go on one of our elaborate or extended vacations to Europe or send Cedric and Latrice to private school. We're bankrupt, JoJo. Literally. The house is being foreclosed on next week."

JoJo gasped.

That mansion in their super-fancy neighborhood? The one JoJo had never been invited to but had found pictures of online?

Wow. Double wow.

"What happened?"

The question came out before she could stop herself.

But Delcine either didn't hear or more likely deigned not to answer and instead just fiddled with a piece of the toilet paper, twisting it around her finger.

"And if that's not bad enough, or embarrassing enough, Winslow is about to be indicted."

"Indicted? Oh, my God. What did he do?"

Delcine snorted, a most unladylike sound that under different circumstances might have amused JoJo. "What didn't he do is the better question."

She stared at the wall for a moment, her lips quivering, and a moment later the tears were falling again.

JoJo, at a loss for how to relate to this Delcine, sat there for a moment. Then she did what her instincts prompted her to do. She gathered her sister in her arms and let her cry.

The two sat like that for a while, JoJo rocking and holding Delcine, while the older of the two alternated between wails and sniffles.

"What the hell is going on in here? What's all this noise?"

Lester appeared in the doorway, wearing a white T-shirt and boxers.

"Go away, Lester."

The nearly identical command from both women made him frown and the sisters look at each other.

A moment later, they both fell backward on the bed laughing as the years between them rolled away.

"Too much damn estrogen in this house," Lester muttered as he walked away.

Clayton snuggled closer to Archer on their king-size bed at the inn. With several plump pillows at his back, Archer was sitting up, and Clayton lounged casually, using Archer as his pillow. Both men were bare chested but wearing matching blue-cotton pajama pants—one of Archer's purchases from earlier in the day.

It was the time late in the evening when work was done—the laptop computer closed and files put aside; the novels, one on each nightstand, forgotten for now with pages book-marked for later, when the storyline of a thriller, Archer's, or a literary classic, Clayton's, would again beckon.

Now, however, quiet time ruled.

"I'm glad you found Mama and Daddy's graves. I wouldn't have known where to begin looking," Clayton said. Then, "We learned a lot today."

Archer, his fingers idly caressing Clayton's chest, murmured a sound that could have been assent or disagreement, depending on the interpretation.

"What?" Clayton said.

When Archer failed to respond, Clayton twisted a bit to see his partner's face. Then, so that he wasn't contorted on the bed, he hitched himself over a bit, pulled one of the pillows from behind Archer and, lying on his stomach, folded his arms under it.

"What did that sound mean?"

Archer took a moment to stretch and then re-arranged the pillows at his back, tossing a couple of them toward the foot of the big bed as he got himself settled.

He had come to a couple of conclusions. Factoring in what he already knew—and continued to keep from Clayton—his suppositions now seemed to have even more merit than ever. What initially seemed preposterous to him had to now be viewed in a different light. A much different light.

"Did it strike you as odd that the good reverend was at the cemetery today?"

Clayton, his head resting on his pillow, said, "Not particularly. Maybe there was a funeral or something."

"There was no funeral," Archer said.

Clayton looked up. "And you know this because . . ."

"Because there weren't any of those tents or chairs or even any flowers on any graves to indicate a service had recently ended. He was there specifically in the place he wanted to be."

That made Clayton sit up, propping up on one elbow.

"He was at Ana Mae's gravesite."

Archer lifted a brow and regarded Clayton. "Yes, he was."

When Archer didn't say anything else, Clayton sighed. "Oh, all right. I'll play along. This is one of those lawyer things of yours where I'm supposed to figure out what seems so readily evident or apparent to the legal eagle?"

Archer smiled. "No. It's not a lawyer thing. Of mine or anybody else's. What it is, at least to me, is curious."

"How so?"

"Why was he at Ana Mae's grave today?"

"Paying respects, I figure," Clayton said.

"Why?"

Clayton groaned and flipped over onto his back. "Come on, Arch. I'm too tired for the mental games."

Since Archer was in no position to make any assumptions or break a confidence, he decided to let it go—for now. He might do a bit of his own investigating tomorrow. In the meantime, with Clayton clearly so amenable, he had another far better idea of how they should spend the next hour or so.

Archer splayed a hand on his partner's bare chest, then let that hand wander in a leisurely southern direction. "Then how about another type of game?"

When the giggling finally subsided, JoJo and Delcine were on Ana Mae's bed facing each other.

"I never did thank you," Delcine said.

That surprised JoJo.

"Thank me? For what?"

"For keeping in touch through the years," Delcine said. "You remember my birthday and the kids'. That's very nice, especially since I know I have been less than . . . ," she paused for a moment, searching for the right word. "Sisterly," she finally said.

JoJo shrugged.

"None of us was ever really close," she said. "At least not after we grew up. With Mama and Daddy gone, there just wasn't anything to keep us tied to this place."

"Ana Mae stayed," Delcine pointed out.

"Yes, she did. But Ana Mae, she was different than

us. She always was. Like even though she was older, at least so much older than me, she always was so . . ."

"Grounded?"

"Yeah," JoJo said. "Rooted here. Like she was just born to be here. In Drapersville. Like the rest of the country or anywhere else just never appealed to her—never even occurred to her."

"Well," Delcine said, "we know from David Bell that *something* in Ohio appealed to her."

JoJo chuckled at that one. "You really think he's her son's father?"

"I don't see how it could be anybody else. The man was, as the kids say, tore up from the floor up at the funeral, and you heard him on the phone," Delcine said sitting up and tucking one leg under the other on the bed. "Ana Mae was his heart and soul. And he's estranged from his twenty-something-year-old son. Ana Mae didn't know where her son was. I think Mr. Bell is the same man and that we should just give up this foolishness of suspecting every man in town who is about the right age of being her secret child."

JoJo made a sound that could have been agreement.

In her years in Las Vegas, although she had spent many of them as a performer, JoJo had also learned how to tend bar. For a while after losing her last gig, bartending was the way she paid the bills. That experience let her know that Delcine might be taking the long way around but would eventually get back to the topic of her troubled marriage and their dire financial state.

It didn't take as long as she thought it might.

"Who would have thought that of the four of us, Ana Mae would be the one with all the money?" Delcine asked.

"What do you mean?"

Delcine sat up and scooted back, bracing herself against the headboard of Ana Mae's double bed.

"Clay's a successful doctor, married to a successful lawyer . . ."

"Isn't it a little odd to think of them as being married? I mean married like, like a man and a woman married. Is it like two husbands or is Clay the wife?"

That earned a little snort-laugh from Delcine. "I suppose it works just like any other relationship."

JoJo nodded. "I'm glad he found Archer. They're a good couple."

"Unlike the matches we made."

This time it was JoJo who snorted. "Exactly. I was hoping to dump Lester. All I needed to do was save up enough money to pay a lawyer. I'll never get rid of him now that he knows there are millions of dollars in play that he could possibly lay claim to. That's why he argued so hard to get us back in the hunt after I lost the quilt."

Delcine sighed. "With us, I hate to admit it and am even embarrassed to say, it wasn't love that brought us together. Winslow and I have always been strategic partners. It made sense professionally and socially for us to marry.

"For him, a loving wife and two perfect children all but ensured that he would be on the right side of the equation at promotion time and in power-networking situations. On the surface, where many if not most of the Beltway's married populace reside, all is well. Underneath, though . . . ," Delcine said, drawing up her knees and wrapping her hands around them on the bed, ". . . underneath the façade, all it is is deception and regret and infidelity."

"He cheated on you?" JoJo asked.

Delcine shook her head. "Not the way you're probably thinking, but in essence, yes. He cheated and got caught. Or will just as soon as that grand jury indictment is handed down."

"What did he do?" JoJo asked, repeating the question that when asked earlier sent her older sister on an extended crying jag.

"It is all rather complicated—not to mention convoluted, if you ask me—but it boils down to influence peddling and kickbacks on housing projects. There's also been something in the paper about budget allocations, but I swear, we haven't seen a penny in any extra or unaccounted-for income."

"What about your house, the foreclosure situation, I mean?" JoJo said.

"Unless about thirty-five grand materializes in the next few days . . . ," Delcine sighed, then closed her eyes. "I don't even have a backup plan. I should be at home packing or something, but . . ."

"Like me, you're hoping for a financial miracle."

It may have been the bleakly wistful tone in her voice, or maybe it was just the words, but Delcine reached for her sister's hands. "Bad stuff going on with you too?"

JoJo nodded.

Then she held out her left hand and wiggled her fingers. "I had to pawn my wedding and engagement rings just to afford the fare to get here for Ana Mae's funeral. There's gonna be no divorcing Lester and no getting away as long as there's a chance I could claim any of Ana Mae's money."

For a few moments, neither of the Futrell sisters said

anything, each woman lost in her own dismal thoughts about her marriage and her financial situation.

Then Delcine, again adopting the airs she usually assumed, said, "We need to go see Mr. Rollings tomorrow and end this quilt treasure-hunt farce."

"You've solved all nine blocks?" JoJo asked.

A steely resolve—or maybe it was blind ambition with a double shot of greed and that snooty air of entitlement—filled Delcine's eyes. She smiled, but it was once again one of those condescending smile-snarls that set JoJo's teeth on edge.

Marguerite was back, and the Delcine of yester-year had been squashed beyond recognition.

With a confident jut of her chin, Marguerite declared, "I have all the information I need to lay claim to the inheritance left by Ana Mae."

20

The Gathering

Rollings had not anticipated hearing from the Futrell siblings for quite a while. Since the debacle with that idiot Lester digging up the backyard, he had kept pretty close tabs on the comings and goings of the Futrells and their significant others.

Winslow Foster, the one who never said much, had scurried back to Maryland or Washington, D.C., leaving his wife to mourn—or celebrate—on her own. The gay lawyer spent most of his days shopping, and a word to County Sheriff Dan Daughtry had ensured that the sleazy one from Las Vegas didn't stir up any trouble in Drapersville, Ahoskie, or anywhere else in the county. Something about that one just set wrong with Rollings and the sheriff. So keeping tabs on Lester Coston just made good sense.

"Dad?"

"In here, son."

Rollings was proud of his son, as proud as a father could be. He would one day inherit the law firm, the mortuary services business, and the other enterprises that the Rollings family had built from nothing and groomed until they thrived. He, of course, had had help. And so would his son. All Trey had to do was keep his nose clean and his mouth shut.

The latter, so far, had proven less of a concern than Rollings anticipated. Trey quickly and early on figured out the benefits of keeping some family secrets within the family. In both the legal and the death industries, perception counted for a lot. If you looked the part, people tended to believe what their eyes told them. Rarely did anyone delve deeper. And for lo these many years, that had been to Rollings's advantage.

"Thank you, Ana Mae," he murmured as Trey came in.

This morning, Rollings worked on the legal side of the street. Buttoned down in his uniform—three-piece suit, conservative tie, and wing tips—he approved of Trey's wardrobe choices for the day.

Tall like his father, Trey sported the blue blazer and gray slacks and shirt of a mortuary intern. Although he had completed law school—Wake Forest, of course—and passed the North Carolina state bar exam in a top percentile, Trey's education was not yet complete.

Another young man may have balked at the very notion of remaining in a small North Carolina town that some called backward to learn the family funeral business once he had the impressive legal credentials to work at any large firm of his choosing, but Trey Rollings's temperament did not run along those lines. He got that passivity from his mother. It was one trait, along with her fair complexion and eye color, that Rollings sometimes wished were not stamped on him. While nothing could be done about the skin, brown contact lenses took care of the eyes.

But all in all, he remained pleased with his son. He just needed to keep Trey otherwise occupied while the Futrells were all in town and talking to Ana Mae's friends. The faster they got done with Ana Mae's little venture, the faster Rollings could again breathe easy. For all of these years, no one to Rollings's knowledge had ever suspected anything. And if they did, they'd kept it to themselves.

"I was just passing through," Trey said. "Maria said to tell you Mrs. Marguerite Foster called. She and her brother and sister would like to see you as soon as possible."

Rollings briefly wondered if Ana Mae had somehow heard and acted on his request. If the Futrells wanted to meet, they were probably ready to present their findings.

"Thank you, Trey. How are things going on the other side?"

Trey Rollings lounged against the doorjamb. "Good, really good, actually. We're going out to the Campbell's in about twenty minutes. They want to have a memorial service in their backyard instead of here or in a church. We're going to see what we need to do to facilitate that."

Rollings nodded. "Be sure to suggest the cooling misters along with the large tent. It will be hot, and if they plan on anything longer than fifteen or twenty minutes, it will be pretty much unbearable out there."

"Cha-ching."

"Trey. Decorum, please."

"It's just us, Dad. And besides, that is why you're suggesting those misters."

His son had him there.

When it came to profits and making money, Trey had inherited his father's skills and none of his biological mother's indifference to money, even though she was rolling in it these days. Trey's biological mother was content with life's basics, tending to her garden or just watching the day go by without accomplishing a single thing. It had been a while since he'd visited Nell Fisher. Their sons looked nothing alike, which helped in the complicated agreement Rollings, his wife, and Nell had come to all those years ago: Nell would raise Jeremy as her only son, and the Rollingses would raise Trey.

While his sons knew of each other, they lived separate lives—one family in Ahoskie and the other in Drapersville.

Ana Mae had known his secret. And to this day, Rollings didn't know if she'd sussed it out on her own or if Nell had told her. If he were given to bets, he'd put money on the former. Ana Mae had been a wise woman, and he knew she had reason to relate.

"Dad? You all right?"

Rollings blinked. He focused in on Trey, leaving the past where it belonged.

"I'm fine," he said. "I'm fine. Make sure you highly recommend the misters to the Campbells."

The profit margin would be slim enough on the Campbell funeral, so they would need to increase it on value-enhanced services. In this case, though, those cooling misters would be true value added as the family and friends of Reed Campbell said their farewells to him. It was one of those hot summer days that made a person just want to sit under the cool shade of a big tree with an icy pitcher of sweet tea at the ready.

The image reminded him of another summer, one long before Trey was conceived, and the cool sweet tea he enjoyed with a special girl . . .

The swing on the front porch could hold three people, but two could cozily share it. He liked spending time with her. She had a way of making him feel important. She believed in him when few others thought he would ever amount to much, given his humble background. They were a lot alike in that regard, but she had two parents who loved her even though her daddy wasn't always around much.

The other thing he liked about her was that Ana Mae could keep a secret. They had never been lovers. She knew she wasn't his type. But they had been close, practically best friends, way back then before their lives took separate paths. Everett went on to study law and mortuary science. Ana Mae took after her mother and became a domestic. She'd gone to her grave still keeping his secrets, and in return, he kept hers.

"Hey, Dad? You all right?"

Rollings blinked again, then shook off the reverie. "I'm fine, son. I am just fine. You should get along now or you won't have much time for lunch before the Campbell family consultation."

"All right. See you later," Trey said, departing.

Rollings watched him go and continued to stare at the spot where Trey had stood long after he'd left the office.

Sitting back in his chair, he steepled his hands, resting his chin on the point where his fingers met. He sat that way for a bit in quiet contemplation, and then, as if speaking to someone right in the understated but luxurious law office with him, he said, "Just like your son Howard, my boys—both of my boys, Jeremy and Trey—turned out to be good young men," he told the empty room. "All three of them are good men, Ana Mae. I'm really, really proud of all of them."

Rosalee Jenkins couldn't get off work until two o'clock. She hadn't had a chance to talk to Reverend Toussaint about what she'd discovered while rummaging through the old archives at the *Drapersville Times & Review*. She had been stunned to discover that the paper had that sort of information, let alone published it. That no one remembered it she found even more remarkable.

Then again, a whole lot was going on across the country back then. So much bad stuff on the TV and on the front pages of not just big-city papers like the *News & Observer* out of Charlotte or the *Atlanta Journal Constitution* farther south. Even the Northern papers like the *Washington Post* and the *New York Times* were paying a lot of attention.

It would have been easy, not to mention likely, that somebody would have overlooked a little item like that in a small-town weekly paper. If Rosalee hadn't been specifically looking for it, she would have missed it too.

She wanted to tell Reverend Toussaint what she'd found, but it didn't look like she would be able to before the meeting at Everett Rollings's office. Apparently, one of the Futrells was ready to claim the money.

When Rosalee arrived at the Rollings and Associates law office, everyone was there already—all of the heirs who were at that first gathering, which seemed so very long ago but actually took place just a little more than a week earlier.

JoJo and Lester. Clayton and his boyfriend, husband, man. Delcine, in another one of her don't–even–think-about-messing–with-me power suits, but not her husband.

Someone over at the barbershop said they spotted him in that big Lincoln headed toward the interstate a day or so ago. Since no one had seen hide nor hair of him since and they'd checked out of their hotel, the odds were that Delcine was gonna lose the race to claim Ana Mae's money.

Although it didn't seem pertinent to her—interesting, but not pertinent—the information Rosalee found over at the newspaper office would help Ana Mae's longtime friend Toussaint le Baptiste the most.

Reverend Toussaint wore a rather dazed expression on his face. Occupying a chair at the foot end of the table, he had his Bible with him, and his hands were clasped together as if in prayer on top of the holy book. He seemed riveted by Ana Mae's quilt, which was again on display near the head of the table.

Next to the reverend sat a smug-looking and -acting Delcine. She came across as if she had all of the answers and would dare anyone to say differently. In an empty chair between JoJo and her sister were their purses; Delcine's big and expensive designer bag—one of those numbers that cost an amount of money any normal person would use to pay three or four months' worth of rent—and JoJo's knockoff, an identical bag to the one Rosalee saw at the flea market not too long ago.

As usual, JoJo was in something too tight and too short, and her eye makeup had been applied with a too-heavy hand.

JoJo's husband, Lester, prowled the conference room, looking at the books, staring at the fish, and pausing every now and then to scowl at either his wife or the quilt. He probably thought his slicked-back hair gave him a cool, Rat Pack look. What it screamed, at least to Rosalee, was hide your purse and your car keys or they might mysteriously turn up missing.

What JoJo saw in that loser was beyond Rosalee—or any of the folks over at Junior's Bar and Grille or at the barbershop.

As she moved toward the empty chair next to Clayton's gorgeous man, Archer, Rosalee greeted the room.

"Hey, everybody."

Clayton nodded at her. Delcine didn't even look in her direction, and Rosalee couldn't be sure if Reverend Toussaint had even heard her.

"Hi, Rosalee," JoJo said.

Archer smiled at her and rose. He pulled the chair out for Rosalee and got her settled.

"Thank you," she said, a little surprised and flattered at the attention from such a good-looking man, even if he was a blond-haired, blue-eyed white boy.

Before Rosalee could spend any more time thinking about Archer, Everett Rollings came in.

"Good afternoon," he said. "Thank you all for gathering on such short notice."

His assistant, the ever-efficient and mostly silent Maria, came in, handed Rollings a manila file and a remote control, and then slipped out just as quietly. Rollings pulled out the chair at the head of the table near the quilt stand.

"Mr. Coston, if you'd have a seat, please, we can begin."

For just a moment, it seemed Lester might protest. Apparently deciding to keep it cool, he headed around the table toward a seat near his wife. A glance at JoJo quelled that notion, though. He took the chair across from Delcine and between the Reverend and Clayton.

"I understand that you have succeeded in your quest," Rollings said.

"What we have succeeded in," Delcine said, as usual taking the role of spokeswoman for the family, "is deciding to end this little farce. We have spent the better part of a week running around this godforsaken town talking to people who knew Ana Mae. What that exercise has gotten us is precious little except wasted time."

"On the contrary, Delcine," Clayton said, leaning forward and bracing his elbows on the table, his hands clasped. "I've learned more about Ana Mae this week since she's been gone than I ever did while she was alive."

"I did, too," JoJo said quietly. "I met and talked to a lot of her friends."

Delcine's brows knit. "Friends? When?"

JoJo glanced at Reverend Toussaint, whose attention was on Clayton. "What I learned," she said, "is that she lived her life with honor and integrity. That's something we should all try to do."

She directed the word *all* specifically toward her husband, who frowned at her.

"What?" Lester said.

"Shut up, Lester." The simultaneous exclamations came from JoJo and Delcine.

"Now you two wait just one . . ."

Rollings held up a hand. "That's enough," he said. "Mr. Coston, Mr. Futrell-Dahlgren, and Mrs. Jenkins, you are here as guests of the four principal heirs. You can be uninvited as easily as you were invited."

Lester sat back in a huff. He wasn't happy, but he also wasn't going to let his mouth . . . or his wife . . . cheat him out of his share of three point eight mil.

Rollings nodded toward Clayton. "Dr. Futrell, you were saying?"

Clay let his hands drop to the top of the table. "My sister was a remarkable woman, Mr. Rollings. That's something I believe you already knew. She possessed a generous spirit and a grace that is uncommon today."

"That's true," JoJo said. "Reverend le Baptiste will probably know where the Scripture is in the Bible, but Ana Mae was just like the virtuous woman."

"The virgin woman? Wasn't that Jesus' mother or wife or something?"

Five sets of eyes turned Lester's way, each gaze displaying varying degrees of incredulity and contempt.

Lester held up both of his hands in surrender, then ran his fingers across his mouth in his familiar zipping-it-shut motion.

"Thank you," JoJo muttered, with a glare across the table at her husband. She then turned her attention back to Rollings, while also glancing at the minister for confirmation. "The virtuous woman was worth more than rubies. Isn't that right, Reverend le Baptiste?"

He nodded. "You're correct, Sister Josephine." He opened his Bible and was flipping through to the citation even as he told them the Scripture reference. "In the book of Proverbs in the Old Testament is where you'll find it," he said. "Proverbs 31, starting with the tenth verse and going to the thirty-first. Who can find a *virtuous woman? for her price is far above rubies."*

JoJo nodded. "That's it," she said. "That was Ana Mae. It goes on and on listing all of the things a virtuous woman does for her family and for her friends. Ana Mae was just like it's described in the Bible. That's what I found out about our sister this week."

"Strength and honor are her clothing," Reverend Toussaint said, still reading from his Bible. *"And she shall rejoice in time to come. She openeth her mouth with wisdom; and in her tongue is the law of kindness.* That's from verses twenty-five and twenty-six."

"Amen," JoJo intoned.

Archer looked at Clayton with a raised eyebrow but, apparently remembering Mr. Rollings's admonition, refrained from saying anything.

Reverend Toussaint, his head still in his Bible, kept reading, "A little later on is something else you should hear. *Favour is deceitful, and beauty is vain: but a woman that feareth the Lord, she shall be praised.* May the Lord add a special blessing to the hearers of his word."

Lester rolled his eyes.

Rollings nodded as if he were a college professor eliciting responses to a query from a less-than-enthusiastic hall of undergraduates. "Anything else, Mrs. Coston?"

JoJo nodded. "I just wanted to thank Reverend le Baptiste for yesterday."

That got Lester stirring again. "Yesterday? What happened with her yesterday?" His suspicious gaze flicked over the preacher.

"He showed me around the school at the church

and I met some of the . . . ," she paused, and then JoJo smiled. "I met some of Ana Mae's good friends."

"Was there anything else you would like to add, Mrs. Coston or Dr. Futrell?"

They both shook their heads.

"Mrs. Foster?"

"I think this week was an enormous waste of time and energy," Delcine said.

Rollings neither agreed nor disagreed with the surly comment. "Reverend?"

Reverend Toussaint cleared his throat. He made a production of closing his Bible and then pushing it a few inches to the side. He rose then and walked from one side of the table to the other.

"In all my years in ministry," he said, as if warming up for what could likely be a protracted sermon, "rarely have I come across a situation like this. I have counseled people from all walks of life. And I have performed many a wedding, baptism, and funeral. But never," he said, moving toward Ana Mae's quilt at the head of the table, "never have I had the death of a church member affect me so profoundly."

Rollings scooted his chair back to give Reverend Toussaint some room.

The minister stood in front of *The Legacy of Ana Mae Futrell* for a moment, as if mesmerized by the skill and creativity that the quilter put into the project.

"Ana Mae Futrell was a virtuous woman," he said. "She was a good woman who always believed in doing the right thing—even at her own personal cost, and even when doing the right thing may not have seemed at all like the right thing to do."

He stared at the quilt, and then reached out a hand to trace the flowers and the leaves surrounding the big tree at the heart and center of the quilt block on the bottom row.

"I know what this quilt means, Mr. Rollings. Both Josephine and Clayton were right in what they said, but I know what Ana Mae was trying to especially say. I know what else she wanted conveyed to all of the people in this room."

Rosalee held up her hand like a pupil in a classroom.

"Yes, Mrs. Jenkins?" Rollings said.

"Mr. Rollings, before this goes any further, I need to speak with the reverend. In private," she added.

Reverend Toussaint turned from his study of the needlework to Rosalee. "You need to speak with me?"

"Yes, Reverend." She looked toward Rollings for permission.

He nodded, and Rosalee scooted her chair back and hopped up before Archer could again play Sir Gallant.

Rosalee led Reverend Toussaint out of the conference room. When the door closed behind them, Delcine was the first to speak.

"Now that those two, neither of whom is any blood relation to Ana Mae, are gone, can you please tell us how her money is going to be divided?"

Impassive as always, Rollings looked at her. "The same way as was outlined following your sister's funeral, Mrs. Foster. Ana Mae decreed that the person who deciphers the meaning of her quilt will receive the inheritance she left."

"I should have taken the ten grand," JoJo said.

"That's crazy talk," Lester said. He chanced a glance in Rollings's direction as if daring the man to try to keep him quiet again. "There's millions at stake for us."

"Wrong, Lester. There's no us in this."

He slammed a hand on the table. "Don't even try to cut me out now, Josephine. If it hadn't been for me a week ago saving your ass after you threw away that piece of whatever the hell it is," he said indicating the quilt on the stand. "If it hadn't been for me bargaining us back into the game, you wouldn't have a leg to stand on."

"This is not a game, Lester. It's about my sister."

"JoJo?"

The quiet query came from Archer.

She glanced at her brother-in-law.

"If you need it," Archer said, "you have representation."

"Representation? What the hell does that mean?" Lester demanded.

He ran a hand through his hair, and then the light apparently dawned in his none-too-bright head.

"Don't even pull that shit on me!"

"Mr. Coston," Rollings said.

"Don't you Mr. Coston me," Lester said. "That fag over there is telling my wife to divorce me. Probably so he can get a hold of more of Annie Mae's money."

"Her name was Ana Mae." That deadly quiet clarification came from Delcine.

"And you, you're just a stuck-up bitch who wouldn't know . . ."

The door to the conference room opened then, and a man whose occupation could only be bouncer or bodyguard entered.

"Hello, Clyde. Mr. Coston, I warned you about your standing and presence here. You have violated the goodwill of this law firm. Please vacate the premises," Rollings said quietly.

Getting red in the face, Lester stood his ground. "I'm not going any damn where as long as she thinks she's gonna take my money."

Rollings nodded toward his employee standing near the open door. The bodyguard-cum-bouncer took two steps forward and toward Lester.

Sizing up the man, Lester took a step back. Six feet eight or so inches of muscle and sinew demanded some respect.

"This isn't over, JoJo," Lester bellowed. "You are not cheating me out of that money. It's mine. You hear that, you fat cow. It's mine!"

The bodyguard grabbed for his arm, but Lester yanked away, stomping out of the office. "You'll be hearing from my fucking lawyer. That's for damn sure, JoJo."

"Go to hell, Lester." JoJo didn't even sound weary.

"I'll see you there, you bitch. Get off of me, you son of a . . ."

In the conference room, they heard the word *bitch,* but it was muffled, as if Lester suddenly needed air to breathe rather than to hurl empty threats and insults.

"I think I'll be needing that representation, Archer."

"You've got it, sis. Pro bono."

She smiled at him, then ducked her head and swiped at a tear she hoped no one saw.

A moment later, though, Delcine pressed a tissue into her hand while exchanging places with the purses that had been in the chair between them. Delcine remained seated next to JoJo.

By the time Reverend Toussaint and Rosalee returned, the atmosphere in the conference room had lost much of its toxicity.

Clayton had taken the position before the quilt, studying Ana Mae's needlework. JoJo and Delcine sat together in a position that indicated they were or had been either crying together or comforting each other. And Archer hovered over the back of their chairs as if protecting them from some unseen harm.

"What happened to Lester?" Rosalee asked.

"He's departed," Mr. Rollings said.

He did not elaborate.

Instead, Rollings looked up at Reverend Toussaint. "Are the two of you prepared to continue?"

The minister eyed Rollings, the look not as benevolent as one might expect, but Reverend Toussaint only nodded.

Rosalee and Reverend Toussaint took their seats, along with Archer, who remained on the side of the table with the sisters.

"I was just reiterating to Mrs. Foster and the others that the terms of Ana Mae's last will and testament have not in any way changed since last week. The person who will ultimately claim Miss Futrell's estate is the one who . . ."

Reverend Toussaint interrupted him.

"As I said, Mr. Rollings, I know what message Ana Mae was conveying to us all. And I would like, at this time, to assign any and all portion coming to me for solving the clues of the quilt to Dr. Clayton Futrell."

"What?" from Delcine.

"Huh?" from JoJo.

"What the hell?" from Clayton.

The responses, variations on the same theme, echoed around the room before Rollings could reestablish any sort of order.

Archer, who maintained his position near the sisters, was the only one who didn't seem fazed. As a matter of fact, he smiled.

"Between Mr. Rollings here, all of the employees in his firm, and Mr. Archer over there, I think enough lawyers are present and accounted for," Reverend Toussaint said. "Mr. Rollings, if you have some sort of paper that needs to be signed, I'd be happy to oblige right here and now to make it official."

Archer's gaze connected with Clayton's confused one.

"Reverend Toussaint, that is, well," Clayton said, "I was going to say that is very generous of you, but in light of what exactly is at stake here, I think I'd better amend that to say it is very preposterous of you. I don't even know you. What would make you say something like that, even if you—especially if you think you know what all of the quilt squares mean?"

"I think it is within my rights to say I want someone else to have any assets coming to me. Is that correct, Mr. Rollings?"

"Yes, but . . ."

"There is no but, Mr. Rollings," Reverend Toussaint said. "I assign any and all profits, proceeds, money, and anything else that would or will come to me from the estate of Miss Ana Mae Futrell to Dr. Clayton Futrell. And I'll sign any papers you lawyers come up with that will attest to that."

"But why?" JoJo asked.

"Are you sure?" Rollings asked at the same time.

"More sure than I've ever been of anything in my life," Reverend Toussaint said.

"As you wish," Rollings said.

"But why?" Clayton wanted to know.

"Because I know what all of this means," he said going to the quilt.

"Eight of the blocks simply tell the story of Ana Mae's life and times here in Drapersville, the things she loved, like her cats and the children at the church school. But it's this one," he said pointing to the anchor block in the eighth position, with the heart and the word Howard in the middle of it. "This is the one that really matters the most. Look at how the tree in this block covers everything else. I know not only who Ana Mae's son Howard is, I also know where he is."

"Oh, for the love of God, sit down," Delcine cried. "Howard is our mother's maiden name. She was Georgette Howard Futrell. This wild goose chase has not yielded any missing or estranged son. There's no record of any birth at the hospital or the courthouse."

"How would you know?" JoJo said.

Smirking, Delcine sat back.

"Because I checked," she said. "We need that money, at least a portion of it. And neither Winslow nor I was about to let some unknown entity swoop in here to lay claim to our sister's financial legacy."

"Howard is not an unknown entity, Sister Delcine."

The quiet words came from Reverend Toussaint, who had finally stopped staring at the quilt Ana Mae created and was now studying Clayton with an intensity that made the younger man squirm.

"Is something wrong, Reverend?"

His face suddenly radiating with a light and a joy that seemed to bubble up inside of him, Reverend Toussaint beamed and shook his head.

Across the table, Archer got up, patted JoJo on the shoulder, and then returned to his husband's side. Since Reverend Toussaint was approaching from the front,

Archer positioned himself at Clayton's back. He placed a comforting and supporting hand on Clayton's right shoulder.

"What?" Clayton said, glancing over his shoulder and up at Archer.

Archer nodded toward Reverend Toussaint.

"Nothing is wrong, son," the minister said, speaking to Clayton. "We lived our entire lives right here in Drapersville, and I never suspected, not even once."

The older man just beamed at Clayton, positively beamed, his smile and his eyes as bright as a child's on Christmas morning.

"Suspected what?" Clayton asked.

"That I had a son. That you were my son. Howard is you, Clayton. You are Ana Mae's precious Howard."

21

Ana Mae's Story

"Shut the front door!"

The outburst came from Ana Mae's holy rolling best friend Rosalee Jenkins, whose eyes were wide and her mouth dropped open.

"Have you completely lost your mind?" Delcine demanded jumping up. "Clay is our brother. I remember when he was born."

"Do you?"

The quiet question came from Everett Rollings. It held the sort of intensity and seriousness that gave everyone in the room more than a moment's pause.

Delcine recovered first.

"Wh-what are you saying, Mr. Rollings?" she asked.

"Yes, what are you saying?" JoJo echoed. "Clay can't be Ana Mae's son."

The man at the center of the pandemonium remained sitting stock-still and staring at Toussaint le

Baptiste as if the man had suddenly sprouted two heads, horns, and wings.

Leaning forward and rubbing his partner's arm, Archer tried to rouse him. "Clay, honey?"

But Rosalee was up and out of her seat, pacing the room and talking to either the Lord or Ana Mae, it was hard to tell which.

"Lord, have mercy. Lord, have mercy," she said, shaking first her head and then her fist heavenward. "Of all the secrets. Why? Why'd you keep it from me, Ana Mae? We were like sisters."

A gasp sounded in the conference room then. Those who weren't wrapped up in their own mental calisthenics—trying to make sense of Reverend Toussaint claiming to be Clayton's father—turned to stare at JoJo.

"Does that mean you're our sister too?" JoJo asked Rosalee. "Was Mama hiding some other big family secret?"

"Your sister?" Rosalee demanded. "Hell, no."

Ana Mae's best friend was beside herself, fit to be tied or both.

The profanity finally got to the preacher. "Sister Rosalee. The Lord doesn't like that language."

"The Lord?" Delcine squealed. "The Lord doesn't like lying and adultery and fornication and fraud and whatever else other thing you're standing over there claiming to be the gospel truth. There is no way on this earth that Clayton was Ana Mae's child. We all grew up together. We lived in the same house. Ana Mae was not pregnant."

"Yes," Reverend Toussaint said. "Yes, she was. And I know when."

"Oh, my God." Clayton dropped his head into his hands, moaning. "Oh, my God."

Archer rounded the chair and squatted down next to Clayton, taking his partner's hands in his. He didn't know what to say, so he just held on, hopefully giving Clay the support he needed to accept this new reality.

Archer had known one of Ana Mae's secrets. As a client, she came to him, insisting on paying the law firm's exorbitant but standard rates so everything would be aboveboard. Archer had known one secret—that Ana Mae was Clayton's biological mother—and had carried it with him for the better part of a year. Keeping that knowledge from Clay had almost cost him their relationship.

While Archer knew that Clay was Ana Mae's son, even he was stunned to discover Clayton's true parentage on the paternal side.

"Oh, my God," Clayton mumbled again.

Archer lifted their joined hands and pressed a kiss on Clayton's palms.

"Oh, for the love of God," Rosalee said. "Get a room."

"Rosalee."

The admonition came from Rollings, who no one noticed had left his seat.

He had apparently pressed another one of his unseen buttons that summoned bodyguards and electronics. A five foot by five foot white screen now took the place of honor at the head of the table. Rollings or his in-and-out assistant had pushed the quilt stand to the side.

Delcine groaned. "Not Ana Mae from the grave again."

"Oh, she was very much alive when she recorded these messages for you," Rollings said.

Clayton looked up at Reverend Toussaint. "I don't get it," he said. "How can you be my father?"

"Hey, everybody!"

The room went dark just as Ana Mae's face popped up on the screen. She was smiling and waving from her porch again. Since she had on the same dress as the previous viewing, this message had obviously been recorded on the same day as the other.

"I have a headache," Delcine said.

"You're not the only one, sis," Clayton replied. Then he turned to look at Delcine, realizing belatedly that maybe she wasn't his sister, but his . . . aunt?

"If you're watching this part," Ana Mae said, "it's because somebody there has figured it all out. If I were a betting woman—and I'm not . . . ," she added, lifting the King James Version of the Holy Bible that rested on the round table near the glass pitcher of lemonade with fresh-cut lemons floating around inside. ". . . But if I were a betting woman, I'd say it was either Too Sweet or JoJo who figured it all out."

"I love you, Ana Mae," Reverend Toussaint murmured softly.

Only Clayton heard the declaration.

"Me?" JoJo exclaimed. "She thought I was smart enough to figure it out? Wow! Ana Mae had more faith in me than I have in myself."

"Shhh," Delcine demanded.

". . . so that's why I'm first gonna speak to Too Sweet."

The preacher rose, approaching the screen and Ana Mae's image on it as if she were right there in the law firm's conference room with them.

"Yes, Ana Mae?"

She leaned forward in the rocking chair and smiled.

"I never meant to deceive you, Toussaint," she said. "We had that one magical, magical night together. And we were both so young. When I found out I was pregnant, I was scared to death. Scared to tell you, scared to tell my Mama. But she figured it out when she didn't see any evidence of my cycle coming around."

Ana Mae paused, refilled her glass of lemonade, and took a sip. With a lace-edged handkerchief, she dabbed at her mouth, replaced the glass on the table, and then continued with her story.

"You were gonna be heading off to that camp soon. Remember?"

"Yes, I was just about to turn seventeen," Toussaint said, more to Ana Mae than to the people in the room with him, who were intently listening and watching. "It was a pre-college camp at Fayetteville State University."

"You were gonna go be somebody. Go to college. Do good things in the world. The last thing you needed to drag you down was a fourteen-year-old pregnant girlfriend."

"Holy shit," JoJo exclaimed. "Fourteen?"

She too had moved closer and, like Reverend Toussaint, remained standing while the video played.

"Daddy had been through on one of his little pop-in trips, and that's when Mama got the idea," Ana Mae said. "Everybody knew Daddy came home whenever he felt like it, and usually left Mama pregnant with another baby. And just about the time I started to show, we went away. All of us."

"Oh, my God."

This time it was Delcine making the exclamation.

"I remember that," she said. "We moved up to Portsmouth or Suffolk or somewhere."

"Mama packed us all up and told the neighbors we were gonna stay a little closer to where Daddy was working for a while in Virginia. But Daddy wasn't there. Ever. It was just me and Mama, Delcine, and JoJo, who was practically just a baby herself."

On the screen, Ana Mae reached down to the table and picked up a heavy cardstock fan from the Holy Ghost Church of the Good Redeemer and started fanning herself a bit with it. It had clearly been warm the day she'd recorded her message to them. Condensation formed and dripped from not only the pitcher, but the glass at its side.

"Baby girl, I think you may have been going on two about then," Ana Mae said.

"Yeah," JoJo said. "There's about eighteen months between me and Clay. But I don't remember any of this."

"You were too little," Delcine said. "But I remember. After a little while up there, Mama said we, Ana Mae and I, were getting a little pudgy, and she told us we needed to diet a bit. But you weren't pudgy, Ana Mae. You were pregnant with a baby. It all makes sense now."

"Shh, we're missing what she's saying," JoJo said.

". . . so I hope you bear me no ill will after all these years," Ana Mae was saying, still addressing her long-ago lover. "Mama said it was for the best, and . . . well, it seemed like the right thing at the time."

"Oh, Ana Mae."

"Clayton, honey, I hope you don't hate me for the way we deceived you."

Ana Mae paused for a moment, using her hankie to dab at her eyes. "It was . . . it was a deception that kept you close. I could be your sister-mama. Teaching you and loving you while we both grew up together. It was an easy lie for Mama. Folks here in town were used to Daddy's comings and goings. I think half of 'em thought he had another family somewhere else. And he probably did, for all I know."

"Oh, dear God." That was Delcine.

"But why not just tell me. Sometime. Anytime along the way. Even when Mama, er"—Clayton looked around—"even when my grandmother died, why still keep up the lies?"

"It was easier," Reverend Toussaint said.

And as if she'd anticipated the question, on the screen the Ana Mae they all knew answered the same question. "By that time, by the time Mama died, I mean, it was habit. Delcine was gone, JoJo was gone, and Clayton, honey, you were so miserable in North Carolina that by then I knew telling you would just be pointless. For all that it mattered to the world, I was just your big sister. That's the way it needed to be."

She paused for a moment, wiped at her eyes again, and said softly. "I'm so sorry."

"She was always there for you, Clay," Archer said quietly.

"There as my sister, not my mother."

"Did it really make a difference?" Archer asked. "You were well and truly loved. And she helped you in every way she could. Didn't you tell me she sent you money the whole time you were in college?"

Clayton nodded. "Envelopes with little notes. Ten dollars here, and 'I'm so proud of you,' scrawled on a piece of paper. A twenty there with a little clipped comic from the newspaper or a flower pressed from her garden."

It was Clayton who was crying now.

A box of tissues appeared on the table. Archer thanked Rollings and then plucked a couple out of the box to press them into Clayton's hands.

"Oh, my God," he said.

"What?"

Clayton looked around for Rollings. "Did she pay for my medical school?"

Rollings nodded. "Part of it."

"I got these 'scholarships' from some North Carolina group that I'd never even heard of. I figured it was something I'd applied for and forgot about. I wasn't about to turn down any money with all the loans I had."

"The Granam Foundation," Rollings supplied.

"Yes," Clayton said. "That's it. I could never find any information about it, though. No address or phone number. No one to thank."

"The what?"

"Granna Mae," JoJo said on an almost whisper. "It was all right there. Right in front of us."

"What is a granamay?" Delcine demanded. She did not at all like being kept in the dark, and there were so many secrets being revealed right here and now that were making her plenty angry.

"Ana Mae," JoJo said. "The kids at the church school called her Granna Mae. She was their adopted grandmother. All of them."

"And after the lottery ticket thing happened, she set up a foundation to supply scholarship aid for students at the Good Redeemer Academy," Reverend Toussaint said. "She felt guilty about buying the ticket in the first place and wanted to make sure its proceeds went to worthy causes."

"Like The Haven and the kids and Jeremy Fisher," JoJo said.

Rosalee and Reverend Toussaint glanced at each other, but neither said anything.

"Granam," Archer deduced, "is an acronym of sorts, a combination of Good Redeemer, maybe even Good Redeemer Academy and part of her name, Ana Mae."

". . . so that's my story," Ana Mae was saying on the screen.

"Mr. Rollings, could you rewind please? We missed a lot of that."

"Well, I'll be god-damned," Rosalee said. She'd apparently finally managed to get herself together. "Eddie Spencer called it."

"Rosalee!"

"Will y'all stop saying my name like y'all all ain't never heard a swear word? This is all just too much for me to take. Ana Mae had and kept more secrets than the CIA."

"Still waters run deep," Reverend Toussaint said.

"What did Eddie Spencer call?" Mr. Rollings said.

Rosalee flushed, clearly guilty of something. "Well, there were, uh, some wagers going on over at Junior's. This whole Ana Mae treasure hunt thing, it's all a lot of people are talking about. There hasn't been this much excitement in Drapersville since those hippies accidentally set fire to the general store that Eddie Spencer's mama used to run back in the day."

When she said hippies, she cast her gaze in Rollings's direction again.

"I still don't get it," Clayton said.

"Neither do I," Delcine chimed in.

"What was the point of the deception?"

"I believe I can answer that," Mr. Rollings said.

"Me too," Rosalee said. "I found it in the old newspaper files over at the *Times & Review.* They got all the papers from way back to the very first one."

"Sister Rosalee," Reverend Toussaint said, with a note of caution in his voice that no one in the room missed.

"This doesn't have anything to do with that," Rosalee said, with an unguarded nod toward the funeral director-cum-lawyer.

"I beg your pardon," Rollings said.

Rosalee waved a hand, dismissing that exchange as an aside. "There was a county prosecutor back in the day . . ."

"Are we going to spend the entire afternoon talking about 'back in the day'?" Delcine groused.

"Those who don't know their history are destined to repeat it," Archer murmured.

Delcine cut her eyes at her brother-in-law but didn't say anything.

"It was in the early 1970s," Mr. Rollings said. "The fallout from the Summer of Love and all that it ushered in was more than Prosecutor Grayson could handle. With all of the hippies still running through town, turning the stately and historic Draper Building into what he accounted as a commune with around-the-clock orgies, Grayson dusted off a little-used North Carolina state statute and put the kibosh on fornication. He prosecuted at least three people."

"On what charges?" Archer asked. "And how were the charges enforced?"

"The bedroom police," Rosalee said.

"The bedroom police," Reverend Toussaint murmured. "Lord, have mercy, I haven't heard that in years."

The lawyer in Archer had to know. "What was it?"

"A merry band of Bible-toting deputies, hand-picked by Grayson."

"The stories were all over the papers," Rosalee said. "I saw some of them over at the newspaper building."

"That's because the law, at least as interpreted by Prosecutor Grayson and old Judge Harper painted a broad stroke," Rollings said. "The charge was 'lewd and indecent behavior that threatened the moral fiber of the community.' "

"Oh, for goodness sakes," Archer said.

"Now you see why I had to get the hell up out of Drapersville, North Carolina?" Clayton said. "Even though by the time I was coming along, and coming out, that law had been shoved back in a closet where it belonged, there was still a pervasive atmosphere here that frowned upon anything deemed outside the norm."

"And a fourteen-year-old pregnant black girl was definitely something outside the norm."

JoJo, who had been picking at a chip in her long, painted nails, said, "I have to give her credit, though."

"Who?" Clayton wanted to know.

"Mama. That she even thought about that law and what was going on in town. How it might affect her child and her unborn grandchild."

Reverend Toussaint started to nod. "And along come me and Ana Mae, two teenagers who have nothing to do with the hippies, but surely fit the definition of what the judge and the prosecutor were gunning for. Miss Georgette must have panicked."

"She did," Rollings said. "And so she loaded up her car with her toddler, her young daughter, and her pregnant fourteen-year-old and moved them across the state border to Suffolk, which at the time was another small country town a world away from here. Ana Mae could have the baby, and when the Futrells finally got back to Drapersville, with Georgette toting a newborn, no one would be the wiser since everyone knew about her on-again, off-again relationship with her husband."

"There was no reason for anyone to think anything except what they saw," Clayton said. "And I became permanent brother to Ana Mae, Delcine, and JoJo."

Rollings aimed the remote to rewind and started the video again at the part they'd missed. Ana Mae, in her own rambling words, recapped the same story they'd just pieced together.

". . . So that's my story," Ana Mae said. "While I could make a guess, I don't know which one of you will get it. I hope you'll do what's right, though. And you'll know what's right when the time comes. But this," she said reaching forward and pulling something from the front porch railing—the very quilt that was now displayed in the conference room. "This quilt tells the whole story. My story. It took me a long time to make it, but it was a labor of love. I never stopped loving you, Too Sweet. We went our separate ways and had our own lives, but you were always my one and only even though there was a time when there were a lot of stories running around about me for a while there. Yeah, I had a lot of boyfriends, but when I refused to," she shrugged, "well, you know, when I wouldn't sleep with 'em, they got mad, called me names, and said ugly things. But you, Toussaint, you were always my one and only."

Ana Mae hugged the quilt to her bosom, smiled at the camera, and then the screen went white again.

The tissue box made the rounds at the table.

Everyone, including Everett Rollings, was outright crying or sniffling. Everyone except Delcine, who had a bigger loss on her hands.

She had passed on the ten thousand dollars—a sure thing—for the chance to get her hands on Ana Mae's millions. And now it was looking like she would be shut out—shut out by a preacher that Ana Mae slept with one time more than thirty years ago. That just was not right.

"It's not right," she said aloud.

"What's not right?" JoJo said, fanning her eyes with one hand and with the other trying to either secure or take off one of her false eyelashes that had come unglued.

"That, that preacher who doesn't even pastor a church gets all of Ana Mae's money. It's not right."

"I don't want it," Reverend Toussaint said. "That's why I'm giving anything that may have come to me for figuring out the quilt's story over to Clayton. Ana Mae gave me a precious, precious gift. She gave me a son. She and Miss Georgette could have gotten rid of you with some back-alley abortion or given you up for adoption. But instead, they brought you back here where both of us, me and Ana Mae, could see you grow up. And there's no dollar amount I can ever, or would if I could, put on that."

Archer squeezed Clayton's hand and gave a little nod.

Clayton, still a little wary, rose. "When you put it that way, Reverend, I sort of get it."

For a moment, the two men stood together awkwardly. Then Clayton, deciding or realizing that the moment and the decision was his to make, tentatively held out a hand to Toussaint le Baptiste. The minister took it and shook it, and before Clayton could back away, Toussaint pulled his son into a hearty embrace.

JoJo started crying again.

Mr. Rollings and Archer smiled.

Rosalee looked heavenward, shaking her head.

Only Delcine still sat pouting. "This is just so wrong. I don't get it."

22

All the Pieces Together

"What don't you get, Delcine? Even I've figured out this whole thing, and I'm the slow one of the bunch."

"You're not slow, JoJo," Archer said. "Your thinking is contemplative and deliberate."

"Thank you, Archer."

"But it was Reverend Toussaint who figured out that Ana Mae's son was Clayton," Archer added.

"About that," Clayton said. "My name isn't Howard. I have my birth certificate, and there's no Howard on it anywhere."

They all looked toward Mr. Rollings, who nodded.

"What you have is an official duplicate," the lawyer told Clayton. "Not necessarily usual, but not unheard of. They are issued when an original document is lost or destroyed—for example, in a fire or hurricane."

"So what's the significance of the name Howard—other than it being mama's maiden name?"

"I think I can answer that," Reverend Toussaint said. "I don't know why it never occurred to me before. Howard is such a common name here."

"He's right," Rollings said. "Just as an example, my middle name is Howard."

"Well, we sure ran into enough Howards that were dead ends," Delcine grumbled. "That cop. Your son," she said, nodding toward Rollings.

"And there was Emily Daniels's Howard," Clayton said.

"If you open the county phone book, you'll see at least two columns of Howards," Rollings added.

Reverend Toussaint shook his head. "No," he said. "I think she wanted her son named after his father, and she remembered that Howard was almost my name. My father wanted me named that. But my mother, who had roots in Haiti, wanted me named for one of her national heroes. So I became Toussaint. Howard may have been Ana Mae's indirect way of naming her son . . . our son . . . after me. It was a name we almost had in common."

"The quilt," Delcine said. "What was the purpose of the quilt? All we did was run around town talking to people who knew Ana Mae. There were no clues about the money."

"Talking to people who knew Ana Mae was the whole thing, just like Reverend Toussaint said," Clayton said. "Don't you see?"

Delcine grabbed her big purse and plopped it into her lap. "Clearly not."

"The clues, the nine blocks in the quilt were the

clues. Everything we'd need to find out more about Ana Mae was right there in the fabric, in the images she created. The quilt was about how she lived, what she loved, and what she spent her time on this earth doing."

Delcine didn't look convinced and sought out Mr. Rollings. "It couldn't be that simple," she said.

"It was that simple," he assured her.

"But . . ."

"Shoot, I knew that the first time I looked at the thing," Rosalee said. "It's as clear as day and would be to anyone who knew Ana Mae."

"And that's just it," Clayton said softly, both awe and respect reflected in his voice. "We didn't know Ana Mae."

Before Delcine could get out her next whiny complaint, Reverend Toussaint strode forward, pulling the quilt and its stand out again so all could see.

"It was a diversion," he said. "All a diversion." He pointed to the block in the bottom row that had the trunk and lower leaves of the big tree appliquéd. "It's about the tree," he said. "See how its branches, leaves, and flowers encompass the entire quilt. That was a clue for me. As was this," he said, pointing to the heart with *HOWARD* in the middle of it.

"Seeing that is what made it all eventually click for me," he said. "But not until you read that book to the children, Sister Josephine. I hadn't thought about that tree in years, let alone its significance to me and to Ana Mae. We are, after all, talking thirty-some years ago. I'm a different man than I was at seventeen. This block and that message, *HOWARD* inside a heart, was just for me. None of you would ever have known its true significance. Not with your family name on your mama's side being Howard. I'm the only one who could decipher what this meant."

He then told them about carving their initials in an old oak one night, an old oak just like the one Ana Mae had reproduced in fabric and stitches.

"And these clues were for the rest of us to figure out," Clayton said, approaching the quilt and the father he never knew.

"The Scripture on the back, on the label," Reverend Toussaint said, flipping it over for them to see. " 'Love must be sincere. Hate what is evil. Cling to what is good. Be devoted to one another in brotherly love.' That's what she wanted you, us, to remember."

"That's what I don't understand, Clay," Delcine said, this time her voice almost the whine they remembered from their childhood in Drapersville.

Clayton held out a hand to her. On a heavy sigh and with a much-put-out huff, Delcine put her big purse aside and got up to peer at the quilt with Clayton.

"Some of them we figured out as a group," he said. "The scratch-off lottery ticket that began it all, at least the financial part of the story."

For all of her book education and time in the Washington, D.C., area as a real housewife, not one portrayed on TV, Delcine remained slow on the uptake. "All we did was talk to the people at the store where she got the ticket."

Clayton nodded. "That's it. If what I'm thinking is right—and Mr. Rollings, I'm sure, will tell us if we're not—that's what this whole quote/unquote treasure hunt was all about. It wasn't, like Lester thought, digging for actual buried treasure. Like Mr. Rollings said, the money is all in bank or brokerage accounts. The treasure was finding out who our sister was."

He paused, frowned a bit, and then amended his last statement. "Well, for me, who my mother was."

JoJo bent over to untie the straps on her high heels, which were, as usual, killing her feet. She gathered up and dropped the sexy and not really appropriate for daytime shoes on top of her bag, then padded barefoot over to the quilt. Without thinking or asking, she hopped up on the conference table, closer to her siblings, one leg dangling as if she were perched on top of a baby grand piano while a crooner wooed her.

Reverend Toussaint and Archer glanced at each other, both shrugged, and they too moved closer to be able to see the detail.

"Well, don't y'all leave me," Rosalee said. "I had something to do with this too."

With a welcoming arm out to her, Reverend Toussaint opened a hole.

Watching them, Mr. Rollings smiled. The small group looked like a family at the moment. That's the picture he wished his deceased client could have seen. He glanced up and the smile grew wry as he realized Ana Mae was probably seeing it unfold just as he was.

"The clues we all figured out as a group or as a group talking to Ana Mae's friends, neighbors, and townspeople were these," Clayton said, pointing to the scratch-off lottery ticket and the Matthew 25 Scripture reference. "Ana Mae took the money, the talents, she'd been given via the lottery and made the money grow. She took her five talents and made them ten."

"Did y'all notice a sheriff's deputy car outside the house since that day?" Rosalee asked.

The lawyer replied, "Given the commotion caused by Mr. Coston and all of the neighborhood assembled out in the yard and on the street, Sheriff Daughtry and I decided to head off any treasure hunters bent on digging up the yard to find a chest full of gold coins."

"Thank you, Mr. Rollings," JoJo said. "I'm still sleeping in that house, and it would be mighty disconcerting to wake up in the middle of the night to hear somebody digging out there."

Rollings nodded, then stepped out of the conference room for a moment. When he returned, his efficient and quiet assistant, Maria, bore a tray with small bottles of water and cups for coffee.

"It will be just a few minutes, sir. They're on the way here now. And the other delivery will be here in about fifteen minutes. They're just putting the finishing touches on."

"Excellent," Rollings murmured. "And Mr. Coston, do you know where he went?"

"I called the sheriff's office when you buzzed and when Clyde came in here. He stopped over at Junior's and has just been making a nuisance of himself. A deputy's on him, though."

"Thank you."

"Another one we worked as a group was the bucket and the mop," Clayton resumed, commenting about the quilt. "That's that Fisher boy and his invention. Ana Mae invested in him and his company, and together they made a killing when he sold it to the Zorin Corporation."

"What about the animals?" JoJo asked.

"That one was me," Rosalee said, laying claim to one of the blocks. "Baby Sue and Diamond Jim came from The Haven. Ana Mae spent almost as much time there as she did at the church and at the Good Redeemer Academy."

"And Emily Daniels from the shelter stopped by the house with an award for Ana Mae," Clayton added.

"Ooh, ooh!" JoJo exclaimed. "I got that one."

"Which one?" Delcine asked.

JoJo pointed to the seventh block of Jesus and the little children.

"Ana Mae loved those kids," JoJo said. "Jesus represents the church, or maybe the church and the school, and the little kids are all of her adopted grandchildren. They all published a book, Ana Mae and the Good Redeemer Academy kids."

She sent a flirtatious smile Reverend Toussaint's way.

He blushed and cleared his throat.

Archer saved him by pointing out the teapot and teacup. "We found the tea shop where she gets her special blend. It's lovely," he said. "It's a bit of a drive, but well worth it. And they simply adore Ana Mae there. We're on their mailing list now, by the way," he told Clayton in an aside. "They can overnight tea to us."

Rosalee tapped JoJo on the shoulder. "You found that square the day Hetty and Betty Johnson stopped by Ana Mae's house."

"Reverend, you weren't there that day. You've got to come see all of Ana Mae's quilts. She has them all documented in binders with pictures."

Reverend Toussaint, who had been mostly silent while the Futrells and Rosalee worked through the blocks of the quilt, realized they'd skipped one.

"What about the first block?" he asked. "The chicken."

"Ana Mae made the best fried chicken in the

county. Even that old shrew Lizbeth Hornsby had to admit it," Rosalee practically cackled. "You shoulda seen her old prune face when Ana Mae got awarded the blue ribbon at the county fair last year. That was a sight to behold. You remember, Reverend. I see you over there smiling."

Reverend Toussaint couldn't hide the grin at that memory. But Rosalee told them the rest of what happened that day.

"You'd a thought Lizbeth got a lemon stuck in her mouth her face was so scrunched up." She was still chuckling when Archer spoke up.

"That doesn't seem to fit the pattern," he said.

"What pattern?"

"Well, look," he said, pointing to the corresponding quilt blocks as he made his case. "In each one of these, there's a story that was either relayed to one of you or that you found out. No one talked to this Lizbeth chicken lady, right?"

The Futrells and Rosalee shook their heads in the negative.

"So that means there must be something else about the chicken. A clue or person we haven't talked to or found yet."

"That would be me," a new voice said from the conference room door.

All of the heads turned as Rollings got up to greet the newcomer.

"Mr. Bell, I presume?" he asked holding out a hand.

The man who'd boo-hooed all over the church at Ana Mae's funeral bounded into the room.

Trailing behind him was a young man, about twenty-five or so years old, with short spiky brown hair and multiple piercings and tattoos. His jeans, strategically ripped, had the expensive look of a designer's interpretation of grunge rather than the honest to goodness wear and tear of a favorite pair of Levis.

David Bell—David Z. Bell, Chairman and CEO of the Zorin Corporation in Ohio—pumped Rollings's hand. "I don't know how you did it, Mr. Rollings, or how Ana Mae did it, but thank you," he said. "Thank you so much for giving me back my son."

Rollings dipped his head as if offering a regal blessing. "I'd like to take the credit," Rollings said. "But it's Miss Futrell who found him."

"Is that Granna Mae?" The young man asked. "Is that who this Ms. Futrell is?"

Reverend Toussaint and JoJo exchanged a look.

"Another adopted grandchild?" JoJo asked him.

Reverend Toussaint shrugged.

"One thing is for sure about Ana Mae," Clayton said in an aside to Archer, "she believed in picking up strays along the way, whether people or animals or projects."

"The virtuous woman," Reverend Toussaint intoned.

"May I have your attention, everyone?" Rollings said. "I believe most of you met David Bell during Miss Futrell's homegoing service. This is his son, Theodore Edgerton."

"Teddy," the young man said. "Theodore Edgerton Bell sounds like some stuffy-ass lawyer." He glanced at Rollings in his three-piece suit, then added, "No offense, dude."

"None taken, Mr. Bell. I've taken the liberty of

having dinner ordered and delivered from Junior's Bar and Grille. Despite the name, they make an excellent barbeque."

"Any fried chicken?" David Bell asked.

"None like Ana Mae's," Rosalee said.

"There sure wasn't," Bell said.

"Ana Mae always brought you chicken," JoJo said. "You mentioned that when we all talked on the phone. They weren't paying attention," she added with a nod toward Clayton and Delcine, "but I heard you."

Bell nodded, beaming, as he rubbed his substantial belly. "Yes, she did. And on more than one occasion we went to the butcher shop for fresh chicken that she fried up right in my kitchen."

JoJo went to the quilt and pointed to the block with the plate of fried chicken. "This quilt block is about you," she told Bell. "Every one of these blocks represents something Ana Mae loved."

While JoJo pointed out all the elements of the quilt for Bell, Maria transformed the conference room table into a dining table. She'd either found one somewhere in the office or run out and purchased a tablecloth to protect the conference room table. Then with the help of Junior himself, who wasn't going to trust this special delivery to any of his regular drivers—they would, undoubtedly, fail to glean any important information on the goings on that had everybody wondering who was gonna win the pool—laid out a spread of Carolina-style ribs and pulled pork, his special sauce, coleslaw, baked beans, potato salad, homemade rolls, and several gallons of sweet tea.

"There's some red velvet cake and a sweet potato pie for dessert," Junior said.

He hovered, hoping for an invitation to stay. But

Rollings thanked him, and efficient Maria hustled him out of the conference room, closing the door behind them.

"A heart attack on a plate," Delcine muttered when Junior left, noting the lack of a single fresh green dish.

But she, like all the others, ended up sucking the bones on the melt-in-your-mouth ribs.

Conversation at the table was pretty much nonexistent until both David Bell and Reverend Toussaint almost simultaneously sat back with a "Whew!" and rubbed their stomachs.

"Now that's what you call good Southern eatin'," the CEO said.

Teddy, looking around for more ribs, eyed the quarter rack still on Delcine's plate.

"Here," she said, passing the plate across to him. "You pack it away just like my son."

"Thank you. Granna Mae said the food in Carolina was good, but she never said it was this good." He sent a sly glance in his father's direction. "I see why the two of you had a 'special' relationship."

"Now, Teddy, you're giving these folks the wrong impression," David Bell said. He looked at the people gathered around the table. "I . . . I meant what I said at Ana Mae's funeral and then later on the phone with you all. That woman meant the world to me.

"She knew Teddy and I were—well, I suppose estranged is the polite way to put it. What I didn't know is that she'd launched a search for him."

"I wasn't lost, Dad."

"You were lost to me. I didn't know where you were or what had become of you."

Teddy spread his hands out in a look-at-me gesture. "I'm fine, clearly."

Twin snorts came from opposite ends of the table as both Rosalee and Delcine let their opinions about tattoos and piercings be known without saying a single word.

"Granna Mae accepted me for who I am," he said.

"And what, exactly, are you?" Delcine asked.

"An artist," the young man replied.

"And a quite accomplished one, if I may say so myself," the proud father declared.

"Granna Mae was my patron."

"The virtuous woman," Reverend Toussaint intoned at the same time Archer muttered, but with a smile, "Here we go again."

By the end of dessert, David Bell explained to them all his fried chicken connection to Ana Mae Futrell.

"She never would let us fly her in for our annual board meetings," he said. "She'd just get on that Greyhound bus and ride all those hours up to Columbus. And she always brought with her, just for me, a basket of her fried chicken. Best meals I ever ate were with Ana Mae sitting in our corporate dining room and in the kitchen at my house.

"She also showed me, last year, the big blue ribbon she won for beating out some little scrawny woman named Lizbeth Hornsby, who thought she could fry up some chicken better than my Ana Mae."

That elicited laughs around the table.

Rosalee got up and came around the table to tap Everett Rollings on the shoulder. "Can I talk to you for a minute," she said. "In private."

"Of course," he said. "We can talk in my office."

Rosalee grabbed her handbag and followed Mr.

Rollings through a door that he held open for her. When they were alone, he folded his arms across his chest.

"You and the reverend were giving me quite a few stares earlier," Rollings told her. "I assume that you want to explain what was on your mind."

"You assume right, Mr. Rollings."

Rosalee opened the clasp on her purse and pulled out a sheet of paper that was folded in quarters.

"I went to the newspaper office to look up some old birth announcements. I got a little distracted 'cause there's a lot of interesting stuff in those old files. Things I'd either forgotten about or never even knew. But that's neither here nor there. You know how the hospital used to send out the names of all the babies born and the newspaper put them in under the birth announcements?"

Rollings nodded. "You thought you could find Ana Mae's son in those old records?"

"Exactly," Rosalee said. "There was no way to keep that information out of the paper back in those days. So I figured I'd go and look through all of the old issues to see if I could find when Ana Mae had a baby."

Rollings smiled. "That was good sleuthing on your part. But as you now know, Ana Mae's son was born in Virginia, not here in North Carolina."

"Uh huh," Rosalee said, unfolding the paper she'd pulled from her pocketbook. "But I came across some other news that knocked me for a loop. I was able to make a copy on the Xerox machine at the newspaper office."

She handed him the paper.

Rollings looked at it, and his smile disappeared. He swallowed hard and cast stricken eyes at Rosalee.

He was so embarrassed that his hands shook. "What are you going to do with this information? Who are you going to tell?"

Rosalee shook her head. "It ain't my business to tell anybody anything, though I kind of reckon that Ana Mae knew that already," she said with a nod toward the photocopied news item.

Everett Rollings's mouth was in a thin line. "Yes, she knew. I was actually just thinking about that quite recently."

"Well, I'm not telling anybody," Rosalee said, "except for Reverend Toussaint. I told him 'cause I needed to ask him what to do."

"That's what you were talking to him about earlier?"

She nodded. "You got lucky," she told him. "With all that was going on around here back then. That was some week."

"The explosions over at the mill," Rollings said nodding. "I remember. There were reporters from all over the East Coast here when that happened. My father provided the services for many of the families who lost loved ones."

"So a little announcement way in the back of the paper probably got overlooked that week. The birth notices weren't even in the usual place on page two, but they were there."

Rosalee indicated the photocopy in his hand. "That Fisher boy is your boy," she said. "I don't know how y'all all managed to keep it quiet all these years. I have one question for you, Mr. Rollings, and you can tell me to mind my own business if you want to."

Rollings pursed his mouth, but nodded.

"Do they know? Your son Trey and that Fisher boy, do they know they brothers?"

"Rosalee, I'd rather not discuss . . ."

She held up a hand to stop him. "That's all right," she told Rollings. "Like I said, I can mind my own business." She nodded toward the photocopied birth announcement he held and said, "I just wanted you to know that there is a public record out there."

"Thank you, Rosalee, for your discretion."

Rosalee shook her head. "Don't thank me," she said. "I reckon if Ana Mae could keep a big secret like she did, I figure I can try."

Back in the conference room, it was close to seven when Rollings brought them all back around to the business of Ana Mae's legacy.

"Mr. Bell, I believe you have a presentation to make."

Bell got up and retrieved a briefcase from the credenza.

"Ana Mae never missed a shareholders' annual meeting. She said she liked getting away on a little vacation every now and then. None of us based in Columbus quite viewed the city as a vacation mecca, but we loved Ana Mae dearly. She kept us grounded. Even though she wasn't a part of the day-to-day operation at Zorin Corporation, she kept us rooted and grounded in the need for our products and always reminded us that we weren't just making money, we were making life better for the millions of people and companies that rely on us for their cleaning needs."

He pulled a framed document from his attaché

case. "We were going to surprise her this year. The board of directors voted to name her our first annual stockholder of the year. So I'd like to present this to . . ." He looked around the room, trying to figure out who was supposed to get it.

Delcine, as the oldest, started to get up, but Everett Rollings cleared his throat . . . loudly. She paused and all eyes turned toward Clayton.

"I guess that would be me," he said, rising.

Bell read the proclamation declaring Ana Mae Futrell the Zorin Corporation's Most Valuable Stockholder.

"We had another little token of appreciation, even though no one had figured out how to make Ana Mae actually take it. I hope you'll accept it, Dr. Futrell. Maybe you and your sisters can work something out."

"What is it?" Rosalee asked.

David Bell grinned. "A real vacation. Two weeks at a resort in the Grand Caymans."

As one, everyone at the table shook his or her head.

To a person, each one knew there was no way Ana Mae would have gotten on a plane to fly over any water to go anywhere. She wouldn't even fly over dry land.

Ana Mae Futrell's life and loves were grounded on God's green earth.

23

A Lasting Legacy

One year later

JoJo came up with the idea.

It was such a good one that Delcine found herself irritated that she failed to think of it first.

Almost a year to the day of Ana Mae's death, *The Legacy of Ana Mae Futrell: A Life of Love in Quilts* was published by the University of North Carolina Press.

While JoJo came up with the idea for the book, Ana Mae had all but written it already, with her binders and notes and photographs of quilts she'd made through the years. All of the recipients of Ana Mae's quilts were delighted to be included in a book featuring her work. Those who still had a quilt made by Ana Mae posed for new pictures and sat for an interview to create a little blurb about why they'd held onto it and what the quilt and Ana Mae had meant in their lives.

Josephine Futrell not only moved back to North Carolina and into the house on Clairmont Road in Drapersville where she, Ana Mae, Clayton, and Delcine grew up, but also took back her maiden name after divorcing Lester. He'd put up a fight about Ana Mae's millions, claiming in the divorce that since Nevada was a community-property state, he was owed half.

It took a team of divorce lawyers from the firm Matthews, Dodson, and Dahlgren of San Francisco to convince him that JoJo had no money since Reverend Toussaint had solved the quilt clues and then given all the money he would have claimed to Clayton, Ana Mae's son.

Still grumbling about being cheated, Lester finally disappeared, much the way Winslow Foster would soon disappear into a federal prison. He'd been convicted on a three-count indictment and was awaiting sentencing. For her part, Delcine and her children were getting settled in a smaller but still impressive Alexandria, Virginia, home that she now owned free and clear—a gift from her brother-nephew.

Until all of the legalities with the ex- or soon-to-be ex-husbands were fully settled, the Futrell sisters enjoyed generous monthly stipends that somehow were deposited into their bank accounts.

JoJo, who wasn't a writer, drafted the foreword and introduction for the book. It was a rambling thank-you letter to her sister.

Archer Futrell-Dahlgren made sure all of the legal documents were in place so one hundred percent of the proceeds of the sale of the book went to Ana Mae's favorite charities and the Granam Foundation's Student Scholarships fund.

Delcine's contribution was a short history of Ana Mae's life and times. Clayton Futrell, who still shied away from the Howard name, wrote the afterword and insisted that the two author photographs on the flap include not just a picture of Ana Mae in her Sunday best, a photo taken on an Easter Sunday, but also the one existing picture of his mother, Ana Mae Futrell, and his father, Toussaint le Baptiste.

It was one of the photos in the memento box JoJo discovered in Ana Mae's closet.

The snapshot, taken on a long-ago Fourth of July, was, Clayton suspected, also the very day he was conceived. In it, a very young Ana Mae gave the camera a shy smile as she waved a small American flag, and a beaming Toussaint had his arm boldly wrapped around her shoulder, declaring to any who would see that she was his girl.

"Thank you, Clayton," Reverend Toussaint said.

"For what?"

The two men were walking together across a lush lawn on a warm but pleasant August day. The resemblance between them was evident now that they and everybody else saw what was right in front of their eyes.

"For not shutting me out of your life this past year. You had every right to."

Clayton shook his head. "How could or would I do that?"

Toussaint just smiled.

"And I want to thank Archer too. He set up everything at the foundation after I resigned from the church."

"That's Archer, Mr. Find It and Fix It," Clayton

said, shaking his head. "He came clean with me not too long after we were all here for Ana Mae's funeral and that video will."

"Came clean?"

Clayton nodded. "He and Ana Mae had been in cahoots with each other for almost a year before she died. Archer and I were going through a rough patch about that time. I thought he was seeing someone else and wanted out of our relationship. It turns out he was wrestling with his conscience and a pretty big conflict of interest. Ana Mae was his client."

"I thought Rollings was her lawyer," Reverend Toussaint said.

Clayton chuckled. "Yeah, he is too. Last summer Lester groused that for a bunch of dirt-poor folks we sure had a lot of lawyers. Anyway, Ana Mae hired Archer to do some legal research for her. Among other things, she wanted my niece Crystal found, and she wanted David Bell's son found."

"She didn't trust Rollings to do that?"

"It wasn't a matter of trust," Clayton looked at the man who was his biological father. "She told Archer she wanted to keep family business in the family, and Archer was family. Just like she considered all of the Good Redeemer Academy students her grandkids, she also claimed Teddy Bell and Jeremy Fisher as her own. If you use Ana Mae's definition of 'family,' I have a whole town of sisters and brothers running around here."

The corner of Toussaint's mouth edged up.

Clayton paused. "There's something else," he said.

Toussaint turned when he realized that Clayton was no longer walking next to him as they crossed the graveyard.

Something that looked like fear flashed in the older man's eyes. "What is it?"

Clayton reached into his suit jacket's inner pocket. He pulled out a piece of paper and held it out, his hand shaking a bit.

"Ana Mae wanted Archer to destroy this," Clayton said, "to leave well enough alone, so to speak. He said he tried to, several times, including while we were here for her funeral, but he couldn't bring himself to do it."

"Wh-what is it?"

Clayton handed the somewhat crinkled paper to Toussaint, who unfolded it but didn't take his eyes off of Clayton.

"It's okay," Clayton said. "Look at it."

When Reverend Toussaint did, his breath caught, and he jerked as if he'd been hit.

"But I thought . . ."

"I did too," Clayton said. "Somehow, Ana Mae got and held on to the original."

The piece of paper was Clayton's original and official birth certificate from the Commonwealth of Virginia. On the line where it said MOTHER was *Ana Mae Berdette Futrell*. At FATHER was neatly printed *Toussaint le Baptiste*. The line for the baby's name read Clayton Howard le Baptiste Futrell.

Toussaint's gaze locked with Clayton's. "I . . . I don't know what to say."

"I wanted you to know," Clayton said. "And," he added with a shrug, "this wasn't something for over the phone."

"Thank you," Toussaint said, clasping his son's shoulder. "Thank you for showing me, for sharing with me that gift from Ana Mae."

They resumed their walk to the area at Antioch

Cemetery where Futrells who'd passed on to glory made their final resting place.

"You didn't need to resign from your position at the church," Clayton said. "You loved the Holy Ghost Church of the Good Redeemer."

"I still do," Reverend Toussaint said. "I'm still a member, just not on the leadership team."

"What happened between you and Ana Mae was a long time ago. A really long time ago. What happened then shouldn't matter now."

As one they paused before Ana Mae's grave at Antioch Cemetery. Both carried long-stemmed red roses.

"People aren't very forgiving in this day and age," Reverend Toussaint said. "Besides, with all of the money coming in to the foundation from Ana Mae's investments and everything else, somebody needed to keep an eye on things and make sure the folks who need it most get what they deserve to make their own stamp on this world of ours."

"Let the dead teach the living," Clayton said.

"Exactly."

The two men stood together, silent for a moment, each lost in his own thoughts about the life and the legacy of the woman they both loved. And then, as one, Clayton and his father placed the roses at Ana Mae Futrell's headstone.

Unfortunately, I had trouble sleeping at night, thanks to Seth. I had been getting up around four each morning since he'd broken up with me. Almost every day I went to work an hour early so I could read the morning newspaper with my coffee so I'd be relaxed by the time my co-workers arrived.

I rarely talked about my personal life with anybody at work, except Lucy. Most of my straitlaced, stuffy co-workers seemed interested only in work so they kept their personal business to themselves too. I had mentioned to my supervisor and a few others that I was engaged but since nobody had asked me about that since I'd told them, I assumed they wouldn't care one way or the other about what had happened between Seth and me so I decided not to mention it unless someone asked. That was one consolation. I planned to take life one day at a time and hope for the best.

Life was too short and even shorter for some folks as I was about to find out.

It was six forty-five A.M. that morning the second week in September when a special news bulletin interrupted the jazz radio station I listened to every morning. I was shocked when the announcer reported that a jet had crashed into one of the World Trade Center twin towers in New York City. I finished my coffee and shuffled down the hall to the break-room to get another cup. When I returned to my office a few minutes later, the same announcer broke into the radio program again. I was getting annoyed because "Caught Up in the Rapture" by Anita Baker had just come on. But when the man said that another plane had hit the other twin tower, I got scared. I didn't find out until an hour later that the plane crashes had been deliberate. By then, some of my co-workers had come in. We all gathered in our conference room to watch the events unfold on a portable TV.

"My sister lives in New York," Donna Handel, one of the teachers, said, choking on a sob.

"My nephew works in one of those buildings," one of the male teachers said.

We all turned to Mrs. Trumble, our birdlike, white-haired principal. "In light of this situation, we'll close for the day until we know more about what's going on," she told us.

People immediately began to scramble out into the hallway, cussing and crying. I turned off my computer, gathered my things, and prepared to leave. The principal and a few other staff members were at the front entrance sending kids back home. I was in such disbelief; I don't even remember the short drive home.

Mama had already called me and left three messages so I called her immediately.

"I know I'll never get on no airplane now," she declared. "You lock your doors and stay inside until we find out what else them terrorists fools done cooked up. In the meantime, you take care of yourself." Mama cleared her throat which told me she had more to say. "Uh, you and Seth still ain't back together?"

"No," I said sharply. "And we won't be."

"Oh, well. Everything happens for a reason. Maybe it wasn't meant for you and him to be together."

"Maybe it wasn't," I agreed. "But I'll do just fine without him, Mama. Don't worry about me."

"You get on with your life, sugar. Don't let this set-back, set you back."

Mama's advice was good, but it was too late. The breakup was always on my mind and the hurt was still as painful as it had been the moment Seth told me our relationship was over. I had been eating like a bird since the last time I saw him. It was so ironic that I had lost another eight pounds because of that.

I did everything I could to keep myself grounded so I wouldn't think about the break-up too much. But I did. I thought about it day and night, every day. I'd even called Seth a few times trying to get him to talk to me. So far, I had not been able to catch up with him and so far he hadn't returned any of my calls.

After we returned to work two days after the attack, I began to work overtime. I knew it would help for me to keep myself busy. I spent more time with my friends, I read books that had been sitting on my bookshelf for months, and I continued to go to the gym.

I had seen Darla Woodson at the gym, but we had not spoken since Seth had dumped me. But the following Monday evening when she climbed onto the treadmill right next to me, she immediately began to walk at a slow pace and talk about her love life.

"Girl, I never thought I could be so happy," she gushed. "I am so in love!"

I was taken aback because Darla didn't seem the least bit concerned about last week's terrorist attacks. That was all everybody at the gym was still talking about. "I can tell. How is your boo doing?" I asked, speaking in a dry tone of voice. I assumed she was avoiding the terrorist issue because it was so painful and she didn't want it to interfere with the state of bliss she was in.

"Oh, he's doing just fine. Everything is going so much better than I even expected!"

"You must have had some weekend," I said, smiling to conceal my smoldering envy. "Did you know anybody in New York or D.C.?"

Darla gave me a puzzled look. "No. Why do you ask?"

"Some of my co-workers had relatives in New York and D.C. They're okay, though."

She gave me another puzzled look. Either this woman had just crawled from under a rock or she had a short memory. Then her eyes suddenly got big. "Oh! Are you talking about the terrorist attacks?"

I nodded.

"I don't know anybody in New York or D.C., but my hairdresser had a sister on the plane that crashed into the north twin tower." Darla shook her head and let out a sorrowful sigh, but her sympathetic gesture didn't seem sincere. "Oh well. We all have to go sometime." That was all she had to say about the biggest tragedy that had ever occurred on American soil in our lifetime. I was stunned and disappointed to know how lax she was. With a huge smile, she waved her hand in my face, pointing to the ring on her finger. "Can you believe this? It was his grandmother's ring."

"It's lovely," I mumbled. Seth had not asked me to return the engagement ring he had given to me. An hour after our break-up I had removed it from my finger and put it in a zip-lock baggie. I stored it in the same kitchen drawer where I kept my other notions, such as my needles and thread, safety pins and such. "You're one lucky girl."

"You don't know the half of it. We got married in his parents' house last Saturday afternoon. We had not planned to take the plunge so soon, but last month all of a sudden, he wanted to do it this month. And that was fine with me." Darla started up the treadmill and began to walk at a slow pace. "Since it was so sudden and unexpected, I had to rush and find a dress. I always wanted to have a big wedding and that's what we had talked about. But, you know, it was real quaint to have a little ceremony in his parents' house with just family and a few close friends."

"That sounds so nice, Darla. Congratulations," I muttered.

An apologetic look suddenly crossed her face. "I'm sorry to be hogging the conversation about me. What have you been up to since the last time I saw you? You look like you've lost a few pounds. Did you find a dress yet? Have you and your fiancé picked a date yet?"

I shook my head. "I won't be needing a wedding dress." I kept my voice strong and my head held high.

Darla gasped. "Oh? What happened? Did you change your mind about getting married?"

"Something like that." I cleared my throat and blinked hard to hold back my tears. I had shed a lot of tears in the last few days, and I didn't want to shed any more. "He broke the engagement." I reorganized my thoughts and kept my chin up. I was determined to keep my wits about me. I refused to show my pain, especially to a person I hardly knew.

"Oh shit! Well, I hope you're still going to be friends with him! Maybe he'll change his mind later on."

I offered a weak smile and shook my head. "I don't think so."

"Well, if you don't mind me asking, what the hell happened?"

"He just said he wasn't ready to get married yet." I forced myself to smile. "It was good while it lasted though. He was so special to me."

"What a shame. How are you handling things?"

"I'm okay, I guess. I still feel a little numb about it, but I'll get over him."

Darla gave me a curious look. "That dude is not telling you something. There has to be a serious reason as to why he called off the wedding other than him not being ready to get married. How long were you guys together?"

"Four years," I said hoarsely.

"And he suddenly calls it quits. Oomph, oomph, oomph! I feel so sorry for what that asshole did to you!"

"We had a lot of good times though." My voice had begun to weaken, no matter how hard I had tried to keep sounding strong.

"He's still an asshole and I hope that he regrets what he did to you someday!"

I exhaled and touched Darla's shoulder. "Thanks, Darla. I appreciate your concern."

"Well, I know I don't know you that well; but would you like to get together for a drink or dinner sometime? That way, we can really have a decent conversation about this. I mean, that is if you'd like to discuss this some more. I have a lot of time on my hands these days. I've already resigned from my boring job, which I hated anyway. We just moved into our new house two days ago so after we finish getting everything in place, you're welcome to come over. I'm sure Seth would love to meet you. Especially after what you just went though. I swear to God, I don't know why some men do the things they do! Thank God there are still some good ones left. Seth is the most sensitive man I've ever known so he'd be a good person for you to talk to."

Even though my eyes were open, everything went black for about two seconds. I could still hear Darla talking, but the only word that really jumped out at me now was her new husband's name: *Seth*. "Your husband is named Seth?"

She nodded vigorously. "He's already told me that we'll name our first son Seth Junior. I'm probably already pregnant. We've been getting busy since we met last April."

"Do you have a picture of your husband?" Had Darla not told me her husband's name was Seth, I would not have been interested in seeing what he looked like.

"Oh, I've got lots of pictures of him and of me together." Darla paused her treadmill and leaned down to lift her gym bag. She rooted around in it for a few seconds and pulled out a wallet and flipped it open. "Here's one we took when we went to the Bahamas. We won't get our wedding pictures until next week."

The picture in front of my burning eyes made my head swim. There was Seth in a floral shirt and a straw hat, standing in front of a palm tree with his arm around Darla. There was a tall glass in his hand with a pine-apple wedge and one of those cute little umbrellas hanging over the lip. The date at the bottom of the photo was the same date that he had told me he had attended that retreat in Sacramento.

"Have you ever seen a more handsome man?" Darla asked, sliding her tongue across her bottom lip.

"Yes," I mumbled. "I have. My ex was just as handsome as yours . . ." My head felt like it was going to explode. I ended my session on the treadmill and retrieved my gym bag off the floor with my hand shaking so hard I almost dropped it. I sniffed and gave Darla a guarded look. "It's been nice talking to you. Good luck."

"I wish you didn't have to rush off. I was going to invite you to join Seth and me for drinks this evening. He's working late so it'll be a couple of hours from now. I'm sure he would love to meet you. He's got a few single friends he could introduce you to."

"Thanks, Darla, but I'll have to decline your invitation. I already have plans for this evening."

"Well, can I get your telephone number so we can keep in touch? If I am pregnant, I don't know how much longer I'll be coming to the gym."

I pretended not to hear Darla's request for my telephone number. I couldn't get out of that gym fast enough. I didn't care if I had to drive fifty miles to another gym I'd never work out in this one again! I sprinted to the nearest exit and I didn't stop until I had made it outside and to the end of the block.

I was in such a daze I couldn't even recall where I had parked. It took me fifteen minutes to locate my car at a meter two blocks from the gym.

With my hands shaking and tears streaming down both sides of my face, I drove to Seth's office. I knew that without an appointment, and since it was after

business hours, the security guard would not allow me to enter the building so I didn't even try. That didn't stop me from going into the underground parking garage.

There were four parking levels. It took me an hour to locate his BMW. I hawked a dollop of spit smack dab in the center of the front windshield. Then I keyed the front, the back, and both sides. Just as I was about to leave and go to a hardware store to purchase something that I could use to slash his tires and bust out every single one of his windows, a man in a gray suit appeared. He didn't see me so I crouched down until I heard him drive away. My plan was to hang around until Seth showed up so I could give him a piece of my mind and a punch in the nose if he provoked me.

I couldn't remain in the garage too long before somebody saw me and got suspicious enough to call security so I left ten minutes later. Catching up with Seth so I could tell him to his face what I thought of him was not going to be easy. Especially with the way he had already been avoiding my phone calls and not returning any of my voice mail messages. Accepting an invitation from Darla to "meet" him so I could bust him in front of her—in the house that should have been my new residence—didn't appeal to me. There was no telling what I would do to him if I confronted him in the new house he'd just purchased. And there was no telling what he would do to me.

I couldn't imagine what he was going to say or do when he found out I knew how he had played me. I cringed when I recalled all the nasty things Darla told me he had said about me. The part about me being lousy in bed was especially hurtful. For all I knew, Darla was in that new house right now stretched out on an expensive couch with a tall drink in her hand telling him about

the poor woman she'd met at the gym whose fiancé had just dumped her. All she had to do was mention my name and a few specific details about me and he and he would put two and two together and realize I was the "poor woman" who'd been dumped!

Since it was going to cost Seth a pretty penny to get his car repaired, I had caused him some pain any-way. Even though he had no idea who the culprit was. That was the only satisfaction I expected to get out of hurting him.

It was enough to suit me for the time being . . .

GREAT BOOKS, GREAT SAVINGS!

When You Visit Our Website:

www.kensingtonbooks.com

You Can Save Money Off The Retail Price
Of Any Book You Purchase!

- All Your Favorite Kensington Authors
- New Releases & Timeless Classics
- Overnight Shipping Available
- eBooks Available For Many Titles
- All Major Credit Cards Accepted

Visit Us Today To Start Saving!
www.kensingtonbooks.com